**WILLIAM SHAKESPEARE** was born in Stratford-upon-Avon in April, 1564, and his birth is traditionally celebrated on April 23. The facts of his life, known from surviving documents, are sparse. He was one of eight children born to John Shakespeare, a merchant of some standing in his community. William probably went to the King's New School in Stratford, but he had no university education. In November 1582, at the age of eighteen, he married Anne Hathaway, eight years his senior, who was pregnant with their first child, Susanna. She was born on May 26, 1583. Twins, a boy, Hamnet (who would die at age eleven), and a girl, Judith, were born in 1585. By 1592 Shakespeare had gone to London, working as an actor and already known as a playwright. A rival dramatist, Robert Greene, referred to him as "an upstart crow, beautified with our feathers." Shakespeare became a principal shareholder and playwright of the successful acting troupe the Lord Chamberlain's men (later, under James I, called the King's men). In 1599 the Lord Chamberlain's men built and occupied the Globe Theatre in Southwark near the Thames River. Here many of Shakespeare's plays were performed by the most famous actors of his time, including Richard Burbage, Will Kempe, and Robert Armin. In addition to his 37 plays, Shakespeare had a hand in others, including *Sir Thomas More* and *The Two Noble Kinsmen*, and he wrote poems, including *Venus and Adonis* and *The Rape of Lucrece*. His 154 sonnets were published, probably without his authorization, in 1609. In 1611 or 1612 he gave up his lodgings in London and devoted more and more of his time to retirement in Stratford, though he continued writing such plays as *The Tempest* and *Henry VIII* until about 1613. He died on April 23, 1616, and was buried in Holy Trinity Church, Stratford. No collected edition of his plays was published during his lifetime, but in 1623 two members of his acting company, John Heminges and Henry Condell, published the great collection now called the First Folio.

**Bantam Shakespeare**
**The Complete Works—29 Volumes**
**Edited by David Bevington**
**With forewords by Joseph Papp on the plays**

*The Poems:* Venus and Adonis, The Rape of Lucrece, The
Phoenix and Turtle, A Lover's Complaint,
the Sonnets

| | |
|---|---|
| *Antony and Cleopatra* | *The Merchant of Venice* |
| *As You Like It* | *A Midsummer Night's Dream* |
| *The Comedy of Errors* | *Much Ado about Nothing* |
| *Hamlet* | *Othello* |
| *Henry IV, Part One* | *Richard II* |
| *Henry IV, Part Two* | *Richard III* |
| *Henry V* | *Romeo and Juliet* |
| *Julius Caesar* | *The Taming of the Shrew* |
| *King Lear* | *The Tempest* |
| *Macbeth* | *Twelfth Night* |

**Together in one volume:**

*Henry VI, Parts One, Two, and Three*
*King John and Henry VIII*
*Measure for Measure, All's Well that Ends Well, and*
*Troilus and Cressida*
*Three Early Comedies:* Love's Labor's Lost, The Two
Gentlemen of Verona, The Merry
Wives of Windsor
*Three Classical Tragedies:* Titus Andronicus, Timon
of Athens, Coriolanus
*The Late Romances:* Pericles, Cymbeline, The Winter's
Tale, The Tempest

**Two collections:**

*Four Comedies:* The Taming of the Shrew, A Midsummer
Night's Dream, The Merchant of Venice,
Twelfth Night
*Four Tragedies:* Hamlet, Othello, King Lear, Macbeth

# William Shakespeare

# THE
# POEMS

Edited by
David Bevington

David Scott Kastan,
James Hammersmith,
and Robert Kean Turner,
Associate Editors

BANTAM BOOKS
TORONTO / NEW YORK / LONDON / SYDNEY / AUCKLAND

**THE POEMS**

*A Bantam Book / published by arrangement
with Scott, Foresman and Company*

*PRINTING HISTORY
Scott, Foresman edition published January 1980
Bantam edition, with newly edited text and substantially revised,
edited, and amplified notes, introductions, and other
materials, published February 1988
Collations checked by Eric Rasmussen.
Additional editorial assistance by Claire McEachern.*

**Library of Congress Cataloging-in-Publication Data**

Shakespeare, William, 1564–1616.
  The poems.

  (A Bantam classic)
  "Bantam edition, with newly edited text and
substantially revised, edited, and amplified notes,
introductions, and other materials"—T.p. verso.
  Bibliography: p.
  Includes index.
  Contents: Venus and Adonis—The rape of Lucrece—
The phoenix and turtle—[etc.]
  I. Bevington, David M.  II. Title.
[PR2841.B48  1988]      821'.3      87–19540
ISBN 0-553-21309-1 (pbk.)

*Published simultaneously in the United States and Canada*

*Bantam Books are published by Bantam Books, a division of Bantam
Doubleday Dell Publishing Group, Inc. Its trademark, consisting of the
words "Bantam Books" and the portrayal of a rooster, is Registered in
U.S. Patent and Trademark Office and in other countries. Marca Regis-
trada. Bantam Books, 1540 Broadway, New York, New York 10036.*

PRINTED IN THE UNITED STATES OF AMERICA

O      0 9 8 7 6 5 4

# Contents

# THE
# POEMS

# The Poems

Most of Shakespeare's nondramatic poems were written early in his career. As a young man in London in the early 1590s, he did what any aspiring writer naturally would do: turned to the writing of amatory poetry, sonnets, and edifying verse narratives in the prevailing genres of the time. Here was the pathway to literary recognition and, one might hope, to the patronage of some influential and generous member of the aristocracy. Shakespeare soon found employment as an actor and writer of plays and no doubt took comfort in his success in the theatrical world; but writing plays then was somewhat like writing movie or television scripts today, often remunerative but usually anonymous. Play scripts were regarded as subliterary; when, some years later, Ben Jonson had the temerity to publish his plays as *operae*, or works, his critics were unsparing in their ridicule of one who confused "works" with "plays." Sonnets and Ovidian amatory verse, on the other hand, were generally recognized as "serious" literary forms.

Cultivated young gentlemen at the Inns of Court, purportedly studying law there but often spending a good deal of their time in literary pursuits, contributed plentifully to the vogue in sonnets, satires, love lyrics, and the like. (John Donne was such a student at the Inns of Court in the late 1590s.) Other aspiring or already recognized writers, including Sir Philip Sidney, Edmund Spenser, Christopher Marlowe, Michael Drayton, Samuel Daniel, Thomas Lodge, and, later in the 1590s, John Marston, Sir John Davies, George Chapman, and Ben Jonson, some of whom were also playwrights, made their mark by writing nondramatic poetry. The classical model provided by such poets as Ovid, Virgil, and Horace added to the sense of propriety in beginning a literary career with the writing of certain kinds of poems such as the eclogue.

Perhaps some enforced leisure in his acting and playwriting career, unwelcomely provided by severe outbreaks of the plague during warmer months in the early 1590s, gave Shakespeare added opportunity and incentive to turn to the writing of nondramatic verse. At any rate, he wrote *Venus and Adonis,* an amatory and even decorously erotic poem in the vein of Ovid, for publication in 1593, carefully seeing it through the press of his Stratford acquaintance Richard Field and assiduously dedicating it to Henry Wriothesley, the young Earl of Southampton. *The Rape of Lucrece* followed in 1594, also from Field's press and also dedicated to Southampton, the dedication on this occasion expressing an increasing sense of confidence and fondness between poet and patron. Whether Southampton substantially assisted Shakespeare in his career we do not know, but that Shakespeare had hopes from this sponsorship seems clear from his way of addressing his aristocratic friend.

Are the sonnets also addressed to Southampton? Although the identity of the friend addressed in Shakespeare's sonnets cannot be assigned with certainty, Southampton is inevitably a likely candidate—young, influential in literary circles, handsome, unmarried until 1598, belonging to a family that no doubt wished to see him settle down with the right wife and beget heirs. It may, however, be mere coincidence that his initials, H. W. (Henry Wriothesley), are the reverse of the mysterious "Mr. W. H." named in the dedication as "the only begetter" of these sonnets. Perhaps the situation described in the sonnets is not autobiographical. At any rate, many if not most of the sonnets must have been written fairly early in Shakespeare's career, when the sonnet form was in vogue. They were not published until 1609, and even then seemingly without Shakespeare's authorization or cooperation, but they were evidently circulated in manuscript among knowledgeable readers, and in fact two of them (138 and 144) made their way into print in 1599, seemingly without Shakespeare's authorization, in a volume published by William Jaggard called *The Passionate Pilgrim.* The sonnets are so extraordinarily fine that we can only wonder at Shakespeare's reluctance or indifference toward publishing, but he may have felt that they were personal, or that the sonnet vogue was past by the time he had written most of them, or that it was the gentlemanly thing to be offhand about publication. (Many of Donne's songs and sonnets were privately circulated in much the same manner some time before they were put into print.) We cannot be sure that the order of the sonnets reflects Shakespeare's final intentions in the matter, since he did not see them through the press, but the overall impression is remarkably cohesive and belies most scholarly efforts to rearrange or disintegrate them.

"The Phoenix and Turtle" and "A Lover's Complaint," published in 1601 and 1609 respectively as parts of volumes largely devoted to other materials and printed seemingly without Shakespeare's cooperation, are probably also early in date of composition, though nothing is known about the circumstances that might have produced them, and the assertion of Shakespeare's authorship is still uncertain though very likely in both cases.

Other nondramatic poems sometimes included in complete collections of Shakespeare's poetry are less certainly vouched for and have been omitted here as of too tenuous a connection to merit inclusion. William Jaggard's *The Passionate Pilgrim*, 1598, mentioned above because it printed two sonnets (138 and 144) some nine years before the sonnets were published as a group, also pirated three lyric passages from Act 4 of *Love's Labor's Lost*, published in that same year (1598). Except for minor textual variants, these texts simply reproduce material available elsewhere in the Shakespeare canon. Plainly Jaggard was capitalizing on Shakespeare's growing reputation by attributing *The Passionate Pilgrim* entirely to him, and doing so most irresponsibly, for a number of poems in the slim volume are manifestly not by Shakespeare at all. Poem 11 of the twenty or twenty-one poems in the volume (number 14 appears as one poem in the original text but is sometimes divided by modern editors) is a sonnet from Bartholomew Griffin's *Fidessa More Chaste Than Kind* (1596), and 4, 6, and 9 are so closely related to it in subject and style that they seem part of a sequence. The obvious resemblance in all four to Shakespeare's *Venus and Adonis* is probably a tribute to that poem's popularity rather than an indication of Shakespeare's authorship of these sonnets. Poems 8 and 20 first appeared in *Poems in Divers Humors*, 1598, by Richard Barnfield. The second of these was reprinted in another popular anthology, *England's Helicon* (1600), in which poem 17 of *The Passionate Pilgrim* also appears and is attributed to the author of poem 20, that is, to Barnfield. (Poem 17 was first published in Thomas Weelkes's *Madrigals*, 1597.) *England's Helicon* also printed a version of poem 19, attributing this famous lyric ("Live with me and be my love") to "Chr. Marlowe," although its Reply (signed "Ignoto") was later said to be by Sir Walter Ralegh. In any case, poem 19 is certainly not by Shakespeare.

These attributions to other poets, most of them fairly reliable, leave only 7, 10, 11, 12, 13, 15, and 18 as possible new works in *The Passionate Pilgrim* to be assigned to Shakespeare's hand. Because of that volume's unreliability, and because most of these otherwise unattributed verses are mediocre, no good reason exists to credit any of them to Shakespeare. If one poem is to be singled out for praise, the usual choice is 12:

> Crabbed age and youth cannot live together.
> Youth is full of pleasance, age is full of care;
> Youth like summer morn, age like winter weather;
> Youth like summer brave, age like winter bare.
> Youth is full of sport, age's breath is short;
>   Youth is nimble, age is lame;
> Youth is hot and bold, age is weak and cold;
>   Youth is wild, and age is tame.
> Age, I do abhor thee; youth, I do adore thee.
>   O, my love, my love is young!
> Age, I do defy thee. O, sweet shepherd, hie thee,
>   For methinks thou stays too long.

Even here we find no unequivocal sign of Shakespeare's genius.

The reliability of attribution to Shakespeare is no stronger in the case of the song, "Shall I die? Shall I fly," transcribed in a manuscript collection of miscellaneous poems probably from the late 1630s and attributed there to Shakespeare by the transcriber. The poem has been noticed before by researchers in its Bodleian Library manuscript but has been passed over in silence as an indifferent piece of work attributed to Shakespeare without authority; another manuscript in the Beinecke Library, Yale University, contains a transcription of the same poem without attribution. Manuscript anthologies, prepared for personal use by literary amateurs fond of assembling their own collection of favorite pieces, were common during the period, and the attributions in them are, for understandable reasons, not infrequently quite wrong. The general accuracy of this particular Bodleian collection is in dispute, and certainly its attributions are not above suspicion. The literary merit of "Shall I die? Shall I fly" is perhaps a matter of opinion, though current interest in it surely derives chiefly from the news media's fascination with the story of a supposed discovery of a new poem by Shakespeare (though in fact the poem had been taken cognizance of by earlier scholars) rather than from anything in the poem itself.

Because it is the kind of poem that virtually any poet of the period could have achieved, and because the attribution is so slenderly based on any reliable authority, it has been omitted here as the poems in *The Passionate Pilgrim* have been. If an editor of a "complete" Shakespeare were to include all writings attributed to Shakespeare during the Renaissance, he or she would have to consider the imposing list of so-called apocryphal plays to which his name was visibly attached, including seven plays actually included in the second printing of the Third Folio of 1664 (*The London Prodigal, The History of Thomas Lord Cromwell*, etc.) along with at least eight others. It is a tribute to Shakespeare's fame that so many works were attributed to him, including some plays now lost. At any rate, a collection of Shakespeare's poems can perhaps better indicate the range of his accomplishment in nondramatic verse if it avoids the distractions of works that are distinctly inferior and have been attributed to him only on the slenderest of authorities.

# VENUS
# AND
# ADONIS

# Introduction

Like most of his contemporaries, Shakespeare apparently did not regard the writing of plays as an elegant literary pursuit. He must have known that he was good at it, and he certainly became famous in his day as a playwright, but he took no pains over the publication of his plays. We have no literary prefaces for them, no indication that Shakespeare saw them through the press. Writing for the theater was rather like writing for the movies today, a profitable and even glamorous venture but subliterary. When Ben Jonson brought out his collected *Works* (mostly plays) during his lifetime, he was jeered at for pretension.

The writing of sonnets and other "serious" poetry, on the other hand, was conventionally a bid for true literary fame. Shakespeare's prefatory epistle to his *Venus and Adonis* betrays an eagerness for recognition. Deferentially he seeks the sponsorship of the Earl of Southampton, in hopes of literary prestige as well as financial support. He speaks of *Venus and Adonis* as "the first heir of my invention," as though he had written no plays earlier, and promises Southampton a "graver labor" to appear shortly. *Venus and Adonis* in 1593 and *The Rape of Lucrece* in 1594 were in fact Shakespeare's first publications. Both were carefully and correctly printed. They were probably composed between June of 1592 and May of 1594, a period when the theaters were closed because of the plague. Shakespeare's belief in their importance to his literary career is confirmed by the reports of his contemporaries. Richard Barnfield singled them out as the works most likely to assure a place for Shakespeare in "fame's immortal book." Francis Meres, in his *Palladis Tamia: Wit's Treasury*, exclaimed in 1598 that "the sweet witty soul of Ovid lives in mellifluous and honey-tongued Shakespeare: witness his *Venus and Adonis*, his *Lucrece*, his sugared sonnets among his private friends, etc." Gabriel Harvey, although preferring *Lucrece* and *Hamlet* as more pleasing to "the wiser sort," conceded that "the younger sort takes much delight in Shakespeare's *Venus and Adonis*." John Weever and still others add further testimonials to the extraordinary reputation of Shakespeare's nondramatic poems.

As Gabriel Harvey's puritanical comment on *Venus and Adonis* suggests, this poem was regarded as amatory and even risqué. It mirrored a current vogue for Ovidian erotic poetry, as exemplified by Thomas Lodge's *Scilla's Metamorphosis*, 1589 (in which an amorous nymph courts a reluctant young man), and by Christopher Marlowe's *Hero and Leander*. This latter poem, left unfinished at Marlowe's death in 1593 and published in 1598 with a continuation by George Chapman, was evidently circulated in manuscript as were so many poems of this sophisticated sort, including Shakespeare's sonnets. Shakespeare may well have been influenced by Marlowe's tone of wryly comic detachment and sensuous grace. He may also have read Michael Drayton's *Endymion and Phoebe* (published in 1595 but written earlier), in which the erotic tradition is somewhat idealized into moral allegory. Most important, however, Shakespeare knew his Ovid, both firsthand and in Golding's English translation (1567). He appears to have combined three mythical tales from the *Metamorphoses*. The narrative outline is to be found in Venus' pursuit of Adonis (Book 10), but the bashful reluctance of the young man is more reminiscent of Hermaphroditus (Book 4) and Narcissus (Book 3). Hermaphroditus pleads youth as his reason for wishing to escape the clutches of the water nymph Salmacis, and so is transformed with her into a single body containing both sexes; Narcissus evades the nymph Echo out of self-infatuation. Shakespeare has thus drawn a composite portrait of male coyness, a subject he was to explore further in the sonnets. Such a theme was suited to a nobleman of Southampton's youth and prospects. In tone it was also well suited to the aristocratic and intellectual set who read such poetry. Shakespeare here aimed at a more refined audience than that for which he wrote plays, though his theatrical audience was generally intelligent and well-to-do. The ornate qualities of *Venus and Adonis* should be judged in the fashionable context of a sophisticated audience.

The poem is, among other things, a tour de force of stylized poetic techniques. The story itself is relatively uneventful, and the characters are static. For two-thirds of the poem, very little happens other than a series of amorous claspings from which Adonis feebly attempts to extricate himself. Even his subsequent fight with the boar and his violent death are occasions for rhetorical pathos rather than for vivid narrative description. The story is essentially a frame. Similarly, we must not expect psychological insight or meaningful self-discovery. The conventions of amatory verse do not encourage a serious interest in character. Venus and Adonis are mouthpieces for contrasting attitudes toward love. They debate a favorite courtly topic in the style of John Lyly. Both appeal to conventional wisdom and speak in *sententiae*, or aphoristic pronouncements. Venus, for example, warning Adonis of the need for caution in pursuing the boar, opines that "Danger deviseth shifts; wit waits on fear" (l. 690). Adonis, pleading his unreadiness for love, cites commonplace analogies: "No fisher but the ungrown fry forbears. / The mellow plum doth fall, the green sticks fast" (ll. 526–527). In substance, their arguments are equally conventional. Venus urges a carpe diem philosophy of seizing the moment of pleasure. "Make use of time, let not advantage slip; / Beauty within itself should not be wasted" (ll. 129–130). She bolsters her claim with an appeal to the "law of nature," according to which all living things are obliged to reproduce themselves; only by begetting can man conquer time and death. Yet however close this position may be to a major theme of the sonnets, it does not go unchallenged. Adonis charges plausibly that Venus is only rationalizing her lust: "O strange excuse, / When reason is the bawd to lust's abuse!" (ll. 791–792). His plea for more time in which to mature and prove his manliness is commendable, however much we may smile at his inability to be aroused by Venus' blandishments. Thus, neither contestant wins the argument. Venus is proved right in her fear that Adonis will be killed by the boar he hunts, but Adonis' rejection of idle lust for manly activity affirms a conventional truth. The debate is in a sense an ingeniously elaborate literary exercise, yet it also allows for reflection on contrasting views of love as sensual and spiritual, absurd and magnificent, funny and serious.

The narrator's persona is central to the ambivalence in the debate. He too speaks in *sententiae*, and his aphorisms appear to sympathize with both contestants. At times, he affirms the irresistible force of love: "What though the rose have prickles, yet 'tis plucked" (l. 574). At other times he laughs at Venus for her vacillation of mood: "Thy weal and woe are both of them extremes. / Despair and hope makes thee ridiculous" (ll. 987–988). Like Ovid's usual persona, the speaker here is both intrigued and amused by love, compelled to heed its power and yet aware of the absurdities. The result is a characteristic Ovidian blend of irony and pathos. The irony is especially evident in the delightful comic touches that undermine the potential seriousness of the action: Venus like an Amazon pulling Adonis off his mount and tucking him under one arm, pouting and blushing; Adonis' horse chasing away after a mare in heat, leaving Adonis to fend for himself; Venus fainting at the thought of the boar and pulling Adonis right on top of her, "in the very lists of love, / Her champion mounted for the hot encounter" (ll. 595–596). These devices distance us from the action and create an atmosphere of elegant entertainment. Yet the poem is also suffused with the rich pathos of sensuous emotion. The sensuousness would cloy without the ironic humor, whereas the humor would seem frivolous without the pathos.

The poem hints at moral allegory, in the manner of Ovidian mythologizing. Venus represents herself as the goddess not only of erotic passion but of eternal love conquering time and death. Because Adonis perversely spurns this ideal, Venus concludes that human beauty must perish and that man's happiness must be subject to mischance. Yet this reading is only one part of the argument and is contradicted by an opposing suggestion that Adonis is the rational principle attempting unsuccessfully to govern man's lust (the boar and Adonis' unbridled horse). These contradictions, which derive from the structure of the poem as a debate, and also from Renaissance Neoplatonism, confirm our impression that the allegory is not the true "meaning" of the poem but is part of an ambiguous view of love as both exalted and earthly, a mystery that we will never comprehend in single terms. The allegory elevates the seriousness, adding poetic dignity to what might otherwise appear to be an unabashedly erotic poem. We should not minimize the sexual teasing or fail to acknowledge our own erotic pleasure in it. Venus' repeated encounters with Adonis take the form of ingeniously varied positions, ending in coital embrace although without consummation. Adonis' passive role invites the male reader to fantasize himself in Adonis' place, being seduced by the goddess of beauty. The famous passage comparing Venus' body to a deer park with "pleasant fountains," "sweet bottom grass," and "round rising hillocks" (ll. 229–240) is graphic through the use of double entendre without being pornographic. The poem is equally explicit in its "banquet" of the five senses (ll. 433–450). This is the "naughty" Ovid of the *Ars Amatoria*.

Shakespeare's poem is an embroidery of poetic flourishes, of "conceits" or ingeniously wrought similes, of artfully constructed digressions such as the narrative of Adonis' horse, and of color symbolism. Images usually are drawn from nature (eagles, birds caught in nets, wolves, berries) or connote burning, blazing, and shining (torches, jewels). The dominant colors are red and white, usually paired antithetically: the red of the rising sun or Adonis' blushing face or Mars' ensign, the white of an alabaster hand or fresh bed linen or "ashy-pale" anger. Ironically, too, the boar's frothy-white mouth is stained with red, and Adonis' red blood blemishes his "wonted lily white." Adonis' flower, the anemone, is reddish-purple and white. A similarly balanced antithesis pervades the play's rhetorical figures, as in the symmetrical repetition of words in grammatically parallel phrases *(parison)*, or in phrases of equal length *(isocolon)*, or in inverted order *(antimetabole)*, or at the beginning and ending of a line *(epanalepsis)*, and so on. These pyrotechnics may at first seem mechanical, but they too have a place in a work of art that celebrates both the erotic and the spiritual in love. Decoration has its function and is not mere embellishment for its own sake.

# Venus and Adonis

*"Vilia miretur vulgus; mihi flavus Apollo Pocula
Castalia plena ministret aqua."*

*To the* RIGHT HONORABLE HENRY WRIOTHESLEY,
*Earl of Southampton, and Baron of Titchfield.*

RIGHT HONORABLE,
   I know not how I shall offend in dedicating my
unpolished lines to your lordship, nor how the
world will censure me for choosing so strong a
prop to support so weak a burden; only if your
honor seem but pleased, I account myself highly
praised, and vow to take advantage of all idle
hours, till I have honored you with some graver
labor. But if the first heir of my invention prove 8
deformed, I shall be sorry it had so noble a god-
father, and never after ear so barren a land, for 10
fear it yield me still so bad a harvest. I leave it to
your honorable survey, and your honor to your
heart's content, which I wish may always answer your own wish and the world's hopeful ex-
pectation.

                              Your honor's in all duty,

                              William Shakespeare.

**Motto: Vilia miretur,** etc. Let the base vulgar admire trash; may golden-
haired Apollo serve me goblets filled from the Castalian spring. (Ovid,
*Amores,* l.15.35–36).
**Dedication: Henry Wriothesley, Earl of Southampton** (A popular and
brilliant young gentleman of nineteen years, already prominent at court.
Subsequent dedications by Shakespeare and others indicate that he was
a genuinely devoted patron of literature throughout his life.)
**8 the first . . . invention** (This phrase has been variously interpreted to
mean Shakespeare's first written work, his first printed work, his first
"invented" work in the sense that the plots of his plays were usually not
original with him, his first work independent of collaborators, or his first
"literary" work, since plays were unliterary in the Elizabethan sense. The
second and last are the most probable.)   **10 ear** plow, cultivate

Even as the sun with purple-colored face
Had ta'en his last leave of the weeping morn,          2
Rose-cheeked Adonis hied him to the chase.          3
Hunting he loved, but love he laughed to scorn.
  Sick-thoughted Venus makes amain unto him,          5
  And like a boldfaced suitor 'gins to woo him.

"Thrice-fairer than myself," thus she began,
"The field's chief flower, sweet above compare,
Stain to all nymphs, more lovely than a man,          9
More white and red than doves or roses are:
  Nature that made thee, with herself at strife,          11
  Saith that the world hath ending with thy life.          12

"Vouchsafe, thou wonder, to alight thy steed,          13
And rein his proud head to the saddlebow.          14
If thou wilt deign this favor, for thy meed          15
A thousand honey secrets shalt thou know.          16
  Here come and sit, where never serpent hisses,
  And being set, I'll smother thee with kisses;

"And yet not cloy thy lips with loathed satiety,
But rather famish them amid their plenty,
Making them red and pale with fresh variety—
Ten kisses short as one, one long as twenty.
  A summer's day will seem an hour but short,
  Being wasted in such time-beguiling sport."          24

---

**2 the weeping morn** i.e., the goddess of the dawn, Aurora, weeping to be left by the sun god. (*Weeping* suggests the dew of morning.) **3 hied him** betook himself, hastened **5 Sick-thoughted** lovesick.  **makes amain** hastens **9 Stain to** eclipsing (in beauty).  **nymphs** i.e., young and beautiful women **11–12 Nature . . . life** i.e., nature strove to surpass herself in making her masterpiece, Adonis, and says that if you die the world will cease. (The story of Adonis' death, and of the anemone that springs from his blood, is a vegetation myth.) **13 Vouchsafe** deign. **alight** alight from **14 the saddlebow** the arch in or the pieces forming the front of the saddle **15 meed** reward **16 honey** i.e., sweet **24 wasted** spent

With this she seizeth on his sweating palm,      25
The precedent of pith and livelihood,      26
And, trembling in her passion, calls it balm,
Earth's sovereign salve, to do a goddess good.      28
     Being so enraged, desire doth lend her force      29
     Courageously to pluck him from his horse.      30

Over one arm the lusty courser's rein,      31
Under her other was the tender boy,
Who blushed and pouted in a dull disdain,      33
With leaden appetite, unapt to toy;      34
     She red and hot as coals of glowing fire,
     He red for shame, but frosty in desire.

The studded bridle on a ragged bough
Nimbly she fastens. O, how quick is love!
The steed is stallèd up, and even now      39
To tie the rider she begins to prove.      40
     Backward she pushed him, as she would be thrust,
     And governed him in strength, though not in lust.

So soon was she along as he was down,      43
Each leaning on their elbows and their hips.
Now doth she stroke his cheek, now doth he frown,
And 'gins to chide, but soon she stops his lips
     And kissing speaks, with lustful language broken,      47
     "If thou wilt chide, thy lips shall never open."

He burns with bashful shame; she with her tears
Doth quench the maiden burning of his cheeks.
Then with her windy sighs and golden hairs
To fan and blow them dry again she seeks.
     He saith she is immodest, blames her miss;      53
     What follows more, she murders with a kiss.

---

**25 sweating** i.e., indicative of youth; not dried with age    **26 precedent**
sign, promise.    **pith and livelihood** sexual strength and vitality
**28 sovereign** efficacious    **29 enraged** ardent    **30 Courageously** lust-
fully.    **pluck** drag    **31 lusty courser's** vigorous horse's    **33 dull** moody,
listless    **34 unapt to toy** undisposed to dally amorously    **39 stallèd**
fastened, secured (as in a stall)    **40 prove** try    **43 along** lying at his
side    **47 broken** interrupted    **53 miss** offense, misconduct

Even as an empty eagle, sharp by fast,                           55
Tires with her beak on feathers, flesh, and bone,               56
Shaking her wings, devouring all in haste,
Till either gorge be stuffed or prey be gone,                    58
   Even so she kissed his brow, his cheek, his chin,
   And where she ends she doth anew begin.

Forced to content, but never to obey,                            61
Panting he lies and breatheth in her face.
She feedeth on the steam as on a prey,
And calls it heavenly moisture, air of grace,
   Wishing her cheeks were gardens full of flowers,
   So they were dewed with such distilling showers.      66

Look how a bird lies tangled in a net,                           67
So fastened in her arms Adonis lies;
Pure shame and awed resistance made him fret,                   69
Which bred more beauty in his angry eyes.
   Rain added to a river that is rank                   71
   Perforce will force it overflow the bank.

Still she entreats, and prettily entreats,
For to a pretty ear she tunes her tale.
Still is he sullen, still he lours and frets,
Twixt crimson shame and anger ashy-pale.
   Being red, she loves him best; and being white,      77
   Her best is bettered with a more delight.            78

Look how he can, she cannot choose but love;
And by her fair immortal hand she swears
From his soft bosom never to remove,                             81
Till he take truce with her contending tears,                    82
   Which long have rained, making her cheeks all wet;
   And one sweet kiss shall pay this countless debt.     84

---

**55 sharp by fast** hungry as a result of fasting   **56 Tires** tears, feeds
ravenously.   **on** at   **58 gorge** stomach   **61 content** acquiesce.   **obey** i.e.,
answer her lust   **66 So** provided that.   **distilling** gently falling, in fine
droplets   **67 Look how** just as   **69 awed** daunted, overborne   **71 rank**
full to overflowing   **77 Being** i.e., he being   **78 more** greater
**81 remove** move, remove herself   **82 take truce** come to terms
**84 countless** beyond reckoning

Upon this promise did he raise his chin,
Like a divedapper peering through a wave,     86
Who, being looked on, ducks as quickly in.
So offers he to give what she did crave;
    But when her lips were ready for his pay,
    He winks and turns his lips another way.     90

Never did passenger in summer's heat     91
More thirst for drink than she for this good turn.
Her help she sees, but help she cannot get;
She bathes in water, yet her fire must burn.     94
    "O, pity," 'gan she cry, "flint-hearted boy!
    'Tis but a kiss I beg. Why art thou coy?

"I have been wooed, as I entreat thee now,
Even by the stern and direful god of war,     98
Whose sinewy neck in battle ne'er did bow,
Who conquers where he comes in every jar;     100
    Yet hath he been my captive and my slave,
    And begged for that which thou unasked shalt have.

"Over my altars hath he hung his lance,
His battered shield, his uncontrollèd crest,     104
And for my sake hath learned to sport and dance,
To toy, to wanton, dally, smile, and jest,     106
    Scorning his churlish drum and ensign red,
    Making my arms his field, his tent my bed.     108

"Thus he that overruled I overswayed,
Leading him prisoner in a red-rose chain.
Strong-tempered steel his stronger strength obeyed,
Yet was he servile to my coy disdain.     112
    O, be not proud, nor brag not of thy might,
    For mastering her that foiled the god of fight!     114

---

**86 divedapper** dabchick, a common English water bird    **90 winks** shuts
his eyes (and winces)    **91 passenger** wayfarer    **94 water** i.e., her
tears.    **fire** (of passion)    **98 direful** inspiring dread    **100 where** wherever.    **jar** fight    **104 uncontrollèd** unconquered, unbowed.    **crest** i.e., of
helmet    **106 toy, wanton** dally, sport amorously    **108 arms** (with a pun
on "weapons")    **112 coy** aloof, teasing    **114 foiled** vanquished

"Touch but my lips with those fair lips of thine—          115
Though mine be not so fair, yet are they red—
The kiss shall be thine own as well as mine.          117
What seest thou in the ground? Hold up thy head.
  Look in mine eyeballs, there thy beauty lies;          119
  Then why not lips on lips, since eyes in eyes?

"Art thou ashamed to kiss? Then wink again,          121
And I will wink; so shall the day seem night.
Love keeps his revels where there are but twain;
Be bold to play, our sport is not in sight.          124
  These blue-veined violets whereon we lean
  Never can blab, nor know not what we mean.          126

"The tender spring upon thy tempting lip          127
Shows thee unripe, yet mayst thou well be tasted.
Make use of time, let not advantage slip;          129
Beauty within itself should not be wasted.          130
  Fair flowers that are not gathered in their prime
  Rot and consume themselves in little time.

"Were I hard-favored, foul, or wrinkled old,          133
Ill-nurtured, crooked, churlish, harsh in voice,
O'erworn, despisèd, rheumatic, and cold,          135
Thick-sighted, barren, lean, and lacking juice,          136
  Then mightst thou pause, for then I were not for
    thee;
  But having no defects, why dost abhor me?

---

115 **Touch** i.e., if you touch   117 **thine . . . mine** i.e., mutual, shared
119 **there . . . lies** i.e., (1) see your beauty reflected there (2) your beauty
lies in my beholding   121 **wink** close the eyes   124 **not in sight** observed by no one   126 **mean** intend   127 **spring** growth (i.e., down)
129 **advantage** opportunity   130 **Beauty . . . wasted** beauty should not
be wasted by being kept to itself   133 **hard-favored** ugly.   **foul** ugly
135 **O'erworn** worn by time   136 **Thick-sighted** dim-eyed

"Thou canst not see one wrinkle in my brow;
Mine eyes are gray and bright and quick in turning;        140
My beauty as the spring doth yearly grow,        141
My flesh is soft and plump, my marrow burning;        142
    My smooth moist hand, were it with thy hand felt,        143
    Would in thy palm dissolve, or seem to melt.

"Bid me discourse, I will enchant thine ear,
Or like a fairy, trip upon the green,        146
Or like a nymph, with long disheveled hair,
Dance on the sands, and yet no footing seen.        148
    Love is a spirit all compact of fire,        149
    Not gross to sink, but light, and will aspire.        150

"Witness this primrose bank whereon I lie;
These forceless flowers like sturdy trees support me.        152
Two strengthless doves will draw me through the sky,        153
From morn till night, even where I list to sport me.        154
    Is love so light, sweet boy, and may it be        155
    That thou shouldst think it heavy unto thee?        156

"Is thine own heart to thine own face affected?        157
Can thy right hand seize love upon thy left?        158
Then woo thyself, be of thyself rejected;        159
Steal thine own freedom and complain on theft.        160
    Narcissus so himself himself forsook,        161
    And died to kiss his shadow in the brook.        162

**140 gray** i.e., blue. **quick in turning** i.e., animated **141 as . . . grow** i.e.,
is perennially renewed, like spring **142 marrow** vital or essential
part. **burning** sexually ardent **143 moist** (Indicative of youth and
passion, as with *sweating* in l. 25.) **146 trip** dance **148 footing** foot-
print **149 compact** composed **150 gross** heavy. (The heavy elements,
earth and water, sink; fire and air rise.) **aspire** rise **152 forceless**
frail **153 doves** (Venus' chariot was depicted as being drawn by
doves.) **154 list** desire **155 light** (1) rising, weightless (2) wanton
**156 heavy** (1) weighty (2) troublous **157 affected** drawn by affection
**158 upon thy left** i.e., by clasping the left hand **159 of** by **160 Steal
. . . freedom** i.e., take your own affections captive. **on** of
**161 Narcissus** a beautiful youth in classical mythology who, leaning
over a pool to drink, fell in love with his reflection and stayed there
until he died. He was afterward changed into a flower. (Ovid, *Metamorphoses,* 3.339–510.) **himself himself forsook** i.e., abandoned himself to
a hopeless passion for himself **162 to kiss** i.e., seeking fruitlessly to
kiss

"Torches are made to light, jewels to wear,
Dainties to taste, fresh beauty for the use,
Herbs for their smell, and sappy plants to bear.          165
Things growing to themselves are growth's abuse.          166
  Seeds spring from seeds, and beauty breedeth
    beauty.
  Thou wast begot; to get it is thy duty.          168

"Upon the earth's increase why shouldst thou feed,
Unless the earth with thy increase be fed?
By law of nature thou art bound to breed,
That thine may live when thou thyself art dead;
  And so, in spite of death, thou dost survive,
  In that thy likeness still is left alive."

By this the lovesick queen began to sweat,          175
For where they lay the shadow had forsook them,
And Titan, tirèd in the midday heat,          177
With burning eye did hotly overlook them,          178
  Wishing Adonis had his team to guide,          179
  So he were like him, and by Venus' side.          180

And now Adonis, with a lazy sprite,          181
And with a heavy, dark, disliking eye,
His louring brows o'erwhelming his fair sight,          183
Like misty vapors when they blot the sky,
  Souring his cheeks, cries, "Fie, no more of love!          185
  The sun doth burn my face; I must remove."          186

---

**165 sappy plants** sap-bearing fruit trees  **166 to themselves** i.e., solely
for their own use  **168 get** beget, procreate  **175 By this** by this time
**177 Titan** the sun god.  **tirèd** attired  **178 overlook** look upon  **179 his
team** i.e., Titan's team of horses  **180 So . . . him** i.e., so that he, Titan,
might be in Adonis' place  **181 lazy sprite** dull spirit  **183 o'erwhelming**
overhanging so as to cover.  **sight** eyes  **185 Souring his cheeks** scowling  **186 remove** move

"Ay me," quoth Venus, "young, and so unkind?     187
What bare excuses mak'st thou to be gone!
I'll sigh celestial breath, whose gentle wind
Shall cool the heat of this descending sun.     190
  I'll make a shadow for thee of my hairs;
  If they burn too, I'll quench them with my tears.

"The sun that shines from heaven shines but warm,
And, lo, I lie between that sun and thee.
The heat I have from thence doth little harm;
Thine eye darts forth the fire that burneth me,
  And were I not immortal, life were done     197
  Between this heavenly and earthly sun.

"Art thou obdurate, flinty, hard as steel?
Nay, more than flint, for stone at rain relenteth.     200
Art thou a woman's son, and canst not feel
What 'tis to love, how want of love tormenteth?
  O, had thy mother borne so hard a mind,
  She had not brought forth thee, but died unkind.     204

"What am I, that thou shouldst contemn me this?     205
Or what great danger dwells upon my suit?     206
What were thy lips the worse for one poor kiss?     207
Speak, fair, but speak fair words, or else be mute.     208
  Give me one kiss, I'll give it thee again,     209
  And one for interest, if thou wilt have twain.

"Fie, lifeless picture, cold and senseless stone,     211
Well-painted idol, image dull and dead,
Statue contenting but the eye alone,
Thing like a man, but of no woman bred!
  Thou art no man, though of a man's complexion,     215
  For men will kiss even by their own direction."     216

---

**187 unkind** unrelenting; unnatural   **190 descending** beating down
**197 were done** would be undone, finished   **200 relenteth** wears slowly
away   **204 unkind** unnaturally unrelenting, not fulfilling her natural
function   **205 contemn** refuse scornfully.  **this** i.e., this request
**206 dwells upon** attends   **207 What** in what way   **208 fair** fair one
**209 Give** if you give   **211 senseless** insensible   **215 complexion** outward
appearance   **216 direction** inclination

This said, impatience chokes her pleading tongue,
And swelling passion doth provoke a pause.
Red cheeks and fiery eyes blaze forth her wrong;                    219
Being judge in love, she cannot right her cause.                    220
   And now she weeps, and now she fain would speak,    221
   And now her sobs do her intendments break.              222

Sometimes she shakes her head and then his hand,                    223
Now gazeth she on him, now on the ground;
Sometimes her arms enfold him like a band.                          225
She would, he will not in her arms be bound;                        226
   And when from thence he struggles to be gone,
   She locks her lily fingers one in one.

"Fondling," she saith, "since I have hemmed thee here              229
Within the circuit of this ivory pale,                             230
I'll be a park, and thou shalt be my deer.                         231
Feed where thou wilt, on mountain or in dale;
   Graze on my lips; and if those hills be dry,
   Stray lower, where the pleasant fountains lie.            234

"Within this limit is relief enough,                               235
Sweet bottom grass and high delightful plain,                      236
Round rising hillocks, brakes obscure and rough,                   237
To shelter thee from tempest and from rain.
   Then be my deer, since I am such a park;
   No dog shall rouse thee, though a thousand bark."         240

**219 blaze forth** proclaim (with a metaphorical sense of "seem to burn,"
"show by their flaming")   **220 Being . . . cause** i.e., although goddess
and hence arbiter of love, Venus cannot prevail in her own case
**221 fain** gladly   **222 do . . . break** interrupt what she intends to say
**223 his hand** (i.e., not in a handshake but in a gesture of frustration)
**225 like a band** as in a bond or fetter   **226 would** i.e., would bind him
**229 Fondling** foolish one   **230 pale** fence (i.e., her arms; the sexual
topography is continued in *fountains, bottom grass, hillocks, brakes,*
etc.)   **231 park** deer preserve.   **deer** (with a pun on *dear*)
**234 fountains** (1) springs (2) breasts   **235 limit** boundary.   **relief**
(1) pasture (2) sexual pleasure   **236 bottom grass** valley grass (with an
allusion to pubic hair)   **237 brakes** thickets (again with sexual suggestion).   **obscure** dark.   **rough** shaggy, dense   **240 rouse** cause to start
from cover

At this Adonis smiles as in disdain,
That in each cheek appears a pretty dimple. 242
Love made those hollows, if himself were slain, 243
He might be buried in a tomb so simple, 244
    Foreknowing well, if there he came to lie,
    Why, there Love lived; and there he could not die. 246

These lovely caves, these round enchanting pits,
Opened their mouths to swallow Venus' liking. 248
Being mad before, how doth she now for wits? 249
Struck dead at first, what needs a second striking?
    Poor queen of love, in thine own law forlorn, 251
    To love a cheek that smiles at thee in scorn!

Now which way shall she turn? What shall she say?
Her words are done, her woes the more increasing;
The time is spent; her object will away,
And from her twining arms doth urge releasing.
    "Pity," she cries, "some favor, some remorse!" 257
    Away he springs and hasteth to his horse.

But, lo, from forth a copse that neighbors by, 259
A breeding jennet, lusty, young, and proud, 260
Adonis' trampling courser doth espy,
And forth she rushes, snorts, and neighs aloud.
    The strong-necked steed, being tied unto a tree,
    Breaketh his rein, and to her straight goes he. 264

---

**242 That** so that   **243 Love** Cupid.  **if** so that if   **244 simple** unadorned   **246 Love** (1) the essence of love, loveliness (2) Cupid himself
**248 Opened . . . liking** i.e., looked so winsome in their dimpling that
Venus was engulfed, swallowed up, by love.  **liking** desire   **249 how . . .
wits** i.e., how may she keep her sanity now   **251 in . . . forlorn** condemned to suffer under your own rule of love   **257 remorse** compas-
sion   **259 copse . . . by** neighboring thicket   **260 breeding** in heat.
**jennet** small Spanish mare.  **lusty** spirited   **264 straight** straightway

Imperiously he leaps, he neighs, he bounds,
And now his woven girths he breaks asunder.
The bearing earth with his hard hoof he wounds,        267
Whose hollow womb resounds like heaven's thunder.
    The iron bit he crusheth 'tween his teeth,
    Controlling what he was controllèd with.

His ears up-pricked, his braided hanging mane
Upon his compassed crest now stand on end;             272
His nostrils drink the air, and forth again,
As from a furnace, vapors doth he send.
    His eye, which scornfully glisters like fire,
    Shows his hot courage and his high desire.          276

Sometimes he trots, as if he told the steps,          277
With gentle majesty and modest pride;
Anon he rears upright, curvets, and leaps,            279
As who should say, "Lo, thus my strength is tried,    280
    And this I do to captivate the eye
    Of the fair breeder that is standing by."

What recketh he his rider's angry stir,               283
His flattering "Holla," or his "Stand, I say"?        284
What cares he now for curb or pricking spur?
For rich caparisons or trappings gay?                 286
    He sees his love, and nothing else he sees,
    For nothing else with his proud sight agrees.

---

**267 bearing** receiving   **272 compassed** arched.   **crest** ridge of the
neck   **276 courage** passion   **277 told** numbered   **279 curvets** raises his
forelegs and then springs with his hind legs before the forelegs reach
the ground   **280 As who should** as one might.   **tried** tested
**283 recketh he** does he care about or pay attention to.   **stir** bustle
**284 flattering** cajoling.   **Holla** stop   **286 caparisons** gaily ornamental
cloth coverings for the saddle and harness

Look when a painter would surpass the life,    289
In limning out a well-proportioned steed,    290
His art with nature's workmanship at strife,
As if the dead the living should exceed,    292
   So did this horse excel a common one
   In shape, in courage, color, pace, and bone.    294

Round-hoofed, short-jointed, fetlocks shag and long,    295
Broad breast, full eye, small head, and nostril wide,
High crest, short ears, straight legs and passing strong,    297
Thin mane, thick tail, broad buttock, tender hide:    298
   Look what a horse should have he did not lack,    299
   Save a proud rider on so proud a back.

Sometimes he scuds far off, and there he stares;
Anon he starts at stirring of a feather;
To bid the wind a base he now prepares,    303
And whe'er he run or fly they know not whether;    304
   For through his mane and tail the high wind sings,
   Fanning the hairs, who wave like feathered wings.

He looks upon his love and neighs unto her;
She answers him as if she knew his mind.
Being proud, as females are, to see him woo her,
She puts on outward strangeness, seems unkind,    310
   Spurns at his love and scorns the heat he feels,    311
   Beating his kind embracements with her heels.    312

---

**289 Look when** just as when    **290 limning out** portraying, drawing
**292 dead** inanimate    **294 bone** frame    **295 fetlocks** lower part of
horses' legs where the tuft of hair grows behind, just above the hoof.
**shag** shaggy    **297 crest** ridge of the neck.    **passing** surpassingly
**298 tender hide** i.e., delicate of hide, not coarse    **299 Look what**
whatever    **303 bid the wind a base** challenge the wind to a contest.
(From the children's game of prisoner's base.)    **304 whe'er** whether.
**whether** which of the two    **310 outward strangeness** seeming coldness.    **unkind** unattracted sexually, not responding to natural feeling
**311 Spurns at** (1) kicks at (2) rejects, repels    **312 kind** (1) affectionate,
passionate (2) prompted by nature

Then, like a melancholy malcontent,
He vails his tail that, like a falling plume,    314
Cool shadow to his melting buttock lent;
He stamps and bites the poor flies in his fume.    316
   His love, perceiving how he was enraged,
   Grew kinder, and his fury was assuaged.

His testy master goeth about to take him,    319
When, lo, the unbacked breeder, full of fear,    320
Jealous of catching, swiftly doth forsake him,    321
With her the horse, and left Adonis there.    322
   As they were mad, unto the wood they hie them,    323
   Outstripping crows that strive to overfly them.    324

All swoll'n with chafing, down Adonis sits,    325
Banning his boisterous and unruly beast;    326
And now the happy season once more fits    327
That lovesick Love by pleading may be blest;    328
   For lovers say the heart hath treble wrong
   When it is barred the aidance of the tongue.    330

An oven that is stopped, or river stayed,    331
Burneth more hotly, swelleth with more rage;
So of concealèd sorrow may be said.    333
Free vent of words love's fire doth assuage;    334
   But when the heart's attorney once is mute,    335
   The client breaks, as desperate in his suit.    336

**314 vails** lowers   **316 fume** anger   **319 testy** irritated.   **goeth about**
makes an effort   **320 unbacked** unbroken, riderless.   **breeder** i.e.,
female in heat   **321 Jealous of catching** fearful of being caught
**322 horse** i.e., stallion   **323 As** as if.   **hie them** hasten   **324 overfly**
**them** fly faster than they can run, or keep pace with them in flight
**325 swoll'n with chafing** puffed with anger   **326 Banning** cursing
**327 fits** is fitting, is suited   **328 Love** i.e., Venus, the goddess of love, not
Cupid, as at ll. 243–246   **330 aidance** help   **331 stopped** stopped up.
**stayed** hindered, dammed   **333 may** it may   **334 love's . . . assuage**
assuages love's fire   **335 the heart's attorney** i.e., the tongue
**336 breaks** (1) goes bankrupt (2) breaks asunder, as the heart is said to
break in rejected love

He sees her coming and begins to glow,
Even as a dying coal revives with wind,
And with his bonnet hides his angry brow,       339
Looks on the dull earth with disturbèd mind,
    Taking no notice that she is so nigh,       341
    For all askance he holds her in his eye.       342

O, what a sight it was, wistly to view       343
How she came stealing to the wayward boy!
To note the fighting conflict of her hue,
How white and red each other did destroy!
    But now her cheek was pale, and by and by       347
    It flashed forth fire, as lightning from the sky.

Now was she just before him as he sat,
And like a lowly lover down she kneels;
With one fair hand she heaveth up his hat,
Her other tender hand his fair cheek feels.
    His tenderer cheek receives her soft hand's print,       353
    As apt as new-fall'n snow takes any dint.       354

O, what a war of looks was then between them!
Her eyes petitioners to his eyes suing,
His eyes saw her eyes as they had not seen them;       357
Her eyes wooed still, his eyes disdained the wooing;
    And all this dumb play had his acts made plain       359
    With tears which, choruslike, her eyes did rain.       360

---

**339 bonnet** hat. **hides . . . brow** (i.e., he pulls his hat down over his brows) **341 Taking** i.e., pretending to take **342 all . . . eye** he watches her out of the corner of his eye **343 wistly** earnestly, attentively **347 But now** a short time ago **353 tenderer** i.e., even more tender than her hand **354 dint** impression **357 as** as if **359 dumb play** dumb show. **his** its. **made plain** explained **360 With** by. **choruslike** i.e., providing a choric interpretation to the dumb show

Full gently now she takes him by the hand,
A lily prisoned in a jail of snow,
Or ivory in an alabaster band,                                        363
So white a friend engirts so white a foe.                             364
  This beauteous combat, willful and unwilling,
  Showed like two silver doves that sit a-billing.           366

Once more the engine of her thoughts began:                          367
"O fairest mover on this mortal round,                               368
Would thou wert as I am, and I a man,
My heart all whole as thine, thy heart my wound!                     370
  For one sweet look thy help I would assure thee,          371
  Though nothing but my body's bane would cure
    thee."                                           372

"Give me my hand," saith he, "why dost thou feel it?"                373
"Give me my heart," saith she, "and thou shalt have it.              374
O, give it me, lest thy hard heart do steel it,                      375
And being steeled, soft sighs can never grave it.                    376
  Then love's deep groans I never shall regard,
  Because Adonis' heart hath made mine hard."

"For shame," he cries, "let go, and let me go!
My day's delight is past, my horse is gone,
And 'tis your fault I am bereft him so.
I pray you hence, and leave me here alone;                           382
  For all my mind, my thought, my busy care,
  Is how to get my palfrey from the mare."                    384

---

**363 band** bond, fetter   **364 So . . . foe** i.e., so white is her passionate
hand thus enclosing his unwilling white hand   **366 Showed** looked
**367 the engine of her thoughts** i.e., her tongue   **368 mover** one who
moves or walks; mortal.   **mortal round** earth   **370 thy heart my wound**
your heart wounded by me as mine is by you   **371 For** in return for.
**thy help . . . thee** I would promise to help you   **372 bane** ruin, death
**373 Give me** i.e., let go   **374 it** i.e., your hand   **375 give . . . it** i.e., give
me your heart, lest your hardness of heart turn it to steel (with a suggestion of *steal*: don't steal your heart from me). Venus goes on to say
that Adonis can also turn *her* heart to steel.   **376 grave** engrave, make
an impression on   **382 hence** i.e., go   **384 palfrey** saddle horse

Thus she replies: "Thy palfrey, as he should,
Welcomes the warm approach of sweet desire.
Affection is a coal that must be cooled,      387
Else, suffered, it will set the heart on fire.      388
     The sea hath bounds, but deep desire hath none;
     Therefore no marvel though thy horse be gone.

"How like a jade he stood, tied to the tree,      391
Servilely mastered with a leathern rein!
But when he saw his love, his youth's fair fee,      393
He held such petty bondage in disdain,
     Throwing the base thong from his bending crest,      395
     Enfranchising his mouth, his back, his breast.      396

"Who sees his true love in her naked bed,      397
Teaching the sheets a whiter hue than white,
But when his glutton eye so full hath fed,      399
His other agents aim at like delight?      400
     Who is so faint that dares not be so bold
     To touch the fire, the weather being cold?

"Let me excuse thy courser, gentle boy;
And learn of him, I heartily beseech thee,
To take advantage on presented joy.      405
Though I were dumb, yet his proceedings teach thee.      406
     O, learn to love; the lesson is but plain,
     And once made perfect, never lost again."      408

---

**387 Affection** passion.   **coal** ember    **388 suffered** permitted to continue    **391 jade** spiritless worn-out nag    **393 fair fee** due reward
**395 base** worthless, paltry.   **bending crest** arching ridge of the neck
**396 Enfranchising** freeing    **397 in . . . bed** i.e., naked in her bed
**399 But when** but that when    **400 agents** organs, senses    **405 on** of.
**presented joy** joy that presents itself    **406 dumb** unable to speak
**408 made perfect** learned completely

"I know not love," quoth he, "nor will not know it,
Unless it be a boar, and then I chase it;
'Tis much to borrow, and I will not owe it;     411
My love to love is love but to disgrace it;     412
   For I have heard it is a life in death,
     That laughs and weeps, and all but with a breath.   414

"Who wears a garment shapeless and unfinished?
Who plucks the bud before one leaf put forth?
If springing things be any jot diminished,     417
They wither in their prime, prove nothing worth.
   The colt that's backed and burdened being young   419
     Loseth his pride and never waxeth strong.

"You hurt my hand with wringing. Let us part
And leave this idle theme, this bootless chat.     422
Remove your siege from my unyielding heart;
To love's alarms it will not ope the gate.     424
   Dismiss your vows, your feignèd tears, your flattery;
     For where a heart is hard they make no battery."   426

"What, canst thou talk?" quoth she. "Hast thou a
     tongue?
O, would thou hadst not, or I had no hearing!
Thy mermaid's voice hath done me double wrong;   429
I had my load before, now pressed with bearing:   430
   Melodious discord, heavenly tune harsh sounding,
     Ear's deep sweet music, and heart's deep sore
       wounding.

**411 borrow** assume as an obligation.   **owe** have to repay   **412 My . . .
disgrace it** my only inclination toward love is a desire to render it
contemptible, discredit it   **414 all . . . breath** all in the same breath
**417 springing** sprouting, immature   **419 backed** broken in   **422 idle**
useless.   **bootless** profitless   **424 alarms** signals of attack   **426 battery**
breach in a fortified wall   **429 mermaid's** siren's   **430 pressed** oppressed, weighted down (making her previous burden of his coy beauty
now unbearable)

"Had I no eyes but ears, my ears would love
That inward beauty and invisible;      434
Or were I deaf, thy outward parts would move      435
Each part in me that were but sensible.      436
     Though neither eyes nor ears, to hear nor see,
     Yet should I be in love by touching thee.

"Say that the sense of feeling were bereft me,
And that I could not see, nor hear, nor touch,
And nothing but the very smell were left me,
Yet would my love to thee be still as much;
     For from the stillitory of thy face excelling      443
     Comes breath perfumed that breedeth love by
       smelling.

"But, O, what banquet wert thou to the taste,
Being nurse and feeder of the other four!
Would they not wish the feast might ever last,
And bid Suspicion double-lock the door,      448
     Lest Jealousy, that sour unwelcome guest,
     Should, by his stealing in, disturb the feast?"

Once more the ruby-colored portal opened,      451
Which to his speech did honey passage yield,      452
Like a red morn, that ever yet betokened
Wreck to the seaman, tempest to the field,      454
     Sorrow to shepherds, woe unto the birds,
     Gusts and foul flaws to herdmen and to herds.      456

---

**434 That . . . invisible** i.e., the unseen beauty of your voice    **435 deaf**
i.e., deaf as well as blind.    **outward parts** i.e., tangible body
**436 sensible** susceptible to sensual impressions    **443 stillitory** still
(used in making perfume).    **excelling** exceedingly beautiful
**448 Suspicion** caution against being detected    **451 portal** i.e., mouth
**452 honey** sweet    **454 Wreck** shipwreck. (A red sun at sunrise
proverbially betokens a storm.)    **tempest to the field** a heavy storm that
beats down the grain    **456 flaws** gusts of wind

This ill presage advisedly she marketh.                                    457
Even as the wind is hushed before it raineth,
Or as the wolf doth grin before he barketh,                                459
Or as the berry breaks before it staineth,
   Or like the deadly bullet of a gun,
   His meaning struck her ere his words begun.

And at his look she flatly falleth down,
For looks kill love, and love by looks reviveth;
A smile recures the wounding of a frown.                                   465
But blessèd bankrupt, that by love so thriveth!                            466
   The silly boy, believing she is dead,                                   467
   Claps her pale cheek, till clapping makes it red;

And all amazed brake off his late intent,                                  469
For sharply he did think to reprehend her,
Which cunning Love did wittily prevent.
Fair fall the wit that can so well defend her!                            472
   For on the grass she lies as she were slain,                            473
   Till his breath breatheth life in her again.

He wrings her nose, he strikes her on the cheeks,                          475
He bends her fingers, holds her pulses hard,                               476
He chafes her lips; a thousand ways he seeks
To mend the hurt that his unkindness marred.                               478
   He kisses her, and she, by her good will,                              479
   Will never rise, so he will kiss her still.                            480

---

**457 ill presage** prediction of storm.   **advisedly** attentively   **459 grin**
bare its teeth   **465 recures** cures   **466 blessèd** fortunate.   **that . . .
thriveth** who prospers so by this gesture of love. (*Love* is sometimes
emended to *loss,* or to *looks.* Venus paradoxically gains what she
wants—Adonis' attention—by her fainting.)   **467 silly** naive
**469 amazed** perplexed, distraught.   **brake** broke   **472 Fair fall** good
luck befall   **473 as** as if   **475 He . . . nose** (A standard first-aid remedy;
briefly stopping the air supply can induce the patient to resume breathing.)   **476 bends her fingers** (as a stimulus or test of consciousness).
**holds . . . hard** takes her pulse   **478 marred** caused to her detriment
**479 good will** consent   **480 so** provided that.   **still** continually

The night of sorrow now is turned to day.
Her two blue windows faintly she upheaveth,
Like the fair sun, when in his fresh array
He cheers the morn and all the earth relieveth;
    And as the bright sun glorifies the sky,
    So is her face illumined with her eye,

Whose beams upon his hairless face are fixed,
As if from thence they borrowed all their shine.
Were never four such lamps together mixed,          489
Had not his clouded with his brow's repine;          490
    But hers, which through the crystal tears gave light,
    Shone like the moon in water seen by night.

"O, where am I?" quoth she, "in earth or heaven,
Or in the ocean drenched, or in the fire?          494
What hour is this? Or morn or weary even?          495
Do I delight to die, or life desire?
    But now I lived, and life was death's annoy;          497
    But now I died, and death was lively joy.          498

"O, thou didst kill me; kill me once again!
Thy eyes' shrewd tutor, that hard heart of thine,          500
Hath taught them scornful tricks and such disdain
That they have murdered this poor heart of mine;
    And these mine eyes, true leaders to their queen,          503
    But for thy piteous lips no more had seen.          504

---

**489 Were never** never before were   **490 repine** repining, dissatisfaction   **494 drenched** drowned   **495 Or** either   **497 death's annoy** i.e., as wretched as death   **498 lively joy** i.e., as joyous as life   **500 shrewd** sharp, harsh   **503 leaders** guides.   **queen** i.e., the heart   **504 But for** were it not for.   **seen** had the power of sight

"Long may they kiss each other, for this cure!                    505
O, never let their crimson liveries wear!                    506
And as they last, their verdure still endure,                    507
To drive infection from the dangerous year!
    That the stargazers, having writ on death,                    509
    May say the plague is banished by thy breath.

"Pure lips, sweet seals in my soft lips imprinted,                    511
What bargains may I make, still to be sealing?                    512
To sell myself I can be well contented,
So thou wilt buy and pay and use good dealing,                    514
    Which purchase if thou make, for fear of slips                    515
    Set thy seal manual on my wax-red lips.                    516

"A thousand kisses buys my heart from me;
And pay them at thy leisure, one by one.
What is ten hundred touches unto thee?                    519
Are they not quickly told and quickly gone?                    520
    Say for nonpayment that the debt should double,
    Is twenty hundred kisses such a trouble?"

"Fair queen," quoth he, "if any love you owe me,                    523
Measure my strangeness with my unripe years.                    524
Before I know myself, seek not to know me.                    525
No fisher but the ungrown fry forbears.                    526
    The mellow plum doth fall; the green sticks fast,
    Or being early plucked is sour to taste.

**505 they** i.e., your lips.    **for** in payment for, as a means of effecting
**506 crimson liveries** uniforms or costumes of crimson.    **wear** wear
out    **507 their verdure** may their fresh fragrance (Alludes to belief in
the efficacy of certain herbs to ward off contagion.)    **509 writ on death**
predicted (by means of astrology) an epidemic of plague    **511 seals . . .
imprinted** stamps that have left their impression on my soft lips
**512 still to be sealing** (1) to continue kissing always (2) to seal a bar-
gain    **514 So** provided that    **515 slips** errors or fraudulent payment
(which Venus suggests they avoid by means of a *seal manual* or seal
placed on the contract of their love)    **516 wax-red** (since wax would be
used in sealing)    **519 touches** i.e., kisses    **520 told** counted    **523 owe**
bear    **524 Measure . . . with** i.e., explain my reserve by    **525 to know
me** (with erotic suggestion)    **526 No . . . forbears** there is no fisherman
who does not throw back immature fish

"Look the world's comforter, with weary gait,                 529
His day's hot task hath ended in the west;
The owl, night's herald, shrieks; 'tis very late;
The sheep are gone to fold, birds to their nest,
    And coal-black clouds that shadow heaven's light
    Do summon us to part and bid good night.

"Now let me say 'Good night,' and so say you;
If you will say so, you shall have a kiss."
"Good night," quoth she, and, ere he says "Adieu,"
The honey fee of parting tendered is.                         538
    Her arms do lend his neck a sweet embrace;
    Incorporate then they seem; face grows to face;           540

Till, breathless, he disjoined, and backward drew
The heavenly moisture, that sweet coral mouth,
Whose precious taste her thirsty lips well knew,
Whereon they surfeit, yet complain on drouth.                 544
    He with her plenty pressed, she faint with dearth,        545
    Their lips together glued, fall to the earth.

Now quick desire hath caught the yielding prey,
And gluttonlike she feeds, yet never filleth;
Her lips are conquerors, his lips obey,
Paying what ransom the insulter willeth,                      550
    Whose vulture thought doth pitch the price so high        551
    That she will draw his lips' rich treasure dry.

And having felt the sweetness of the spoil,                   553
With blindfold fury she begins to forage;
Her face doth reek and smoke, her blood doth boil,            555
And careless lust stirs up a desperate courage,               556
    Planting oblivion, beating reason back,                   557
    Forgetting shame's pure blush and honor's wrack.          558

**529 Look** see how.   **world's comforter** i.e., sun   **538 honey** sweet.
**tendered is** is given   **540 Incorporate** united into one body   **544 on
drouth** of drought, of not having enough   **545 with . . . pressed** oppressed with the plenty she bestowed on him   **550 insulter** boasting
conqueror   **551 vulture** i.e., ravenous.   **pitch** set at a certain level or
point   **553 spoil** plunder, conquest   **555 reek** i.e., steam   **556 careless**
heedless   **557 Planting oblivion** implanting or causing forgetfulness
of all that she ought to remember   **558 wrack** ruin

Hot, faint, and weary, with her hard embracing,
Like a wild bird being tamed with too much handling,
Or as the fleet-foot roe that's tired with chasing,                    561
Or like the froward infant stilled with dandling,                    562
  He now obeys, and now no more resisteth,
  While she takes all she can, not all she listeth.                    564

What wax so frozen but dissolves with temp'ring                    565
And yields at last to every light impression?
Things out of hope are compassed oft with vent'ring,                    567
Chiefly in love, whose leave exceeds commission.                    568
  Affection faints not like a pale-faced coward,                    569
  But then woos best when most his choice is froward.                    570

When he did frown, O, had she then gave over,
Such nectar from his lips she had not sucked.
Foul words and frowns must not repel a lover.                    573
What though the rose have prickles, yet 'tis plucked.
  Were beauty under twenty locks kept fast,
  Yet love breaks through and picks them all at last.                    576

For pity now she can no more detain him;                    577
The poor fool prays her that he may depart.                    578
She is resolved no longer to restrain him,
Bids him farewell, and look well to her heart,                    580
  The which, by Cupid's bow she doth protest,                    581
  He carries thence encagèd in his breast.

**561 with chasing** with being chased   **562 froward** fretful   **564 listeth**
desires   **565 temp'ring** heating and working with the fingers   **567 out
of** beyond.   **compassed** encompassed, accomplished   **568 leave exceeds
commission** liberties go beyond due warrant   **569 Affection** passion.
**faints not** does not relent or fall back   **570 choice is froward** chosen
one is stubborn, obstinate   **573 Foul** hostile, disagreeable   **576 picks
them all** (Picking a lock often has sexual meaning in Shakespeare.)
**577 For pity** appealing to his sense of pity   **578 fool** (An affectionate
term.)   **580 and look well to** i.e., and bids him take good care of
**581 protest** vow, affirm

"Sweet boy," she says, "this night I'll waste in sorrow,     583
For my sick heart commands mine eyes to watch.     584
Tell me, Love's master, shall we meet tomorrow?
Say, shall we, shall we? Wilt thou make the match?"
  He tells her no, tomorrow he intends
  To hunt the boar with certain of his friends.

"The boar!" quoth she, whereat a sudden pale,     589
Like lawn being spread upon the blushing rose,     590
Usurps her cheek. She trembles at his tale
And on his neck her yoking arms she throws.
  She sinketh down, still hanging by his neck;
  He on her belly falls, she on her back.

Now is she in the very lists of love,     595
Her champion mounted for the hot encounter.
All is imaginary she doth prove,     597
He will not manage her, although he mount her;     598
  That worse than Tantalus' is her annoy,     599
  To clip Elysium and to lack her joy.     600

Even as poor birds, deceived with painted grapes,     601
Do surfeit by the eye and pine the maw,     602
Even so she languisheth in her mishaps,
As those poor birds that helpless berries saw.     604
  The warm effects which she in him finds missing     605
  She seeks to kindle with continual kissing.

**583 waste** spend   **584 watch** stay awake   **589 pale** pallor   **590 lawn**
fine linen   **595 lists** tournament field (with erotic suggestion)   **597 she**
**doth prove** that she experiences   **598 manage** control, ride (as one
manages a horse)   **599 Tantalus** a son of Zeus who was punished by
perpetual hunger and thirst with food and drink always in sight yet
untouchable.   **annoy** vexation, torment   **600 clip** embrace.   **Elysium**
blissful afterlife in classical mythology.   **and** and yet   **601 birds . . .**
**grapes** (Allusion to Zeuxis, a Greek painter of the fifth century B.C., so
skillful an artist that birds were said to peck at his picture of a bunch
of grapes.)   **602 pine the maw** starve the stomach   **604 As** like.
**helpless** affording no sustenance   **605 warm effects** sexual response

But all in vain; good queen, it will not be.
She hath assayed as much as may be proved.    608
Her pleading hath deserved a greater fee;    609
She's Love, she loves, and yet she is not loved.
   "Fie, fie," he says, "you crush me, let me go!
   You have no reason to withhold me so."

"Thou hadst been gone," quoth she, "sweet boy, ere
   this,
But that thou toldst me thou wouldst hunt the boar.
O, be advised! Thou know'st not what it is    615
With javelin's point a churlish swine to gore,
   Whose tushes, never sheathed, he whetteth still,    617
   Like to a mortal butcher bent to kill.    618

"On his bow-back he hath a battle set    619
Of bristly pikes, that ever threat his foes;    620
His eyes like glowworms shine when he doth fret;    621
His snout digs sepulchers where'er he goes;
   Being moved, he strikes whate'er is in his way,    623
   And whom he strikes his crooked tushes slay.

"His brawny sides, with hairy bristles armed,
Are better proof than thy spear's point can enter;    626
His short thick neck cannot be easily harmed;
Being ireful, on the lion he will venter.    628
   The thorny brambles and embracing bushes,
   As fearful of him, part, through whom he rushes.    630

**608 assayed** tried.   **proved** experienced, tried   **609 pleading . . . fee** (A legal metaphor; she is *pleading* her own case.)   **615 advised** warned **617 tushes** tusks.   **still** continually   **618 Like to** like.   **mortal** deadly. **bent to kill** intent on killing   **619 bow-back** arched back, but suggestive also of a bowman's quiver.   **battle** i.e., martial array   **620 ever threat** continually threaten   **621 fret** i.e., gnash his teeth   **623 moved** angered   **626 proof** armor   **628 ireful** wrathful.   **venter** venture   **630 As** as if

"Alas, he naught esteems that face of thine,
To which Love's eyes pays tributary gazes,
Nor thy soft hands, sweet lips, and crystal eyne,    633
Whose full perfection all the world amazes;
   But having thee at vantage—wondrous dread!—    635
   Would root these beauties as he roots the mead.    636

"O, let him keep his loathsome cabin still!    637
Beauty hath naught to do with such foul fiends.
Come not within his danger by thy will;    639
They that thrive well take counsel of their friends.
   When thou didst name the boar, not to dissemble,    641
   I feared thy fortune, and my joints did tremble.    642

"Didst thou not mark my face? Was it not white?
Sawest thou not signs of fear lurk in mine eye?
Grew I not faint, and fell I not downright?    645
Within my bosom, whereon thou dost lie,
   My boding heart pants, beats, and takes no rest,
   But, like an earthquake, shakes thee on my breast.

"For where Love reigns, disturbing Jealousy    649
Doth call himself Affection's sentinel,
Gives false alarms, suggesteth mutiny,    651
And in a peaceful hour doth cry 'Kill, kill!'    652
   Distempering gentle Love in his desire,    653
   As air and water do abate the fire.    654

**633 eyne** eyes    **635 at vantage** at a disadvantage    **636 root** root up.
**mead** meadow    **637 keep** occupy.    **cabin** den    **639 danger** i.e., zone of
danger.    **by thy will** intentionally    **641 not to dissemble** to tell you the
plain truth    **642 feared** feared for    **645 downright** forthwith
**649 Jealousy** apprehension    **651 suggesteth mutiny** incites dissension
**652 in a** i.e., disturbing a    **653 Distempering** quenching    **654 abate**
extinguish

"This sour informer, this bate-breeding spy,          655
This canker that eats up Love's tender spring,          656
This carry-tale, dissentious Jealousy,          657
That sometimes true news, sometimes false doth bring,
   Knocks at my heart and whispers in mine ear
   That if I love thee, I thy death should fear;

"And more than so, presenteth to mine eye          661
The picture of an angry chafing boar,
Under whose sharp fangs on his back doth lie
An image like thyself, all stained with gore,
   Whose blood upon the fresh flowers being shed
   Doth make them droop with grief and hang the head.

"What should I do, seeing thee so indeed,          667
That tremble at th' imagination?          668
The thought of it doth make my faint heart bleed,
And fear doth teach it divination.          670
   I prophesy thy death, my living sorrow,
   If thou encounter with the boar tomorrow.

"But if thou needs wilt hunt, be ruled by me;          673
Uncouple at the timorous flying hare,          674
Or at the fox which lives by subtlety,
Or at the roe which no encounter dare.
   Pursue these fearful creatures o'er the downs,          677
   And on thy well-breathed horse keep with thy
      hounds.          678

---

655 **bate-breeding** strife-breeding   656 **canker** cankerworm.   **spring**
young shoot of a plant   657 **carry-tale** spreader of (distressing) talk
661 **more than so** even more than that   667–668 **seeing . . . imagination**
if I should actually see you dead, when merely imagining it makes me
tremble   670 **divination** i.e., power to prophesy   673 **needs wilt** must
674 **Uncouple** unleash the hounds.   **flying** fleeing pursuit   677 **fearful**
full of fears   678 **well-breathed** not easily winded, in good condition

"And when thou hast on foot the purblind hare,     679
Mark the poor wretch, to overshoot his troubles     680
How he outruns the wind and with what care     681
He cranks and crosses with a thousand doubles.     682
    The many musets through the which he goes     683
    Are like a labyrinth to amaze his foes.     684

"Sometimes he runs among a flock of sheep,
To make the cunning hounds mistake their smell,
And sometimes where earth-delving coneys keep,     687
To stop the loud pursuers in their yell,     688
    And sometimes sorteth with a herd of deer.     689
    Danger deviseth shifts; wit waits on fear.     690

"For there his smell with others being mingled,
The hot scent-snuffing hounds are driven to doubt,
Ceasing their clamorous cry till they have singled
With much ado the cold fault cleanly out.     694
    Then do they spend their mouths; echo replies,     695
    As if another chase were in the skies.

"By this, poor Wat, far off upon a hill,     697
Stands on his hinder legs with listening ear,
To hearken if his foes pursue him still.
Anon their loud alarums he doth hear,
    And now his grief may be comparèd well
    To one sore sick that hears the passing bell.     702

**679 on foot** in chase. **purblind** dimsighted   **680 overshoot** run beyond   **681 outruns the wind** i.e., leaves his scent far behind   **682 cranks** twists and turns   **683 musets** gaps in hedge or fence   **684 amaze** bewilder   **687 coneys** rabbits. **keep** dwell   **688 yell** cry   **689 sorteth** consorts, mingles   **690 shifts** tricks.   **wit waits** intelligence attends   **694 cold fault** cold or lost scent   **695 spend their mouths** give the cry on spotting the game   **697 Wat** (A common name applied to the hare.)   **702 sore** very.   **passing bell** bell tolled for a person who has just died

"Then shalt thou see the dew-bedabbled wretch          703
Turn, and return, indenting with the way;          704
Each envious brier his weary legs do scratch,          705
Each shadow makes him stop, each murmur stay;
    For misery is trodden on by many,
    And, being low, never relieved by any.

"Lie quietly, and hear a little more.
Nay, do not struggle, for thou shalt not rise.
To make thee hate the hunting of the boar,
Unlike myself thou hear'st me moralize,          712
    Applying this to that, and so to so;
    For love can comment upon every woe.

"Where did I leave?" "No matter where," quoth he,          715
"Leave me, and then the story aptly ends;
The night is spent." "Why, what of that?" quoth she.
"I am," quoth he, "expected of my friends,          718
    And now 'tis dark, and going I shall fall."
    "In night," quoth she, "desire sees best of all.

"But if thou fall, O, then imagine this,
The earth, in love with thee, thy footing trips,
And all is but to rob thee of a kiss.
Rich preys make true men thieves; so do thy lips          724
    Make modest Dian cloudy and forlorn,          725
    Lest she should steal a kiss and die forsworn.          726

---

**703 dew-bedabbled** sprinkled with dew   **704 indenting** zigzagging
**705 envious** malicious   **712 Unlike . . . moralize** i.e., contrary to the
usual way of the goddess of love, you hear me point out a moral application   **715 leave** leave off. (But Adonis answers with another sense,
"go away from.")   **718 of** by   **724 Rich . . . thieves** i.e., the chance of
rich spoils (*preys*) will make thieves even of honest (*true*) men   **725 Dian**
Diana, goddess of the moon, chastity, and the hunt. (Even Diana would
fall in love with Adonis.)   **cloudy** obscured with clouds; sorrowful
**726 forsworn** i.e., having broken her vow as the goddess of chastity

"Now of this dark night I perceive the reason:    727
Cynthia for shame obscures her silver shine,    728
Till forging Nature be condemned of treason,    729
For stealing molds from heaven that were divine,
   Wherein she framed thee, in high heaven's despite,    731
   To shame the sun by day and her by night.    732

"And therefore hath she bribed the Destinies
To cross the curious workmanship of nature,    734
To mingle beauty with infirmities,
And pure perfection with impure defeature,    736
   Making it subject to the tyranny
   Of mad mischances and much misery;

"As burning fevers, agues pale and faint,    739
Life-poisoning pestilence and frenzies wood,    740
The marrow-eating sickness, whose attaint    741
Disorder breeds by heating of the blood,
   Surfeits, impostumes, grief, and damned despair    743
   Swear Nature's death for framing thee so fair.    744

"And not the least of all these maladies
But in one minute's fight brings beauty under.
Both favor, savor, hue, and qualities,    747
Whereat th' impartial gazer late did wonder,    748
   Are on the sudden wasted, thawed, and done,    749
   As mountain snow melts with the midday sun.

---

**727 of** for    **728 Cynthia** i.e., Diana, the moon    **729 forging** counterfeiting    **731 she** i.e., Nature.   **in . . . despite** in defiance of high heaven
**732 her** i.e., the moon    **734 cross** thwart.   **curious** ingenious
**736 defeature** disfigurement    **739 As** such as    **740 frenzies** seizures.
**wood** mad    **741 The marrow-eating sickness** (probably venereal disease;
love is said to burn or melt the marrow, as in l. 142; hence the *heating
of the blood* in l. 742).   **attaint** infection    **743 impostumes** abscesses
**744 Swear . . . fair** (all these diseases) swear to kill Nature because she
formed you so beautiful    **747 favor** beauty of feature.   **savor** sweetness
of smell.   **hue** (1) color (2) shape    **748 impartial** i.e., uninfluenced by
love.   **late** lately    **749 wasted** wasted away.   **done** destroyed

"Therefore, despite of fruitless chastity,                            751
Love-lacking vestals and self-loving nuns,
That on the earth would breed a scarcity
And barren dearth of daughters and of sons,
   Be prodigal. The lamp that burns by night
   Dries up his oil to lend the world his light.                  756

"What is thy body but a swallowing grave,
Seeming to bury that posterity
Which by the rights of time thou needs must have,
If thou destroy them not in dark obscurity?
   If so, the world will hold thee in disdain,
   Sith in thy pride so fair a hope is slain.                     762

"So in thyself thyself art made away,                                 763
A mischief worse than civil homebred strife,                          764
Or theirs whose desperate hands themselves do slay,
Or butcher sire that reaves his son of life.                          766
   Foul cankering rust the hidden treasure frets,                767
   But gold that's put to use more gold begets."

"Nay, then," quoth Adon, "you will fall again
Into your idle overhandled theme.                                     770
The kiss I gave you is bestowed in vain,
And all in vain you strive against the stream;                        772
   For, by this black-faced night, desire's foul nurse,          773
   Your treatise makes me like you worse and worse.               774

"If love have lent you twenty thousand tongues,
And every tongue more moving than your own,
Bewitching like the wanton mermaids' songs,                          777
Yet from mine ear the tempting tune is blown;
   For know, my heart stands armèd in mine ear
   And will not let a false sound enter there,

---

**751 despite of** in defiance of.   **fruitless** barren   **756 his** its   **762 Sith**
since   **763 thyself art made away** i.e., your futurity is destroyed
**764 mischief** evil   **766 reaves** bereaves   **767 cankering** consuming (like
the cankerworm).   **frets** eats away   **770 idle** profitless   **772 stream**
current   **773 night . . . nurse** i.e., night, the foul nourisher of evil desire   **774 treatise** discourse   **777 mermaids'** i.e., sirens'

"Lest the deceiving harmony should run
Into the quiet closure of my breast;　　　　　　　782
And then my little heart were quite undone,
In his bedchamber to be barred of rest.
　　No, lady, no. My heart longs not to groan,
　　But soundly sleeps, while now it sleeps alone.

"What have you urged that I cannot reprove?　　　787
The path is smooth that leadeth on to danger.
I hate not love but your device in love,　　　　　789
That lends embracements unto every stranger.
　　You do it for increase. O strange excuse,
　　When reason is the bawd to lust's abuse!

"Call it not love, for Love to heaven is fled,
Since sweating Lust on earth usurped his name,
Under whose simple semblance he hath fed　　　795
Upon fresh beauty, blotting it with blame;　　　796
　　Which the hot tyrant stains and soon bereaves,　　797
　　As caterpillars do the tender leaves.

"Love comforteth like sunshine after rain,
But Lust's effect is tempest after sun;
Love's gentle spring doth always fresh remain,
Lust's winter comes ere summer half be done.
　　Love surfeits not, Lust like a glutton dies;
　　Love is all truth, Lust full of forgèd lies.

"More I could tell, but more I dare not say;
The text is old, the orator too green.　　　　　806
Therefore, in sadness, now I will away.　　　　807
My face is full of shame, my heart of teen;　　　808
　　Mine ears, that to your wanton talk attended,
　　Do burn themselves for having so offended."　　　810

---

782 **closure** enclosure　787 **urged** argued for.　**reprove** refute
789 **device** cunning, deceitful conduct　795 **whose** i.e., Love's.　**simple
semblance** guileless appearance.　**he** i.e., Lust　796 **blotting** soiling
797 **bereaves** spoils　806 **The text** the point being explicated (like the
*text* of a sermon).　**green** young, unpracticed　807 **in sadness** seriously,
truly　808 **teen** grief, vexation　810 **burn themselves** blush

With this, he breaketh from the sweet embrace
Of those fair arms which bound him to her breast
And homeward through the dark laund runs apace,                    813
Leaves Love upon her back deeply distressed.
   Look how a bright star shooteth from the sky,
   So glides he in the night from Venus' eye;

Which after him she darts, as one on shore
Gazing upon a late-embarkèd friend,                    818
Till the wild waves will have him seen no more,                    819
Whose ridges with the meeting clouds contend.
   So did the merciless and pitchy night
   Fold in the object that did feed her sight.                    822

Whereat amazed, as one that unaware                    823
Hath dropped a precious jewel in the flood,                    824
Or stonished as night wanderers often are,                    825
Their light blown out in some mistrustful wood,                    826
   Even so confounded in the dark she lay,                    827
   Having lost the fair discovery of her way.                    828

And now she beats her heart, whereat it groans,
That all the neighbor caves, as seeming troubled,
Make verbal repetition of her moans.
Passion on passion deeply is redoubled:                    832
   "Ay me!" she cries, and twenty times "Woe, woe!"
   And twenty echoes twenty times cry so.

She marking them begins a wailing note
And sings extemporally a woeful ditty
How love makes young men thrall and old men dote,                    837
How love is wise in folly, foolish witty.
   Her heavy anthem still concludes in woe,                    839
   And still the choir of echoes answer so.

---

813 laund glade   818 late-embarkèd having recently taken ship
819 have him seen allow him to be seen   822 Fold in enfold, close in
823 amazed dazed, confused.   unaware inadvertently   824 flood body
of flowing water   825 stonished dismayed   826 mistrustful causing
apprehension   827 confounded bewildered   828 the fair . . . way i.e.,
the one who lighted her path.   discovery discoverer   832 Passion
lamentation   837 thrall captive   839 heavy melancholy.   still
continually

Her song was tedious and outwore the night,
For lovers' hours are long, though seeming short.
If pleased themselves, others, they think, delight
In suchlike circumstance, with suchlike sport.
    Their copious stories, oftentimes begun,
    End without audience and are never done.

For who hath she to spend the night withal                    847
But idle sounds resembling parasits,                    848
Like shrill-tongued tapsters answering every call,                    849
Soothing the humor of fantastic wits?                    850
    She says "'Tis so," they answer all "'Tis so,"
    And would say after her, if she said "No."

Lo here the gentle lark, weary of rest,
From his moist cabinet mounts up on high,                    854
And wakes the morning, from whose silver breast                    855
The sun ariseth in his majesty,
    Who doth the world so gloriously behold                    857
    That cedar tops and hills seem burnished gold.

Venus salutes him with this fair good morrow:
"O thou clear god, and patron of all light,                    860
From whom each lamp and shining star doth borrow
The beauteous influence that makes him bright,                    862
    There lives a son that sucked an earthly mother                    863
    May lend thee light, as thou dost lend to other."                    864

---

**847 withal** with    **848 parasits** parasites, flattering attendants
**849 tapsters** waiters in taverns    **850 Soothing . . . wits** i.e., complying
with the whim of capricious tavern customers    **854 moist cabinet** dewy
dwelling, nest    **855 whose silver breast** (Aurora, the dawn, is personified as a goddess bidding farewell to her lover, the sun.)    **857 behold**
i.e., shine upon    **860 clear** bright    **862 influence** a supposed flowing or
streaming of an ethereal fluid from a celestial body, influencing human
destiny. (An astrological term.)    **863 a son** i.e., Adonis.    **sucked** suckled
from    **864 May** who may

This said, she hasteth to a myrtle grove,
Musing the morning is so much o'erworn,                    866
And yet she hears no tidings of her love.
She hearkens for his hounds and for his horn.
  Anon she hears them chant it lustily,                    869
  And all in haste she coasteth to the cry.                870

And as she runs, the bushes in the way
Some catch her by the neck, some kiss her face,
Some twine about her thigh to make her stay.
She wildly breaketh from their strict embrace,            874
  Like a milch doe, whose swelling dugs do ache,          875
  Hasting to feed her fawn hid in some brake.             876

By this, she hears the hounds are at a bay,               877
Whereat she starts, like one that spies an adder
Wreathed up in fatal folds just in his way,              879
The fear whereof doth make him shake and shudder;
  Even so the timorous yelping of the hounds
  Appalls her senses and her spirit confounds.

For now she knows it is no gentle chase,
But the blunt boar, rough bear, or lion proud,
Because the cry remaineth in one place,
Where fearfully the dogs exclaim aloud.
  Finding their enemy to be so curst,                     887
  They all strain court'sy who shall cope him first.      888

---

866 **Musing** wondering (that).    **o'erworn** advanced    869 **chant** i.e.,
sound    870 **coasteth to** approaches    874 **strict** tight    875 **milch doe**
female deer producing milk.    **dugs** udders    876 **brake** thicket    877 **By
this** by this time.    **at a bay** i.e., faced by their quarry, which, being
cornered, has turned to make its stand    879 **folds** coils    887 **curst**
savage    888 **strain court'sy** are punctiliously polite, stand upon ceremony; i.e., they hold back.    **cope** cope with

This dismal cry rings sadly in her ear,     889
Through which it enters to surprise her heart,     890
Who, overcome by doubt and bloodless fear,     891
With cold-pale weakness numbs each feeling part.     892
    Like soldiers, when their captain once doth yield,     893
    They basely fly and dare not stay the field.     894

Thus stands she in a trembling ecstasy,     895
Till, cheering up her senses all dismayed,
She tells them 'tis a causeless fantasy     897
And childish error that they are afraid;
    Bids them leave quaking, bids them fear no more—
    And with that word she spied the hunted boar,

Whose frothy mouth, bepainted all with red,
Like milk and blood being mingled both together,
A second fear through all her sinews spread,     903
Which madly hurries her she knows not whither.
    This way she runs, and now she will no further,
    But back retires to rate the boar for murther.     906

A thousand spleens bear her a thousand ways;     907
She treads the path that she untreads again;     908
Her more than haste is mated with delays,     909
Like the proceedings of a drunken brain,
    Full of respects, yet naught at all respecting,     911
    In hand with all things, naught at all effecting.     912

**889 dismal** foreboding ill    **890 surprise** assail suddenly    **891 bloodless fear** i.e., fear that causes the blood to draw to the heart and desert the features, leaving one *cold, pale,* and *weak* (l. 892)    **892 feeling part** bodily part and organ of sense    **893 when . . . yield** once their commanding officer has yielded    **894 stay the field** remain in the battlefield and stand against the onslaught    **895 ecstasy** agitated state    **897 them** i.e., her senses    **903 sinews** nerves    **906 rate** berate    **907 spleens** impulses    **908 untreads** retraces    **909 mated** confounded, checked **911 respects** designs, considerations.    **naught at all respecting** i.e., heedless    **912 In hand with** busy about

Here kenneled in a brake she finds a hound,                    913
And asks the weary caitiff for his master,                    914
And there another licking of his wound,
'Gainst venomed sores the only sovereign plaster;                    916
   And here she meets another sadly scowling,
   To whom she speaks, and he replies with howling.

When he hath ceased his ill-resounding noise,
Another flapmouthed mourner, black and grim,                    920
Against the welkin volleys out his voice;                    921
Another and another answer him,
   Clapping their proud tails to the ground below,
   Shaking their scratched ears, bleeding as they go.

Look how the world's poor people are amazed                    925
At apparitions, signs, and prodigies,
Whereon with fearful eyes they long have gazed,
Infusing them with dreadful prophecies;                    928
   So she at these sad signs draws up her breath
   And, sighing it again, exclaims on Death.                    930

"Hard-favored tyrant, ugly, meager, lean,
Hateful divorce of love!"—thus chides she Death—                    932
"Grim-grinning ghost, earth's worm, what dost thou
   mean                    933
To stifle beauty and to steal his breath,
   Who, when he lived, his breath and beauty set
   Gloss on the rose, smell to the violet?                    936

---

**913 kenneled** hiding as if in its kennel   **914 caitiff** wretch   **916 only
sovereign plaster** best all-curing application   **920 flapmouthed** having
broad, hanging lips or jowls   **921 welkin** sky   **925 Look how** just as
**928 Infusing them with** attributing to them.   **prophecies** prophetic
qualities   **930 exclaims on** denounces   **932 divorce** terminator
**933 Grim-grinning** i.e., grinning like a skull.   **worm** i.e., cankerworm,
consumer of flowers (with the suggestion also of worms that devour
corpses)   **936 smell** i.e., and gave smell

"If he be dead—O no, it cannot be,
Seeing his beauty, thou shouldst strike at it!                     938
O yes, it may; thou hast no eyes to see,                           939
But hatefully at random dost thou hit.
   Thy mark is feeble age, but thy false dart          941
   Mistakes that aim and cleaves an infant's heart.

"Hadst thou but bid beware, then he had spoke,                     943
And, hearing him, thy power had lost his power.                    944
The Destinies will curse thee for this stroke;
They bid thee crop a weed, thou pluck'st a flower.
   Love's golden arrow at him should have fled,
   And not Death's ebon dart, to strike him dead.          948

"Dost thou drink tears, that thou provok'st such
   weeping?
What may a heavy groan advantage thee?
Why hast thou cast into eternal sleeping
Those eyes that taught all other eyes to see?
   Now Nature cares not for thy mortal vigor,             953
   Since her best work is ruined with thy rigor."         954

Here overcome, as one full of despair,
She vailed her eyelids, who, like sluices, stopped                956
The crystal tide that from her two cheeks fair
In the sweet channel of her bosom dropped;                        958
   But through the floodgates breaks the silver rain,
   And with his strong course opens them again.           960

---

**938 Seeing** i.e., that, seeing   **939 no eyes** (The eye sockets of the skull of
Death are empty.)   **941 mark** target   **943 bid beware** i.e., issued a
warning of the approach of Death.   **he** i.e., Adonis   **944 his** its
**948 ebon** ebony, black   **953 cares . . . vigor** does not fear your deadly
power   **954 with** by   **956 vailed** lowered.   **who** which.   **stopped**
stopped up   **958 channel** i.e., cleavage   **960 his** its

O, how her eyes and tears did lend and borrow!    961
Her eye seen in the tears, tears in her eye,
Both crystals, where they viewed each other's sorrow,   963
Sorrow that friendly sighs sought still to dry;   964
   But like a stormy day, now wind, now rain,
   Sighs dry her cheeks, tears make them wet again.

Variable passions throng her constant woe,
As striving who should best become her grief.   968
All entertained, each passion labors so   969
That every present sorrow seemeth chief,
   But none is best; then join they all together,   971
   Like many clouds consulting for foul weather.   972

By this, far off she hears some huntsman hallow;   973
A nurse's song ne'er pleased her babe so well.
The dire imagination she did follow   975
This sound of hope doth labor to expel;
   For now reviving joy bids her rejoice
   And flatters her it is Adonis' voice.

Whereat her tears began to turn their tide,   979
Being prisoned in her eye like pearls in glass;
Yet sometimes falls an orient drop beside,   981
Which her cheek melts, as scorning it should pass,   982
   To wash the foul face of the sluttish ground,   983
   Who is but drunken when she seemeth drowned.   984

---

**961 lend and borrow** i.e., reflect each other   **963 crystals** i.e., mirrors
**964 friendly** i.e., consoling   **968 As** as if.  **who** which (passion).
**become** suit   **969 entertained** having been admitted   **971 best**
supreme   **972 consulting for** cooperating to produce   **973 By this** by
this time.  **hallow** halloo   **975 follow** pursue in her thoughts   **979 turn**
**their tide** ebb   **981 orient** shining.  **beside** to one side   **982 melts** i.e.,
dries.  **as** as if   **983 foul** dirty   **984 Who . . . drowned** i.e., the sluttish
earth would seem as though made drunk by her tears, which in her
produce a more innocent effect of drowning

O hard-believing love, how strange it seems      985
Not to believe, and yet too credulous!      986
Thy weal and woe are both of them extremes.
Despair and hope makes thee ridiculous:      988
   The one doth flatter thee in thoughts unlikely,      989
   In likely thoughts the other kills thee quickly.

Now she unweaves the web that she hath wrought;
Adonis lives, and Death is not to blame;
It was not she that called him all to naught.      993
Now she adds honors to his hateful name:
   She clepes him king of graves and grave for kings,      995
   Imperious supreme of all mortal things.      996

"No, no," quoth she, "sweet Death, I did but jest.
Yet pardon me, I felt a kind of fear
Whenas I met the boar, that bloody beast,      999
Which knows no pity, but is still severe.      1000
   Then, gentle shadow—truth I must confess—      1001
   I railed on thee, fearing my love's decesse.      1002

"'Tis not my fault; the boar provoked my tongue.
Be wreaked on him, invisible commander.      1004
'Tis he, foul creature, that hath done thee wrong;
I did but act, he's author of thy slander.      1006
   Grief hath two tongues, and never woman yet      1007
   Could rule them both without ten women's wit."

**985-986 O . . . credulous** i.e., love is at once too skeptical and too credulous   **988 Despair and hope** i.e., the rapid oscillation between despair and hope   **989 The one** i.e., hope   **993 all to naught** wholly evil   **995 clepes** names, calls   **996 Imperious supreme** imperial ruler   **999 Whenas** when   **1000 still severe** incessantly ruthless   **1001 shadow** specter   **1002 railed on** reviled.   **decesse** decease   **1004 wreaked** revenged.   **invisible commander** i.e., Death, a specter that orders our final destiny   **1006 act** i.e., act as agent   **1007 two tongues** i.e., a double tongue, twice as loud and hard to control as a usual tongue. (Women are conventionally unable to rule their tongues in any case.)

Thus hoping that Adonis is alive,
Her rash suspect she doth extenuate;                    1010
And that his beauty may the better thrive,
With Death she humbly doth insinuate;                   1012
  Tells him of trophies, statues, tombs, and stories    1013
   His victories, his triumphs, and his glories.

"O Jove," quoth she, "how much a fool was I
To be of such a weak and silly mind
To wail his death who lives and must not die
Till mutual overthrow of mortal kind!                   1018
  For, he being dead, with him is beauty slain,
   And, beauty dead, black chaos comes again.

"Fie, fie, fond love, thou art as full of fear          1021
As one with treasure laden, hemmed with thieves;        1022
Trifles, unwitnessèd with eye or ear,                   1023
Thy coward heart with false bethinking grieves."        1024
  Even at this word she hears a merry horn,
   Whereat she leaps that was but late forlorn.        1026

As falcon to the lure, away she flies—
The grass stoops not, she treads on it so light—
And in her haste unfortunately spies
The foul boar's conquest on her fair delight;
  Which seen, her eyes, as murdered with the view,    1031
   Like stars ashamed of day, themselves withdrew;    1032

Or, as the snail, whose tender horns being hit,
Shrinks backward in his shelly cave with pain,
And there, all smothered up, in shade doth sit,
Long after fearing to creep forth again;
  So, at his bloody view, her eyes are fled
   Into the deep dark cabins of her head,

---

**1010 rash suspect** too hasty suspicion (of Death).   **extenuate** excuse,
make light of   **1012 insinuate** ingratiate herself   **1013 trophies** memorial monuments.   **stories** narrates, relates   **1018 mutual** i.e., univer-
sal   **1021 fond** foolish   **1022 hemmed with** hemmed about by
**1023-1024 Trifles . . . grieves** mere trifles, not actually seen by eye or
heard by ear, grieve your cowardly heart with false imaginings
**1026 leaps** i.e., leaps for joy.   **late** lately   **1031 as** as if   **1032 ashamed
of** put to shame by.   **withdrew** i.e., closed

Where they resign their office and their light
To the disposing of her troubled brain,                                    1040
Who bids them still consort with ugly night                                1041
And never wound the heart with looks again—                                1042
    Who, like a king perplexèd in his throne,                              1043
    By their suggestion gives a deadly groan.                              1044

Whereat each tributary subject quakes,                                     1045
As when the wind, imprisoned in the ground,                               1046
Struggling for passage, earth's foundation shakes,
Which with cold terror doth men's minds confound.
    This mutiny each part doth so surprise                                  1049
    That from their dark beds once more leap her eyes;

And, being opened, threw unwilling light
Upon the wide wound that the boar had trenched
In his soft flank, whose wonted lily white                                 1053
With purple tears, that his wound wept, was drenched.
    No flower was nigh, no grass, herb, leaf, or weed,
    But stole his blood and seemed with him to bleed.                      1056

This solemn sympathy poor Venus noteth.
Over one shoulder doth she hang her head.
Dumbly she passions, franticly she doteth;                                 1059
She thinks he could not die, he is not dead.
    Her voice is stopped, her joints forget to bow;                        1061
    Her eyes are mad that they have wept till now.                         1062

Upon his hurt she looks so steadfastly
That her sight, dazzling, makes the wound seem three;                     1064
And then she reprehends her mangling eye,
That makes more gashes where no breach should be.
    His face seems twain, each several limb is doubled;
    For oft the eye mistakes, the brain being troubled.

**1040 disposing** direction, ordering    **1041 still consort** always remain
**1042 with looks** by looking    **1043 Who** which, i.e., the heart    **1044 By
their suggestion** incited by the eyes    **1045 tributary subject** i.e., subordinate part of the body    **1046 wind . . . ground** (The common Elizabethan explanation of earthquakes; cf. *1 Henry IV*, 3.1.30.)    **1049 surprise**
attack suddenly    **1053 wonted** customary    **1056 But stole** that did not
steal    **1059 passions** shows grief    **1061 forget to bow** are paralyzed
(with grief)    **1062 till now** before now (in a lesser cause)    **1064 dazzling**
being dazzled

"My tongue cannot express my grief for one,
And yet," quoth she, "behold two Adons dead!
My sighs are blown away, my salt tears gone;
Mine eyes are turned to fire, my heart to lead.
    Heavy heart's lead, melt at mine eyes' red fire!
    So shall I die by drops of hot desire.       1074

"Alas, poor world, what treasure hast thou lost!
What face remains alive that's worth the viewing?
Whose tongue is music now? What canst thou boast
Of things long since, or anything ensuing?       1078
    The flowers are sweet, their colors fresh and trim,
    But true sweet beauty lived and died with him.

"Bonnet nor veil henceforth no creature wear!       1081
Nor sun nor wind will ever strive to kiss you.
Having no fair to lose, you need not fear;       1083
The sun doth scorn you, and the wind doth hiss you.
    But when Adonis lived, sun and sharp air
    Lurked like two thieves, to rob him of his fair.

"And therefore would he put his bonnet on,
Under whose brim the gaudy sun would peep;       1088
The wind would blow it off and, being gone,       1089
Play with his locks. Then would Adonis weep;
    And straight, in pity of his tender years,       1091
    They both would strive who first should dry his
      tears.

"To see his face the lion walked along
Behind some hedge, because he would not fear him;       1094
To recreate himself when he hath song,       1095
The tiger would be tame and gently hear him;
    If he had spoke, the wolf would leave his prey
    And never fright the silly lamb that day.       1098

**1074 So shall I die** (Venus imagines a terrible death by melted lead.)
**1078 Of . . . ensuing** past or to come    **1081 Bonnet nor veil** neither hat
nor veil (worn to guard a fair complexion, regarded as particularly
beautiful, against the sun)    **1083 fair** beauty. (Also in l. 1086.)
**1088 gaudy** brilliantly shining    **1089 being gone** it (the hat) being
gone    **1091 straight** at once    **1094 would not fear** did not wish to
frighten    **1095 To recreate . . . song** whenever he sang for his own
recreation    **1098 silly** innocent

"When he beheld his shadow in the brook,
The fishes spread on it their golden gills;
When he was by, the birds such pleasure took
That some would sing, some other in their bills    1102
   Would bring him mulberries and ripe-red cherries;
   He fed them with his sight, they him with berries.

"But this foul, grim, and urchin-snouted boar,    1105
Whose downward eye still looketh for a grave,    1106
Ne'er saw the beauteous livery that he wore—    1107
Witness the entertainment that he gave.    1108
   If he did see his face, why then I know
   He thought to kiss him, and hath killed him so.

"'Tis true, 'tis true! Thus was Adonis slain:
He ran upon the boar with his sharp spear,
Who did not whet his teeth at him again,    1113
But by a kiss thought to persuade him there;    1114
   And, nuzzling in his flank, the loving swine
   Sheathed unaware the tusk in his soft groin.

"Had I been toothed like him, I must confess,
With kissing him I should have killed him first;
But he is dead, and never did he bless
My youth with his—the more am I accurst."
   With this, she falleth in the place she stood,    1121
   And stains her face with his congealèd blood.

---

**1102 other** others   **1105 urchin-snouted** having a snout like a hedgehog
**1106 still** continually.   **for a grave** i.e., as if for a grave in which to bury
victims. (Compare l. 622, where the boar's snout *digs sepulchers*
as it roots in the earth.)   **1107 livery** i.e., outside appearance
**1108 entertainment** treatment, reception   **1113 again** in return
**1114 persuade** win over, or persuade to stay   **1121 place** place where

She looks upon his lips, and they are pale;
She takes him by the hand, and that is cold;
She whispers in his ears a heavy tale,                          1125
As if they heard the woeful words she told;
   She lifts the coffer-lids that close his eyes,           1127
   Where, lo, two lamps, burnt out, in darkness lies;

Two glasses, where herself herself beheld                       1129
A thousand times, and now no more reflect,
Their virtue lost, wherein they late excelled,                  1131
And every beauty robbed of his effect.                          1132
   "Wonder of time," quoth she, "this is my spite,        1133
   That, thou being dead, the day should yet be light.

"Since thou art dead, lo, here I prophesy:
Sorrow on love hereafter shall attend.
It shall be waited on with jealousy,                            1137
Find sweet beginning but unsavory end,
   Ne'er settled equally, but high or low,                1139
   That all love's pleasure shall not match his woe.       1140

"It shall be fickle, false, and full of fraud,
Bud and be blasted in a breathing while;                        1142
The bottom poison, and the top o'erstrawed                      1143
With sweets that shall the truest sight beguile.
   The strongest body shall it make most weak,
   Strike the wise dumb and teach the fool to speak.

---

**1125 heavy** sad    **1127 coffer-lids** lids covering chests of treasure, i.e.,
eyelids    **1129 glasses** mirrors    **1131 virtue** power (to see and to reflect)    **1132 his** its    **1133 time** i.e., the ages, human existence.    **spite**
torment, vexation    **1137 It** love.    **with** by    **1139 Ne'er . . . low** i.e., (love
will be) never equal between the two lovers; they will be from high and
low social stations    **1140 his** its    **1142 blasted** blighted.    **breathing
while** i.e., short time    **1143 The bottom** i.e., the substance, what is
inside.    **top** surface.    **o'erstrawed** strewn over

"It shall be sparing and too full of riot,                    1147
Teaching decrepit age to tread the measures;                  1148
The staring ruffian shall it keep in quiet,                   1149
Pluck down the rich, enrich the poor with treasures;
    It shall be raging mad and silly mild,                    1151
    Make the young old, the old become a child.

"It shall suspect where is no cause of fear;                  1153
It shall not fear where it should most mistrust;
It shall be merciful and too severe,
And most deceiving when it seems most just;                   1156
    Perverse it shall be where it shows most toward,          1157
    Put fear to valor, courage to the coward.

"It shall be cause of war and dire events
And set dissension twixt the son and sire,
Subject and servile to all discontents,                       1161
As dry combustious matter is to fire.
    Sith in his prime Death doth my love destroy,             1163
    They that love best their loves shall not enjoy."

By this, the boy that by her side lay killed                  1165
Was melted like a vapor from her sight,
And in his blood that on the ground lay spilled
A purple flow'r sprung up, checkered with white,              1168
    Resembling well his pale cheeks and the blood
    Which in round drops upon their whiteness stood.

---

1147 sparing . . . riot i.e., both niggardly and excessive   1148 tread the
measures dance. (An inappropriate action for the old.)   1149 staring
looking savage, glaring   1151 silly innocently   1153 is there is
1156 just trustworthy   1157 Perverse stubborn, contrary.   toward
tractable   1161 Subject . . . discontents (love will be) both the cause and
the unwilling slave of every kind of dissension   1163 Sith since
1165 By this by this time   1168 flow'r i.e., anemone

She bows her head, the new-sprung flower to smell,
Comparing it to her Adonis' breath,
And says within her bosom it shall dwell,
Since he himself is reft from her by death.    1174
 She crops the stalk, and in the breach appears
 Green dropping sap, which she compares to tears.

"Poor flower," quoth she, "this was thy father's
  guise—           1177
Sweet issue of a more sweet-smelling sire—   1178
For every little grief to wet his eyes;     1179
To grow unto himself was his desire,     1180
 And so 'tis thine; but know, it is as good
 To wither in my breast as in his blood.

"Here was thy father's bed, here in my breast;
Thou art the next of blood, and 'tis thy right.
Lo, in this hollow cradle take thy rest;
My throbbing heart shall rock thee day and night.
 There shall not be one minute in an hour
 Wherein I will not kiss my sweet love's flower."

Thus weary of the world, away she hies
And yokes her silver doves, by whose swift aid
Their mistress, mounted, through the empty skies  1191
In her light chariot quickly is conveyed,    1192
 Holding their course to Paphos, where their queen 1193
 Means to immure herself and not be seen.

---

**1174 reft** bereft  **1177 guise** manner, way  **1178 Sweet issue** i.e., you,
the anemone, who are the sweet offspring  **1179 For . . . eyes** i.e., to
weep compassionately at every little sorrow  **1180 To grow unto himself** i.e., to mature self-made and independent  **1191–1192 mounted . . .
conveyed** is quickly conveyed, mounted in her light chariot, through the
empty skies  **1193 Paphos** Venus' dwelling in Cyprus

# Date and Text

On April 18, 1593, "a booke intituled, Venus and Adonis" was entered to Richard Field in the Stationers' Register, the official record book of the London Company of Stationers (booksellers and printers), and was published by him the same year. The quarto contains a dedication written by Shakespeare to the Earl of Southampton. The text seems to have been carefully supervised through the press, and based on the author's manuscript. The poem was very popular, and was reprinted nine times before Shakespeare's death. The First Folio of 1623, being limited to plays, did not include it or any other nondramatic poems. Contemporary references are numerous: Francis Meres and Richard Barnfield in 1598, Gabriel Harvey in 1598–1601, and John Weever in 1599, among others. Shakespeare probably wrote this poem shortly before its publication, since his intention was to present it to Southampton. The theaters closed from June 1592 to May 1594, giving Shakespeare a period of enforced leisure in which to write poetry.

# Textual Notes

These textual notes are not a historical collation; they are simply a record of departures in this edition from the copy text. The reading adopted in this edition appears in boldface, followed by the rejected reading from the copy text, i.e., the quarto of 1593. Only major alterations in punctuation are noted. Corrections of minor and obvious typographical errors are not indicated.

Copy text: the quarto of 1593.

**185 Souring** So wring   **304 whe'er** where   **457 marketh.** marketh,
**458 raineth,** raineth:   **570 woos** woes   **601 as** so   **680 overshoot** ouer-shut
**748 th'** the th'   **873 twine** twin'd   **1013 stories** stories,   **1027 falcon**
Faulcons   **1031 as** are   **1054 was** had

# THE RAPE
# OF
# LUCRECE

# Introduction

*The Rape of Lucrece* is closely related to *Venus and Adonis*. The two were published about a year apart, in 1593 and 1594, both printed by Richard Field. Both are dedicated to the young Earl of Southampton, Henry Wriothesley, whose confidence and friendship Shakespeare appears to have gained during the interim between the two poems; the dedicatory preface to *The Rape of Lucrece* expresses assurance that the poem will be accepted. Stylistically the two poems are of a piece, alike reliant on Petrarchan ornament and rhetorical showmanship, alike steeped in Ovidian pathos. Yet they are complementary rather than similar in attitude and subject. *The Rape of Lucrece* appears to be the "graver labor" promised to Southampton in the dedication of the earlier poem, a planned sequel in which love would be subjected to a darker treatment. *Venus and Adonis* is chiefly about sensual pleasure, whereas *The Rape of Lucrece* is about heroic chastity. The first poem is amatory, erotic, and amusing despite its sad end; the second is moral, declamatory, and lugubrious. As Gabriel Harvey observed (c. 1598–1601), "The younger sort takes much delight in Shakespeare's *Venus and Adonis*, but his *Lucrece* and his *Tragedy of Hamlet, Prince of Denmark* have it in them to please the wiser sort."

Harvey's pairing of this poem with *Hamlet* suggests that, to Harvey at least, Shakespeare aspires to sublime effects in *Lucrece*. For his verse pattern Shakespeare chooses the seven-line rhyme royal stanza, traditionally used for tragic expression, as in Geoffry Chaucer's *Troilus and Criseyde* and several of the more formal *Canterbury Tales*, in John Lydgate's *The Fall of Princes* (1430–1438) and its continuation in *A Mirror for Magistrates* (1559), in Samuel Daniel's *The Complaint of Rosamond*, and others. Although Shakespeare turns to Ovid once again as his chief source, he chooses a tale of ravishment, suicide, and vengeance rather than one of titillating amatory pursuit. The story of Lucrece had gained wide currency in the ancient and medieval worlds as an exemplum of chaste conduct in women. Shakespeare seems to have known Livy's *History of Rome* (Book 1,

chaps. 57–59), though he relied primarily on Ovid's *Fasti*
(2, 721–852). Among later versions he may have known
Chaucer's *The Legend of Good Women* and a translation of
Livy in William Painter's *The Palace of Pleasure* (1566,
1575). He encountered other "complaints" in *A Mirror for
Magistrates* and in Daniel's *The Complaint of Rosamond*,
and it is to this well-established genre that *Lucrece* belongs.
The poem had the desired effect of enhancing Shakespeare's reputation for elegant poetry; it was reprinted five
times during his lifetime and was frequently admired by his
contemporaries. *Venus and Adonis* was, to be sure, more
popular still (it was reprinted nine times during Shakespeare's lifetime), but no one in Shakespeare's day seems to
have regarded *Lucrece* as anything other than a noble work.

To understand the poem in terms of its own generic sense
of form, we must recognize its conventions and not expect it
to be other than what it professes to be. As in *Venus and
Adonis*, plot and character are secondary. Although the
story outlined in "The Argument" is potentially sensa-
tional and swift-moving, Shakespeare deliberately cuts
away most of the action. We do not see Lucius Tarquinius'
murder of his father-in-law and tyrannical seizure of Rome,
or Collatinus' rash boasting of his wife Lucrece's virtue in
the presence of the King's lustful son Sextus Tarquinius.
Nor, at the conclusion of the story, do we learn much about
the avenging of Lucrece's rape. Shakespeare's focus is on
the attitudes of the two protagonists immediately before
and after the ravishment. Even here, despite opportunities
for psychological probing, Shakespeare's real interest is
not in the characters themselves so much as in the social
ramifications of their actions. As Coppélia Kahn has shown
(in *Shakespeare Studies 9*), the rape serves as a means of
examining the nature of marriage in a patriarchal society
where competition for ownership and struggles for power
characterize men's attitudes toward politics and sex. Using
Rome as a familiar mirror for English customs, Shakespeare presents Lucrece as a heroine acting to uphold the
institution of marriage. It is she who acquires the stain
through being violated and she who must pay the cost of
wifely duty in marriage. Like a number of Shakespeare's
later heroines, such as Imogen in *Cymbeline*, Lucrece is
portrayed as beautiful but not alluring, restrained even in

her marriage bed. She arranges her death so as to make the most of its social implications.

Along with his interest in patriarchy and violence, Shakespeare frames the story of *The Rape of Lucrece* in terms of the political events that lead to the founding of the Roman republic. The corruption of the Tarquins raises issues about Roman values generally, and the poem ends with a strong repudiation of the old order. The villain of the poem is at once rapist and tyrant; the resolution is both a vindication of women as victims and a movement toward republicanism. To be sure, the patriarchy that has dictated the conditions of Lucrece's life and honor will remain intact in the republic; the wife is still her husband's possession, and her greatest obligation to state and family must be to ensure that the husband's honor remains unbesmirched. Nonetheless, the assumptions of Roman hierarchy have been held up to scrutiny.

Shakespeare casts his narrative in the form of a series of rhetorical disputations, each a set piece presented as a debate or as a formal declamation. The debates are built around familiar antitheses: honor versus lust, rude will versus conscience, "affection" versus reason, nobility versus baseness, and so on. Many of the images are similarly arranged in contrasting pairs: dove and owl, daylight and darkness, clear and cloudy weather, white and red. Tarquin debates with himself the reasons for and against rape; Lucrece tries to persuade him of the depravity of his course; Lucrece ponders suicide. These debates generate in turn a number of rhetorical apostrophes to marital fidelity (ll. 22–28), to the ideal of kingship as a moral example to others (ll. 610–637), to Night (ll. 764–812), to Opportunity (ll. 876–924), and to Time (ll. 925–1022). Another rhetorical formula, perhaps the most successful in the poem, is the use of structural digression. The most notable describes a painting of Troy with obvious relevance to Lucrece's sad fate: Troy is a city destroyed by a rape, Paris achieves his selfish pleasure at the expense of the public good, Sinon wins his sinister victory through deceitful appearance.

Throughout, the poem's ornament strives after heightened and elaborate effects. The comparisons, or "conceits" as the Elizabethans called them, are intentionally contrived and reliant on ingenious wordplay. Shakespeare puns on

the word "will," for example, as he does in the Sonnets,
where he takes advantage of his own first name being Will
(see Sonnet 135), and in *Venus and Adonis* (see ll. 365, 369).
In *The Rape of Lucrece*, the word is central to Shakespeare's
depiction of Tarquin, as we see the ravisher holding a disputation between "frozen conscience and hot-burning will"
(l. 247), forcing the locks "between her chamber and his
will" (l. 302), feeding ravenously "in his will his willful eye"
(l. 417), and the like. These and other passages often frame
the word in a polarity of "will" and "heart," and range over
numerous meanings that include inclination, desire, appetite, sexual lust, request or command, volition, pleasure,
permission, good will, spontaneity. The fact that the word
rhymes with "kill" and "ill" adds to its usefulness. Another
kind of "conceit" found throughout *The Rape of Lucrece*—
one that arises integrally from the poem's deepest
concerns—is the extended military metaphor of a city under siege. Tarquin's heart beats an alarum, Lucrece's
breasts are "round turrets" made pale by the assault
(ll. 432–441), and, in her subsequent death, she is likened
to a "late-sacked island" surrounded by rivers of her
own blood (l. 1740). Elsewhere she is a house that has been
pillaged, "Her mansion battered by the enemy"
(ll. 1170–1171). Classical allusions are of course common,
notably to the story of the rape of Philomel or Philomela
(ll. 1079, 1128, etc.). Rhetorical devices of antithesis are displayed with the same ornate versatility as in *Venus and
Adonis*. In a poem on a serious subject, these devices may
seem overly contrived to us. We should nevertheless recognize them as conventional in the genre to which *The Rape of
Lucrece* belongs. We find a similar blending of the sensuous
and the moral in the sometimes grotesque conceits of the
Catholic poet Robert Southwell (d. 1595) and in the later ba-
roque paradoxes of Richard Crashaw (d. 1649). Among
Shakespeare's dramatic works, *Titus Andronicus* seems
closest to *The Rape of Lucrece* in its pathos, refined sensa-
tionalism, and use of classical allusion and specifically in
the character of Lavinia, whose misfortunes and chaste dignity so much resemble those of Lucrece.

Throughout *The Rape of Lucrece*, we find a consciousness of the poem's own artistry. In Lucrece's tragic plight,
Shakespeare explores art's ability to articulate through its

various means of expression. Especially in the long passage on the painting of the fall of Troy (ll. 1366–1568), Lucrece shows an understandable anxiety about art's ability to deceive. The painting is in some ways more realistic than life itself; the figures in the painting seem to move and are so cunningly rendered that they "mock the mind" (l. 1414). The imaginary work is "Conceit deceitful" (l. 1423), able through synecdoche (using the part to represent the whole) to suggest a series of general truths lying behind the particulars that are shown. This power of art to deceive is most troublesome in the case of Sinon, the betrayer of Troy—"In him the painter labored with his skill / To hide deceit" (ll. 1506–1507)—and has succeeded with such devastating effect that the viewer cannot tell from Sinon's mild appearance that he is in fact capable of limitless evil. In his capacity for deception, Sinon is like Tarquin, the seemingly attractive courtier who has ravaged Lucrece. Art is thus capable of misrepresentation for purposes of evil; its persuasive power, its imaginative vision, can be perverted to wrong ends. Seen through such art, Rome too is at once a great source of civilization and a nation whose values are cast seriously in doubt. *The Rape of Lucrece* thus grapples with issues of serious consequence, ones that also concerned Shakespeare in his early plays (such as *Titus Andronicus*) and indeed throughout his career as dramatist.

# The Rape of Lucrece

*To the* RIGHT HONORABLE HENRY WRIOTHESLEY, *Earl of Southampton, and Baron of Titchfield.*

The love I dedicate to your lordship is without end; whereof this pamphlet without beginning is ² but a superfluous moiety. The warrant I have of ³ your honorable disposition, not the worth of my untutored lines, makes it assured of acceptance. What I have done is yours; what I have to do is yours; being part in all I have, devoted yours. ⁷ Were my worth greater, my duty would show greater; meantime, as it is, it is bound to your lordship, to whom I wish long life still length- ¹⁰ ened with all happiness.

Your lordship's in all duty,

William Shakespeare.

## THE ARGUMENT

Lucius Tarquinius, for his excessive pride surnamed Superbus, after he had caused his own father-in-law ² Servius Tullius to be cruelly murdered and, contrary to the Roman laws and customs, not requiring or ⁴ staying for the people's suffrages, had possessed ⁵

---

**Dedication.**
**2 without beginning** i.e., beginning *in medias res,* in the middle of the action   **3 moiety** part.   **warrant** assurance   **7 being . . . have** since you are part of everything I have done and have to do   **10 still** continually

**The Argument.**
**2 Superbus** "the Proud"   **4 requiring** requesting   **5 suffrages** consent

himself of the kingdom, went, accompanied with
his sons and other noblemen of Rome, to besiege
Ardea. During which siege, the principal men of the
army meeting one evening at the tent of Sextus Tarquinius, the King's son, in their discourses after
supper everyone commended the virtues of his own
wife; among whom Collatinus extolled the incom-
parable chastity of his wife Lucretia. In that pleasant 13
humor they all posted to Rome; and intending, by 14
their secret and sudden arrival, to make trial of that
which everyone had before avouched, only Colla- 16
tinus finds his wife, though it were late in the night,
spinning amongst her maids; the other ladies were
all found dancing and reveling, or in several dis- 19
ports. Whereupon the noblemen yielded Collatinus 20
the victory and his wife the fame. At that time Sextus Tarquinius, being inflamed with Lucrece's beauty,
yet smothering his passions for the present, de-
parted with the rest back to the camp; from whence
he shortly after privily withdrew himself, and was, 25
according to his estate, royally entertained and 26
lodged by Lucrece at Collatium. The same night he
treacherously stealeth into her chamber, violently
ravished her, and early in the morning speedeth
away. Lucrece, in this lamentable plight, hastily dis-
patcheth messengers, one to Rome for her father,
another to the camp for Collatine. They came, the
one accompanied with Junius Brutus, the other with
Publius Valerius; and finding Lucrece attired in
mourning habit, demanded the cause of her sorrow. 35
She, first taking an oath of them for her revenge,
revealed the actor and whole manner of his dealing, 37
and withal suddenly stabbed herself. Which done,
with one consent they all vowed to root out the
whole hated family of the Tarquins; and, bearing the
dead body to Rome, Brutus acquainted the people
with the doer and manner of the vile deed, with a
bitter invective against the tyranny of the King,

---

13 **pleasant** merry  14 **posted** hastened  16 **avouched** affirmed
19–20 **several disports** various pastimes  25 **privily** secretly  26 **estate**
rank  35 **habit** attire  37 **actor** doer

wherewith the people were so moved that with one consent and a general acclamation the Tarquins were all exiled and the state government changed from kings to consuls.

From the besiegèd Ardea all in post,                    1
Borne by the trustless wings of false desire,           2
Lust-breathèd Tarquin leaves the Roman host,            3
And to Collatium bears the lightless fire               4
Which, in pale embers hid, lurks to aspire              5
    And girdle with embracing flames the waist
    Of Collatine's fair love, Lucrece the chaste.

Haply that name of "chaste" unhapp'ly set               8
This bateless edge on his keen appetite,                9
When Collatine unwisely did not let                    10
To praise the clear unmatchèd red and white
Which triumphed in that sky of his delight,            12
    Where mortal stars, as bright as heaven's beauties, 13
    With pure aspects did him peculiar duties.         14

For he the night before, in Tarquin's tent,
Unlocked the treasure of his happy state;              16
What priceless wealth the heavens had him lent
In the possession of his beauteous mate;
Reck'ning his fortune at such high proud rate          19
    That kings might be espousèd to more fame,
    But king nor peer to such a peerless dame.

1 **Ardea** a city twenty-four miles south of Rome.  **post** haste
2 **trustless** treacherous  3 **Lust-breathèd** excited by lust  4 **Collatium** a
city about ten miles east of Rome.  **lightless** i.e., smoldering invisibly
5 **aspire** rise, i.e., break into flames  8 **Haply** perchance.  **unhapp'ly**
(1) unhappily (2) by mischance  9 **bateless** not to be blunted  10 **let**
forbear  12 **sky** i.e., Lucrece's face  13 **mortal stars** i.e., Lucrece's eyes
14 **aspects** (1) looks (2) astrologically favorable position.  **peculiar**
exclusively for him  16 **Unlocked the treasure** i.e., opened and revealed
(in conversation) the riches  19 **high proud** making him highly proud

O happiness enjoyed but of a few!
And, if possessed, as soon decayed and done                        23
As is the morning silver melting dew
Against the golden splendor of the sun!
An expired date, canceled ere well begun.                          26
   Honor and beauty in the owner's arms
   Are weakly fortressed from a world of harms.

Beauty itself doth of itself persuade                               29
The eyes of men without an orator;
What needeth then apology be made
To set forth that which is so singular?
Or why is Collatine the publisher
   Of that rich jewel he should keep unknown
   From thievish ears, because it is his own?

Perchance his boast of Lucrece's sovereignty                        36
Suggested this proud issue of a king;                              37
For by our ears our hearts oft tainted be.
Perchance that envy of so rich a thing,                             39
Braving compare, disdainfully did sting                            40
   His high-pitched thoughts, that meaner men should
     vaunt                                  41
   That golden hap which their superiors want.        42

But some untimely thought did instigate
His all too timeless speed, if none of those.                      44
His honor, his affairs, his friends, his state,                    45
Neglected all, with swift intent he goes
To quench the coal which in his liver glows.                       47
   O rash false heat, wrapped in repentant cold,
   Thy hasty spring still blasts and ne'er grows old!    49

---

**23 done** done with   **26 date** period of time   **29 of itself** by its own
nature   **36 sovereignty** supremacy   **37 Suggested** tempted. **issue**
offspring, son (i.e., Tarquin)   **39 Perchance that** i.e., perhaps it was that
**40 Braving compare** defying comparison   **41 meaner** less nobly born
**42 hap** fortune.   **want** lack   **44 timeless** unseemly, unseasonable
**45 state** position   **47 liver** (Regarded as the seat of the passions.)
**49 blasts** is blighted (by cold winds)

When at Collatium this false lord arrived,
Well was he welcomed by the Roman dame,
Within whose face beauty and virtue strived
Which of them both should underprop her fame.
When virtue bragged, beauty would blush for shame;
   When beauty boasted blushes, in despite
    Virtue would stain that o'er with silver white.

But beauty, in that white entitulèd      57
From Venus' doves, doth challenge that fair field.      58
Then virtue claims from beauty beauty's red,
Which virtue gave the golden age to gild      60
Their silver cheeks, and called it then their shield,
   Teaching them thus to use it in the fight,
    When shame assailed, the red should fence the white.   63

This heraldry in Lucrece' face was seen,
Argued by beauty's red and virtue's white.      65
Of either's color was the other queen,
Proving from world's minority their right.      67
Yet their ambition makes them still to fight,      68
   The sovereignty of either being so great
    That oft they interchange each other's seat.

This silent war of lilies and of roses,
Which Tarquin viewed in her fair face's field,
In their pure ranks his traitor eye encloses,      73
Where, lest between them both it should be killed,
The coward captive vanquishèd doth yield
   To those two armies that would let him go,
    Rather than triumph in so false a foe.

---

**57 entitulèd** entitled, having a claim   **58 doves** (Venus' chariot was drawn by white doves.)   **challenge** claim.   **field** (1) battlefield (2) the surface of the shield, where the armorial device is displayed   **60 gild** i.e., cover with a blush of modesty. (Gold and red were often considered interchangeable as colors.)   **63 fence** defend   **65 Argued** disputed, and demonstrated   **67 world's minority** the long-ago *golden age*, mentioned in l. 60 (i.e., their right is as old as the doves of Venus and the first blush)   **68 still** always   **73 encloses** surrounds, overwhelms

Now thinks he that her husband's shallow tongue,
The niggard prodigal that praised her so,                                   79
In that high task hath done her beauty wrong,
Which far exceeds his barren skill to show.
Therefore that praise which Collatine doth owe                              82
   Enchanted Tarquin answers with surmise,                    83
   In silent wonder of still-gazing eyes.

This earthly saint, adorèd by this devil,
Little suspecteth the false worshiper,
For unstained thoughts do seldom dream on evil;
Birds never limed no secret bushes fear.                                    88
So, guiltless, she securely gives good cheer                               89
   And reverend welcome to her princely guest,
   Whose inward ill no outward harm expressed.

For that he colored with his high estate,                                   92
Hiding base sin in pleats of majesty,                                       93
That nothing in him seemed inordinate                                       94
Save sometimes too much wonder of his eye,
Which, having all, all could not satisfy;
   But, poorly rich, so wanteth in his store                   97
   That, cloyed with much, he pineth still for more.

But she, that never coped with stranger eyes,                              99
Could pick no meaning from their parling looks,                           100
Nor read the subtle shining secrecies
Writ in the glassy margins of such books.                                 102
She touched no unknown baits, nor feared no hooks;
   Nor could she moralize his wanton sight                     104
   More than his eyes were opened to the light.                105

**79 niggard prodigal** unwisely lavish yet coming too short in praise
**82 doth owe** i.e., must still render, having fallen short on previous
occasions   **83 answers** renders.   **surmise** visual contemplation
**88 limed** snared with birdlime, a sticky substance placed on branches
**89 securely** unsuspiciously   **92 that he colored** i.e., he disguised his
harmful intent   **93 pleats** cunning folds, concealments   **94 That** so that
**97 so ... store** feels such a craving despite the abundance   **99 stranger
eyes** eyes of a stranger   **100 parling** speaking, conferring   **102 glassy
... books** (Refers to the custom of printing explanatory comments in
book margins; cf. *Romeo and Juliet*, 1.3.87.)   **104 moralize** interpret.
**sight** looking   **105 than** than that

He stories to her ears her husband's fame,     106
Won in the fields of fruitful Italy,
And decks with praises Collatine's high name,
Made glorious by his manly chivalry
With bruisèd arms and wreaths of victory.     110
    Her joy with heaved-up hand she doth express
    And, wordless, so greets heaven for his success.

Far from the purpose of his coming thither
He makes excuses for his being there.
No cloudy show of stormy blustering weather
Doth yet in his fair welkin once appear,     116
Till sable Night, mother of dread and fear,     117
    Upon the world dim darkness doth display
    And in her vaulty prison stows the day.

For then is Tarquin brought unto his bed,
Intending weariness with heavy sprite;     121
For, after supper, long he questionèd     122
With modest Lucrece, and wore out the night.
Now leaden slumber with life's strength doth fight,
    And everyone to rest himself betakes,
    Save thieves and cares and troubled minds that
      wakes.

As one of which doth Tarquin lie revolving     127
The sundry dangers of his will's obtaining;     128
Yet ever to obtain his will resolving,
Though weak-built hopes persuade him to abstaining.
Despair to gain doth traffic oft for gaining;     131
    And when great treasure is the meed proposed,     132
    Though death be adjunct, there's no death supposed.     133

---

**106 stories** relates    **110 bruisèd arms** armor battered in combat
**116 welkin** sky, i.e., appearance, face    **117 sable** black    **121 Intending**
pretending. **sprite** spirit    **122 questionèd** conversed    **127 revolving**
considering    **128 his will's obtaining** obtaining his will    **131 Despair**
**. . . gaining** i.e., even a despairing hope often perversely undertakes to
venture for gain; or, despair of success again and again changes place
with a will to succeed    **132 meed** reward    **133 adjunct** adjoined,
resultant. **supposed** thought of

Those that much covet are with gain so fond          134
That what they have not, that which they possess          135
They scatter and unloose it from their bond,          136
And so, by hoping more, they have but less;
Or, gaining more, the profit of excess          138
    Is but to surfeit, and such griefs sustain          139
    That they prove bankrupt in this poor-rich gain.

The aim of all is but to nurse the life
With honor, wealth, and ease in waning age;
And in this aim there is such thwarting strife          143
That one for all or all for one we gage:          144
As life for honor in fell battle's rage,          145
    Honor for wealth; and oft that wealth doth cost
    The death of all, and all together lost.

So that in venturing ill we leave to be          148
The things we are for that which we expect;          149
And this ambitious foul infirmity,          150
In having much, torments us with defect          151
Of that we have. So then we do neglect
    The thing we have, and all for want of wit          153
    Make something nothing by augmenting it.

Such hazard now must doting Tarquin make,
Pawning his honor to obtain his lust,
And for himself himself he must forsake.          157
Then where is truth, if there be no self-trust?
When shall he think to find a stranger just,
    When he himself himself confounds, betrays
    To slanderous tongues and wretched hateful days?

---

**134 fond** infatuated   **135 what** for what   **136 bond** possession
**138 profit of excess** advantage of having more than enough   **139 such
griefs sustain** i.e., to sustain such griefs as accompany surfeit   **143 And**
yet   **144 gage** stake, risk   **145 As** such as.   **fell** fierce   **148 leave to be**
cease being   **149 expect** i.e., hope to be   **150 infirmity** i.e., covetousness
**151 In having much** though we have much.   **defect** the imagined defi-
ciency   **153 want of wit** lack of common sense   **157 for ... forsake** i.e.,
he must forsake his honorable self to satisfy his lustful self

Now stole upon the time the dead of night,
When heavy sleep had closed up mortal eyes.
No comfortable star did lend his light, 164
No noise but owls' and wolves' death-boding cries.
Now serves the season that they may surprise
  The silly lambs. Pure thoughts are dead and still, 167
  While lust and murder wakes to stain and kill.

And now this lustful lord leapt from his bed,
Throwing his mantle rudely o'er his arm;
Is madly tossed between desire and dread;
Th' one sweetly flatters, th' other feareth harm;
But honest fear, bewitched with lust's foul charm,
  Doth too too oft betake him to retire, 174
  Beaten away by brainsick rude desire.

His falchion on a flint he softly smiteth, 176
That from the cold stone sparks of fire do fly;
Whereat a waxen torch forthwith he lighteth,
Which must be lodestar to his lustful eye; 179
And to the flame thus speaks advisedly: 180
  "As from this cold flint I enforced this fire,
  So Lucrece must I force to my desire."

Here pale with fear he doth premeditate
The dangers of his loathsome enterprise,
And in his inward mind he doth debate
What following sorrow may on this arise.
Then, looking scornfully, he doth despise
  His naked armor of still-slaughtered lust, 188
  And justly thus controls his thoughts unjust: 189

**164 comfortable** cheering, benevolent. **his** its **167 silly** helpless, defenseless **174 betake . . . retire** i.e., (honest fear) retires in confusion. **him** himself **176 falchion** curved sword **179 lodestar** the guiding polestar **180 advisedly** deliberately **188 His . . . lust** his poor defense against his own lust, which is continually being slaughtered, i.e., temporarily satiated, but never killed; or, his insatiable and vulnerable lust, which will be his only poor armor once he has committed the rape **189 justly** accurately, closely

"Fair torch, burn out thy light, and lend it not
To darken her whose light excelleth thine;
And die, unhallowed thoughts, before you blot
With your uncleanness that which is divine.
Offer pure incense to so pure a shrine.
    Let fair humanity abhor the deed
    That spots and stains love's modest snow-white weed.  196

"O shame to knighthood and to shining arms!
O foul dishonor to my household's grave!                198
O impious act, including all foul harms!                199
A martial man to be soft fancy's slave!                 200
True valor still a true respect should have;            201
    Then my digression is so vile, so base,             202
    That it will live engraven in my face.

"Yea, though I die, the scandal will survive
And be an eyesore in my golden coat;                     205
Some loathsome dash the herald will contrive            206
To cipher me how fondly I did dote;                     207
That my posterity, shamed with the note,                208
    Shall curse my bones, and hold it for no sin
    To wish that I their father had not been.

"What win I, if I gain the thing I seek?
A dream, a breath, a froth of fleeting joy.
Who buys a minute's mirth to wail a week?
Or sells eternity to get a toy?                         214
For one sweet grape who will the vine destroy?
    Or what fond beggar, but to touch the crown,
    Would with the scepter straight be strucken down?   217

196 weed garment (i.e., chastity)  198 my household's grave memorial
tomb of my forebears  199 including encompassing  200 fancy's love's,
infatuation's  201 true respect i.e., proper consideration for virtue
202 digression falling away (from honor)  205 coat coat of arms
206 dash bar, stroke (devised by the heralds to indicate something
dishonorable in the pedigree)  207 cipher express in characters, indicate.  fondly foolishly  208 note stigma, the heraldic bar (l. 206)
214 toy trifle  217 straight at once

"If Collatinus dream of my intent,
Will he not wake and in a desperate rage
Post hither, this vile purpose to prevent?                    220
This siege that hath engirt his marriage,                     221
This blur to youth, this sorrow to the sage,
    This dying virtue, this surviving shame,
    Whose crime will bear an ever-during blame?              224

"O, what excuse can my invention make
When thou shalt charge me with so black a deed?
Will not my tongue be mute, my frail joints shake,
Mine eyes forgo their light, my false heart bleed?           228
The guilt being great, the fear doth still exceed;
    And extreme fear can neither fight nor fly,
    But cowardlike with trembling terror die.

"Had Collatinus killed my son or sire,
Or lain in ambush to betray my life,
Or were he not my dear friend, this desire
Might have excuse to work upon his wife,
As in revenge or quittal of such strife;                     236
    But as he is my kinsman, my dear friend,
    The shame and fault finds no excuse nor end.

"Shameful it is; ay, if the fact be known,                   239
Hateful it is. There is no hate in loving.
I'll beg her love. But she is not her own.                   241
The worst is but denial and reproving.
My will is strong, past reason's weak removing.
    Who fears a sentence or an old man's saw                 244
    Shall by a painted cloth be kept in awe."               245

220 **Post** hasten   221 **engirt** engirdled, as in a siege   224 **ever-during**
everlasting   228 **forgo their light** lose their power of vision   236 **quittal**
requital   239 **fact** deed   241 **she . . . own** i.e., she is not entirely independent, since she has duties to her husband   244 **Who** whoever.   **sentence** moral sentiment.   **saw** saying, proverb   245 **painted cloth** wall
hanging in which moral tales and maxims were sometimes depicted.
(Cf. ll. 1366–1456, where such a painted cloth is described.)

Thus, graceless, holds he disputation                          246
'Tween frozen conscience and hot-burning will,
And with good thoughts makes dispensation,                     248
Urging the worser sense for vantage still,
Which in a moment doth confound and kill
   All pure effects, and doth so far proceed     251
   That what is vile shows like a virtuous deed.

Quoth he, "She took me kindly by the hand
And gazed for tidings in my eager eyes,
Fearing some hard news from the warlike band
Where her belovèd Collatinus lies.
O, how her fear did make her color rise!
   First red as roses that on lawn we lay,       258
   Then white as lawn, the roses took away.

"And how her hand, in my hand being locked,
Forced it to tremble with her loyal fear!
Which struck her sad, and then it faster rocked,
Until her husband's welfare she did hear;
Whereat she smilèd with so sweet a cheer
   That had Narcissus seen her as she stood        265
   Self-love had never drowned him in the flood.

"Why hunt I then for color or excuses?                          267
All orators are dumb when beauty pleadeth;
Poor wretches have remorse in poor abuses;                      269
Love thrives not in the heart that shadows dreadeth.           270
Affection is my captain, and he leadeth;                        271
   And when his gaudy banner is displayed,
   The coward fights and will not be dismayed.      273

**246 graceless** lacking in social and divine grace    **248 makes dispensation** dispenses, sets aside    **251 effects** impulses    **258 lawn** fine white
linen    **265 Narcissus** youth who fell in love with his own reflection in
the water (but who would have fallen in love with Lucrece if he had
seen her)    **267 color** pretext    **269 Poor . . . abuses** i.e., only lowborn
cowardly men feel remorse for their paltry misdeeds    **270 shadows** i.e.,
the chimeras of conscience    **271 Affection** passion    **273 The coward**
i.e., even the coward

"Then, childish fear, avaunt! Debating, die!　　　274
Respect and reason, wait on wrinkled age!　　　275
My heart shall never countermand mine eye.　　　276
Sad pause and deep regard beseems the sage;　　　277
My part is youth, and beats these from the stage.
　　Desire my pilot is, beauty my prize;
　　Then who fears sinking where such treasure lies?"

As corn o'ergrown by weeds, so heedful fear　　　281
Is almost choked by unresisted lust.
Away he steals with open listening ear,
Full of foul hope and full of fond mistrust,　　　284
Both which, as servitors to the unjust,
　　So cross him with their opposite persuasion　　　286
　　That now he vows a league, and now invasion.　　　287

Within his thought her heavenly image sits,
And in the selfsame seat sits Collatine.
That eye which looks on her confounds his wits;　　　290
That eye which him beholds, as more divine,　　　291
Unto a view so false will not incline,
　　But with a pure appeal seeks to the heart,　　　293
　　Which once corrupted takes the worser part;

And therein heartens up his servile powers,　　　295
Who, flattered by their leader's jocund show,　　　296
Stuff up his lust, as minutes fill up hours;
And as their captain, so their pride doth grow,
Paying more slavish tribute than they owe.
　　By reprobate desire thus madly led,
　　The Roman lord marcheth to Lucrece' bed.

---

**274 avaunt** begone　**275 Respect** circumspection.　**wait on** attend,
accompany　**276 heart** (Here, *moral sense;* cf. ll. 293 ff., where the heart
is corrupted.)　**277 Sad** serious, reflective　**281 corn** grain　**284 fond**
foolish　**286 cross** thwart　**287 league** treaty (of peace)　**290 confounds
his wits** i.e., overwhelms reason with lust　**291 as more divine** i.e., as
representing reason　**293 seeks** applies　**295 servile powers** base passions, appetites. (The image is the common one of the faculties as an
army: the heart as captain of the sensible soul commands all the affections to serve him. Cf. ll. 433 ff., below.)　**296 jocund** sprightly

The locks between her chamber and his will,
Each one by him enforced, retires his ward;                          303
But, as they open, they all rate his ill,                            304
Which drives the creeping thief to some regard.                      305
The threshold grates the door to have him heard;
    Night-wandering weasels shriek to see him there;                 307
    They fright him, yet he still pursues his fear.                  308

As each unwilling portal yields him way,
Through little vents and crannies of the place
The wind wars with his torch to make him stay
And blows the smoke of it into his face,
Extinguishing his conduct in this case;                              313
    But his hot heart, which fond desire doth scorch,
    Puffs forth another wind that fires the torch.

And being lighted, by the light he spies
Lucretia's glove, wherein her needle sticks.
He takes it from the rushes where it lies,                           318
And gripping it, the needle his finger pricks,
As who should say, "This glove to wanton tricks
    Is not inured. Return again in haste;
    Thou seest our mistress' ornaments are chaste."

But all these poor forbiddings could not stay him;                   323
He in the worst sense consters their denial.                         324
The doors, the wind, the glove, that did delay him,
He takes for accidental things of trial,                             326
Or as those bars which stop the hourly dial,                         327
    Who with a lingering stay his course doth let                    328
    Till every minute pays the hour his debt.


303 **retires his ward** draws back its guard, i.e., the locking bolt
304 **rate his ill** chide his evil (by creaking)   305 **regard** caution
307 **weasels** (Weasels were sometimes kept in houses as rat catchers.)
308 **his fear** i.e., the cause of his fear   313 **conduct** conductor, i.e., his
torch   318 **rushes** reeds used as floor covering   323 **stay** restrain
324 **consters** construes   326 **accidental . . . trial** i.e., accidents that test
his resolve, not portents   327 **bars . . . dial** minute marks on a clock
face at which the minute hand seems to pause slightly   328 **Who**
which.   **his** its.   **let** hinder

"So, so," quoth he, "these lets attend the time,                330
Like little frosts that sometimes threat the spring,
To add a more rejoicing to the prime,                           332
And give the sneapèd birds more cause to sing.                  333
Pain pays the income of each precious thing;                    334
  Huge rocks, high winds, strong pirates, shelves, and
    sands                                     335
  The merchant fears, ere rich at home he lands."

Now is he come unto the chamber door
That shuts him from the heaven of his thought,
Which with a yielding latch, and with no more,
Hath barred him from the blessèd thing he sought.
So from himself impiety hath wrought                            341
  That for his prey to pray he doth begin,
  As if the heavens should countenance his sin.

But in the midst of his unfruitful prayer,
Having solicited th' eternal power
That his foul thoughts might compass his fair fair,            346
And they would stand auspicious to the hour,                   347
Even there he starts. Quoth he, "I must deflower.             348
  The powers to whom I pray abhor this fact;            349
  How can they then assist me in the act?

"Then Love and Fortune be my gods, my guide!
My will is backed with resolution.
Thoughts are but dreams till their effects be tried;
The blackest sin is cleared with absolution;
Against love's fire fear's frost hath dissolution.
  The eye of heaven is out, and misty night             356
  Covers the shame that follows sweet delight."

---

**330 these . . . time** i.e., these hindrances (like the minute marks) are part
of the passage of time    **332 more** greater.    **prime** spring    **333 sneapèd**
nipped or pinched with cold    **334 pays . . . of** is the price of obtaining
**335 shelves** sandbars    **341 So . . . wrought** impiety has so wrested him
away from his true nature    **346 compass** encompass, possess.    **fair fair**
virtuous fair one    **347 they** i.e., that they, the eternal powers of heaven
**348 starts** i.e., is startled, taken aback    **349 fact** deed    **356 out** extin-
guished

This said, his guilty hand plucked up the latch,
And with his knee the door he opens wide.
The dove sleeps fast that this night owl will catch.
Thus treason works ere traitors be espied.
Who sees the lurking serpent steps aside;                    362
    But she, sound sleeping, fearing no such thing,
    Lies at the mercy of his mortal sting.                   364

Into the chamber wickedly he stalks,
And gazeth on her yet unstainèd bed.
The curtains being close, about he walks,
Rolling his greedy eyeballs in his head.
By their high treason is his heart misled,
    Which gives the watchword to his hand full soon
    To draw the cloud that hides the silver moon.           371

Look as the fair and fiery-pointed sun,                      372
Rushing from forth a cloud, bereaves our sight,
Even so, the curtain drawn, his eyes begun
To wink, being blinded with a greater light.                375
Whether it is that she reflects so bright                    376
    That dazzleth them, or else some shame supposed;
    But blind they are, and keep themselves enclosed.

O, had they in that darksome prison died,
Then had they seen the period of their ill!                  380
Then Collatine again by Lucrece' side
In his clear bed might have reposèd still.                   382
But they must ope, this blessèd league to kill,             383
    And holy-thoughted Lucrece to their sight               384
    Must sell her joy, her life, her world's delight.

**362 Who** whoever   **364 mortal** deadly   **371 draw the cloud** i.e., draw
back the bedcurtains   **372 Look as** just as   **375 wink** shut   **376 reflects**
shines   **380 period** end.   **ill** wrongdoing   **382 clear** pure, innocent
**383 league** i.e., marriage   **384 to their sight** for the sake of what they
(his eyes) will see

Her lily hand her rosy cheek lies under,
Cozening the pillow of a lawful kiss, 387
Who, therefore angry, seems to part in sunder,
Swelling on either side to want his bliss; 389
Between whose hills her head entombèd is;
   Where, like a virtuous monument, she lies, 391
   To be admired of lewd unhallowed eyes.

Without the bed her other fair hand was, 393
On the green coverlet, whose perfect white
Showed like an April daisy on the grass,
With pearly sweat resembling dew of night.
Her eyes, like marigolds, had sheathed their light,
   And canopied in darkness sweetly lay,
   Till they might open to adorn the day.

Her hair, like golden threads, played with her breath—
O modest wantons, wanton modesty!
Showing life's triumph in the map of death 402
And death's dim look in life's mortality. 403
Each in her sleep themselves so beautify 404
   As if between them twain there were no strife,
   But that life lived in death and death in life.

Her breasts like ivory globes circled with blue,
A pair of maiden worlds unconquerèd,
Save of their lord no bearing yoke they knew,
And him by oath they truly honorèd.
These worlds in Tarquin new ambition bred,
   Who, like a foul usurper, went about
   From this fair throne to heave the owner out.

**387 Cozening** cheating   **389 to want his** i.e., protesting the lack of its
**391 monument** effigy on a tomb   **393 Without** on the outside of
**402 the map of death** i.e., sleep. (*Map* means "image, picture.")
**403 life's mortality** life's least-living aspect, i.e., sleep   **404 Each** i.e.,
life and death

What could he see but mightily he noted?
What did he note but strongly he desired?
What he beheld, on that he firmly doted,
And in his will his willful eye he tired.                    417
With more than admiration he admired
　　Her azure veins, her alabaster skin,
　　Her coral lips, her snow-white dimpled chin.


As the grim lion fawneth o'er his prey,                    421
Sharp hunger by the conquest satisfied,
So o'er this sleeping soul doth Tarquin stay,
His rage of lust by gazing qualified—                    424
Slacked, not suppressed, for standing by her side,
　　His eye, which late this mutiny restrains,                    426
　　Unto a greater uproar tempts his veins.


And they, like straggling slaves for pillage fighting,                    428
Obdurate vassals fell exploits effecting,                    429
In bloody death and ravishment delighting,
Nor children's tears nor mothers' groans respecting,
Swell in their pride, the onset still expecting.                    432
　　Anon his beating heart, alarum striking,
　　Gives the hot charge and bids them do their liking.


His drumming heart cheers up his burning eye,
His eye commends the leading to his hand;                    436
His hand, as proud of such a dignity,
Smoking with pride, marched on to make his stand
On her bare breast, the heart of all her land;
　　Whose ranks of blue veins, as his hand did scale,                    440
　　Left their round turrets destitute and pale.


**417 will** lust.　**tired** (1) exhausted (2) glutted, fed ravenously. (A term
from falconry.)　**421 fawneth** shows delight　**424 qualified** softened,
abated　**426 late** lately, a moment ago　**428 slaves** i.e., base-born sol-
diers　**429 fell** fierce.　**effecting** i.e., on the verge of carrying out
**432 pride** lust.　**still** continually　**436 commends** entrusts, commissions
**440 scale** ascend (as in military attack)

They, mustering to the quiet cabinet                                442
Where their dear governess and lady lies,
Do tell her she is dreadfully beset,
And fright her with confusion of their cries.
She, much amazed, breaks ope her locked-up eyes,
    Who, peeping forth this tumult to behold,
    Are by his flaming torch dimmed and controlled.     448

Imagine her as one in dead of night
From forth dull sleep by dreadful fancy waking,
That thinks she hath beheld some ghastly sprite,
Whose grim aspect sets every joint a-shaking.
What terror 'tis! But she, in worser taking,             453
    From sleep disturbèd, heedfully doth view
    The sight which makes supposèd terror true.

Wrapped and confounded in a thousand fears,
Like to a new-killed bird she trembling lies.
She dares not look; yet, winking, there appears     458
Quick-shifting antics, ugly in her eyes.                459
Such shadows are the weak brain's forgeries,
    Who, angry that the eyes fly from their lights,     461
    In darkness daunts them with more dreadful sights.

His hand, that yet remains upon her breast—
Rude ram, to batter such an ivory wall!—             464
May feel her heart—poor citizen!—distressed,
Wounding itself to death, rise up and fall,
Beating her bulk, that his hand shakes withal.         467
    This moves in him more rage and lesser pity
    To make the breach and enter this sweet city.

442 **mustering** gathering. **cabinet** i.e., heart   448 **controlled** overpowered   453 **taking** state of agitation   458 **winking** closing the eyes
459 **antics** phantoms, fantastic appearances, shapes   461 **fly ... lights**
i.e., refuse to send out the beams, which enable the eyes to see
464 **ram** battering ram   467 **bulk** i.e., chest, breast.   **that** so that

First, like a trumpet, doth his tongue begin
To sound a parley to his heartless foe,                        471
Who o'er the white sheet peers her whiter chin,
The reason of this rash alarm to know,
Which he by dumb demeanor seeks to show;                       474
  But she with vehement prayers urgeth still           475
  Under what color he commits this ill.                 476

Thus he replies: "The color in thy face,                       477
That even for anger makes the lily pale,
And the red rose blush at her own disgrace,
Shall plead for me and tell my loving tale.
Under that color am I come to scale                            481
  Thy never-conquered fort; the fault is thine,
  For those thine eyes betray thee unto mine.

"Thus I forestall thee, if thou mean to chide:
Thy beauty hath ensnared thee to this night,
Where thou with patience must my will abide—
My will that marks thee for my earth's delight,
Which I to conquer sought with all my might.
  But as reproof and reason beat it dead,               489
  By thy bright beauty was it newly bred.

"I see what crosses my attempt will bring;                     491
I know what thorns the growing rose defends;
I think the honey guarded with a sting;                        493
All this beforehand counsel comprehends.
But will is deaf and hears no heedful friends;
  Only he hath an eye to gaze on beauty
  And dotes on what he looks, 'gainst law or duty.       497

---

**471 a parley** a summoning of the defenders to a negotiation.   **heartless**
spiritless, wanting courage   **474 dumb demeanor** dumb show
**475 urgeth** cries out to know   **476 color** pretext   **477 color** hue (punning on the previous line)   **481 color** banner (punning on l. 476)   **489 as**
as soon as   **491 crosses** vexations   **493 think the honey** know the honey
to be   **497 looks** sees

"I have debated, even in my soul,
What wrong, what shame, what sorrow I shall breed,
But nothing can affection's course control          500
Or stop the headlong fury of his speed.
I know repentant tears ensue the deed,              502
  Reproach, disdain, and deadly enmity;
  Yet strive I to embrace mine infamy."

This said, he shakes aloft his Roman blade,
Which, like a falcon towering in the skies,
Coucheth the fowl below with his wings' shade,      507
Whose crooked beak threats if he mount he dies.     508
So under his insulting falchion lies                509
  Harmless Lucretia, marking what he tells
  With trembling fear, as fowl hear falcons' bells.  511

"Lucrece," quoth he, "this night I must enjoy thee.
If thou deny, then force must work my way,
For in thy bed I purpose to destroy thee.
That done, some worthless slave of thine I'll slay,
To kill thine honor with thy life's decay;          516
  And in thy dead arms do I mean to place him,
  Swearing I slew him, seeing thee embrace him.

"So thy surviving husband shall remain
The scornful mark of every open eye,                520
Thy kinsmen hang their heads at this disdain,
Thy issue blurred with nameless bastardy;           522
And thou, the author of their obloquy,
  Shalt have thy trespass cited up in rhymes
  And sung by children in succeeding times.

---

**500 affection's** passion's   **502 ensue** follow upon   **507 Coucheth** causes
to couch, i.e., remain concealed   **508 Whose** i.e., the falcon's.   **he** i.e.,
the fowl   **509 insulting** exulting in triumph   **511 bells** (Falcons had
bells attached to their feet.)   **516 To kill . . . decay** i.e., to destroy your
honor even while also taking your life   **520 open eye** i.e., observer
**522 issue blurred** offspring tarnished.   **nameless** the father's name
being unknown

"But if thou yield, I rest thy secret friend.          526
The fault unknown is as a thought unacted;
A little harm done to a great good end
For lawful policy remains enacted.          529
The poisonous simple sometimes is compacted          530
  In a pure compound; being so applied,          531
  His venom in effect is purified.

"Then, for thy husband and thy children's sake,
Tender my suit. Bequeath not to their lot          534
The shame that from them no device can take,          535
The blemish that will never be forgot,
Worse than a slavish wipe or birth hour's blot.          537
  For marks descried in men's nativity
  Are nature's faults, not their own infamy."

Here with a cockatrice' dead-killing eye          540
He rouseth up himself and makes a pause,
While she, the picture of pure piety,
Like a white hind under the gripe's sharp claws,          543
Pleads, in a wilderness where are no laws,
  To the rough beast that knows no gentle right,          545
  Nor aught obeys but his foul appetite.

---

**526 rest** remain.   **friend** lover   **529 For ... enacted** is accepted as a
legal expedient   **530 simple** ingredient, drug.   **compacted** mixed
**531 pure** i.e., benign, medically efficacious   **534 Tender** regard
**535 device** heraldic motto   **537 slavish wipe** brand with which slaves
were marked.   **birth hour's blot** unsightly birthmark   **540 cockatrice**
the basilisk, said to be hatched by a serpent from a cock's egg and to
kill by its breath and the rays it emitted from its eyes   **543 hind** female
deer.   **gripe's** vulture's, or griffin's   **545 gentle right** the right that
should be given to the weak and noble. (*Gentle* means both "weak" and
"nobly born.")

But when a black-faced cloud the world doth threat,
In his dim mist th' aspiring mountains hiding,
From earth's dark womb some gentle gust doth get,    549
Which blow these pitchy vapors from their biding,    550
Hindering their present fall by this dividing;    551
    So his unhallowed haste her words delays,    552
    And moody Pluto winks while Orpheus plays.    553

Yet, foul night-waking cat, he doth but dally,
While in his hold-fast foot the weak mouse panteth.
Her sad behavior feeds his vulture folly,    556
A swallowing gulf that even in plenty wanteth.    557
His ear her prayers admits, but his heart granteth
    No penetrable entrance to her plaining;    559
    Tears harden lust, though marble wear with raining.

Her pity-pleading eyes are sadly fixed
In the remorseless wrinkles of his face;    562
Her modest eloquence with sighs is mixed,
Which to her oratory adds more grace.
She puts the period often from his place,    565
    And midst the sentence so her accent breaks    566
    That twice she doth begin ere once she speaks.

She conjures him by high almighty Jove,
By knighthood, gentry, and sweet friendship's oath,    569
By her untimely tears, her husband's love,
By holy human law and common troth,    571
By heaven and earth, and all the power of both,
    That to his borrowed bed he make retire    573
    And stoop to honor, not to foul desire.    574

**549 doth get** comes into being  **550 pitchy** black.  **their biding** where
they hang  **551 their present fall** i.e., the imminent onset of the storm
**552 So . . . delays** thus her words delay his unhallowed haste  **553 winks**
closes his eyes.  **Orpheus** husband of Eurydice who went to the underworld for her and charmed Pluto, ruler of the underworld, with his playing the lyre  **556 vulture folly** ravenous lewdness and madness  **557 gulf**
maw, belly.  **wanteth** craves insatiably  **559 plaining** lamentation
**562 wrinkles** i.e., frowns  **565 his place** its place (in the sentence; i.e., she
speaks in broken phrases)  **566 accent** speech  **569 gentry** nobleness of
birth and breeding  **571 troth** good faith  **573 borrowed** lent him for the
night  **574 stoop** (Plays on the meanings "subject oneself," "debase
oneself," and "stoop to the lure or prey" like a falcon.)

Quoth she, "Reward not hospitality
With such black payment as thou hast pretended.          576
Mud not the fountain that gave drink to thee;
Mar not the thing that cannot be amended.               578
End thy ill aim before thy shoot be ended;              579
  He is no woodman that doth bend his bow        580
  To strike a poor unseasonable doe.             581

"My husband is thy friend; for his sake spare me.
Thyself art mighty; for thine own sake leave me.
Myself a weakling; do not then ensnare me.
Thou look'st not like deceit; do not deceive me.
My sighs, like whirlwinds, labor hence to heave thee.
  If ever man were moved with woman's moans,
  Be movèd with my tears, my sighs, my groans;

"All which together, like a troubled ocean,
Beat at thy rocky and wreck-threatening heart,
To soften it with their continual motion;
For stones dissolved to water do convert.               592
O, if no harder than a stone thou art,
  Melt at my tears, and be compassionate!
  Soft pity enters at an iron gate.

"In Tarquin's likeness I did entertain thee.
Hast thou put on his shape to do him shame?
To all the host of heaven I complain me.
Thou wrong'st his honor, wound'st his princely name.
Thou art not what thou seem'st; and if the same,        600
  Thou seem'st not what thou art, a god, a king;
  For kings like gods should govern everything.

---

**576 pretended** proposed  **578 amended** returned to its former
purity  **579 shoot** shooting, hunting  **580 woodman** huntsman
**581 unseasonable** in foal or not yet bearing, out of the hunting season
**592 stones . . . convert** i.e., stones are worn away in time by water.
**convert** change  **600 if the same** i.e., if you are actually Tarquin

"How will thy shame be seeded in thine age,                    603
When thus thy vices bud before thy spring?
If in thy hope thou dar'st do such outrage,                    605
What dar'st thou not when once thou art a king?
O, be remembered, no outrageous thing                         607
  From vassal actors can be wiped away;                  608
  Then kings' misdeeds cannot be hid in clay.            609

"This deed will make thee only loved for fear,                610
But happy monarchs still are feared for love.                 611
With foul offenders thou perforce must bear,                  612
When they in thee the like offenses prove.
If but for fear of this, thy will remove;                     614
  For princes are the glass, the school, the book,      615
  Where subjects' eyes do learn, do read, do look.

"And wilt thou be the school where Lust shall learn?
Must he in thee read lectures of such shame?
Wilt thou be glass wherein it shall discern
Authority for sin, warrant for blame,
To privilege dishonor in thy name?                            621
  Thou back'st reproach against long-living laud        622
  And mak'st fair reputation but a bawd.

"Hast thou command? By Him that gave it thee,                 624
From a pure heart command thy rebel will.
Draw not thy sword to guard iniquity,
For it was lent thee all that brood to kill.                  627
Thy princely office how canst thou fulfill,
  When, patterned by thy fault, foul Sin may say        629
  He learned to sin, and thou didst teach the way?

**603 be seeded** ripen   **605 in thy hope** i.e., while you are yet only heir to
the kingdom   **607 be remembered** bear in mind   **608 vassal actors** i.e.,
vassals or ordinary subjects who commit crimes   **609 in clay** i.e., even
in death   **610 loved for fear** i.e., obeyed out of fear   **611 still . . . love**
i.e., always are regarded with reverential awe stemming from love
**612 With . . . bear** i.e., you will have to put up with others' foul offenses
**614 but** only.   **thy will remove** dissuade your lust   **615 glass** mirror
and paradigm   **621 privilege** license   **622 Thou back'st** you support.
**laud** praise   **624 Him** i.e., God   **627 that brood** i.e., the progeny of evil
**629 patterned** shown a precedent

"Think but how vile a spectacle it were
To view thy present trespass in another.
Men's faults do seldom to themselves appear;
Their own transgressions partially they smother.          634
This guilt would seem death-worthy in thy brother.
    O, how are they wrapped in with infamies
    That from their own misdeeds askance their eyes!       637

"To thee, to thee, my heaved-up hands appeal,             638
Not to seducing lust, thy rash relier.                    639
I sue for exiled majesty's repeal;                        640
Let him return, and flattering thoughts retire.           641
His true respect will prison false desire                 642
    And wipe the dim mist from thy doting eyne,           643
    That thou shalt see thy state and pity mine."

"Have done," quoth he. "My uncontrollèd tide
Turns not, but swells the higher by this let.             646
Small lights are soon blown out; huge fires abide,
And with the wind in greater fury fret.
The petty streams that pay a daily debt
    To their salt sovereign, with their fresh falls' haste   650
    Add to his flow but alter not his taste."

"Thou art," quoth she, "a sea, a sovereign king;
And lo, there falls into thy boundless flood
Black lust, dishonor, shame, misgoverning,
Who seek to stain the ocean of thy blood.
If all these petty ills shall change thy good,
    Thy sea within a puddle's womb is hearsed,            657
    And not the puddle in thy sea dispersed.

**634 partially** showing partiality toward themselves.   **smother** conceal
**637 askance** avert   **638 heaved-up** raised   **639 thy rash relier** on which
you rashly rely; or, which rashly relies on you in your present emotional
state   **640 repeal** recall from exile   **641 and flattering thoughts retire**
i.e., and let those thoughts that flatter and egg on lust go away   **642 His
true respect** true respect for him; or, his true judgment.   **prison** imprison   **643 eyne** eyes   **646 let** hindrance   **650 salt sovereign** i.e., the
sea   **657 hearsed** buried, coffined

"So shall these slaves be king, and thou their slave;          659
Thou nobly base, they basely dignified;
Thou their fair life, and they thy fouler grave;
Thou loathèd in their shame, they in thy pride.
The lesser thing should not the greater hide;
   The cedar stoops not to the base shrub's foot,
   But low shrubs wither at the cedar's root.

"So let thy thoughts, low vassals to thy state—"
"No more," quoth he, "by heaven, I will not hear thee.
Yield to my love; if not, enforcèd hate,                      668
Instead of love's coy touch, shall rudely tear thee.          669
That done, despitefully I mean to bear thee
   Unto the base bed of some rascal groom,                    671
   To be thy partner in this shameful doom."

This said, he sets his foot upon the light,
For light and lust are deadly enemies;
Shame folded up in blind concealing night,
When most unseen, then most doth tyrannize.
The wolf hath seized his prey, the poor lamb cries;
   Till with her own white fleece her voice controlled        678
   Entombs her outcry in her lips' sweet fold.                679

For with the nightly linen that she wears
He pens her piteous clamors in her head,
Cooling his hot face in the chastest tears
That ever modest eyes with sorrow shed.
O, that prone lust should stain so pure a bed!                684
   The spots whereof could weeping purify,                    685
   Her tears should drop on them perpetually.

---

**659 these slaves** i.e., lust, dishonor, etc.; see l. 654   **668 enforcèd hate**
force impelled by hatred   **669 coy** gentle   **671 groom** servant
**678–679 Till . . . fold** until, overmastering her voice with her own night-
wear, he buries her outcry as though in the fold of her sweet lips. (*Fold*
refers to her folded or compressed lips and to a sheepfold; hence *pens*
in l. 681.)   **684 prone** eager, headlong   **685 could weeping** if weeping
could

But she hath lost a dearer thing than life,
And he hath won what he would lose again.
This forcèd league doth force a further strife;
This momentary joy breeds months of pain;
This hot desire converts to cold disdain.                          691
   Pure Chastity is rifled of her store,
    And Lust, the thief, far poorer than before.

Look as the full-fed hound or gorgèd hawk,                        694
Unapt for tender smell or speedy flight,                          695
Make slow pursuit, or altogether balk                            696
The prey wherein by nature they delight;
So surfeit-taking Tarquin fares this night.
   His taste delicious, in digestion souring,
    Devours his will, that lived by foul devouring.

O, deeper sin than bottomless conceit                            701
Can comprehend in still imagination!
Drunken Desire must vomit his receipt                            703
Ere he can see his own abomination.
While Lust is in his pride, no exclamation                       705
   Can curb his heat or rein his rash desire,
    Till like a jade Self-will himself doth tire.             707

And then with lank and lean discolored cheek,
With heavy eye, knit brow, and strengthless pace,
Feeble Desire, all recreant, poor, and meek,                     710
Like to a bankrupt beggar wails his case.                        711
The flesh being proud, Desire doth fight with Grace,             712
   For there it revels, and when that decays,                713
    The guilty rebel for remission prays.                     714

---

**691 converts** changes   **694 Look as** just as   **695 tender smell** delicate
scent   **696 balk** turn away from, let slip   **701 bottomless conceit**
limitless imagination   **703 his receipt** what it has swallowed
**705 exclamation** protest   **707 jade** untrained or unbroken horse
**710 recreant** craven, cowed   **711 Like to** like   **712 proud** i.e., stubborn,
willful   **713 there** i.e., in the flesh.   **when that decays** when the reveling
in pleasure subsides   **714 The guilty . . . prays** i.e., the flesh prays for
forgiveness

So fares it with this faultful lord of Rome,
Who this accomplishment so hotly chased;
For now against himself he sounds this doom,                     717
That through the length of times he stands disgraced.
Besides, his soul's fair temple is defaced,
    To whose weak ruins muster troops of cares
    To ask the spotted princess how she fares.                   721

She says her subjects with foul insurrection                     722
Have battered down her consecrated wall,
And by their mortal fault brought in subjection                  724
Her immortality, and made her thrall
To living death and pain perpetual,
    Which in her prescience she controllèd still,                727
    But her foresight could not forestall their will.            728

Ev'n in this thought through the dark night he stealeth,
A captive victor that hath lost in gain,                         730
Bearing away the wound that nothing healeth,
The scar that will, despite of cure, remain,
Leaving his spoil perplexed in greater pain.                     733
    She bears the load of lust he left behind,
    And he the burden of a guilty mind.

He like a thievish dog creeps sadly thence;
She like a wearied lamb lies panting there.
He scowls and hates himself for his offense;
She, desperate, with her nails her flesh doth tear.
He faintly flies, sweating with guilty fear;
    She stays, exclaiming on the direful night;                  741
    He runs, and chides his vanished, loathed delight.

---

**717 sounds this doom** pronounces this judgment   **721 spotted princess**
i.e., his contaminated soul, of whom the *temple*, l. 719, is the body
**722 subjects** i.e., the senses   **724 mortal** deadly   **727–728 Which . . .
will** i.e., she could foresee the inevitable coming of pain and death but
could do nothing to prevent it   **730 captive victor** i.e., Tarquin, who has
triumphed over Lucrece and thus gained perpetual durance in sin
**733 spoil** prey, i.e., Lucrece   **741 exclaiming on** denouncing

He thence departs a heavy convertite;                743
She there remains a hopeless castaway.
He in his speed looks for the morning light;
She prays she never may behold the day.
"For day," quoth she, "night's scapes doth open lay,                747
    And my true eyes have never practiced how
    To cloak offenses with a cunning brow.

"They think not but that every eye can see
The same disgrace which they themselves behold;
And therefore would they still in darkness be,
To have their unseen sin remain untold.
For they their guilt with weeping will unfold,                754
    And grave, like water that doth eat in steel,                755
    Upon my cheeks what helpless shame I feel."

Here she exclaims against repose and rest                757
And bids her eyes hereafter still be blind.                758
She wakes her heart by beating on her breast,
And bids it leap from thence, where it may find
Some purer chest to close so pure a mind.                761
    Frantic with grief thus breathes she forth her spite                762
    Against the unseen secrecy of night:

"O comfort-killing Night, image of hell,
Dim register and notary of shame,                765
Black stage for tragedies and murders fell,                766
Vast sin-concealing chaos, nurse of blame!                767
Blind muffled bawd, dark harbor for defame,                768
    Grim cave of death, whisp'ring conspirator
    With close-tongued treason and the ravisher!                770

---

**743 heavy convertite** sad penitent   **747 scapes** transgressions
**754 unfold** reveal   **755 grave** engrave.   **water** i.e., aqua fortis, nitric
acid   **757 exclaims against** reproaches   **758 still** forever   **761 close**
enclose   **762 spite** vexation   **765 register** registrar.   **notary** recorder
**766 Black stage** (Referring seemingly to a practice of hanging the stage
with black for the performance of a tragedy.)   **767 blame** evil
**768 defame** infamy   **770 close-tongued** closemouthed, secretive of
speech

"O hateful, vaporous, and foggy Night,
Since thou art guilty of my cureless crime,
Muster thy mists to meet the eastern light,
Make war against proportioned course of time;     774
Or if thou wilt permit the sun to climb
  His wonted height, yet ere he go to bed
  Knit poisonous clouds about his golden head.

"With rotten damps ravish the morning air;
Let their exhaled unwholesome breaths make sick
The life of purity, the supreme fair,     780
Ere he arrive his weary noontide prick;     781
And let thy musty vapors march so thick
  That in their smoky ranks his smothered light
  May set at noon and make perpetual night.

"Were Tarquin Night, as he is but Night's child,
The silver-shining queen he would distain;     786
Her twinkling handmaids too, by him defiled,     787
Through Night's black bosom should not peep again.
So should I have copartners in my pain;
  And fellowship in woe doth woe assuage,
  As palmers' chat makes short their pilgrimage.     791

"Where now I have no one to blush with me,     792
To cross their arms and hang their heads with mine,     793
To mask their brows and hide their infamy;     794
But I alone alone must sit and pine,     795
Seasoning the earth with showers of silver brine,
  Mingling my talk with tears, my grief with groans,
  Poor wasting monuments of lasting moans.     798

---

**774 proportioned** i.e., orderly in the regulated interchange of day and
night   **780 life** life-giving essence.   **supreme fair** i.e., the sun
**781 arrive** arrive at.   **prick** mark (as on a dial)   **786 queen** i.e., moon.
**distain** stain, soil   **787 handmaids** i.e., stars   **791 palmers'** pilgrims'
**792 Where** whereas   **793–794 To cross . . . infamy** (Folding the arms
and pulling the hat over the brows were conventional gestures of grief.)
**795 I alone alone** only I alone   **798 monuments** tokens, mementos

"O Night, thou furnace of foul reeking smoke!
Let not the jealous Day behold that face
Which underneath thy black all-hiding cloak
Immodestly lies martyred with disgrace!                     802
Keep still possession of thy gloomy place,
     That all the faults which in thy reign are made
     May likewise be sepulchered in thy shade.

"Make me not object to the telltale Day.                    806
The light will show charactered in my brow                  807
The story of sweet chastity's decay,                        808
The impious breach of holy wedlock vow.
Yea, the illiterate, that know not how
     To cipher what is writ in learnèd books,                811
     Will quote my loathsome trespass in my looks.           812

"The nurse, to still her child, will tell my story,
And fright her crying babe with Tarquin's name;
The orator, to deck his oratory,                            815
Will couple my reproach to Tarquin's shame;
Feast-finding minstrels, tuning my defame,                  817
     Will tie the hearers to attend each line,
     How Tarquin wrongèd me, I Collatine.

"Let my good name, that senseless reputation,              820
For Collatine's dear love be kept unspotted.
If that be made a theme for disputation,                    822
The branches of another root are rotted,                    823
And undeserved reproach to him allotted
     That is as clear from this attaint of mine             825
     As I, ere this, was pure to Collatine.

---

**802 martyred** i.e., disfigured   **806 object** a thing perceived, object of
gossip   **807 charactered** inscribed   **808 decay** ruin   **811 cipher** deci-
pher, read   **812 quote** note, observe   **815 deck** adorn   **817 Feast-
finding** searching out feasts at which to sing   **820 senseless** impalpable
**822–823 If . . . rotted** i.e., if my reputation comes in question then
Collatine's will also be attacked   **825 attaint** stain, imputation of
dishonor

"O unseen shame, invisible disgrace!
O unfelt sore, crest-wounding, private scar!                    828
Reproach is stamped in Collatinus' face,
And Tarquin's eye may read the mot afar,                        830
How he in peace is wounded, not in war.
  Alas, how many bear such shameful blows,
  Which not themselves but he that gives them knows!

"If, Collatine, thine honor lay in me,
From me by strong assault it is bereft;
My honey lost, and I, a dronelike bee,
Have no perfection of my summer left,                           837
But robbed and ransacked by injurious theft.
  In thy weak hive a wandering wasp hath crept
  And sucked the honey which thy chaste bee kept.

"Yet am I guilty of thy honor's wrack;
Yet for thy honor did I entertain him.
Coming from thee, I could not put him back,
For it had been dishonor to disdain him.
Besides, of weariness he did complain him,
  And talked of virtue. O unlooked-for evil,
  When virtue is profaned in such a devil!

"Why should the worm intrude the maiden bud?
Or hateful cuckoos hatch in sparrows' nests?
Or toads infect fair founts with venom mud?
Or tyrant folly lurk in gentle breasts?                         851
Or kings be breakers of their own behests?                     852
  But no perfection is so absolute
  That some impurity doth not pollute.

---

**828 crest-wounding** disgraceful to the crest, or device above the shield
in one's coat of arms    **830 mot** motto    **837 Have . . . left** have nothing
left of the honey I perfected in the summer    **851 gentle** noble (in rank
and temperament)    **852 behests** biddings, injunctions

"The agèd man that coffers up his gold
Is plagued with cramps and gouts and painful fits,
And scarce hath eyes his treasure to behold,
But like still-pining Tantalus he sits,                    858
And useless barns the harvest of his wits,                    859
    Having no other pleasure of his gain
    But torment that it cannot cure his pain.

"So then he hath it when he cannot use it,
And leaves it to be mastered by his young,
Who in their pride do presently abuse it.                    864
Their father was too weak, and they too strong,
To hold their cursèd-blessèd fortune long.
    The sweets we wish for turn to loathèd sours
    Even in the moment that we call them ours.

"Unruly blasts wait on the tender spring;
Unwholesome weeds take root with precious flowers;
The adder hisses where the sweet birds sing;
What virtue breeds iniquity devours.
We have no good that we can say is ours,
    But ill-annexèd Opportunity                    874
    Or kills his life or else his quality.                    875

"O Opportunity, thy guilt is great!
'Tis thou that execut'st the traitor's treason;
Thou sets the wolf where he the lamb may get;
Whoever plots the sin, thou 'point'st the season.                    879
'Tis thou that spurn'st at right, at law, at reason;
    And in thy shady cell, where none may spy him,
    Sits Sin, to seize the souls that wander by him.

---

**858 still-pining** continually starving.  **Tantalus** a son of Zeus who was
punished by perpetual hunger and thirst with unreachable food and
drink always in sight. (Renaissance commentators on Ovid glossed
Tantalus as a usurer; hence the image of ll. 859 ff.)  **859 barns** stores, as
in a barn  **864 presently** immediately  **874 ill-annexèd** joined to the
good for an evil purpose.  **Opportunity** chance or circumstance
**875 Or . . . quality** either destroys that good thing or else destroys its
nature that makes it good  **879 'point'st** appointest

"Thou makest the vestal violate her oath;
Thou blowest the fire when temperance is thawed;
Thou smother'st honesty, thou murderest troth.      885
Thou foul abettor, thou notorious bawd,
Thou plantest scandal and displacest laud.      887
    Thou ravisher, thou traitor, thou false thief,
    Thy honey turns to gall, thy joy to grief!

"Thy secret pleasure turns to open shame,
Thy private·feasting to a public fast,
Thy smoothing titles to a ragged name,      892
Thy sugared tongue to bitter wormwood taste.
Thy violent vanities can never last.
    How comes it then, vile Opportunity,
    Being so bad, such numbers seek for thee?

"When wilt thou be the humble suppliant's friend,
And bring him where his suit may be obtained?
When wilt thou sort an hour great strifes to end?      899
Or free that soul which wretchedness hath chained?
Give physic to the sick, ease to the pained?
    The poor, lame, blind, halt, creep, cry out for thee,
    But they ne'er meet with Opportunity.

"The patient dies while the physician sleeps;
The orphan pines while the oppressor feeds;      905
Justice is feasting while the widow weeps;
Advice is sporting while infection breeds.      907
Thou grant'st no time for charitable deeds.
    Wrath, envy, treason, rape, and murder's rages,
    Thy heinous hours wait on them as their pages.

---

**885 honesty** chastity.    **troth** honesty    **887 laud** praise    **892 smoothing**
flattering.    **ragged** faulty, irregular    **899 sort** choose, appoint
**905 pines** starves    **907 Advice** i.e., medical advice.    **sporting** taking idle
pleasure

"When Truth and Virtue have to do with thee,
A thousand crosses keep them from thy aid.          912
They buy thy help; but Sin ne'er gives a fee,          913
He gratis comes; and thou art well apaid          914
As well to hear as grant what he hath said.          915
  My Collatine would else have come to me
  When Tarquin did, but he was stayed by thee.

"Guilty thou art of murder and of theft,
Guilty of perjury and subornation,
Guilty of treason, forgery, and shift,          920
Guilty of incest, that abomination—
An accessory by thine inclination          922
  To all sins past and all that are to come,
  From the creation to the general doom.          924

"Misshapen Time, copesmate of ugly Night,          925
Swift subtle post, carrier of grisly care,          926
Eater of youth, false slave to false delight,
Base watch of woes, sin's packhorse, virtue's snare!          928
Thou nursest all, and murderest all that are.
  O, hear me then, injurious, shifting Time!
  Be guilty of my death, since of my crime.          931

"Why hath thy servant Opportunity
Betrayed the hours thou gav'st me to repose,
Canceled my fortunes, and enchainèd me
To endless date of never-ending woes?          935
Time's office is to fine the hate of foes,          936
  To eat up errors by opinion bred,          937
  Not spend the dowry of a lawful bed.

---

**912 crosses** hindrances   **913 buy** i.e., have to pay for   **914 apaid** satisfied   **915 As . . . as** both to hear and   **920 shift** fraud   **922 inclination** natural disposition   **924 general doom** Doomsday, Day of Judgment   **925 copesmate** companion, accomplice   **926 post** messenger   **928 watch** crier, one who announces woes   **931 since of** i.e., since you are guilty of   **935 date** duration   **936 office is** function ideally is.   **fine** punish, or put an end to   **937 opinion** popular rumor

"Time's glory is to calm contending kings,
To unmask falsehood and bring truth to light,
To stamp the seal of time in agèd things,
To wake the morn and sentinel the night,          942
To wrong the wronger till he render right,
  To ruinate proud buildings with thy hours,
  And smear with dust their glittering golden towers;

"To fill with wormholes stately monuments,
To feed oblivion with decay of things,
To blot old books and alter their contents,        948
To pluck the quills from ancient ravens' wings,    949
To dry the old oak's sap and cherish springs,      950
  To spoil antiquities of hammered steel,
  And turn the giddy round of Fortune's wheel;

"To show the beldam daughters of her daughter,     953
To make the child a man, the man a child,          954
To slay the tiger that doth live by slaughter,
To tame the unicorn and lion wild,
To mock the subtle in themselves beguiled,         957
  To cheer the plowman with increaseful crops,     958
  And waste huge stones with little waterdrops.    959

"Why work'st thou mischief in thy pilgrimage,
Unless thou couldst return to make amends?
One poor retiring minute in an age                 962
Would purchase thee a thousand thousand friends,
Lending him wit that to bad debtors lends.         964
  O, this dread night, wouldst thou one hour come
    back,
  I could prevent this storm and shun thy wrack!   966

---

**942 sentinel** stand guard over   **948 blot** erase, obliterate   **949 To pluck . . . wings** i.e., to end even the existence of long-lived ravens
**950 springs** new growth, shoots   **953 beldam** old woman   **954 a child** i.e., in the second childishness of old age   **957 subtle . . . beguiled** crafty who are foiled by their own cleverness   **958 increaseful** fruitful
**959 waste** wear away   **962 retiring** returning (thereby allowing men an opportunity to undo some evil)   **964 Lending . . . lends** i.e., giving the person who has made loans to poor credit risks an opportunity to reconsider   **966 prevent** anticipate, forestall

"Thou ceaseless lackey to Eternity,                          967
With some mischance cross Tarquin in his flight!            968
Devise extremes beyond extremity
To make him curse this cursèd crimeful night.
Let ghastly shadows his lewd eyes affright,
    And the dire thought of his committed evil
    Shape every bush a hideous shapeless devil.

"Disturb his hours of rest with restless trances;           974
Afflict him in his bed with bedrid groans;                  975
Let there bechance him pitiful mischances,
To make him moan, but pity not his moans.
Stone him with hardened hearts harder than stones,
    And let mild women to him lose their mildness,
    Wilder to him than tigers in their wildness.

"Let him have time to tear his curlèd hair,
Let him have time against himself to rave,
Let him have time of Time's help to despair,
Let him have time to live a loathèd slave,
Let him have time a beggar's orts to crave,                 985
    And time to see one that by alms doth live
    Disdain to him disdainèd scraps to give.

"Let him have time to see his friends his foes,
And merry fools to mock at him resort;                      989
Let him have time to mark how slow time goes
In time of sorrow, and how swift and short
His time of folly and his time of sport;
    And ever let his unrecalling crime                      993
    Have time to wail th' abusing of his time.

**967 ceaseless lackey** omnipresent attendant. (The image is of Time as a
footman accompanying humanity on its journey to eternity.)   **968 cross**
thwart   **974 trances** visions, fits   **975 bedrid** bedridden   **985 orts**
refuse, fragments of food   **989 And . . . resort** and merry fools gather
(*resort*) to mock him   **993 unrecalling** that may not be recalled

"O Time, thou tutor both to good and bad,
Teach me to curse him that thou taught'st this ill!          996
At his own shadow let the thief run mad,
Himself himself seek every hour to kill!
Such wretched hands such wretched blood should
    spill;
    For who so base would such an office have
    As slanderous deathsman to so base a slave?          1001

"The baser is he, coming from a king,
To shame his hope with deeds degenerate.          1003
The mightier man, the mightier is the thing
That makes him honored or begets him hate;
For greatest scandal waits on greatest state.          1006
    The moon being clouded presently is missed,          1007
    But little stars may hide them when they list.

"The crow may bathe his coal-black wings in mire,
And unperceived fly with the filth away,
But if the like the snow-white swan desire,
The stain upon his silver down will stay.
Poor grooms are sightless night, kings glorious day.          1013
    Gnats are unnoted wheresoe'er they fly,
    But eagles gazed upon with every eye.

"Out, idle words, servants to shallow fools,          1016
Unprofitable sounds, weak arbitrators!
Busy yourselves in skill-contending schools;          1018
Debate where leisure serves with dull debaters;
To trembling clients be you mediators.
    For me, I force not argument a straw,          1021
    Since that my case is past the help of law.

---

**996 that** to whom   **1001 slanderous** despised, contemptible.   **deaths-
man** executioner   **1003 his hope** the hope men had of him as heir to the
crown   **1006 waits . . . state** potentially attends those of most exalted
rank   **1007 presently** at once   **1013 grooms** i.e., lowborn persons.   **are**
are like.   **sightless** making things invisible; pitch dark   **1016 Out** (An
exclamation of disapproval.)   **1018 in . . . schools** i.e., among scholars
who perennially debate with words   **1021 force** value.   **a straw** i.e., a
straw's worth

"In vain I rail at Opportunity,
At Time, at Tarquin, and uncheerful Night;
In vain I cavil with mine infamy,                              1025
In vain I spurn at my confirmed despite.                       1026
This helpless smoke of words doth me no right.                 1027
   The remedy indeed to do me good
   Is to let forth my foul-defilèd blood.                     1029

"Poor hand, why quiver'st thou at this decree?
Honor thyself to rid me of this shame!
For if I die, my honor lives in thee,
But if I live, thou liv'st in my defame.
Since thou couldst not defend thy loyal dame,
   And wast afeard to scratch her wicked foe,
   Kill both thyself and her for yielding so."

This said, from her betumbled couch she starteth,
To find some desperate instrument of death;
But this, no slaughterhouse, no tool imparteth               1039
To make more vent for passage of her breath,
Which, thronging through her lips, so vanisheth
   As smoke from Etna, that in air consumes,
   Or that which from dischargèd cannon fumes.

"In vain," quoth she, "I live, and seek in vain
Some happy means to end a hapless life.
I feared by Tarquin's falchion to be slain,                  1046
Yet for the selfsame purpose seek a knife;
But when I feared I was a loyal wife.
   So am I now.—O no, that cannot be!
   Of that true type hath Tarquin rifled me.                 1050

---

**1025 cavil with** raise objections to    **1026 spurn at** (Literally, kick
against.)    **confirmed despite** unavoidable injury    **1027 helpless** affording no help    **1029 let . . . blood** bleed (1) as a *remedy* (l. 1028) for illness,
a standard form of medical treatment (2) as a means of death    **1039 no
slaughterhouse** being no slaughterhouse.    **imparteth** provides
**1046 falchion** curved sword    **1050 type** stamp; example

"O, that is gone for which I sought to live,
And therefore now I need not fear to die.
To clear this spot by death, at least I give 1053
A badge of fame to slander's livery, 1054
A dying life to living infamy.
  Poor helpless help, the treasure stol'n away,
  To burn the guiltless casket where it lay!

"Well, well, dear Collatine, thou shalt not know
The stainèd taste of violated troth;
I will not wrong thy true affection so
To flatter thee with an infringèd oath; 1061
This bastard graft shall never come to growth. 1062
  He shall not boast who did thy stock pollute
  That thou art doting father of his fruit.

"Nor shall he smile at thee in secret thought,
Nor laugh with his companions at thy state,
But thou shalt know thy interest was not bought 1067
Basely with gold, but stol'n from forth thy gate.
For me, I am the mistress of my fate,
  And with my trespass never will dispense 1070
  Till life to death acquit my forced offense. 1071

"I will not poison thee with my attaint, 1072
Nor fold my fault in cleanly coined excuses; 1073
My sable ground of sin I will not paint, 1074
To hide the truth of this false night's abuses.
My tongue shall utter all; mine eyes, like sluices,
  As from a mountain spring that feeds a dale,
  Shall gush pure streams to purge my impure tale."

---

**1053 To clear** i.e., in clearing.   **spot** stain   **1054 fame** good reputation.
**livery** clothing or uniform worn by those in service, bearing a heraldic
*badge* on the sleeve to indicate in whose service the livery is worn.
(Lucrece says that the livery of shame will be partially redeemed by the
badge of an honorable death.)   **1061 flatter** deceive. (Lucrece will not
bear a bastard child that might deceive Collatine with the thought of
being the father.)   **1062 graft** scion   **1067 interest** claim, property
**1070 with . . . dispense** never will pardon my offense. (To *dispense* is to
grant dispensation.)   **1071 acquit** atone for   **1072 attaint** infection
**1073 cleanly coined** cleverly counterfeited   **1074 sable ground** dark
surface on a heraldic device

By this, lamenting Philomel had ended                          1079
The well-tuned warble of her nightly sorrow,
And solemn night with slow sad gait descended
To ugly hell, when, lo, the blushing morrow
Lends light to all fair eyes that light will borrow.           1083
    But cloudy Lucrece shames herself to see,                  1084
    And therefore still in night would cloistered be.


Revealing day through every cranny spies
And seems to point her out where she sits weeping,
To whom she sobbing speaks: "O eye of eyes,
Why pry'st thou through my window? Leave thy
        peeping.
Mock with thy tickling beams eyes that are sleeping.
    Brand not my forehead with thy piercing light,
    For day hath naught to do what's done by night."          1092


Thus cavils she with everything she sees.
True grief is fond and testy as a child,                       1094
Who wayward once, his mood with naught agrees.                 1095
Old woes, not infant sorrows, bear them mild.                  1096
Continuance tames the one; the other wild,
    Like an unpracticed swimmer plunging still,
    With too much labor drowns for want of skill.


So she, deep-drenchèd in a sea of care,
Holds disputation with each thing she views,
And to herself all sorrow doth compare;
No object but her passion's strength renews,                   1103
And as one shifts, another straight ensues.                    1104
    Sometimes her grief is dumb and hath no words,
    Sometimes 'tis mad and too much talk affords.


**1079 Philomel,** i.e., the nightingale. Philomela was raped by her brother-
in-law, Tereus, who cut out her tongue so that she could not disclose his
villainy; she was changed into a nightingale.    **1083 borrow** i.e., make use
of that which heaven lends    **1084 shames** is ashamed    **1092 to do** to do
with    **1094 fond** foolish    **1095 wayward once** i.e., once in a peevish
mood    **1096 them** themselves.    **mild** mildly, calmly    **1103 her . . .
renews** renews the strength of her passion    **1104 shifts** moves, yields
place.    **straight** at once

The little birds that tune their morning's joy
Make her moans mad with their sweet melody,
For mirth doth search the bottom of annoy;          1109
Sad souls are slain in merry company.
Grief best is pleased with grief's society.
   True sorrow then is feelingly suffied          1112
   When with like semblance it is sympathized.      1113

'Tis double death to drown in ken of shore;          1114
He ten times pines that pines beholding food;        1115
To see the salve doth make the wound ache more;
Great grief grieves most at that would do it good;   1117
Deep woes roll forward like a gentle flood,
   Who, being stopped, the bounding banks o'erflows;  1119
   Grief dallied with nor law nor limit knows.        1120

"You mocking birds," quoth she, "your tunes entomb
Within your hollow-swelling feathered breasts,
And in my hearing be you mute and dumb.
My restless discord loves no stops nor rests;        1124
A woeful hostess brooks not merry guests.            1125
   Relish your nimble notes to pleasing ears;        1126
   Distress likes dumps, when time is kept with tears.  1127

"Come, Philomel, that sing'st of ravishment,
Make thy sad grove in my disheveled hair.
As the dank earth weeps at thy languishment,
So I at each sad strain will strain a tear           1131
And with deep groans the diapason bear;              1132
   For burden-wise I'll hum on Tarquin still,        1133
   While thou on Tereus descants better skill.        1134

**1109 search** probe. **annoy** grief, injury   **1112 suffied** contented
**1113 sympathized** matched   **1114 ken** sight   **1115 pines** hungers
**1117 would** which wishes to   **1119 Who** which.   **stopped** dammed up.
**bounding** containing, confining   **1120 dallied** trifled.   **nor . . . nor** neither . . . nor   **1124 restless** agitated (with a pun on the musical sense of having no *stops* or *rests*, i.e., being ceaseless, without pause)   **1125 brooks** enjoys   **1126 Relish** (1) warble, make attractive (2) elaborate with musical
ornamentation.   **pleasing** capable of being pleased   **1127 dumps** mournful
songs   **1131 strain . . . strain** melody . . . force, squeeze   **1132 diapason**
bass accompaniment below the melody   **1133 burden-wise** in the manner of
an undersong or bass (with a play on *burden* meaning "sorrow")
**1134 descants better skill** i.e., sing a musical elaboration in the upper
register with better skill (than my bass accompaniment)

"And whiles against a thorn thou bear'st thy part          1135
To keep thy sharp woes waking, wretched I,
To imitate thee well, against my heart
Will fix a sharp knife to affright mine eye,
Who, if it wink, shall thereon fall and die.          1139
  These means, as frets upon an instrument,          1140
  Shall tune our heartstrings to true languishment.

"And for, poor bird, thou sing'st not in the day,          1142
As shaming any eye should thee behold,          1143
Some dark deep desert seated from the way,          1144
That knows not parching heat nor freezing cold,
Will we find out; and there we will unfold
  To creatures stern sad tunes, to change their kinds.          1147
  Since men prove beasts, let beasts bear gentle
    minds."

As the poor frighted deer, that stands at gaze,          1149
Wildly determining which way to fly,
Or one encompassed with a winding maze,
That cannot tread the way out readily,
So with herself is she in mutiny,
  To live or die which of the twain were better
  When life is shamed and death reproach's debtor.          1155

---

**1135 against a thorn** (According to popular belief, the nightingale
perched deliberately with a thorn against her breast to keep herself
awake.)  **1139 Who** which, i.e., my heart.  **if it wink** i.e., if my eye
should close in sleep  **1140 frets** bars placed on the fingerboards of
stringed instruments to regulate the fingering (with a pun on *frets*
meaning "vexations")  **1142 for** because.  **sing'st not in the day** (One of
the common errors of the time; nightingales sing both by day and by
night.)  **1143 As shaming** as though being ashamed that, or since you
are ashamed that  **1144 desert** deserted place.  **seated from** situated
away from  **1147 kinds** natures  **1149 at gaze** transfixed, bewildered
**1155 death reproach's debtor** i.e., death by suicide would incur
reproach

"To kill myself," quoth she, "alack, what were it
But with my body my poor soul's pollution?                    1157
They that lose half with greater patience bear it
Than they whose whole is swallowed in confusion.             1159
That mother tries a merciless conclusion                      1160
  Who, having two sweet babes, when death takes one,
  Will slay the other and be nurse to none.

"My body or my soul, which was the dearer,
When the one pure, the other made divine?
Whose love of either to myself was nearer,                    1165
When both were kept for heaven and Collatine?
Ay me! The bark pilled from the lofty pine,                   1167
  His leaves will wither and his sap decay;
  So must my soul, her bark being pilled away.

"Her house is sacked, her quiet interrupted,
Her mansion battered by the enemy,
Her sacred temple spotted, spoiled, corrupted,
Grossly engirt with daring infamy.
Then let it not be called impiety
  If in this blemished fort I make some hole               1175
  Through which I may convey this troubled soul.            1176

"Yet die I will not till my Collatine
Have heard the cause of my untimely death,
That he may vow, in that sad hour of mine,
Revenge on him that made me stop my breath.
My stainèd blood to Tarquin I'll bequeath,
  Which by him tainted shall for him be spent,
  And as his due writ in my testament.                      1183

**1157 But . . . pollution** but to add my poor soul's pollution (through
suicide) to that of my body (through the rape)   **1159 confusion** ruin
**1160 conclusion** experiment   **1165 Whose . . . either** love of which of
the two   **1167 pilled** peeled, stripped off, rifled   **1175 fort** i.e., body
**1176 convey** let out   **1183 testament** last will and testament

"My honor I'll bequeath unto the knife
That wounds my body so dishonorèd.
'Tis honor to deprive dishonored life;        1186
The one will live, the other being dead.
So of shame's ashes shall my fame be bred,
    For in my death I murder shameful scorn;
    My shame so dead, mine honor is new born.

"Dear lord of that dear jewel I have lost,        1191
What legacy shall I bequeath to thee?
My resolution, love, shall be thy boast,
By whose example thou revenged mayst be.
How Tarquin must be used, read it in me:
    Myself, thy friend, will kill myself, thy foe,
    And for my sake serve thou false Tarquin so.

"This brief abridgment of my will I make:
My soul and body to the skies and ground;
My resolution, husband, do thou take;
Mine honor be the knife's that makes my wound;
My shame be his that did my fame confound;
    And all my fame that lives disbursèd be        1203
    To those that live and think no shame of me.

"Thou, Collatine, shalt oversee this will.
How was I overseen that thou shalt see it!        1206
My blood shall wash the slander of mine ill;
My life's foul deed my life's fair end shall free it.        1208
Faint not, faint heart, but stoutly say 'So be it.'
    Yield to my hand; my hand shall conquer thee.
    Thou dead, both die, and both shall victors be."

**1186 deprive** take away   **1191 dear jewel** i.e., chastity   **1203 disbursèd**
i.e., paid out as legacies   **1206 overseen** deluded, taken advantage of
(with quibble on *oversee*, l. 1205, i.e., attend to as an executor of an
estate)   **1208 My . . . free it** my life's virtuous end will atone for my
life's foul deed

This plot of death when sadly she had laid,
And wiped the brinish pearl from her bright eyes,
With untuned tongue she hoarsely calls her maid,          1214
Whose swift obedience to her mistress hies;          1215
For fleet-winged duty with thought's feathers flies.
   Poor Lucrece' cheeks unto her maid seem so
   As winter meads when sun doth melt their snow.

Her mistress she doth give demure good morrow          1219
With soft slow tongue, true mark of modesty,
And sorts a sad look to her lady's sorrow,          1221
Forwhy her face wore sorrow's livery;          1222
But durst not ask of her audaciously
   Why her two suns were cloud-eclipsèd so,
   Nor why her fair cheeks over-washed with woe.          1225

But as the earth doth weep, the sun being set,
Each flower moistened like a melting eye,
Even so the maid with swelling drops 'gan wet
Her circled eyne, enforced by sympathy          1229
Of those fair suns set in her mistress' sky,
   Who in a salt-waved ocean quench their light,
   Which makes the maid weep like the dewy night.

A pretty while these pretty creatures stand,          1233
Like ivory conduits coral cisterns filling.          1234
One justly weeps; the other takes in hand          1235
No cause but company of her drops spilling.          1236
Their gentle sex to weep are often willing,
   Grieving themselves to guess at others' smarts,          1238
   And then they drown their eyes or break their hearts.

---

**1214 untuned** discordant   **1215 Whose . . . hies** who in swift obedience
hastens to her mistress   **1219 Her** i.e., to her   **1221 sorts** adapts
**1222 Forwhy** because   **1225 over-washed** overflowed   **1229 circled** i.e.,
circled with red.   **eyne** eyes.   **enforced** compelled   **1233 pretty while**
considerable while   **1234 conduits** (Alludes to conduit spouts and
fountains shaped in the form of human figures; the women's eyes
run like conduits.)   **1235 takes in hand** acknowledges, entertains
**1236 No . . . spilling** i.e., no cause for the shedding of teardrops other
than to keep her mistress company   **1238 to guess at** i.e., merely when
they conjecture

For men have marble, women waxen, minds,                    1240
And therefore are they formed as marble will.              1241
The weak oppressed, th' impression of strange kinds        1242
Is formed in them by force, by fraud, or skill.
Then call them not the authors of their ill,
    No more than wax shall be accounted evil
    Wherein is stamped the semblance of a devil.

Their smoothness, like a goodly champaign plain,           1247
Lays open all the little worms that creep;                 1248
In men, as in a rough-grown grove, remain
Cave-keeping evils that obscurely sleep.                   1250
Through crystal walls each little mote will peep.          1251
    Though men can cover crimes with bold stern looks,
    Poor women's faces are their own faults' books.

No man inveigh against the withered flower,                1254
But chide rough winter that the flow'r hath killed.
Not that devoured, but that which doth devour,
Is worthy blame. O, let it not be hild                     1257
Poor women's faults, that they are so fulfilled            1258
    With men's abuses. Those proud lords, to blame,        1259
    Make weak-made women tenants to their shame.           1260

The precedent whereof in Lucrece view,                     1261
Assailed by night with circumstances strong                1262
Of present death, and shame that might ensue               1263
By that her death, to do her husband wrong.                1264
Such danger to resistance did belong                       1265
    That dying fear through all her body spread;           1266
    And who cannot abuse a body dead?

1240 waxen i.e., soft, impressionable   1241 will wills, wishes   1242 The
weak i.e., when the weak are.   strange kinds natures unlike their own
1247 champaign level, open   1248 Lays open reveals.   worms reptiles,
i.e., blemishes   1250 Cave-keeping remaining concealed in caves
1251 mote speck   1254 No man let no man   1257 hild held
1258 fulfilled filled   1259 lords, to blame lords, who are blameworthy;
or, who are too much to blame (too blame); or, owners of blame (lords to
blame)   1260 tenants i.e., occupying and sharing a shame that is properly men's   1261 precedent proof, example   1262–1263 circumstances
. . . death a situation strongly threatening immediate death   1264 By
that her death by her very death   1265 danger i.e., the danger of being
defamed by Tarquin   1266 dying i.e., paralyzing

By this, mild patience bid fair Lucrece speak                    1268
To the poor counterfeit of her complaining:                      1269
"My girl," quoth she, "on what occasion break
Those tears from thee, that down thy cheeks are
    raining?
If thou dost weep for grief of my sustaining,                    1272
  Know, gentle wench, it small avails my mood.
  If tears could help, mine own would do me good.

"But tell me, girl, when went"—and there she stayed
Till after a deep groan—"Tarquin from hence?"
"Madam, ere I was up," replied the maid,
"The more to blame my sluggard negligence.                       1278
Yet with the fault I thus far can dispense:                       1279
  Myself was stirring ere the break of day,
  And, ere I rose, was Tarquin gone away.

"But, lady, if your maid may be so bold,
She would request to know your heaviness."                        1283
"O, peace!" quoth Lucrece. "If it should be told,
The repetition cannot make it less;
For more it is than I can well express,
  And that deep torture may be called a hell
  When more is felt than one hath power to tell.

"Go, get me hither paper, ink, and pen.
Yet save that labor, for I have them here.
What should I say? One of my husband's men
Bid thou be ready by and by to bear
A letter to my lord, my love, my dear.
  Bid him with speed prepare to carry it;
  The cause craves haste, and it will soon be writ."

**1268 By this** by this time   **1269 counterfeit of her complaining** i.e., the
maid, weeping like her   **1272 of my sustaining** borne by me   **1278 to
blame** at fault   **1279 dispense** give dispensation, find excuse
**1283 know** i.e., know the reason for

Her maid is gone, and she prepares to write,
First hovering o'er the paper with her quill.
Conceit and grief an eager combat fight;          1298
What wit sets down is blotted straight with will;          1299
This is too curious-good, this blunt and ill.          1300
   Much like a press of people at a door
   Throng her inventions, which shall go before.          1302

At last she thus begins: "Thou worthy lord
Of that unworthy wife that greeteth thee,
Health to thy person! Next vouchsafe t' afford—
If ever, love, thy Lucrece thou wilt see—
Some present speed to come and visit me.
   So, I commend me from our house in grief.          1308
   My woes are tedious, though my words are brief."          1309

Here folds she up the tenor of her woe,          1310
Her certain sorrow writ uncertainly.          1311
By this short schedule Collatine may know          1312
Her grief, but not her grief's true quality.
She dares not thereof make discovery,          1314
   Lest he should hold it her own gross abuse,          1315
   Ere she with blood had stained her stained excuse.          1316

Besides, the life and feeling of her passion
She hoards, to spend when he is by to hear her,
When sighs and groans and tears may grace the
    fashion          1319
Of her disgrace, the better so to clear her
From that suspicion which the world might bear her.
   To shun this blot, she would not blot the letter          1322
   With words, till action might become them better.

---

**1298 Conceit** thought (of what she will write). **eager** fierce **1299 wit** intellect. **blotted** canceled. **will** passion, feeling **1300 curious-good** fastidiously, studiedly phrased **1302 which . . . before** contending as to who is to enter first **1308 commend me** ask to be remembered **1309 tedious** prolonged, painful **1310 tenor** gist, summary **1311 uncertainly** i.e., not in precise detail, vaguely **1312 schedule** document, summary **1314 thereof make discovery** i.e., reveal the true extent and nature of her grief **1315 abuse** wrongdoing **1316 had stained** (1) had discolored (2) had given color or credence to. **her stained excuse** i.e., the explanation of her shame **1319 fashion** fashioning **1322 blot . . . blot** stain . . . mar

To see sad sights moves more than hear them told,
For then the eye interprets to the ear
The heavy motion that it doth behold,                                    1326
When every part a part of woe doth bear.                                 1327
'Tis but a part of sorrow that we hear.
   Deep sounds make lesser noise than shallow fords,       1329
   And sorrow ebbs, being blown with wind of words.

Her letter now is sealed, and on it writ,
"At Ardea to my lord with more than haste."
The post attends, and she delivers it,                                   1333
Charging the sour-faced groom to hie as fast
As lagging fowls before the northern blast.                             1335
   Speed more than speed but dull and slow she deems;      1336
   Extremity still urgeth such extremes.                    1337

The homely villain curtsies to her low;                                  1338
And, blushing on her, with a steadfast eye
Receives the scroll without or yea or no,
And forth with bashful innocence doth hie.
But they whose guilt within their bosoms lie
   Imagine every eye beholds their blame;
   For Lucrece thought he blushed to see her shame,

When, silly groom, God wot, it was defect                                1345
Of spirit, life, and bold audacity.
Such harmless creatures have a true respect                              1347
To talk in deeds, while others saucily                                   1348
Promise more speed, but do it leisurely.
   Even so this pattern of the worn-out age                   1350
   Pawned honest looks but laid no words to gage.             1351

---

**1326 heavy motion** sad action  **1327 every part** i.e., of the body
**1329 Deep sounds** deep waters (with pun on *sounds*, i.e., inlets of the
sea, and "noise")  **1333 post** messenger  **1335 lagging** falling behind in
migratory flight  **1336 Speed . . . deems** i.e., she considers even extraordinary speed too tedious and slow  **1337 still** ever  **1338 homely** simple
and unhandsome.  **villain** servant.  **curtsies** bows  **1345 silly** simple
**1347 respect** care  **1348 To talk in deeds** i.e., to express themselves in
deeds only  **1350 pattern . . . age** i.e., example of faithful service in the
good old days  **1351 Pawned . . . gage** i.e., pledged his loyalty word-
lessly through honest looks

His kindled duty kindled her mistrust,                1352
That two red fires in both their faces blazed.
She thought he blushed as knowing Tarquin's lust,
And, blushing with him, wistly on him gazed.          1355
Her earnest eye did make him more amazed.             1356
  The more she saw the blood his cheeks replenish,
  The more she thought he spied in her some blemish.

But long she thinks till he return again,            1359
And yet the duteous vassal scarce is gone.
The weary time she cannot entertain,                 1361
For now 'tis stale to sigh, to weep, and groan.
So woe hath wearied woe, moan tirèd moan,
  That she her plaints a little while doth stay,   1364
  Pausing for means to mourn some newer way.

At last she calls to mind where hangs a piece        1366
Of skillful painting, made for Priam's Troy,         1367
Before the which is drawn the power of Greece,       1368
For Helen's rape the city to destroy,
Threat'ning cloud-kissing Ilion with annoy,          1370
  Which the conceited painter drew so proud       1371
  As heaven, it seemed, to kiss the turrets bowed.

A thousand lamentable objects there,
In scorn of nature, art gave lifeless life.          1374
Many a dry drop seemed a weeping tear,               1375
Shed for the slaughtered husband by the wife.
The red blood reeked, to show the painter's strife,  1377
  And dying eyes gleamed forth their ashy lights
  Like dying coals burnt out in tedious nights.

---

1352 **kindled duty** i.e., blushing obeisance. **mistrust** i.e., fear of her
shame being known   1355 **wistly** intently   1356 **amazed** embarrassed
1359 **long she thinks** she thinks it long   1361 **entertain** occupy
1364 **stay** halt   1366 **piece** picture (evidently in a tapestry)
1367 **made for** depicting   1368 **drawn** drawn up, arrayed.   **power**
army   1370 **cloud-kissing Ilion** i.e., lofty-towered Troy.   **annoy** harm
1371 **conceited** ingenious   1374 **In scorn of** i.e., defiantly rivaling.
**lifeless** inanimate   1375 **dry drop** i.e., drop of paint depicting a tear
1377 **strife** rivalry, i.e., with Nature; also the strife depicted in the
painting

There might you see the laboring pioneer                    1380
Begrimed with sweat and smearèd all with dust;
And from the towers of Troy there would appear
The very eyes of men through loopholes thrust,
Gazing upon the Greeks with little lust.                    1384
   Such sweet observance in this work was had           1385
   That one might see those far-off eyes look sad.

In great commanders grace and majesty
You might behold, triumphing in their faces;
In youth, quick bearing and dexterity;                      1389
And here and there the painter interlaces
Pale cowards marching on with trembling paces,
   Which heartless peasants did so well resemble         1392
   That one would swear he saw them quake and
      tremble.

In Ajax and Ulysses, O, what art
Of physiognomy might one behold!
The face of either ciphered either's heart;                 1396
Their face their manners most expressly told.
In Ajax' eyes blunt rage and rigor rolled,
   But the mild glance that sly Ulysses lent
   Showed deep regard and smiling government.             1400

There pleading might you see grave Nestor stand,            1401
As 'twere encouraging the Greeks to fight,
Making such sober action with his hand
That it beguiled attention, charmed the sight.
In speech, it seemed, his beard, all silver white,
   Wagged up and down, and from his lips did fly
   Thin winding breath, which purled up to the sky.       1407

**1380 pioneer** digger of trenches and mines   **1384 lust** pleasure, delight
**1385 sweet observance** i.e., verisimilitude created with loving attention
to detail   **1389 quick** lively   **1392 heartless** cowardly   **1396 ciphered**
showed, expressed   **1400 deep . . . government** profound wisdom and
the complacency arising from passions being under the command of
reason   **1401 pleading** making a persuasive oration   **1407 purled**
curled

About him were a press of gaping faces,
Which seemed to swallow up his sound advice,
All jointly listening, but with several graces,          1410
As if some mermaid did their ears entice;
Some high, some low, the painter was so nice.          1412
    The scalps of many, almost hid behind,          1413
    To jump up higher seemed, to mock the mind.          1414

Here one man's hand leaned on another's head,
His nose being shadowed by his neighbor's ear;
Here one being thronged bears back, all boll'n and red;          1417
Another, smothered, seems to pelt and swear;          1418
And in their rage such signs of rage they bear
    As, but for loss of Nestor's golden words,          1420
    It seemed they would debate with angry swords.

For much imaginary work was there,          1422
Conceit deceitful, so compact, so kind,          1423
That for Achilles' image stood his spear
Gripped in an armèd hand; himself, behind,
Was left unseen, save to the eye of mind.
    A hand, a foot, a face, a leg, a head,
    Stood for the whole to be imaginèd.

And from the walls of strong-besiegèd Troy,
When their brave hope, bold Hector, marched to field,
Stood many Trojan mothers, sharing joy
To see their youthful sons bright weapons wield;
And to their hope they such odd action yield          1433
    That through their light joy seemèd to appear,
    Like bright things stained, a kind of heavy fear.

---

**1410 with several graces** i.e., in differing attitudes   **1412 Some . . . low**
some tall, some short.   **nice** accurate, particular   **1413 scalps** heads of
hair   **1414 to mock the mind** (The artistic illusion deceives the mind of
the viewer into thinking he sees the movement of those in the back of
the crowd who are jumping higher to catch Nestor's oration.)
**1417 thronged** crowded.   **bears** pushes.   **boll'n** swollen up   **1418 pelt**
scold   **1420 but . . . words** i.e., were it not that they would thereby miss
Nestor's speech   **1422 imaginary work** work of the imagination
**1423 Conceit deceitful** artful contrivance, techniques.   **compact** eco-
nomical and well composed.   **kind** natural   **1433 they . . . yield** they
add such actions and emotions at odds with the joy

And from the strand of Dardan where they fought      1436
To Simois' reedy banks the red blood ran,      1437
Whose waves to imitate the battle sought
With swelling ridges; and their ranks began
To break upon the gallèd shore, and then      1440
    Retire again, till, meeting greater ranks,
    They join and shoot their foam at Simois' banks.

To this well-painted piece is Lucrece come,
To find a face where all distress is stelled.      1444
Many she sees where cares have carvèd some,
But none where all distress and dolor dwelled,
Till she despairing Hecuba beheld,      1447
    Staring on Priam's wounds with her old eyes,
    Which bleeding under Pyrrhus' proud foot lies.

In her the painter had anatomized      1450
Time's ruin, beauty's wrack, and grim care's reign.
Her cheeks with chaps and wrinkles were disguised;      1452
Of what she was no semblance did remain.
Her blue blood, changed to black in every vein,
    Wanting the spring that those shrunk pipes had fed,      1455
    Showed life imprisoned in a body dead.

On this sad shadow Lucrece spends her eyes,      1457
And shapes her sorrow to the beldam's woes,      1458
Who nothing wants to answer her but cries      1459
And bitter words to ban her cruel foes.      1460
The painter was no god to lend her those;
    And therefore Lucrece swears he did her wrong,
    To give her so much grief and not a tongue.

---

**1436 strand** shore    **1437 Simois** river near Troy    **1440 gallèd** eroded
**1444 stelled** portrayed, engraved    **1447 Hecuba** Queen of Troy, wife of
King Priam    **1450 anatomized** laid open, dissected    **1452 chaps** cracks
and lines in the skin.   **disguised** disfigured    **1455 spring** i.e., source of
blood and life.   **pipes** i.e., veins    **1457 shadow** image, likeness
**1458 shapes** likens, compares.   **beldam's** old woman's    **1459 wants to
answer her** i.e., lacks in order to be perfectly like Lucrece in her sorrow
**1460 ban** curse

"Poor instrument," quoth she, "without a sound,
I'll tune thy woes with my lamenting tongue,                    1465
And drop sweet balm in Priam's painted wound,
And rail on Pyrrhus that hath done him wrong,
And with my tears quench Troy that burns so long,
    And with my knife scratch out the angry eyes
    Of all the Greeks that are thine enemies.

"Show me the strumpet that began this stir,
That with my nails her beauty I may tear.
Thy heat of lust, fond Paris, did incur                        1473
This load of wrath that burning Troy doth bear.
Thy eye kindled the fire that burneth here,
    And here in Troy, for trespass of thine eye,
    The sire, the son, the dame, and daughter die.

"Why should the private pleasure of some one
Become the public plague of many moe?                          1479
Let sin, alone committed, light alone                          1480
Upon his head that hath transgressèd so;
Let guiltless souls be freed from guilty woe.
    For one's offense why should so many fall,
    To plague a private sin in general?                        1484

"Lo, here weeps Hecuba, here Priam dies,
Here manly Hector faints, here Troilus swounds,                1486
Here friend by friend in bloody channel lies,                 1487
And friend to friend gives unadvisèd wounds,                  1488
And one man's lust these many lives confounds.
    Had doting Priam checked his son's desire,
    Troy had been bright with fame and not with fire."

---

**1465 tune** sing   **1473 fond** doting   **1479 moe** more   **1480 alone committed** committed by one person alone.   **light** alight   **1484 in general**
collectively, publicly. (Lucrece wonders why it should be necessary to
punish the general public for an individual's sin.)   **1486 swounds**
swoons   **1487 channel** gutter   **1488 unadvisèd wounds** wounds they
never intended for each other

Here feelingly she weeps Troy's painted woes,
For sorrow, like a heavy-hanging bell,
Once set on ringing, with his own weight goes;                    1494
Then little strength rings out the doleful knell.
So Lucrece, set a-work, sad tales doth tell
  To penciled pensiveness and colored sorrow;                    1497
  She lends them words, and she their looks doth
    borrow.

She throws her eyes about the painting round,
And who she finds forlorn she doth lament.                    1500
At last she sees a wretched image bound,                    1501
That piteous looks to Phrygian shepherds lent.                    1502
His face, though full of cares, yet showed content;
  Onward to Troy with the blunt swains he goes,                    1504
  So mild that patience seemed to scorn his woes.                    1505

In him the painter labored with his skill
To hide deceit and give the harmless show                    1507
An humble gait, calm looks, eyes wailing still,                    1508
A brow unbent that seemed to welcome woe;
Cheeks neither red nor pale, but mingled so
  That blushing red no guilty instance gave,                    1511
  Nor ashy pale the fear that false hearts have.

But, like a constant and confirmèd devil,
He entertained a show so seeming just,                    1514
And therein so ensconced his secret evil,                    1515
That jealousy itself could not mistrust                    1516
False-creeping craft and perjury should thrust
  Into so bright a day such black-faced storms,
  Or blot with hell-born sin such saintlike forms.

**1494 his** its   **1497 penciled** painted.   **colored** painted   **1500 who** whoever   **1501 image** i.e., of Sinon, betrayer of Troy.   **bound** onward bound   **1502 piteous . . . lent** i.e., drew pitying looks from Phrygian shepherds. (Sinon deceived humble Trojans into pitying him as a deserter from the Greeks, thereby persuading them to admit the wooden horse.)   **1504 blunt swains** rustic peasants   **1505 patience** i.e., his patience.   **scorn** make light of   **1507 harmless show** outwardly harmless appearance   **1508 still** continually   **1511 guilty instance** symptom of guilt   **1514 entertained a show** kept up an appearance   **1515 ensconced** hid   **1516 jealousy** suspicion.   **mistrust** suspect (that)

The well-skilled workman this mild image drew
For perjured Sinon, whose enchanting story          1521
The credulous old Priam after slew;          1522
Whose words like wildfire burnt the shining glory          1523
Of rich-built Ilion, that the skies were sorry,
   And little stars shot from their fixèd places,
   When their glass fell wherein they viewed their faces.          1526

This picture she advisedly perused,          1527
And chid the painter for his wondrous skill,
Saying, some shape in Sinon's was abused;          1529
So fair a form lodged not a mind so ill.
And still on him she gazed, and gazing still,
   Such signs of truth in his plain face she spied          1532
   That she concludes the picture was belied.          1533

"It cannot be," quoth she, "that so much guile—"
She would have said "can lurk in such a look";
But Tarquin's shape came in her mind the while,
And from her tongue "can lurk" from "cannot" took.
"It cannot be" she in that sense forsook,
   And turned it thus: "It cannot be, I find,
   But such a face should bear a wicked mind.

"For even as subtle Sinon here is painted,
So sober-sad, so weary, and so mild,
As if with grief or travel he had fainted,          1543
To me came Tarquin armèd, so beguiled          1544
With outward honesty, but yet defiled
   With inward vice. As Priam him did cherish,
   So did I Tarquin; so my Troy did perish.

**1521 For** to represent.  **enchanting** bewitching  **1522 The . . . slew**
subsequently brought about the slaughter of credulous old Priam
**1523 wildfire** a highly inflammable mixture of tar, sulfur, grease, etc.,
used in war  **1526 glass** mirror (i.e., rich-built Troy)  **1527 advisedly**
studiously  **1529 some shape** i.e., the figure of some other person.
**abused** slanderously portrayed  **1532 plain** honest  **1533 belied** falsi-
fied  **1543 travel** (The quarto's *trauaile* also contains the idea of "travail," labor.)  **1544 armèd** equipped, accoutered.  **beguiled** concealed
or disguised by guile

"Look, look, how listening Priam wets his eyes,
To see those borrowed tears that Sinon sheeds!     1549
Priam, why art thou old and yet not wise?
For every tear he falls a Trojan bleeds.     1551
His eye drops fire, no water thence proceeds;
    Those round clear pearls of his, that move thy pity,
    Are balls of quenchless fire to burn thy city.

"Such devils steal effects from lightless hell,     1555
For Sinon in his fire doth quake with cold,
And in that cold hot-burning fire doth dwell.
These contraries such unity do hold     1558
Only to flatter fools and make them bold.     1559
    So Priam's trust false Sinon's tears doth flatter     1560
    That he finds means to burn his Troy with water."     1561

Here, all enraged, such passion her assails
That patience is quite beaten from her breast.
She tears the senseless Sinon with her nails,     1564
Comparing him to that unhappy guest     1565
Whose deed hath made herself herself detest.
    At last she smilingly with this gives o'er:
    "Fool, fool!" quoth she, "his wounds will not be
        sore."

**1549 borrowed** counterfeited.   **sheeds** sheds   **1551 he** i.e., Sinon.   **falls** lets fall   **1555 Such devils** (The ability to weep without real tears— *effects*—was attributed to devils.)   **1558–1561 These . . . water** i.e., this illusory coinciding of contraries, hot and cold, is designed to encourage and embolden fools, just as Sinon hoodwinks Priam into a false sense of security; thus false Sinon's tears lull Priam into misplaced trust, so that Sinon finds means to burn Priam's Troy by use of false tears. (*Fools,* l. 1559, can perhaps refer to Priam or to Sinon, and much of the grammar is ingeniously reversible.)   **1559, 1560 flatter** encourage with false hopes   **1564 senseless** inanimate; unfeeling   **1565 unhappy** causing unhappiness

Thus ebbs and flows the current of her sorrow,
And time doth weary time with her complaining.
She looks for night, and then she longs for morrow,
And both she thinks too long with her remaining.
Short time seems long in sorrow's sharp sustaining;          1573
   Though woe be heavy, yet it seldom sleeps,          1574
   And they that watch see time how slow it creeps.          1575

Which all this time hath overslipped her thought
That she with painted images hath spent,
Being from the feeling of her own grief brought          1578
By deep surmise of others' detriment,          1579
Losing her woes in shows of discontent.          1580
   It easeth some, though none it ever cured,
   To think their dolor others have endured.

But now the mindful messenger, come back,          1583
Brings home his lord and other company,
Who finds his Lucrece clad in mourning black,
And round about her tear-distainèd eye          1586
Blue circles streamed, like rainbows in the sky.
   These water galls in her dim element          1588
   Foretell new storms to those already spent.          1589

Which when her sad-beholding husband saw,
Amazedly in her sad face he stares.
Her eyes, though sod in tears, looked red and raw,          1592
Her lively color killed with deadly cares.
He hath no power to ask her how she fares;
   Both stood like old acquaintance in a trance,
   Met far from home, wond'ring each other's chance.          1596

---

**1573 in . . . sustaining** when it is sustained by sharp sorrow
**1574 heavy** exhausting; sorrowful     **1575 watch** stay awake
**1578 brought** made mindful     **1579 surmise** conjecture, contemplation
**1580 shows of discontent** representations of sorrow, i.e., the painted
scene of Troy's woe     **1583 mindful** diligent     **1586 tear-distainèd** tear-
stained     **1588 water galls** fragments of rainbow, secondary rainbows
(foretelling stormy weather).     **dim** cloudy.     **element** sky, i.e., face or eye
**1589 to** besides     **1592 sod** sodden, steeped     **1596 wond'ring . . . chance**
wondering about each other's fortune; or, each wondering at the chance
that has brought him to the other

At last he takes her by the bloodless hand,
And thus begins: "What uncouth ill event                    1598
Hath thee befall'n, that thou dost trembling stand?
Sweet love, what spite hath thy fair color spent?          1600
Why art thou thus attired in discontent?                    1601
    Unmask, dear dear, this moody heaviness,                1602
    And tell thy grief, that we may give redress."

Three times with sighs she gives her sorrow fire            1604
Ere once she can discharge one word of woe.                 1605
At length addressed to answer his desire,                   1606
She modestly prepares to let them know
Her honor is ta'en prisoner by the foe,
    While Collatine and his consorted lords                 1609
    With sad attention long to hear her words.              1610

And now this pale swan in her watery nest                   1611
Begins the sad dirge of her certain ending:
"Few words," quoth she, "shall fit the trespass best,
Where no excuse can give the fault amending.
In me more woes than words are now depending,               1615
    And my laments would be drawn out too long,
    To tell them all with one poor tirèd tongue.

"Then be this all the task it hath to say:
Dear husband, in the interest of thy bed                    1619
A stranger came, and on that pillow lay
Where thou wast wont to rest thy weary head;
And what wrong else may be imaginèd
    By foul enforcement might be done to me,
    From that, alas, thy Lucrece is not free.

---

**1598 uncouth** unknown, strange   **1600 spite** injury.   **spent** expended,
taken away   **1601 attired** wrapped up   **1602 Unmask** reveal
**1604–1605 Three . . . woe** (The metaphor is that of discharging firearms
by means of a match.)   **1606 addressed** prepared   **1609 consorted**
companion   **1610 sad** serious   **1611 swan** (Alludes to the belief that the
swan, ordinarily without a song, sings beautifully at its own death.)
**1615 depending** belonging, suspended, or pending (?)   **1619 in the
interest** claiming possession

"For in the dreadful dead of dark midnight,
With shining falchion in my chamber came
A creeping creature with a flaming light,
And softly cried, 'Awake, thou Roman dame,
And entertain my love! Else lasting shame       1629
  On thee and thine this night I will inflict,
  If thou my love's desire do contradict.

"'For some hard-favored groom of thine,' quoth he,   1632
'Unless thou yoke thy liking to my will,
I'll murder straight, and then I'll slaughter thee   1634
And swear I found you where you did fulfill
The loathsome act of lust, and so did kill
  The lechers in their deed. This act will be
  My fame and thy perpetual infamy.'

"With this, I did begin to start and cry;
And then against my heart he set his sword,
Swearing, unless I took all patiently,
I should not live to speak another word;
So should my shame still rest upon record,
  And never be forgot in mighty Rome
  Th' adulterate death of Lucrece and her groom.    1645

"Mine enemy was strong, my poor self weak,
And far the weaker with so strong a fear.
My bloody judge forbade my tongue to speak;
No rightful plea might plead for justice there.
His scarlet lust came evidence to swear            1650
  That my poor beauty had purloined his eyes;
  And when the judge is robbed the prisoner dies.

---

**1629 entertain** receive  **1632 hard-favored** ugly  **1634 straight** at once
**1645 adulterate** adulterous  **1650 came evidence** supplied evidence

"O, teach me how to make mine own excuse!
Or at the least this refuge let me find:
Though my gross blood be stained with this abuse,
Immaculate and spotless is my mind.
That was not forced, that never was inclined
    To accessory yieldings, but still pure     1658
    Doth in her poisoned closet yet endure."     1659

Lo, here, the hopeless merchant of this loss,     1660
With head declined and voice dammed up with woe,     1661
With sad set eyes and wreathèd arms across,
From lips new waxen pale begins to blow     1663
The grief away that stops his answer so.
    But, wretched as he is, he strives in vain;
    What he breathes out his breath drinks up again.

As through an arch the violent roaring tide     1667
Outruns the eye that doth behold his haste,
Yet in the eddy boundeth in his pride
Back to the strait that forced him on so fast—
In rage sent out, recalled in rage, being past—
    Even so his sighs, his sorrows, make a saw,     1672
    To push grief on and back the same grief draw.     1673

Which speechless woe of his poor she attendeth,     1674
And his untimely frenzy thus awaketh:     1675
"Dear lord, thy sorrow to my sorrow lendeth
Another power; no flood by raining slaketh.     1677
My woe too sensible thy passion maketh     1678
    More feeling-painful. Let it then suffice     1679
    To drown one woe, one pair of weeping eyes.

1658 accessory yieldings i.e., as an accessory to crime   1659 poisoned
closet i.e., violated body   1660 merchant of this loss i.e., owner who
has sustained this loss, Collatine   1661 declined lowered, bent down
1663 new waxen newly turned   1667 arch i.e., of a bridge, such as
London Bridge or Clopton Bridge   1672 saw i.e., sawlike back-and-forth
motion   1673 and . . . draw and draw the same grief back. (Collatine
breathes and sighs, in and out.)   1674 Which . . . attendeth i.e., to which
speechless woe of Collatine poor Lucrece pays heed   1675 And . . .
awaketh and awakens him from his ill-timed distraction   1677 Another
power added strength.   no . . . slaketh no flood is lessened by more
rain   1678–1679 My . . . painful your passionate grief makes my woe,
already too keenly felt, even more painfully perceived

"And for my sake, when I might charm thee so, 1681
For she that was thy Lucrece, now attend me:
Be suddenly revengèd on my foe, 1683
Thine, mine, his own. Suppose thou dost defend me 1684
From what is past. The help that thou shalt lend me
  Comes all too late, yet let the traitor die;
    For sparing justice feeds iniquity. 1687

"But ere I name him, you fair lords," quoth she,
Speaking to those that came with Collatine,
"Shall plight your honorable faiths to me, 1690
With swift pursuit to venge this wrong of mine;
For 'tis a meritorious fair design
  To chase injustice with revengeful arms.
    Knights, by their oaths, should right poor ladies'
      harms."

At this request, with noble disposition
Each present lord began to promise aid,
As bound in knighthood to her imposition, 1697
Longing to hear the hateful foe bewrayed. 1698
But she, that yet her sad task hath not said, 1699
  The protestation stops. "O, speak," quoth she, 1700
    "How may this forcèd stain be wiped from me?

"What is the quality of my offense, 1702
Being constrained with dreadful circumstance? 1703
May my pure mind with the foul act dispense, 1704
My low-declinèd honor to advance? 1705
May any terms acquit me from this chance? 1706
  The poisoned fountain clears itself again,
    And why not I from this compellèd stain?"

1681 **so** i.e., in the person of my former self, still unravished
1683 **suddenly** quickly   1684 **his own** i.e., his own worst enemy
1687 **sparing** too lenient.   **feeds iniquity** encourages wrongdoing
1690 **plight** pledge   1697 **imposition** injunction   1698 **bewrayed** revealed, named   1699 **her . . . said** had not yet finished her sad task of
speaking   1700 **protestation** resolution   1702 **quality** nature
1703 **with dreadful circumstance** in a situation filled with dread
1704 **with . . . dispense** be able to free itself from the foul deed
1705 **advance** raise up   1706 **terms** mitigating grounds

With this they all at once began to say
Her body's stain her mind untainted clears,
While with a joyless smile she turns away
The face, that map which deep impression bears          1712
Of hard misfortune, carved in it with tears.
  "No, no," quoth she, "no dame hereafter living
  By my excuse shall claim excuse's giving."          1715

Here with a sigh, as if her heart would break,
She throws forth Tarquin's name: "He, he," she says,
But more than "he" her poor tongue could not speak;
Till after many accents and delays,          1719
Untimely breathings, sick and short assays,
  She utters this: "He, he, fair lords, 'tis he,
  That guides this hand to give this wound to me."

Even here she sheathèd in her harmless breast
A harmful knife, that thence her soul unsheathed.
That blow did bail it from the deep unrest          1725
Of that polluted prison where it breathed.
Her contrite sighs unto the clouds bequeathed
  Her wingèd sprite, and through her wounds doth fly
  Life's lasting date from canceled destiny.          1729

Stone-still, astonished with this deadly deed,
Stood Collatine and all his lordly crew,
Till Lucrece' father, that beholds her bleed,
Himself on her self-slaughtered body threw,
And from the purple fountain Brutus drew          1734
  The murderous knife, and, as it left the place,
  Her blood, in poor revenge, held it in chase;

---

**1712 map** i.e., image   **1715 By . . . giving** will be able to claim the
right to offer (give) an excuse using my excuse as her precedent
**1719 accents** sounds expressive of emotion   **1725 bail it** pay for its
release   **1729 Life's . . . destiny** i.e., the life that now has a perpetual
existence, its subjugation to corporeal existence having been canceled
**1734 Brutus** Lucius Junius Brutus, whose brother had been killed by
the father of the Tarquin in this poem

And bubbling from her breast, it doth divide
In two slow rivers, that the crimson blood
Circles her body in on every side,
Who, like a late-sacked island, vastly stood          1740
Bare and unpeopled in this fearful flood.
   Some of her blood still pure and red remained,
   And some looked black, and that false Tarquin
     stained.

About the mourning and congealèd face
Of that black blood a watery rigol goes,              1745
Which seems to weep upon the tainted place;
And ever since, as pitying Lucrece' woes,
Corrupted blood some watery token shows,
   And blood untainted still doth red abide,
   Blushing at that which is so putrified.

"Daughter, dear daughter," old Lucretius cries,
"That life was mine which thou hast here deprived.    1752
If in the child the father's image lies,
Where shall I live now Lucrece is unlived?            1754
Thou wast not to this end from me derived.
   If children predecease progenitors,
   We are their offspring, and they none of ours.

"Poor broken glass, I often did behold               1758
In thy sweet semblance my old age new born;
But now that fair fresh mirror dim and old
Shows me a bare-boned death by time outworn.         1761
O, from thy cheeks my image thou hast torn,
   And shivered all the beauty of my glass,
   That I no more can see what once I was!

---

**1740 late-sacked** recently pillaged.   **vastly** having been desolated
**1745 rigol** rim of serum   **1752 deprived** taken away   **1754 unlived**
bereft of life   **1758 glass** mirror (i.e., Lucrece, the image of her father)
**1761 death** death's-head, skull

"O Time, cease thou thy course and last no longer,
If they surcease to be that should survive!     1766
Shall rotten Death make conquest of the stronger
And leave the faltering feeble souls alive?
The old bees die, the young possess their hive.
   Then live, sweet Lucrece, live again and see
   Thy father die, and not thy father thee!"

By this, starts Collatine as from a dream,
And bids Lucretius give his sorrow place;     1773
And then in key-cold Lucrece' bleeding stream     1774
He falls, and bathes the pale fear in his face,     1775
And counterfeits to die with her a space,     1776
   Till manly shame bids him possess his breath
   And live to be revengèd on her death.

The deep vexation of his inward soul
Hath served a dumb arrest upon his tongue,     1780
Who, mad that sorrow should his use control,
Or keep him from heart-easing words so long,
Begins to talk; but through his lips do throng
   Weak words, so thick come in his poor heart's aid,     1784
   That no man could distinguish what he said.

Yet sometimes "Tarquin" was pronouncèd plain,
But through his teeth, as if the name he tore.
This windy tempest, till it blow up rain,
Held back his sorrow's tide, to make it more.
At last it rains, and busy winds give o'er;
   Then son and father weep with equal strife
   Who should weep most, for daughter or for wife.

---

**1766 surcease** cease    **1773 give . . . place** yield him precedence in sorrowing    **1774 key-cold** i.e., cold as steel    **1775 pale fear** fearful pallor    **1776 counterfeits to die** gives the appearance of dying.    **a space** for a period of time    **1780 dumb arrest** injunction to be silent    **1784 thick** thickly, fast

The one doth call her his, the other his,
Yet neither may possess the claim they lay.                    1794
The father says, "She's mine." "O, mine she is,"
Replies her husband. "Do not take away
My sorrow's interest. Let no mourner say                    1797
   He weeps for her, for she was only mine,
   And only must be wailed by Collatine."

"O," quoth Lucretius, "I did give that life
Which she too early and too late hath spilled."                    1801
"Woe, woe," quoth Collatine, "She was my wife,
I owed her, and 'tis mine that she hath killed."                    1803
"My daughter" and "my wife" with clamors filled
   The dispersed air, who, holding Lucrece' life,
   Answered their cries, "my daughter" and "my wife."

Brutus, who plucked the knife from Lucrece' side,
Seeing such emulation in their woe,
Began to clothe his wit in state and pride,                    1809
Burying in Lucrece' wound his folly's show.                    1810
He with the Romans was esteemèd so
   As silly jeering idiots are with kings,                    1812
   For sportive words and uttering foolish things.

But now he throws that shallow habit by,                    1814
Wherein deep policy did him disguise,                    1815
And armed his long-hid wits advisedly
To check the tears in Collatinus' eyes.
"Thou wrongèd lord of Rome," quoth he, "arise!
   Let my unsounded self, supposed a fool,                    1819
   Now set thy long-experienced wit to school.

---

**1794 possess . . . lay** take possession of what they claim (since she
is dead)   **1797 interest** claim to possession   **1801 late** recently
**1803 owed** owned   **1809 state** dignity   **1810 folly's show** pretense of
folly. (Brutus feigned madness to escape the fate of his brother; see
l. 1734, note.)   **1812 silly jeering idiots** i.e., innocent court jesters
**1814 habit** cloak and disposition   **1815 policy** cunning
**1819 unsounded** unplumbed, unexplored

"Why, Collatine, is woe the cure for woe?
Do wounds help wounds, or grief help grievous deeds?
Is it revenge to give thyself a blow
For his foul act by whom thy fair wife bleeds?
Such childish humor from weak minds proceeds.          1825
   Thy wretched wife mistook the matter so
   To slay herself, that should have slain her foe.

"Courageous Roman, do not steep thy heart
In such relenting dew of lamentations,
But kneel with me and help to bear thy part
To rouse our Roman gods with invocations
That they will suffer these abominations—          1832
   Since Rome herself in them doth stand disgraced—
   By our strong arms from forth her fair streets
     chased.          1834

"Now, by the Capitol that we adore,
And by this chaste blood so unjustly stained,
By heaven's fair sun that breeds the fat earth's store,          1837
By all our country rights in Rome maintained,          1838
And by chaste Lucrece' soul that late complained
   Her wrongs to us, and by this bloody knife,
   We will revenge the death of this true wife."

This said, he struck his hand upon his breast,
And kissed the fatal knife, to end his vow;
And to his protestation urged the rest,          1844
Who, wondering at him, did his words allow.          1845
Then jointly to the ground their knees they bow,
   And that deep vow which Brutus made before
   He doth again repeat, and that they swore.

**1825 humor** disposition   **1832 suffer** permit   **1834 chased** i.e., to be
chased away   **1837 fat** fertile   **1838 country rights** rights we have as a
people   **1844 protestation** resolution   **1845 allow** approve

When they had sworn to this advisèd doom,          1849
They did conclude to bear dead Lucrece thence,
To show her bleeding body thorough Rome,          1851
And so to publish Tarquin's foul offense;          1852
Which being done with speedy diligence,
   The Romans plausibly did give consent          1854
   To Tarquin's everlasting banishment.

---

**1849 advisèd doom** considered judgment   **1851 thorough** throughout
**1852 publish** make public   **1854 plausibly** with applause

# Date and Text

Shakespeare promised a "graver labor" to Southampton in his dedication of *Venus and Adonis,* 1593, and *The Rape of Lucrece* is almost surely that promised sequel. It was registered in the Stationers' Register, the official record book of the London Company of Stationers (booksellers and printers), by John Harrison on May 9, 1594, and issued that same year as "printed by Richard Field, for Iohn Harrison." The printed text was probably based on Shakespeare's manuscript. Although not quite as popular as *Venus and Adonis,* the poem was reprinted five times during Shakespeare's lifetime. Contemporaries of Shakespeare who allude favorably to the poem include W. Har and Michael Drayton in 1594, William Covell in 1595, Francis Meres in 1598, Gabriel Harvey in 1598–1601, John Weever in 1599, and others. The date of composition of the poem is well fixed between the publication of *Venus and Adonis* in 1593 and that of *The Rape of Lucrece* itself in 1594.

# Textual Notes

These textual notes are not a historical collation; they are simply a record of departures in this edition from the copy text. The reading adopted in this edition appears in boldface, followed by the rejected reading from the copy text, i.e., the quarto of 1594. Only major alterations in punctuation are noted. Corrections of minor and obvious typographical errors are not indicated.

Copy text: the corrected quarto of 1594 [Q corr.] A number of corrected readings are however rejected as sophistications; see text notes below at ll. 24, 31, 50, 125, 126.

**24 morning** [Q uncorr.] mornings [Q corr.]   **31 apology** [Q uncorr.] Apologies [Q corr.]   **50 Collatium** [Q uncorr., Colatium] Colatia [Q corr.]   **125 himself betakes** [Q uncorr.] themselues betake [Q corr.]   **126 wakes** [Q uncorr.] wake [corr.]   **555 panteth** pateth   **560 wear** were   **688 lose** loose [also at ll. 979 and 1158]   **922 inclination** inclination.   **1126 Relish** Ralish   **1129 hair** heare   **1249 remain** remaine.   **1251 peep** peepe,   **1312 schedule** Cedule   **1350 this pattern of the** the pattern of this [in four copies of Q; it is uncertain which is the corrected state]   **1386 far-off** farre of   **1543 travel** trauaile   **1544 so** to

**1580 Losing** Loosing   **1648 forbade** forbod   **1660 here** heare   **1662 wreathed** wretched   **1680 one woe** on woe   **1713 in it** it in   **1768 faltering** foultring

# THE
# PHOENIX
# AND
# TURTLE

# Introduction

"The Phoenix and Turtle" first appeared in a collection of poems called *Loves Martyr: Or, Rosalins Complaint* by Robert Chester (1601). This quarto volume offered various poetic exercises about the phoenix and the turtle "by the best and chiefest of our modern writers." The poem assigned to Shakespeare has been universally accepted as his and is one of his most remarkable productions. With a deceptively simple diction, in gracefully pure tetrameter quatrains and triplets, the poem effortlessly evokes the transcendental ideal of a love existing eternally beyond death. The occasion is an assembly of birds to observe the funeral rites of the phoenix and the turtle. The phoenix, legendary bird of resurrection from her own ashes, once more finds life through death in the company of the turtledove, emblem of pure constancy in affection. Their spiritual union becomes a mystical oneness in whose presence Reason stands virtually speechless. Baffled human discourse must resort to paradox in order to explain how two beings become one essence, "Hearts remote yet not asunder." Mathematics and logic are "confounded" by this joining of two spirits into a "concordant one." This paradox of oneness echoes scholastic theology and its expounding of the doctrine of the Trinity, although, somewhat in the manner of John Donne's poetry, this allusion is more a part of the poem's serious wit than its symbolic meaning. The poignant brevity of this vision is rendered all the more mysterious by our not knowing what if any human tragedy may have prompted this metaphysical affirmation.

# The Phoenix and Turtle

Let the bird of loudest lay                               1
On the sole Arabian tree                                 2
Herald sad and trumpet be,                               3
To whose sound chaste wings obey.                        4

But thou shrieking harbinger,                            5
Foul precurrer of the fiend,                             6
Augur of the fever's end,                                7
To this troop come thou not near.

From this session interdict
Every fowl of tyrant wing,                              10
Save the eagle, feathered king;
Keep the obsequy so strict.

Let the priest in surplice white,
That defunctive music can,                              14
Be the death-divining swan,                             15
Lest the requiem lack his right.                        16

---

**Title: Phoenix** mythical bird that was thought to be consumed in flame
and reborn in its own ashes, symbol of immortality.   **Turtle** turtledove,
symbol of constancy in love

**1 bird . . . lay** the bird (possibly the nightingale) of loudest song   **2 sole
Arabian tree** (The phoenix was thought to build its nest in a unique tree
in Arabia.)   **3 sad** solemn.   **trumpet** trumpeter   **4 chaste wings** i.e., the
wings of the good birds that are being summoned.   **obey** are obedient
**5 shrieking harbinger** i.e., screech owl   **6 precurrer** forerunner
**7 Augur . . . end** i.e., prognosticator of death   **10 fowl . . . wing**
bird of prey   **14 defunctive** funereal.   **can** knows, has skill in
**15 death-divining swan** (Alludes to the belief that the swan foresees its
own death and sings when it is about to die.)   **16 his right** its proper
ceremony, or its proper due (referring either to the *requiem* or to the
*swan*)

And thou treble-dated crow,                                    17
That thy sable gender mak'st                                    18
With the breath thou giv'st and tak'st,                         19
'Mongst our mourners shalt thou go.

Here the anthem doth commence.
Love and constancy is dead;
Phoenix and the turtle fled
In a mutual flame from hence.

So they loved, as love in twain                                25
Had the essence but in one,
Two distincts, division none;                                   27
Number there in love was slain.                                 28

Hearts remote yet not asunder,
Distance and no space was seen
Twixt this turtle and his queen;
But in them it were a wonder.                                   32

So between them love did shine,                                 33
That the turtle saw his right                                   34
Flaming in the phoenix' sight;                                  35
Either was the other's mine.                                    36

**17 treble-dated** i.e., living thrice as long as the normal span of life
**18–19 That . . . tak'st** (Cf. *Hortus Sanitatis*, Bk. 3, sec. 34, in Seager's
*Natural History in Shakespeare's Time:* "They [ravens] are said to
conceive and to lay eggs at the bill. The young become black on the
seventh day.")   **18 sable gender** black offspring   **25 So . . . as** they so
loved that   **27 distincts** separate or individual persons or things
**28 Number . . . slain** i.e., their love, being of one essence, paradoxically
renders the very concept of number meaningless; "one is no number"
**32 But . . . wonder** this phenomenon, had it been seen anywhere but in
them, would have seemed amazing   **33 So** in such a way   **34 his right**
his true nature, what pertained uniquely and rightly to him; or, what
was due to him   **35 sight** eyes   **36 mine** i.e., very own. (The phoenix
and turtle are so merged in one another's identity that each contains
the other's being.)

Property was thus appalled 37
That the self was not the same; 38
Single nature's double name 39
Neither two nor one was called. 40

Reason, in itself confounded, 41
Saw division grow together, 42
To themselves yet either neither, 43
Simple were so well compounded, 44

That it cried, "How true a twain 45
Seemeth this concordant one! 
Love hath reason, Reason none, 47
If what parts can so remain." 48

Whereupon it made this threne 49
To the phoenix and the dove, 
Co-supremes and stars of love, 51
As chorus to their tragic scene.

### THRENOS

Beauty, truth, and rarity, 53
Grace in all simplicity, 
Here enclosed, in cinders lie. 55

Death is now the phoenix' nest, 
And the turtle's loyal breast 
To eternity doth rest,

**37–38 Property . . . same** i.e., the very idea of a peculiar or essential quality was thus confounded by the paradoxical revelation here that each lover's identity was merged into the other's and was no longer itself   **39–40 Single . . . called** i.e., their nature was at once so single and double that it could not properly be called either one or two **41–44 Reason . . . compounded** i.e., Reason, which proceeds by making discriminations between separate entities, is confounded when it beholds a paradoxical union of such entities, each at once discrete and fused into a single being, at once a simple (i.e., made of one substance) and a compound   **45 it** i.e., Reason   **47–48 Love . . . remain** i.e., Love, which ordinarily lacks reason, is reasonable, and Reason itself lacks reason, if two that can be disunited or parted nevertheless remain thus in union   **49 threne** lamentation, funeral song (from Greek *threnos*) **51 Co-supremes** joint rulers   **53 truth** constancy in love (also in l. 62) **55 enclosed** i.e., enclosed in *this urn* (l. 65)

Leaving no posterity;
'Twas not their infirmity, 60
It was married chastity. 61

Truth may seem, but cannot be; 62
Beauty brag, but 'tis not she; 63
Truth and beauty buried be. 64

To this urn let those repair
That are either true or fair;
For these dead birds sigh a prayer.

---

**60–61 'Twas . . . chastity** i.e., it was not a defect in them to leave no posterity, but an emblem of their mystical eternal trothplight
**62–64 Truth . . . be** i.e., fidelity and beauty as known to mortal perception are only illusory, for their ideal incarnation now lies buried with the phoenix and turtle

# Date and Text

"The Phoenix and Turtle" first appeared in a volume with the following title:

LOVES MARTYR: OR, ROSALINS COMPLAINT. *Allegorically shadowing the truth of Loue,* in the constant Fate of the Phoenix *and* Turtle. . . . by ROBERT CHESTER. . . . *To these are added some new compositions, of seuerall moderne Writers whose names are subscribed to their seuerall workes, vpon the first subiect: viz. the* Phoenix *and* Turtle.

The date 1601 appears on a separate title page. One poem is signed "William Shake-speare," others John Marston, George Chapman, and Ben Jonson.

# A LOVER'S
# COMPLAINT

# Introduction

Thomas Thorpe published "A Lover's Complaint" in his 1609 quarto of Shakespeare's *Sonnets,* ascribing the poem to "William Shake-speare" in its title heading (sig. K$^v$). The ascription must not be given too much weight, for Thorpe evidently did not have Shakespeare's authorization to publish the sonnets and may possibly have added the last two sonnets from some other source. Yet Thorpe's edition remains the only objective evidence we have, and its authority has never been convincingly refuted. The modern tendency to dismiss "A Lover's Complaint" as unworthy of Shakespeare's genius rests on subjective judgment and on stylistic "tests" that are too often proved unreliable. In fact the density of metaphor and energy of wordplay are stylistically and intellectually very much like that of his known work. The poem was never ascribed to anyone else during Shakespeare's lifetime. On balance, the evidence is in favor of his authorship, though the issue will continue to remain in doubt.

The poem's genre, the "complaint" of a forsaken maiden, is conventional, along with the pastoral setting, the catalog of the fickle lover's features, and the sententious warnings against blind passion. The poem did not add to Shakespeare's contemporary reputation. Still, it cannot safely be assigned to any other Elizabethan poet. Nor does it read like a mere effusion of Shakespeare's youth. Though written in *The Rape of Lucrece*'s seven-line rhyme royal stanza, the poem eschews Ovidian and Petrarchan conceit for an occasional richness and complexity of metaphor.

# A Lover's Complaint

From off a hill whose concave womb reworded                1
A plaintful story from a sistering vale,                   2
My spirits t' attend this double voice accorded,          3
And down I laid to list the sad-tuned tale;               4
Ere long espied a fickle maid full pale,                  5
Tearing of papers, breaking rings a-twain,                6
Storming her world with sorrow's wind and rain.

Upon her head a platted hive of straw,                    8
Which fortified her visage from the sun,                  9
Whereon the thought might think sometimes it saw          10
The carcass of a beauty spent and done.                   11
Time had not scythèd all that youth begun,
Nor youth all quit, but spite of heaven's fell rage       13
Some beauty peeped through lattice of seared age.         14

Oft did she heave her napkin to her eyne,                 15
Which on it had conceited characters,                     16
Laund'ring the silken figures in the brine
That seasoned woe had pelleted in tears,                  18
And often reading what contents it bears;
As often shrieking undistinguished woe,                   20
In clamors of all size, both high and low.

---

**1 concave womb** hollow-shaped hillside.   **reworded** echoed   **2 plaintful story** i.e., mournful sound (which turns out to be the grieving of a maiden).   **sistering** neighboring   **3 attend** listen to.   **double** (because echoed).   **accorded** inclined, consented   **4 list** listen to.   **sad-tuned** i.e., sung in a minor key   **5 fickle** i.e., perturbed, moody   **6 papers** i.e., love letters   **8 platted hive** i.e., woven hat   **9 fortified** protected   **10 the thought** the mind; that which thinks   **11 carcass** decaying lifeless remnant.   **spent** consumed   **13 all quit** deserted every part.   **fell** deadly, cruel   **14 seared** dried up   **15 heave** lift.   **napkin** handkerchief.   **eyne** eyes   **16 conceited characters** fanciful or emblematic devices   **18 seasoned** (1) matured (2) salted.   **pelleted** formed into small globules   **20 undistinguished woe** incoherent cries of grief

Sometimes her leveled eyes their carriage ride,          22
As they did battery to the spheres intend;          23
Sometimes, diverted, their poor balls are tied          24
To th' orbèd earth; sometimes they do extend          25
Their view right on; anon their gazes lend          26
To every place at once, and, nowhere fixed,          27
The mind and sight distractedly commixed.          28

Her hair, nor loose nor tied in formal plat,          29
Proclaimed in her a careless hand of pride;          30
For some, untucked, descended her sheaved hat,          31
Hanging her pale and pinèd cheek beside;          32
Some in her threaden fillet still did bide,          33
And, true to bondage, would not break from thence,
Though slackly braided in loose negligence.

A thousand favors from a maund she drew          36
Of amber, crystal, and of beaded jet, ·          37
Which one by one she in a river threw,
Upon whose weeping margent she was set,          39
Like usury applying wet to wet,          40
Or monarch's hands that lets not bounty fall
Where want cries some, but where excess begs all.          42

**22 her ... ride** i.e., her eyes, directed and aimed like a cannon, swiveled about as on a gun carriage  **23 As ... intend** as if they did intend to direct their fire against the heavens  **24 balls** eyeballs  **24–25 are ... earth** seem fixed to the orb-shaped earth, to the ground  **26 right on** straight in front of her  **26–27 lend ... once** i.e., roll distractedly everywhere  **28 The mind ... commixed** her mind and sight wildly confused or mingled  **29 nor ... nor** neither ... nor.  **in formal plat** neatly braided  **30 careless ... pride** hand careless of appearances  **31 descended** hung from.  **sheaved** straw  **32 Hanging ... beside** hanging beside her pale cheek wasted with pining  **33 threaden fillet** i.e., ribbon binding her hair  **36 favors** love tokens.  **maund** woven basket with handles  **37 beaded jet** jet beads  **39 weeping margent** moist bank (though *weeping* also applies to her)  **40 usury** i.e., adding money to money; she adds tears to the river's water  **42 Where ... all** i.e., (not) where the needy cry out for some charity, but where the rich beg all the bounty there is

Of folded schedules had she many a one,    43
Which she perused, sighed, tore, and gave the flood;    44
Cracked many a ring of posied gold and bone,    45
Bidding them find their sepulchers in mud;
Found yet more letters sadly penned in blood,
With sleided silk feat and affectedly    48
Enswathed and sealed to curious secrecy.    49

These often bathed she in her fluxive eyes,    50
And often kissed, and often 'gan to tear;
Cried, "O false blood, thou register of lies,    52
What unapprovèd witness dost thou bear!    53
Ink would have seemed more black and damnèd here!"
This said, in top of rage the lines she rents,    55
Big discontent so breaking their contents.    56

A reverend man that grazed his cattle nigh—    57
Sometime a blusterer, that the ruffle knew    58
Of court, of city, and had let go by
The swiftest hours, observèd as they flew—    60
Towards this afflicted fancy fastly drew,    61
And, privileged by age, desires to know
In brief the grounds and motives of her woe.

43 **schedules** papers containing writing, i.e., letters   44 **gave the flood**
threw in the stream   45 **posied** inscribed with a motto   48 **sleided**
separated into threads.   **feat** featly, adroitly.   **affectedly** lovingly
49 **Enswathed . . . secrecy** wrapped about (with the silk) and sealed
(with wax) into careful secrecy   50 **fluxive** flowing   52 **blood** i.e., the
blood in which the letters were written (l. 47), but with a sense also
of the *blood* or passion that has played her *false*.   **register** record
53 **unapprovèd** unconfirmed, false   55 **in top of** in the height of.   **rents**
rends, tears   56 **discontent . . . contents** (with a play of antithesis)
57 **reverend** aged   58 **Sometime** at one time.   **blusterer** boisterous
fellow.   **ruffle** commotion, bustle   60 **swiftest hours** i.e., time of
youth.   **observèd as they flew** (This man has let his youth go by and
disappear, but not without observing and learning from the years as
they flew.)   61 **fancy** i.e., amorous passion, and the person expressing
it.   **fastly** (1) quickly (2) in close proximity

So slides he down upon his grainèd bat,      64
And comely-distant sits he by her side,      65
When he again desires her, being sat,      66
Her grievance with his hearing to divide.      67
If that from him there may be aught applied      68
Which may her suffering ecstasy assuage,      69
'Tis promised in the charity of age.

"Father," she says, "though in me you behold      71
The injury of many a blasting hour,      72
Let it not tell your judgment I am old;
Not age, but sorrow, over me hath power.
I might as yet have been a spreading flower,      75
Fresh to myself, if I had self-applied      76
Love to myself and to no love beside.

"But, woe is me! Too early I attended      78
A youthful suit—it was to gain my grace—      79
O, one by nature's outwards so commended      80
That maidens' eyes stuck over all his face.      81
Love lacked a dwelling and made him her place;      82
And when in his fair parts she did abide,
She was new lodged and newly deified.

"His browny locks did hang in crooked curls,
And every light occasion of the wind      86
Upon his lips their silken parcels hurls.      87
What's sweet to do, to do will aptly find;      88
Each eye that saw him did enchant the mind,
For on his visage was in little drawn      90
What largeness thinks in Paradise was sawn.      91

---

**64 So . . . bat** and so he lowers himself by means of his club or staff that is worn and showing the grain   **65 comely-distant** a: a decorous distance   **66 being** he being   **67 divide** share   **68 If that** if   **69 ecstasy** frenzy (of grief)   **71 Father** i.e., old man   **72 blasting** blighting, withering   **75 spreading** unfolding   **76 Fresh to myself** i.e., like a flower that lives and dies unseen and unplucked   **78 attended** heeded   **79 grace** favor   **80 nature's outwards** the physical appearance given him by nature   **81 stuck over** i.e., were glued to   **82 Love** Venus   **86 occasion** i.e., stirring   **87 Upon . . . hurls** (the wind) tosses the *silken parcels*, the curls, against his lips   **88 to do will aptly find** i.e., will find a doer or an occasion   **90 in little** in miniature   **91 What . . . sawn** what one supposes was seen in full scale in Paradise

"Small show of man was yet upon his chin;
His phoenix down began but to appear          93
Like unshorn velvet on that termless skin          94
Whose bare outbragged the web it seemed to wear.          95
Yet showed his visage by that cost more dear;          96
And nice affections wavering stood in doubt          97
If best were as it was, or best without.          98

"His qualities were beauteous as his form,          99
For maiden-tongued he was, and thereof free;          100
Yet, if men moved him, was he such a storm          101
As oft twixt May and April is to see,          102
When winds breathe sweet, unruly though they be.
His rudeness so with his authorized youth          104
Did livery falseness in a pride of truth.          105

"Well could he ride, and often men would say,
'That horse his mettle from his rider takes.          107
Proud of subjection, noble by the sway,          108
What rounds, what bounds, what course, what stop he
    makes!'          109
And controversy hence a question takes,          110
Whether the horse by him became his deed,          111
Or he his manage by th' well-doing steed.          112

**93 phoenix** i.e., suggesting his unique perfection (since only one phoenix, a mythical bird, exists at one time)   **94 termless** indescribable;
youthful   **95 bare outbragged** bareness surpassed.   **web** i.e., covering,
the downy beard   **96 cost** (1) expense (2) rich covering; i.e., his face
seemed lovelier because of its rich or silken covering.   **dear** (1) costly
(2) lovely   **97 nice affections** carefully discriminating tastes, inclina-
tions   **98 without** i.e., lacking the downy beard   **99 qualities were**
manner was as   **100 maiden-tongued** modest of speech, soft-spoken.
**free** eloquent; innocent   **101 moved** i.e., to anger   **102 to see** to be
seen   **104–105 His . . . truth** his roughness, privileged by his youth,
thereby did dress falseness in a magnificent garment or concealment of
truth   **107 mettle** vigor and strength of spirit   **108 noble by the sway**
made noble by the way he's controlled   **109 stop** sudden check in a
horse's "career" or trial gallop at full speed. (All the terms here are
terms of *manage*, l. 112, the schooling or handling of a horse.)
**110 takes** takes up, considers   **111–112 Whether . . . steed** whether it
was owing to his horsemanship that his horse acted so becomingly or
whether he seemed such a good rider because he had so good a horse

"But quickly on this side the verdict went:
His real habitude gave life and grace                          114
To appertainings and to ornament,
Accomplished in himself, not in his case.                      116
All aids, themselves made fairer by their place,               117
Came for additions, yet their purposed trim                    118
Pieced not his grace, but were all graced by him.              119

"So on the tip of his subduing tongue
All kind of arguments and question deep,
All replication prompt and reason strong,                      122
For his advantage still did wake and sleep.                    123
To make the weeper laugh, the laugher weep,
He had the dialect and different skill,                        125
Catching all passions in his craft of will,                    126

"That he did in the general bosom reign                        127
Of young, of old, and sexes both enchanted,
To dwell with him in thoughts, or to remain
In personal duty, following where he haunted.                  130
Consents bewitched, ere he desire, have granted,              131
And dialogued for him what he would say,                      132
Asked their own wills, and made their wills obey.             133

---

**114 habitude** constitution, temperament   **116 case** conditions and
circumstances, e.g., the possession of so good a horse   **117 place** i.e.,
place near to him or on his person   **118 Came for additions** came in for
consideration as additional graces.   **purposed trim** intended function
as adornment   **119 Pieced** mended, augmented   **122 replication** reply.   **reason strong** persuasive argument   **123 still** continually.   **wake
and sleep** i.e., work in varying moods, now actively, now insinuatingly
**125 dialect** manner of expression.   **different** varied, readily adaptable
**126 passions** (1) passions of his hearers (2) passions incorporated into
his moving speech.   **craft of will** skill in persuasion   **127 That** so
that.   **general bosom** hearts of all   **130 In personal duty** i.e., like a
personal servant.   **haunted** frequented   **131–133 Consents . . . obey** i.e.,
women have consented to his will before he even asked them, and have
made up his love speeches to them for him, and have made themselves
obey their own desires

"Many there were that did his picture get
To serve their eyes, and in it put their mind,          135
Like fools that in th' imagination set
The goodly objects which abroad they find          137
Of lands and mansions, theirs in thought assigned,          138
And laboring in more pleasures to bestow them          139
Than the true gouty landlord which doth owe them;          140

"So many have, that never touched his hand,          141
Sweetly supposed them mistress of his heart.          142
My woeful self, that did in freedom stand,
And was my own fee simple, not in part,          144
What with his art in youth, and youth in art,
Threw my affections in his charmèd power,          146
Reserved the stalk and gave him all my flower.

"Yet did I not, as some my equals did,          148
Demand of him, nor being desired yielded;          149
Finding myself in honor so forbid,          150
With safest distance I mine honor shielded.          151
Experience for me many bulwarks builded          152
Of proofs new-bleeding, which remained the foil          153
Of this false jewel, and his amorous spoil.          154

135 **in it . . . mind** let their minds become engrossed with it
137 **objects** i.e., of sight.   **abroad** round about them, in the world
138 **theirs . . . assigned** imagining those possessions to be their own
139 **laboring . . . them** striving to derive more pleasure from them
140 **owe** own   141 **So many** thus many persons, many women
142 **them** themselves   144 **was . . . part** i.e., had total control of my own
destiny, not partial control, as of land held in freehold   146 **charmèd**
**power** power to charm or cast a spell   148 **my equals** i.e., of those
equal to me in age and station   149 **Demand . . . yielded** i.e., ask him to
take me, or yield myself to him the moment he desired me to   150 **in**
**honor so forbid** forbidden by (maidenly) honor to do so (i.e., to yield
at once)   151 **With safest distance** by staying at a safe distance
152–153 **Experience . . . new-bleeding** i.e., the experience of those
recently undone in love by him provided me with many defenses
153 **foil** dark background used to show off the brilliance of a jewel
154 **this false jewel** i.e., the young man.   **spoil** plunder; that which is
spoiled

"But, ah, who ever shunned by precedent
The destined ill she must herself assay?                    156
Or forced examples, 'gainst her own content,             157
To put the by-past perils in her way?                       158
Counsel may stop awhile what will not stay;            159
For when we rage, advice is often seen                     160
By blunting us to make our wits more keen.             161

"Nor gives it satisfaction to our blood                     162
That we must curb it upon others' proof,                  163
To be forbade the sweets that seems so good          164
For fear of harms that preach in our behoof.           165
O appetite, from judgment stand aloof!                    166
The one a palate hath that needs will taste,            167
Though Reason weep and cry, 'It is thy last.'

"For further I could say 'This man's untrue,'           169
And knew the patterns of his foul beguiling;          170
Heard where his plants in others' orchards grew,    171
Saw how deceits were gilded in his smiling;           172
Knew vows were ever brokers to defiling;              173
Thought characters and words merely but art,        174
And bastards of his foul adulterate heart.

156 assay learn by experience    157 forced proffered, urged.    content
i.e., presumed happiness in love    158 To . . . way to raise as objections
(to her own love happiness) the past perils (of others)    159 stay remain
stopped forever    160 rage i.e., in passion    161 By . . . keen i.e., in
attempting to stop us, merely making us all the more ingenious and
eager    162 blood passion    163 proof experience    164 seems i.e.,
seem    165 preach in our behoof i.e., offer us good advice aimed at
benefiting us    166 O appetite . . . aloof i.e., beware lest passion over-
whelm reason by its immediacy    167 The one i.e., passion, *appetite*.
needs will taste insists upon gratification    169 say . . . untrue tell of
this man's faithlessness    170 knew . . . beguiling i.e., had examples of
his treachery before me    171 plants i.e., children illegitimately begot-
ten.    orchards gardens    172 gilded given a gilded (false) surface
173 brokers panders    174 characters and words i.e., the written and
spoken word.    art artifice

"And long upon these terms I held my city,     176
Till thus he 'gan besiege me: 'Gentle maid,
Have of my suffering youth some feeling pity,
And be not of my holy vows afraid.
That's to ye sworn to none was ever said;     180
For feasts of love I have been called unto,     181
Till now did ne'er invite, nor never woo.     182

"'All my offenses that abroad you see     183
Are errors of the blood, none of the mind.
Love made them not. With acture they may be,     185
Where neither party is nor true nor kind.     186
They sought their shame that so their shame did find;
And so much less of shame in me remains     188
By how much of me their reproach contains.     189

"'Among the many that mine eyes have seen,
Not one whose flame my heart so much as warmed,     191
Or my affection put to th' smallest teen,     192
Or any of my leisures ever charmed.     193
Harm have I done to them, but ne'er was harmed;
Kept hearts in liveries, but mine own was free,     195
And reigned, commanding in his monarchy.

---

**176 city** citadel (of chastity)   **180 That's** that which is   **181–182 For . . . woo** I have been invited to other feasts of love before now, but never until now did I do the inviting and the wooing   **183 abroad** in the world around us   **185–186 With . . . kind** they may be physically performed where neither partner is faithful or truly in love   **188–189 And . . . contains** i.e., and I am all the less to blame by how little their reproaches really accuse me (rather than themselves)   **191 Not one . . . warmed** i.e., there is not one whose flame of passion so much as warmed my heart   **192 Or . . . teen** or gave my affection the least sorrow (*teen*)   **193 Or . . . charmed** or put a spell on any of my times of leisure   **195 in liveries** in the uniform of a person in service, i.e., almost enslaved

" 'Look here what tributes wounded fancies sent me,      197
Of pallid pearls and rubies red as blood,
Figuring that they their passions likewise lent me      199
Of grief and blushes, aptly understood
In bloodless white and the encrimsoned mood—      201
Effects of terror and dear modesty,      202
Encamped in hearts but fighting outwardly.      203

" 'And, lo, behold these talents of their hair,      204
With twisted metal amorously impleached,      205
I have received from many a several fair,      206
Their kind acceptance weepingly beseeched,      207
With th' annexions of fair gems enriched,      208
And deep-brained sonnets that did amplify      209
Each stone's dear nature, worth, and quality.

" 'The diamond? Why, 'twas beautiful and hard,
Whereto his invised properties did tend;      212
The deep-green emerald, in whose fresh regard      213
Weak sights their sickly radiance do amend;      214
The heaven-hued sapphire and the opal blend      215
With objects manifold—each several stone,      216
With wit well blazoned, smiled or made some moan.      217

---

**197 wounded fancies** i.e., doting young women   **199 Figuring** symboliz-
ing   **201 mood** mode, form, emotional state (i.e., blushing)   **202 Effects**
the signs or results.   **dear** precious; deeply felt   **203 but fighting
outwardly** and only feigning resistance   **204 talents** i.e., treasures,
riches. (Literally, coins or valuable metal plates.)   **205 impleached**
intertwined   **206 a several fair** different beautiful ladies   **207 Their
kind . . . beseeched** who have besought me with their tears to accept
their gifts kindly   **208 annexions** additions   **209 deep-brained** intri-
cate.   **amplify** enlarge upon, go into detail about   **212 Whereto . . .
tend** toward which its invisible properties incline. (*Invised,* used nowhere else, is of uncertain meaning.) The young man too is beautiful
and hard.   **213 regard** aspect, sight   **214 radiance** power of vision. (The
emerald helps repair weak vision to those who look at it, just as the
young man refreshes the eyes by his beauty.)   **215–216 blend . . . manifold** blended with many colors (?) or, blended with (or that blends with)
many objects presented to the sight (?)   **217 blazoned** proclaimed,
cataloged (in the accompanying sonnets)

" 'Lo, all these trophies of affections hot,                        218
Of pensived and subdued desires the tender,                        219
Nature hath charged me that I hoard them not,
But yield them up where I myself must render,
That is, to you, my origin and ender;                              222
For these, of force, must your oblations be,                       223
Since, I their altar, you enpatron me.                             224

" 'O, then, advance of yours that phraseless hand,                 225
Whose white weighs down the airy scale of praise!                  226
Take all these similes to your own command,                        227
Hallowed with sighs that burning lungs did raise;                  228
What me, your minister, for you obeys,                             229
Works under you; and to your audit comes                          230
Their distract parcels in combinèd sums.                          231

" 'Lo, this device was sent me from a nun,
Or sister sanctified, of holiest note,                            233
Which late her noble suit in court did shun,                      234
Whose rarest havings made the blossoms dote;                      235
For she was sought by spirits of richest coat,                    236
But kept cold distance, and did thence remove                     237
To spend her living in eternal love.                              238

**218 affections** passions   **219 pensived** saddened.   **tender** offering
**222 ender** end, conclusion. (You are the source of my life and that
without which I cannot live.)   **223 of force** perforce.   **your oblations**
offerings made at the altar of love for you   **224 Since . . . me** since I am
the altar (on which these gifts are offered), and you are my patron saint
(to whom the altar is dedicated)   **225 phraseless** which no words can
describe   **226 weighs . . . praise** i.e., outweighs in the scales any praise
that can be offered to it in airy words   **227 similes** i.e., symbolic
love tokens or gems accompanied by symbolic explanation in the
sonnets   **228 Hallowed** consecrated.   **burning** i.e., hot with passion
**229–230 What . . . you** i.e., whatever obeys me and is at my command
as your minister or agent acting on your authority is thus yours also
**230 audit** accounting   **231 distract** separate   **233 note** reputation
**234 Which . . . shun** i.e., who recently shunned the attendance at court
to which her noble rank entitled her.   **suit in** attendance at   **235 Whose
. . . dote** i.e., whose rare gift of beauty made the young courtiers (in the
blossom of their life) dote on her   **236 spirits** spirited young men.
**coat** coat of arms, i.e., descent   **237 remove** depart   **238 living**
lifetime.   **eternal love** love of the eternal God (i.e., she became a nun)

" 'But, O my sweet, what labor is 't to leave          239
The thing we have not, mast'ring what not strives,          240
Paling the place which did no form receive,          241
Playing patient sports in unconstrainèd gyves?          242
She that her fame so to herself contrives,          243
The scars of battle scapeth by the flight
And makes her absence valiant, not her might.          245

" 'O, pardon me, in that my boast is true!          246
The accident which brought me to her eye
Upon the moment did her force subdue,          248
And now she would the cagèd cloister fly.          249
Religious love put out religion's eye.          250
Not to be tempted, would she be immured,          251
And now to tempt all liberty procured.          252

" 'How mighty then you are, O, hear me tell!
The broken bosoms that to me belong          254
Have emptied all their fountains in my well,          255
And mine I pour your ocean all among.
I strong o'er them, and you o'er me being strong,          257
Must for your victory us all congest,          258
As compound love to physic your cold breast.          259

---

**239–242 what . . . gyves** i.e., how can it be called a difficult thing to give
up something we haven't tried yet, mastering an emotion that offers no
resistance, *paling*, or fencing, in the heart upon which no lover has yet
made any impression, patiently pretending to endure restraints that in
fact impose no restraint and that one is not obliged to endure
**243 fame . . . contrives** devises for herself a reputation (for renouncing
love)   **245 makes . . . might** i.e., shows valor only in avoiding temptation, not in confronting it directly   **246 my boast** i.e., that she could
resist me only by fleeing, not when she saw me   **248 Upon the moment** at once   **249 would . . . fly** wished to flee the locked convent
**250 Religious . . . eye** i.e., love of me put out love of the divine
**251–252 Not . . . procured** before, she wished to be shut up from
temptation, but now she sought liberty to venture everything. (The
quarto reads *enur'd* for *immured*, and perhaps should be *inured*, habit-
uated.)   **254 bosoms** i.e., hearts   **255 well** spring, stream   **257 strong**
victorious   **258 for** because of.   **us all** i.e., my admirers and myself.
**congest** gather together   **259 compound love** i.e., love compounded
of the various loves of myself and my former loves. (*Compound*
also has the suggestion of a drug.)   **physic** cure

" 'My parts had power to charm a sacred nun,                    260
Who, disciplined, ay, dieted in grace,                         261
Believed her eyes when they t' assail begun,                   262
All vows and consecrations giving place.
O most potential love! Vow, bond, nor space,                   264
In thee hath neither sting, knot, nor confine,                 265
For thou art all, and all things else are thine.

" 'When thou impressest, what are precepts worth               267
Of stale example? When thou wilt inflame,                      268
How coldly those impediments stand forth
Of wealth, of filial fear, law, kindred, fame!
Love's arms are peace, 'gainst rule, 'gainst sense,
      'gainst shame,                                           271
And sweetens, in the suffering pangs it bears,                 272
The aloes of all forces, shocks, and fears.                    273

" 'Now all these hearts that do on mine depend,
Feeling it break, with bleeding groans they pine,              275
And, supplicant, their sighs to you extend                     276
To leave the battery that you make 'gainst mine,               277
Lending soft audience to my sweet design,
And credent soul to that strong-bonded oath                    279
That shall prefer and undertake my troth.'                     280

**260 parts** qualities    **261 disciplined** subjected to religious discipline.
**dieted** nourished, controlled    **262 assail** i.e., assail her heart
**264 potential** powerful    **264–265 Vow . . . confine** against you vows have
no strength (*sting*), bonds have no binding force (*knot*), and space is no
barrier or impediment (*confine*)    **267 thou impressest** you make an
impression on a heart, or conscript it into your service    **267–268 what
. . . example** of what worth are moralistic warnings based on stale old
instances    **271 Love's . . . shame** i.e., love's might enforces its own
peace in the teeth of reason, good sense, and decorum    **272 it bears**
that it (love) brings, the pangs that lovers must suffer    **273 aloes** i.e.,
bitterness.    **forces** acts of force.    **shocks** clashes    **275 break** i.e., break
in disappointment at the threat of rejection by the woman now ad-
dressed.    **bleeding groans** (Each groan was thought to cost the heart a
drop of blood.)    **276 supplicant** as suppliants    **277 leave** leave off
**279 credent** believing, trusting    **280 prefer** advance.    **undertake** guar-
antee, see through to the end

"This said, his watery eyes he did dismount,                281
Whose sights till then were leveled on my face;             282
Each cheek a river running from a fount
With brinish current downward flowed apace.
O, how the channel to the stream gave grace!                285
Who glazed with crystal gate the glowing roses             286
That flame through water which their hue encloses.

"O father, what a hell of witchcraft lies                   288
In the small orb of one particular tear!                    289
But with the inundation of the eyes
What rocky heart to water will not wear?
What breast so cold that is not warmèd here?
O cleft effect! Cold modesty, hot wrath,                    293
Both fire from hence and chill extincture hath.            294

"For, lo, his passion, but an art of craft,                 295
Even there resolved my reason into tears;                   296
There my white stole of chastity I daffed,                  297
Shook off my sober guards and civil fears;                  298
Appear to him as he to me appears,                          299
All melting; though our drops this difference bore:        300
His poisoned me, and mine did him restore.

---

**281 dismount** remove from its mount, lower (as with an artillery
piece)  **282 leveled on** aimed at  **285 channel . . . stream** i.e., cheek to
the flow of tears  **286 Who** which, i.e., the stream of tears.  **gate** i.e., a
protective layer  **288 father** i.e., the old man to whom she is talking
**289 particular** single  **293 cleft** twofold.  **wrath** passion (the wrath of
love)  **294 extincture** extinguishing  **295 passion** passionate wooing.
**but an art** merely an artifice  **296 resolved** dissolved  **297 daffed**
doffed, put off  **298 guards** defenses.  **civil** decorous, grave
**299 Appear** I did appear  **300 drops** i.e., tears (which here have medicinal qualities)

"In him a plenitude of subtle matter,                    302
Applied to cautels, all strange forms receives,          303
Of burning blushes, or of weeping water,
Or swooning paleness; and he takes and leaves,           305
In either's aptness, as it best deceives,                306
To blush at speeches rank, to weep at woes,              307
Or to turn white and swoon at tragic shows;

"That not a heart which in his level came                309
Could scape the hail of his all-hurting aim,             310
Showing fair nature is both kind and tame;               311
And, veiled in them, did win whom he would maim.         312
Against the thing he sought he would exclaim;
When he most burnt in heart-wished luxury,               314
He preached pure maid and praised cold chastity.         315

"Thus merely with the garment of a grace                 316
The naked and concealèd fiend he covered,                317
That th' unexperient gave the tempter place,             318
Which like a cherubin above them hovered.                319
Who, young and simple, would not be so lovered?          320
Ay me! I fell, and yet do question make                  321
What I should do again for such a sake.                   322

302 **subtle matter** matter capable of being variously impressed or
formed  303 **cautels** crafty devices  305 **takes and leaves** i.e., uses one
and avoids the other  306 **In either's aptness** whichever is more appro-
priate  307 **rank** gross  309 **That** so that.  **level** range and aim. (Continues the metaphor of siege.)  310 **Could** that could.  **hail** i.e., of
artillery  311 **Showing . . . tame** i.e., his aim being to represent his true
nature as loving and docile  312 **And . . . maim** and, disguised thus in
kindness and docility, or in *blushes, weeping,* and *paleness* (ll. 304–305),
won the heart of the woman he intended to harm  314 **heart-wished
luxury** deeply desired lechery  315 **pure maid** as if he were an un-
touched virgin  316 **with . . . grace** with a charming outward show or
appearance (perhaps suggesting also one of the three Graces)  317 **The
naked . . . covered** he covered his fiendish inner self with concealment
318 **inexperient** inexperienced.  **place** entry  319 **Which . . . hovered**
who, resembling a cherub, hovered over his victims as though offering
them protection  320 **simple** naive.  **be so lovered** surrender to a lover
like him  321 **question make** i.e., ask myself  322 **for such a sake** for
someone like him, or for the sake of falling into such pleasure—however
brief

"O, that infected moisture of his eye, 323
O, that false fire which in his cheek so glowed,
O, that forced thunder from his heart did fly, 325
O, that sad breath his spongy lungs bestowed, 326
O, all that borrowed motion seeming owed, 327
Would yet again betray the fore-betrayed,
And new pervert a reconcilèd maid!" 329

---

**323 infected** infectious **325 forced** feigned. **from** that from
**326 spongy lungs** lungs that are spongelike (as all lungs are; perhaps
with the suggestion of "blown up with flattery and pretended grief")
**327 borrowed . . . owed** pretended action that seemed in earnest. **owed**
owned, his own **329 reconcilèd** penitent

# Date and Text

*A Lover's Complaint* first appeared in Thomas Thorpe's 1609 edition of the sonnets. It may have been printed from the same transcript as that used to print the sonnets. The poem is not mentioned on the title page of the volume, but has its own head-title on sig. K$^v$: "A Louers complaint. By William Shake-speare." For the reliability of this attribution, see the Introduction to *A Lover's Complaint*.

# Textual Notes

These textual notes are not a historical collation; they are simply a record of departures in this edition from the copy text. The reading adopted in this edition appears in boldface, followed by the rejected reading from the copy text, i.e., the quarto of 1609. Only major alterations in punctuation are noted. Corrections of minor and obvious typographical errors are not indicated.

Copy text: the Sonnet quarto of 1609 [Q].

**7 sorrow's** sorrowes,   **14 lattice** lettice   **37 beaded** bedded   **51 'gan** gaue
**95 wear** were   **103 breathe** breath   **112 manage** mannad'g   **118 Came** Can
**164 forbade** forbod   **182 woo** vovv   **198 pallid** palyd   **204 hair**
heir   **205 metal** mettle   **228 Hallowed** Hollowed   **251 immured** enur'd
**252 procured** procure   **260 nun** Sunne   **293 O** Or   **303 strange** straing

# SONNETS

# Introduction

Shakespeare seems to have cared more about his reputation as a lyric poet than as a dramatist. He contributed to the major nondramatic genres of his day: to amatory Ovidian narrative in *Venus and Adonis*, to the Complaint in *The Rape of Lucrece*, to philosophical poetry in "The Phoenix and Turtle." He cooperated in the publication of his first two important poems, dedicating them to the young Earl of Southampton with a plea to him for sponsorship. To write poetry in this vein was more fashionable than to write plays, which one did mainly for money.

A poet with ambitions of this sort simply had to write a sonnet sequence. Sonneteering was the rage in England in the early and mid 1590s. Based on the sonneteering tradition of Francesco Petrarch, Sir Thomas Wyatt, and others, and gaining new momentum in 1591 with the publication of Sir Philip Sidney's *Astrophel and Stella*, the vogue ended almost as suddenly as it began, in 1596 or 1597. The sonnet sequences of this brief period bear the names of most well-known and minor poets of the day: *Amoretti* by Edmund Spenser (1595), *Delia* by Samuel Daniel (1591 and 1592), *Caelica* by Fulke Greville (not published until 1633), *Idea's Mirror* by Michael Drayton (1594), *Diana* by Henry Constable (1592), *Phyllis* by Thomas Lodge (1593), and the more imitative sequences of Barnabe Barnes, Giles Fletcher, William Percy, Bartholomew Griffin, William Smith, and Robert Tofte.

Shakespeare wrote sonnets during the heyday of the genre, for in 1598 Francis Meres, in his *Palladis Tamia: Wit's Treasury*, praised Shakespeare's "sugared sonnets among his private friends." Even though they were not printed at the time, we know from Meres's remark that they were circulated in manuscript among the cognoscenti and commanded respect. Shakespeare may actually have preferred to delay the publication of his sonnets, not through indifference to their literary worth but through a desire not to seem too professional. The "courtly makers" of the English Renaissance, those gentlemen whose chivalric accomplishments were supposed to include versifying, looked on

the writing of poetry as an avocation designed to amuse
one's peers or to court a lady. Publication was not quite
genteel, and many such authors affected dismay when their
verses were pirated into print. The young wits about London of the 1590s, whether aristocratic or not, sometimes
imitated this fashion. Like young John Donne, they sought
the favorable verdict of their fellow wits at the Inns of Court
(where young men studied law) and professed not to care
about wider recognition. Whether Shakespeare was motivated in this way we do not know, but in any event his much-
sought-after sonnet sequence was not published until 1609,
long after the vogue had passed. The publisher, Thomas
Thorpe, seems not to have obtained Shakespeare's authorization. Two sonnets, numbers 138 and 144, had been pirated
ten years earlier by William Jaggard in *The Passionate Pilgrim*, 1599, a little anthology with some poems by Shakespeare and some wrongly attributed to him. The sonnets
were not reprinted until 1640, either because the sonnet
vogue had passed or because Thorpe's edition had been
suppressed.

The unexplained circumstances of publication have given
rise to a host of vexing and apparently unanswerable questions. Probably no puzzle in all English literature has provoked so much speculation and produced so little
agreement. To whom are the sonnets addressed? Do they
tell a consistent story, and if so do they tell us anything
about Shakespeare's life? The basic difficulty is that we
cannot be sure that the order in which Thorpe published
the sonnets represents Shakespeare's intention, nor can we
assume that Thorpe spoke for Shakespeare when he dedicated the sonnets to "Mr. W. H." As they stand, most of the
first 126 sonnets appear to be addressed in warm friendship to a handsome young aristocrat, whereas sonnets
127–152 speak of the poet's dark-haired mistress. Yet the
last two sonnets, 153–154, seem unrelated to anything previous, and cast some doubt on the reliability of the ordering. Within each large grouping of the sonnets, moreover,
we find evident inconsistencies: jealousies disappear and
suddenly reappear, the poet bewails his absolute rejection
by the friend and then speaks a few sonnets later of harmo-
nious affection as though nothing had happened, and so on.
Some sonnets are closely linked to their predecessors,

some are apparently disconnected (although even here we must allow for the real possibility that Shakespeare intends juxtaposition and contrast). We cannot be sure if the friend of sonnets 1–126 is really one person or several. We can only speculate that the unhappy love triangle described in 40–42, in which the friend has usurped the poet's mistress, can be identified with the love triangle of the "Dark Lady" sonnets, 127–152. Most readers sense a narrative continuity of the whole, yet find blocks of sonnets stubbornly out of place. The temptation to rearrange the order has proved irresistible, but no alternative order has ever won acceptance. The consensus is that Thorpe's order is at times suspect, but may have more rationale than at first appears. It is, in any case, the only authoritative order we have.

No less frustrating is Thorpe's dedication "To the Only Begetter of These Ensuing Sonnets, Mr. W. H." Given the late and unauthorized publication, we cannot assume that Thorpe speaks for Shakespeare. Quite possibly he is only thanking the person who obtained the sonnets for him, making publication possible. Mundanely enough, Mr. W. H. could be William Hall, an associate of Thorpe's in the publishing business. Yet Elizabethan usage affords few instances of "begetter" in this sense of "obtainer." Recently, Donald Foster has offered new and persuasive arguments for the idea that "Mr. W. H." is only a typographical error of a common sort, and that Thorpe meant to say "Mr. W. S.," Master William Shakespeare. In this case, "begetter" would mean simply "creator." This solution has a wonderful neatness about it, but other readers have wondered if it answers the seeming contradiction that Thorpe speaks of "Mr. W. H." and "our ever-living poet" in the dedication as though they are two people. Thorpe offers to Mr. W. H. "that eternity promised by our ever-living poet," as though Mr. W. H. were the very subject of those sonnets whom Shakespeare vows to immortalize.

This interpretation of "begetter" as "inspirer" has prompted many enthusiasts to search for a Mr. W. H. in Shakespeare's life, a nobleman who befriended him. The chief candidates are two. First is the young Earl of Southampton, to whom Shakespeare had dedicated *Venus and Adonis* and *The Rape of Lucrece*. The dedication to the second of these poems bespeaks a warmth and gratitude that had been lacking in the first. The Earl's name, Henry Wriothesley, yields initials that are the reverse of W. H. If this correspondence seems unconvincing, W. H. could stand for Sir William Harvey, third husband of Mary, Lady Southampton, the young Earl's mother. Some researchers would have us believe that Shakespeare wrote the sonnets for Lady Southampton, especially those urging a young man (her son) to marry and procreate. This entire case is speculative, however, and we have no evidence that Shakespeare had any dealings whatever with Southampton after *The Rape of Lucrece*. The plain ascription "Mr. W. H." seems an oddly uncivil way for Thorpe to have addressed an earl. If meant for Southampton, the sonnets must have been written fairly early in the 1590s, for they give no hint of Southampton's later career: his courtship of Elizabeth Vernon, her pregnancy and their secret marriage in 1598, his later involvement in Essex's Irish campaign and abortive uprising against Queen Elizabeth. Those literary sleuths who stress similarities to the Southampton relationship are too willing to overlook dissimilarities.

The second chief candidate for Mr. W. H. is William Herbert, third Earl of Pembroke, to whom, along with his brother, Shakespeare's colleagues dedicated the First Folio of 1623. In 1595 Pembroke's parents were attempting to arrange his marriage with Lady Elizabeth Carey, granddaughter of the first Lord Hunsdon, who was Lord Chamberlain and patron of Shakespeare's company. In 1597 another alliance was attempted with Bridget Vere, granddaughter of Lord Burghley. In both negotiations, young Pembroke objected to the girl in question. This hypothesis requires, however, an uncomfortably late date for the sonnets, and postulates a gap in age between Shakespeare and Pembroke that would have afforded little opportunity for genuine friendship. Pembroke was only fifteen in 1595, Shakespeare thirty-one. Besides, no evidence whatever supports the claim other than historical coincidence. The common initials W. H. can be made to produce other candidates as well, such as the Lincolnshire lawyer named William Hatcliffe proposed (to no one's satisfaction) by Leslie Hotson. Hotson wants to date most of the sonnets before 1589, since Hatcliffe came to London in 1587–1588. When such speculations are constructed on the single enigmatic testimonial of the dedication by Thomas Thorpe, who may well have had no connection with Shakespeare, we are left with a case that would not be worth describing had it not captured the imagination of so many researchers.

Biographical identifications have also been proposed for the various personages in the sonnet sequence, predictably with no better success. The rival poet, with "the proud full sail of his great verse" (86), has been linked to Christopher Marlowe (who died in 1593), George Chapman, and others. The sequence gives us little to go on, other than that the rival poet possesses a considerable enough talent to intimidate the author of the sonnets and ingratiate himself with the author's aristocratic friend. No biographical circumstances even distantly resembling this rivalry have come to light. Various candidates have also been found for the "Dark Lady." One is Mary Fitton, a lady-in-waiting at court who bore a child by Pembroke in 1601. Again, we have no evidence that Shakespeare knew her, nor is he likely to have carried on an affair with one of such high rank. A. L. Rowse has proposed Emilia Lanier, wife of Alfonso Lanier and daughter of a court musician named Bassano, a woman of suitably dark complexion perhaps but whose presumed connection with Shakespeare rests only on the reported rumor that she was a mistress of Lord Hunsdon. We are left finally without knowing who any of these people were, or whether indeed Shakespeare was attempting to be biographical at all.

The same irresolution afflicts the dating of the sonnets. Do they give hints of a personal chronicle extending over some years, following Thorpe's arrangement of the sonnets or some alternative order? Sonnet 104 speaks of three years having elapsed since the poet met his friend. Are there other signposts that relate to contemporary events? A line in Sonnet 107 ("The mortal moon hath her eclipse endured") is usually linked to the death of Queen Elizabeth (known as Diana or Cynthia) in 1603, though Leslie Hotson prefers to see in it an allusion to the Spanish Armada, shaped for sea battle in a moonlike crescent when it met defeat in 1588. The newly built pyramids in Sonnet 123 remind Hotson of the obelisks built by Pope Sixtus V in Rome, 1586–1589; other researchers have discovered pyramids erected on London's streets in 1603 to celebrate the

coronation of James I. As these illustrations suggest, speculative dating can be used to support a hypothesis of early or
late composition. The wary consensus of most scholars is
that the sonnets were written over a number of years, a
large number certainly before 1598 but some perhaps later
and even up to the date of publication in 1609.

However fruitless this quest for nonexistent certainties,
it does at least direct us to a meaningful critical question:
should we expect sonnets of this "personal" nature to be at
least partly autobiographical? Shakespeare's sonnets have
struck many readers as cries from the heart, voicing at
times fears of rejection, self-hatred, humiliation, and at
other times a serene gratitude for reciprocated affection.
This power of expression may, however, be a tribute to
Shakespeare's dramatic gift rather than evidence of personal involvement. Earlier sonnet sequences, both Elizabethan and pre-Elizabethan, had established a variety of
artistic conventions that tended to displace biography. Petrarch's famous *Rime*, or sonnets, later collected in his
*Canzoniere*, though addressed to Laura in two sequences
(during her life and after her death), idealized her into the
unapproachable lady worshiped by the self-abasing and
miserable lover. Petrarch's imitators—Serafino Aquilano,
Pietro Bembo, Ludovico Ariosto, and Torquato Tasso
among the Italians, Clement Marot, Joachim du Bellay,
Pierre de Ronsard, and Philippe Desportes among the
French Pléiade—reworked these conventions in countless
variations. In England the fashion was taken up by Sir
Thomas Wyatt, the Earl of Surrey, George Gascoigne,
Thomas Watson, and others. Spenser's *Amoretti* and Sidney's *Astrophel and Stella*, though inspired at least in part
by real women in the poets' lives, are also deeply concerned
with theories of writing poetry. Rejection of the stereo-
typed attitudes and relationships that had come to domi-
nate the typical Petrarchan sonnet sequence is evidence not
of biographical literalism in art but of a new insistence on
lifelike emotion in art; as Sidney's muse urges him, "look in
thy heart and write." Thus, both the Petrarchan and the
anti-Petrarchan schools avoid biographical writing for its
own sake. This is essentially true of all Elizabethan sonneteering, from Drayton's serious pursuit of Platonic abstrac-

tion in his *Idea's Mirror* to the facile chorusing of lesser sonnet writers about Diana, Phyllis, Zepheria, or Fidessa.

The "story" connecting the individual poems of an Elizabethan sonnet sequence is never very important or consistent, even when we can be sure of the order in which the sonnets were written. Dante had used prose links in his *La Vita Nuova* (c. 1282) to stress narrative continuity, and so had Petrarch, but this sturdy framework had been abandoned by the late sixteenth century. Rather than telling a chronological story, the typical Elizabethan sonnet sequence offers a thematically connected series of lyrical meditations, chiefly on love but also on poetic theory, the adversities of fortune, death, or what have you. The narrative events mentioned from time to time are not the substance of the sequence but the mere occasion for meditative reflection. Attitudes need not be consistent throughout, and the characters need not be consistently motivated like dramatis personae in a play.

Shakespeare's sonnet sequence retains these conventions of Elizabethan sonneteering and employs many archetypal situations and themes that had been explored by his predecessors and contemporaries. His emphasis on friendship seems new, for no other sequence addressed a majority of its sonnets to a friend rather than to a mistress, but even here the anti-Petrarchan quest for spontaneity and candor is in the best Elizabethan tradition of Sidney and Spenser. Besides, the exaltation of friendship over love was itself a widespread Neoplatonic commonplace recently popularized in the writings of John Lyly. Shakespeare's sequence makes use of the structural design found in contemporary models. Even though we cannot reconstruct a rigorously consistent chronological narrative from the sonnets, we can discern overall patterns out of which the poet's emotional crises arise and upon which he constructs his meditative lyrics. Certain groupings, such as the sonnets addressed to the "Dark Lady," 127–152, achieve a plausible cohesion in which the individual sonnets comment on one another through reinforcement or antithetical design and are thus enhanced by their context; a case can be made, in other words, for the order of the poems as Thorpe printed them. Even the last two sonnets, 153 and 154, have their defenders (see Michael J. B. Allen's essay in *Shakespeare Survey*,

1978). Juxtaposition is a favorite technique in Shakespeare's plays, and we must remember that he alone among
the major Elizabethan sonneteers wrote for the stage.

Taking note of such considerations, we can account for
most of the situations portrayed in Shakespeare's sonnets
by postulating four figures: the poet-speaker himself, his
friend, his mistress, and a rival poet. The order of events in
this tangled relationship is not what the poet wishes to describe; instead, he touches upon this situation from time to
time as he explores his own reaction to love in its various
aspects.

The poet's relationship to his friend is a vulnerable one.
This friend to whom he writes is aristocratic, handsome,
younger than he is. The poet is beholden to this friend as a
sponsor and must consider himself as subservient no matter how deep their mutual affection. Even at its happiest,
their relationship is hierarchical. The poet abases himself
in order to extol his friend's beauty and virtues (52–54,
105–106). He confesses that his love would be idolatry, except that the friend's goodness excels all poetic hyperbole.
As the older of the two, the poet sententiously urges his
young friend to marry and eternize his beauty through the
engendering of children (1–17). Such a course, he argues, is
the surest way to conquer devouring Time, the enemy of all
earthly beauty and love. Yet elsewhere the poet exalts his
own art as the surest defense against Time (55, 60, 63–65,
etc.). These conclusions are nominally contradictory, offering procreation in one instance and poetry in another as the
best hope for immortality, but thematically the two are obviously related. In even the happiest of the sonnets, such as
those giving thanks for "the marriage of true minds" (116,
123), the consciousness of devouring Time is inescapable. If
love and celebratory poetry can sometimes triumph over
Time, the victory is all the more precious because it is
achieved in the face of such odds.

Love and perfect friendship are a refuge for the poet
faced with hostile fortune and an indifferent world. He is
too often "in disgrace with fortune and men's eyes" (29),
oppressed by his own failings, saddened by the facile success of opportunists (66–68), ashamed of having sold himself cheap in his own profession (110–111). If taken

biographically, this could mean that Shakespeare was not happy about his career as actor and playwright, but the motif makes complete sense in the sonnet sequence without resort to biography. A biographical reading also raises the question of homosexual attraction, as urged recently anew by Joseph Pequigney in his *Such Is My Love* (University of Chicago Press, 1985). The bawdy reference in Sonnet 20.12 to the friend's possession of "one thing to my purpose nothing" would seem to militate against the idea of a consummated homosexual relationship, while conversely many sonnets (such as 138) do point to the poet's consummation with his mistress. Still, the bond between poet and friend is extraordinarily strong. The poet is pathetically dependent on his friend. Occasional absences torture him with the physical separation, even though he realizes that pure love of the spirit ought not to be hampered by distance or time (43–51). The absence is especially painful when the poet must confess his own disloyalty (117–118). The chronology of these absences cannot be worked out satisfactorily, but the haunting theme of separation is incessant, overwhelming. By extension it includes the fear of separation through death (71–73, 126). The concern with absence is closely related to the poet's obsession with devouring Time.

All the poet's misfortunes would be bearable if love were constant, but his dependency on the aristocratic friend leaves him at the mercy of that friend's changeable mood. The poet must not complain when his well-born friend entertains a rival poet (78–86) or forms other emotional attachments, even with the poet's own mistress (40–42). These disloyalties evoke outbursts of jealousy. The poet vacillates between forgiveness and recrimination. Sometimes even his forgiveness is self-loathing, in which the poet confesses he would take back the friend on any terms (93–95). At times the poet grovels, conceding that he deserves no better treatment (57–58), but at other times his stored-up resentment bursts forth (93–95). The poet's fears, though presented in no clear chronological order, run the gamut from a fatalistic sense that rejection will come one day (49) to an abject and bitter final farewell (87). Sometimes he is tormented by jealousy (61), sometimes by self-hate (88–89).

The sonnets addressed to the poet's mistress, the "Dark Lady," similarly convey fear, self-abasement, and a panicky

awareness of loss of self-control. In rare moments of happiness, the poet praises her dark features as proof of her being a real woman, not a Petrarchan goddess (130). Too often,
however, her lack of ideal beauty reminds the poet of his
irrational enchantment (148–150). She is tyrannous, disdainful, spiteful, disloyal, a "female evil" (144) who has
tempted away from the poet his better self, his friend. The
poet is distressed not so much by her perfidy as by his own
self-betrayal; he sees bitterly that he offends his nobler reason by his attachment to the rebellious flesh. He worships
what others abhor, and perjures himself by swearing to
what he knows to be false (150–152). His only hope for escape is to punish his flesh and renounce the vanity of all
worldly striving (146), but this solution evades him as he
plunges helplessly back into the perverse enslavement of a
sickened appetite.

   This sketch of only some themes of the sequence may suggest the range and yet the interconnection of Shakespeare's
meditations on love, friendship, and poetry. Patterns are
visible, even if the exact chronology (never important in the
Elizabethan sonnet sequence) cannot be determined. This
patterning is equally evident in matters of versification and
imagery. The sonnets are written throughout in the "Shake-
spearean" or English form, *abab cdcd efef gg.* (Number 126,
written entirely in couplets, is an exception, perhaps because it was intended as the envoy to the series addressed to
the poet's friend.) This familiar sonnet form, introduced by
Wyatt and developed by Sidney, differs markedly from the
octave-sestet division of the Petrarchan, or Italian, sonnet.
The English form of three quatrains and a concluding couplet lends itself to a step-by-step development of idea and
image, culminating in an epigrammatic two-line conclusion
that may summarize the thought of the preceding twelve
lines or give a sententious interpretation of the images developed up to this point. Sonnet 7 pursues the image of the
sun at morning, noon, and evening through three quatrains,
one for each phase of the day, and then in the couplet "applies" the image to the friend's unwillingness to beget children. Sonnet 29 moves from resentment of misfortune to a
rejoicing in the friend's love, and rhetorically mirrors this
sudden elevation of mood in the image of the lark "at break
of day arising / From sullen earth." Shakespeare's rhetori-

cal and imagistic devices exploit the sonnet structure he inherited and perfected, and remind us again of the strong element of convention and artifice in these supremely "personal" sonnets. The recurring images—the canker on the rose, the pleading of a case at law, the seasonal rhythms of summer and winter, the alternations of day and night, the harmonies and dissonances of music—also testify to the artistic unity of the whole and to the artist's extraordinary discipline in evoking a sense of helpless loss of self-control.

# Sonnets

## 1

From fairest creatures we desire increase,
That thereby beauty's rose might never die,
But as the riper should by time decease,
His tender heir might bear his memory;                    4
But thou, contracted to thine own bright eyes,
Feed'st thy light's flame with self-substantial fuel,
Making a famine where abundance lies,
Thyself thy foe, to thy sweet self too cruel.            8
Thou that art now the world's fresh ornament
And only herald to the gaudy spring,
Within thine own bud buriest thy content,
And, tender churl, mak'st waste in niggarding.          12
    Pity the world, or else this glutton be,
    To eat the world's due, by the grave and thee.

1 • 1 **increase** procreation  **3 as** just as, while  **4 bear his memory** i.e.,
immortalize him by bearing his features  **5 contracted** engaged, es-
poused  **6 self-substantial** of your own substance  **10 only** unique.
**herald to** messenger of  **11 thy content** (1) that which is contained in
you; potential fatherhood (2) contentment  **12 mak'st . . . niggarding**
squander your substance by being miserly. (An oxymoron, like *tender
churl*, youthful old miser.)  **14 the world's due** i.e., the offspring you
owe to posterity.  **by . . . thee** (consumed) by death and by your willfully
remaining childless

## 2

When forty winters shall besiege thy brow
And dig deep trenches in thy beauty's field,
Thy youth's proud livery, so gazed on now,
Will be a tattered weed, of small worth held.     4
Then being asked where all thy beauty lies,
Where all the treasure of thy lusty days,
To say within thine own deep-sunken eyes
Were an all-eating shame and thriftless praise.     8
How much more praise deserved thy beauty's use
If thou couldst answer, "This fair child of mine
Shall sum my count and make my old excuse,"
Proving his beauty by succession thine.     12
   This were to be new made when thou art old,
   And see thy blood warm when thou feel'st it cold.

**2·2 trenches** i.e., wrinkles.   **field** (1) meadow (2) battlefield (3) heraldic background   **4 weed** garment (with a play on a *weed* growing in *beauty's field*, l. 2)   **6 lusty** (1) vigorous (2) lustful   **7 deep-sunken** i.e., with age   **8 all-eating shame** shameful gluttony, and one that would consume you with shame.   **thriftless praise** (1) praise of extravagance (2) idle praise   **9 deserved . . . use** would the proper investment and employment of your beauty deserve   **11 sum . . . excuse** even my account and make amends (for growing old, or for consuming beauty during my life) in my old age   **12 thine** i.e., derived from you   **13 were** would be

# 3

Look in thy glass, and tell the face thou viewest
Now is the time that face should form another,
Whose fresh repair if now thou not renewest
Thou dost beguile the world, unbless some mother.          4
For where is she so fair whose uneared womb
Disdains the tillage of thy husbandry?
Or who is he so fond will be the tomb
Of his self-love, to stop posterity?                          8
Thou art thy mother's glass, and she in thee
Calls back the lovely April of her prime;
So thou through windows of thine age shalt see,
Despite of wrinkles, this thy golden time.                   12
   But if thou live remembered not to be,
    Die single, and thine image dies with thee.

---

**3 · 1 glass** mirror   **3 fresh repair** youthful condition   **4 beguile** cheat.
**unbless some mother** withhold the happiness of childbearing from
some woman   **5 uneared** untilled, uncultivated   **6 husbandry** cultiva-
tion (with obvious suggestion of "playing the husband")   **7 fond** foolish.   **will be** i.e., that he will be   **9 thy mother's glass** the image of your
mother   **11 windows of thine age** i.e., eyes dimmed by advancing
years   **13 remembered not to be** in such a way as not to be remembered, without children

# 4

Unthrifty loveliness, why dost thou spend
Upon thyself thy beauty's legacy?
Nature's bequest gives nothing, but doth lend,
And being frank she lends to those are free.                    4
Then, beauteous niggard, why dost thou abuse
The bounteous largess given thee to give?
Profitless usurer, why dost thou use
So great a sum of sums, yet canst not live?                     8
For having traffic with thyself alone,
Thou of thyself thy sweet self dost deceive.
Then how, when Nature calls thee to be gone,
What acceptable audit canst thou leave?                         12
   Thy unused beauty must be tombed with thee,
   Which, usèd, lives th' executor to be.

---

**4 · 1 Unthrifty** (1) prodigal (2) unavailing  **4 frank** liberal, bounteous.
**are free** who are generous  **7 use** (1) use up (2) fail to invest for profit.
(See Sonnet 6.5 and note.)  **8 live** (1) have a livelihood (2) live in your
posterity  **9 traffic** commerce. (The commercial and financial metaphor
hints at sexual self-fascination.)  **10 deceive** cheat  **13 unused**
(1) unemployed (2) not invested for profit  **14 lives** would live (in your
son)

# 5

Those hours, that with gentle work did frame
The lovely gaze where every eye doth dwell,
Will play the tyrants to the very same
And that unfair which fairly doth excel;                                    4
For never-resting Time leads summer on
To hideous winter and confounds him there,
Sap checked with frost and lusty leaves quite gone,
Beauty o'ersnowed and bareness everywhere.                                  8
Then, were not summer's distillation left
A liquid prisoner pent in walls of glass,
Beauty's effect with beauty were bereft,
Nor it nor no remembrance what it was.                                      12
　　But flowers distilled, though they with winter meet,
　　Leese but their show; their substance still lives
　　　sweet.

**5 • 1 frame** make　**2 gaze** object of gazes　**3 play . . . to** oppress
**4 unfair** make unlovely.　**fairly** (1) in beauty (2) truly, honestly
**6 confounds** destroys　**7 lusty** vigorous　**9 summer's distillation** distilled perfume of flowers　**10 walls of glass** glass containers　**11 with
. . . bereft** would be lost along with beauty itself　**12 Nor it nor no**
(leaving behind) neither it (beauty) nor any　**14 Leese** lose.　**still**
(1) notwithstanding (2) always

# 6

Then let not winter's ragged hand deface
In thee thy summer ere thou be distilled.
Make sweet some vial; treasure thou some place
With beauty's treasure ere it be self-killed.                              4
That use is not forbidden usury
Which happies those that pay the willing loan;
That's for thyself to breed another thee,
Or ten times happier, be it ten for one.                                  8
Ten times thyself were happier than thou art,
If ten of thine ten times refigured thee;
Then what could death do, if thou shouldst depart,
Leaving thee living in posterity?                                        12
    Be not self-willed, for thou art much too fair
      To be death's conquest and make worms thine heir.

---

**6·1 ragged** rough   **3 vial** (with suggestion of a womb).   **treasure** enrich   **5 use** lending money at interest   **6 happies** makes happy.   **pay
. . . loan** willingly borrow on these terms and repay the loan   **7 That's
. . . thee** i.e., such would be the case if you were to sire a child like
you   **8 Or . . . one** i.e., or indeed the happy mother (of l. 6) would be ten
times happier were she to bear you ten children instead of one. (*Ten for
one* alludes to the highest legal rate of interest, one for ten.)   **9 Ten . . .
art** i.e., ten children of yours would be a tenfold blessing and would
make you happier   **10 refigured** duplicated, copied   **13 self-willed**
(1) obstinate (2) bequeathed to self

# 7

Lo, in the orient when the gracious light
Lifts up his burning head, each under eye
Doth homage to his new-appearing sight,
Serving with looks his sacred majesty;                       4
And having climbed the steep-up heavenly hill,
Resembling strong youth in his middle age,
Yet mortal looks adore his beauty still,
Attending on his golden pilgrimage;                          8
But when from highmost pitch, with weary car,
Like feeble age, he reeleth from the day,
The eyes, 'fore duteous, now converted are
From his low tract and look another way.                     12
    So thou, thyself outgoing in thy noon,
    Unlooked on diest, unless thou get a son.

1 orient east.   light i.e., sun   2 under earthly   9 pitch highest point
s of a falcon's flight before it attacks).   car chariot (of the sun god)
4 converted turned away   12 tract course   14 get beget

# 8

Music to hear, why hear'st thou music sadly?
Sweets with sweets war not, joy delights in joy.
Why lov'st thou that which thou receiv'st not gladly,
Or else receiv'st with pleasure thine annoy?           4
If the true concord of well-tunèd sounds,
By unions married, do offend thine ear,
They do but sweetly chide thee, who confounds
In singleness the parts that thou shouldst bear.        8
Mark how one string, sweet husband to another,
Strikes each in each by mutual ordering,
Resembling sire and child and happy mother
Who, all in one, one pleasing note do sing;             12
    Whose speechless song, being many, seeming one,
    Sings this to thee: "Thou single wilt prove none."

8 • 1 **Music to hear** i.e., you whom it is music to hear.  **sadly** gravely;
without joy  **4 thine annoy** what annoys you  **6 married** i.e., harmo-
nized  **7–8 who . . . bear** you who destroy, by playing a single part only,
the harmony (i.e., marriage) that you should sustain  **9 sweet husband**
i.e., paired, as on the double strings of the lute, one string vibrating
sympathetically to the other  **10 each in each** i.e., with double reso-
nance, sounding mutually  **13 Whose** i.e., the strings'.  **being . . . one**
i.e., making harmony out of several voices  **14 Thou . . . none** (Alludes
to the proverb, "One is no number." The single person who dies without posterity leaves nothing of himself behind.)

# 9

Is it for fear to wet a widow's eye
That thou consum'st thyself in single life?
Ah, if thou issueless shalt hap to die,
The world will wail thee like a makeless wife;                    4
The world will be thy widow and still weep
That thou no form of thee hast left behind,
When every private widow well may keep,
By children's eyes, her husband's shape in mind.                 8
Look what an unthrift in the world doth spend
Shifts but his place, for still the world enjoys it;
But beauty's waste hath in the world an end,
And, kept unused, the user so destroys it.                        12
   No love toward others in that bosom sits
    That on himself such murd'rous shame commits.

---

**9 • 3 issueless** without offspring   **4 makeless** mateless, i.e., widowed
**5 still** constantly, always   **7 private** individual, as distinguished from
the whole world   **8 By** by means of   **9 Look what** whatever.   **unthrift**
spendthrift   **10 his** its.   **enjoys** uses, keeps in circulation   **12 user** i.e.,
he who should use it (with a suggestion of a *usurer* who is miserly)

## 10

For shame, deny that thou bear'st love to any,
Who for thyself art so unprovident!
Grant, if thou wilt, thou art beloved of many,
But that thou none lov'st is most evident;                        4
For thou art so possessed with murd'rous hate
That 'gainst thyself thou stick'st not to conspire,
Seeking that beauteous roof to ruinate
Which to repair should be thy chief desire.                       8
O, change thy thought, that I may change my mind!
Shall hate be fairer lodged than gentle love?
Be, as thy presence is, gracious and kind,
Or to thyself at least kindhearted prove:                        12
   Make thee another self, for love of me,
   That beauty still may live in thine or thee.

---

**10•6 thou stick'st** you scruple  **9 thought** intention.  **change my mind**
no longer believe as I have until now  **11 presence** appearance, bearing

# 11

As fast as thou shalt wane, so fast thou grow'st
In one of thine from that which thou departest;
And that fresh blood which youngly thou bestow'st
Thou mayst call thine when thou from youth
    convertest.                                      4
Herein lives wisdom, beauty, and increase;
Without this, folly, age, and cold decay.
If all were minded so, the times should cease
And threescore year would make the world away.      8
Let those whom Nature hath not made for store,
Harsh, featureless, and rude, barrenly perish;
Look whom she best endowed she gave the more,
Which bounteous gift thou shouldst in bounty cherish.   12
   She carved thee for her seal, and meant thereby
   Thou shouldst print more, not let that copy die.

---

**11 · 1–2 thou grow'st . . . departest** i.e., you become, through a child of
your own, what you cease to be in yourself   **3 youngly** in youth   **4 thou
. . . convertest** you change from youth (to old age)   **7 minded so** sharing
your intention (to have no children).   **times** succeeding generations
**8 year** years   **9 for store** as a source of supply   **10 Harsh** hard-
favored.   **featureless** having no attractive features or appearance.   **rude**
rudely fashioned   **11 Look whom** whomever   **13 seal** stamp from
which impressions are made

# 12

When I do count the clock that tells the time,
And see the brave day sunk in hideous night;
When I behold the violet past prime,
And sable curls all silvered o'er with white;                4
When lofty trees I see barren of leaves
Which erst from heat did canopy the herd,
And summer's green, all girded up in sheaves,
Borne on the bier with white and bristly beard,             8
Then of thy beauty do I question make
That thou among the wastes of time must go,
Since sweets and beauties do themselves forsake
And die as fast as they see others grow;                    12
    And nothing 'gainst Time's scythe can make defense
    Save breed, to brave him when he takes thee hence.

**12 · 1 tells** (1) announces (2) counts   **2 brave** splendid   **4 sable** black
**6 erst** formerly   **7 girded** bundled   **8 bier** i.e., harvest cart (but with
suggestion of funeral bier).   **beard** i.e., the tufted grain (but suggesting
also a dead man laid out for burial)   **9 do ... make** I discuss with
myself   **14 breed** offspring.   **brave him** defy Time

# 13

O, that you were yourself! But, love, you are
No longer yours than you yourself here live.
Against this coming end you should prepare,
And your sweet semblance to some other give.                4
So should that beauty which you hold in lease
Find no determination; then you were
Yourself again after yourself's decease,
When your sweet issue your sweet form should bear.          8
Who lets so fair a house fall to decay,
Which husbandry in honor might uphold
Against the stormy gusts of winter's day
And barren rage of death's eternal cold?                    12
   O, none but unthrifts! Dear my love, you know
   You had a father; let your son say so.

---

13 • 1 **yourself** i.e., your eternal self, not vulnerable to Time's decay
2 **here** i.e., here on earth   3 **Against** in anticipation of   6 **determination**
end   10 **husbandry** careful management (with a pun on "being a husband")

## 14

Not from the stars do I my judgment pluck,
And yet methinks I have astronomy,
But not to tell of good or evil luck,
Of plagues, of dearths, or seasons' quality;        4
Nor can I fortune to brief minutes tell,
'Pointing to each his thunder, rain, and wind,
Or say with princes if it shall go well
By oft predict that I in heaven find.        8
But from thine eyes my knowledge I derive,
And, constant stars, in them I read such art
As truth and beauty shall together thrive
If from thyself to store thou wouldst convert.      12
    Or else of thee this I prognosticate:
    Thy end is truth's and beauty's doom and date.

14 · 1 **judgment pluck** derive conclusions   2 **have astronomy** am skilled in astrology   4 **seasons' quality** i.e., what the weather of the seasons will be like   5 **fortune . . . tell** i.e., foretell events to the precise minute   6 **'Pointing** appointing, assigning.  **each** each minute.  **his** its   7 **Or . . . well** or say if things will go well for certain rulers   8 **oft predict** frequent predictions   10–11 **read . . . As** gather such learning as, in effect, that   12 **store** replenishment (through the begetting of children).  **convert** turn   14 **doom and date** limit of duration, destruction

# 15

When I consider every thing that grows
Holds in perfection but a little moment,
That this huge stage presenteth naught but shows
Whereon the stars in secret influence comment;                    4
When I perceive that men as plants increase,
Cheerèd and checked even by the selfsame sky,
Vaunt in their youthful sap, at height decrease,
And wear their brave state out of memory;                         8
Then the conceit of this inconstant stay
Sets you most rich in youth before my sight,
Where wasteful Time debateth with Decay
To change your day of youth to sullied night;                    12
   And all in war with Time for love of you,
   As he takes from you I engraft you new.

15·2 **Holds in perfection** maintains its prime  **3 stage** i.e., the world
**6 Cheerèd and checked** (1) urged on, nourished, and held back, starved
(2) applauded and hissed  **7 Vaunt** boast, exult.  **sap** vigor.  **at height
decrease** i.e., no sooner reach full maturity but they (humans) start to
decline  **8 brave** splendid.  **out of memory** i.e., until forgotten
**9 conceit** notion.  **inconstant stay** mutable duration  **11 wasteful . . .
Decay** i.e., Time and Decay contend to see who can ruin you fastest, or
join forces to do so, debating between them the best procedure  **13 all
in war** I, fighting with might and main  **14 engraft you new** renew you
by grafting, infusing new life into you (by means of my verse)

# 16

But wherefore do not you a mightier way
Make war upon this bloody tyrant, Time,
And fortify yourself in your decay
With means more blessèd than my barren rhyme?        4
Now stand you on the top of happy hours,
And many maiden gardens yet unset
With virtuous wish would bear your living flowers,
Much liker than your painted counterfeit.           8
So should the lines of life that life repair
Which this time's pencil, or my pupil pen,
Neither in inward worth nor outward fair
Can make you live yourself in eyes of men.          12
   To give away yourself keeps yourself still,
   And you must live, drawn by your own sweet skill.

**16 · 4 barren** (1) unable to produce offspring (2) poetically sterile
**6 unset** (1) unplanted (2) unimpregnated   **7 virtuous wish** desire that is
still chaste   **8 liker** more resembling you.   **painted** rendered by art
(including poetry), artificial.   **counterfeit** portrait   **9 lines of life** lin-
eage, i.e., children (whose lineaments are more lifelike than lines of
verse or of a portrait)   **10 this time's pencil** a portraiture done in this
present age.   **pupil** apprenticed, inexpert   **11 fair** beauty   **13 give away
yourself** i.e., beget children.   **keeps** preserves

# 17

Who will believe my verse in time to come
If it were filled with your most high deserts?
Though yet, heaven knows, it is but as a tomb
Which hides your life and shows not half your parts.      4
If I could write the beauty of your eyes
And in fresh numbers number all your graces,
The age to come would say, "This poet lies;
Such heavenly touches ne'er touched earthly faces."       8
So should my papers, yellowed with their age,
Be scorned like old men of less truth than tongue,
And your true rights be termed a poet's rage
And stretchèd meter of an antique song.                   12
    But were some child of yours alive that time,
    You should live twice, in it and in my rhyme.

**17·3 yet** as yet   **4 parts** qualities   **6 numbers** verses   **10 of . . . tongue**
more garrulous than truthful   **11 rage** exaggerated inspiration
**12 stretchèd meter** overstrained poetry, poetic license

## 18

Shall I compare thee to a summer's day?
Thou art more lovely and more temperate.
Rough winds do shake the darling buds of May,
And summer's lease hath all too short a date.　　　　4
Sometimes too hot the eye of heaven shines,
And often is his gold complexion dimmed;
And every fair from fair sometimes declines,
By chance or nature's changing course untrimmed.　　8
But thy eternal summer shall not fade
Nor lose possession of that fair thou ow'st;
Nor shall Death brag thou wanderest in his shade,
When in eternal lines to time thou grow'st.　　　　12
　　So long as men can breathe or eyes can see,
　　So long lives this, and this gives life to thee.

---

**18・4 lease** allotted time.　**date** duration　**5 eye** i.e., sun　**7 fair from
fair**　beautiful thing from beauty　**8 untrimmed** stripped of ornament
and beauty　**10 fair thou ow'st** beauty you own　**12 lines** i.e., of poetry.　**to . . . grow'st** you become incorporated into time, engrafted upon
it　**14 this** i.e., this sonnet

# 19

Devouring Time, blunt thou the lion's paws,
And make the earth devour her own sweet brood;
Pluck the keen teeth from the fierce tiger's jaws,
And burn the long-lived phoenix in her blood;                    4
Make glad and sorry seasons as thou fleet'st,
And do whate'er thou wilt, swift-footed Time,
To the wide world and all her fading sweets.
But I forbid thee one most heinous crime:                        8
O, carve not with thy hours my love's fair brow,
Nor draw no lines there with thine antique pen;
Him in thy course untainted do allow
For beauty's pattern to succeeding men.                          12
    Yet, do thy worst, old Time. Despite thy wrong,
    My love shall in my verse ever live young.

**19・4 phoenix** legendary bird reputed to live for hundreds of years and
then be consumed alive (*in her blood*) in its own ashes from which it is
then reborn   **5 sorry** i.e., miserable, uncomfortable.   **thou fleet'st** you
fleet, hurry   **10 antique** (1) old (2) antic, capricious, fantastic
**11 untainted** (1) unhit in tilting (2) unsullied

## 20

A woman's face with Nature's own hand painted
Hast thou, the master-mistress of my passion;
A woman's gentle heart, but not acquainted
With shifting change, as is false women's fashion;  4
An eye more bright than theirs, less false in rolling,
Gilding the object whereupon it gazeth;
A man in hue, all hues in his controlling,
Which steals men's eyes and women's souls amazeth.  8
And for a woman wert thou first created,
Till Nature, as she wrought thee, fell a-doting,
And by addition me of thee defeated,
By adding one thing to my purpose nothing.  12
   But since she pricked thee out for women's pleasure,
   Mine be thy love and thy love's use their treasure.

**20 · 1 with . . . hand** i.e., without cosmetics  **2 master-mistress** i.e., both master and mistress, male and female.  **passion** love  **4 as . . . fashion** as is the way with women, who are false by nature  **5 rolling** i.e., roving  **6 Gilding** causing to shine brightly  **7 A man . . . controlling** one who has a manly appearance, and has power over all other appearances (suggesting too that he captivates all beholders, and that his *hue* is womanly as well as manly)  **10 fell a-doting** fell infatuatedly in love with you, and so went mildly crazy  **11 defeated** defrauded, deprived  **12 to my purpose nothing** out of line with my wishes  **13 pricked** designated (with bawdy suggestion; the *thing* in l. 12 is a phallus).  **for women's pleasure** to give (sexual) pleasure to women  **14 and . . . treasure** i.e., and let women enjoy the profits of love's *use* (usury) as their treasure (with bawdy suggestion that the lover is to use the *treasure* of their bodies)

# 21

So is it not with me as with that muse,
Stirred by a painted beauty to his verse,
Who heaven itself for ornament doth use
And every fair with his fair doth rehearse,                              4
Making a couplement of proud compare
With sun and moon, with earth and sea's rich gems,
With April's firstborn flowers, and all things rare
That heaven's air in this huge rondure hems.                            8
O, let me, true in love, but truly write,
And then, believe me, my love is as fair
As any mother's child, though not so bright
As those gold candles fixed in heaven's air.                           12
    Let them say more that like of hearsay well;
    I will not praise that purpose not to sell.

**21 · 1 muse** i.e., poet   **2 Stirred** inspired.   **painted** artificial, created by
cosmetics   **3 Who . . . use** i.e., who does not scruple to invoke heaven
itself as an ornament of praise for his mistress   **4 every . . . rehearse**
compares his lady fair with every lovely thing   **5 Making . . . compare**
joining (her) in proud comparison   **8 rondure** sphere.   **hems** encloses,
encircles   **12 gold candles** i.e., stars. (The trite and exaggerated metaphor is of the sort the poet hopes to eschew.)   **13 like . . . well** like to
deal in secondhand or trite expressions   **14 I will . . . sell** i.e., I, who do
not intend to sell as a merchant might, will accordingly not indulge in
extravagant and empty praise

## 22

My glass shall not persuade me I am old
So long as youth and thou are of one date;
But when in thee Time's furrows I behold,
Then look I death my days should expiate.                    4
For all that beauty that doth cover thee
Is but the seemly raiment of my heart,
Which in thy breast doth live, as thine in me.
How can I then be elder than thou art?                       8
O, therefore, love, be of thyself so wary
As I, not for myself, but for thee will,
Bearing thy heart, which I will keep so chary
As tender nurse her babe from faring ill.                    12
   Presume not on thy heart when mine is slain;
   Thou gav'st me thine, not to give back again.

---

**22·1 glass** mirror   **2 of one date** of an age, i.e., young   **4 look I** I
foresee.   **expiate** end   **6 seemly** becoming   **10 will** i.e., will take
care of myself for your sake   **11 Bearing** since I bear.   **chary** carefully   **13 Presume not on** do not expect to receive back

## 23

As an unperfect actor on the stage
Who with his fear is put beside his part,
Or some fierce thing replete with too much rage,
Whose strength's abundance weakens his own heart,          4
So I, for fear of trust, forget to say
The perfect ceremony of love's rite,
And in mine own love's strength seem to decay,
O'ercharged with burden of mine own love's might.          8
O, let my books be then the eloquence
And dumb presagers of my speaking breast,
Who plead for love and look for recompense
More than that tongue that more hath more expressed.       12
    O, learn to read what silent love hath writ.
    To hear with eyes belongs to love's fine wit.

23 • 1 **unperfect** one who has not learned his lines   **2 beside** out of
**3 Or . . . rage** i.e., or some wild animal overfilled with ungovernable
rage   **4 heart** courage   **5 for . . . trust** mistrusting myself.   **forget**
forget how   **9 books** (Possibly refers to the sonnets, or to *Venus and
Adonis* and *The Rape of Lucrece*, or more generally the works of the
persona poet.)   **10 dumb presagers** silent messengers or presenters
**12 more hath more expressed** has more often or more fully said more
**14 fine wit** sharp intelligence

## 24

Mine eye hath played the painter and hath stelled
Thy beauty's form in table of my heart;
My body is the frame wherein 'tis held,
And perspective it is best painter's art.                    4
For through the painter must you see his skill
To find where your true image pictured lies,
Which in my bosom's shop is hanging still,
That hath his windows glazèd with thine eyes.               8
Now see what good turns eyes for eyes have done:
Mine eyes have drawn thy shape, and thine for me
Are windows to my breast, wherethrough the sun
Delights to peep, to gaze therein on thee.                  12
   Yet eyes this cunning want to grace their art:
   They draw but what they see, know not the heart.

**24 · 1 played** acted the part of. **stelled** fixed, installed; or possibly
steeled, i.e., engraved. (The quarto reads *steeld*.) **2 table** tablet, wooden
panel used for painting **3 frame** (1) picture frame (2) bodily frame
**4 perspective** an artist's method of producing a distorted picture that
looks right only from an oblique point of view; or a painter's technique
used to produce the illusion of distance, one thing seeming to lie behind
another; or an optical device for bringing images to the painter's eye
**5 For . . . skill** i.e., you must look through the eyes of me, the skillful
painter **7 bosom's shop** i.e., heart **8 his** its. **glazèd** fitted with glass,
paned. (The friend, looking at the poet's portrait of him engraved in the
poet's heart, sees into that heart.) **13 this cunning want** lack this
skill. **grace** enhance **14 know not** do not perceive the thoughts of.
(The poet cannot see into the heart of the friend.)

## 25

Let those who are in favor with their stars
Of public honor and proud titles boast,
Whilst I, whom fortune of such triumph bars,
Unlooked-for joy in that I honor most.                                    4
Great princes' favorites their fair leaves spread
But as the marigold at the sun's eye,
And in themselves their pride lies burièd,
For at a frown they in their glory die.                                   8
The painful warrior famousèd for fight,
After a thousand victories once foiled,
Is from the book of honor rasèd quite,
And all the rest forgot for which he toiled.                              12
   Then happy I, that love and am beloved
   Where I may not remove nor be removed.

---

**25 · 3 of** from   **4 Unlooked-for** (1) unexpectedly (2) out of the public
eye.   **that** that which   **5 their . . . spread** i.e., flourish, blossom, prosper   **6 But** only   **7 lies burièd** i.e., will die with the ending of their
brief glory   **8 a frown** (1) a prince's frown (2) a cloud obscuring the
sun   **9 painful** enduring much, striving.   **famousèd** renowned.   **fight**
(Reads *worth* in the 1609 quarto; some editors retain, and emend *quite*
in l. 11 to *forth*.)   **11 rasèd** erased   **12 the rest** i.e., his *thousand victories*   **14 remove** i.e., be unfaithful.   **removed** i.e., removed from favor

## 26

Lord of my love, to whom in vassalage
Thy merit hath my duty strongly knit,
To thee I send this written embassage
To witness duty, not to show my wit—                          4
Duty so great, which wit so poor as mine
May make seem bare, in wanting words to show it,
But that I hope some good conceit of thine
In thy soul's thought, all naked, will bestow it;             8
Till whatsoever star that guides my moving
Points on me graciously with fair aspect,
And puts apparel on my tattered loving
To show me worthy of thy sweet respect.                       12
   Then may I dare to boast how I do love thee;
   Till then not show my head where thou mayst
     prove me.

---

**26 • 1 vassalage** allegiance  **4 witness** bear witness to  **6 wanting** lacking  **7 good conceit** good conception, or favorable opinion  **8 all naked** (Modifies *Duty*.)  **bestow** give lodging to  **9 moving** life and deeds  **10 aspect** influence (as of a star)  **14 prove** test

# 27

Weary with toil, I haste me to my bed,
The dear repose for limbs with travel tirèd;
But then begins a journey in my head,
To work my mind when body's work's expirèd. 4
For then my thoughts, from far where I abide,
Intend a zealous pilgrimage to thee,
And keep my drooping eyelids open wide,
Looking on darkness which the blind do see; 8
Save that my soul's imaginary sight
Presents thy shadow to my sightless view,
Which, like a jewel hung in ghastly night,
Makes black night beauteous and her old face new. 12
  Lo, thus by day my limbs, by night my mind,
    For thee and for myself no quiet find.

27 • 2 **travel** (with connotation also of *travail;* spelled *trauaill* in the quarto) **5 from far** i.e., far away from you **6 Intend** direct, set out upon **9 Save** except **10 thy shadow** the image of you

## 28

How can I then return in happy plight
That am debarred the benefit of rest?
When day's oppression is not eased by night,
But day by night, and night by day, oppressed?          4
And each, though enemies to either's reign,
Do in consent shake hands to torture me,
The one by toil, the other to complain
How far I toil, still farther off from thee.            8
I tell the day, to please him, thou art bright
And dost him grace when clouds do blot the heaven;
So flatter I the swart-complexioned night,
When sparkling stars twire not, thou gild'st th' even.  12
 But day doth daily draw my sorrows longer,
  And night doth nightly make grief's strength seem
    stronger.

28 · 4 But . . . oppressed i.e., but experiencing sleeplessness at night and
fatigue during the day   6 consent i.e., mutual agreement   7 the other
to complain i.e., the night by causing me to complain   10 And . . .
heaven i.e., and that you shine in place of the sun when the sun is
overclouded   11 So flatter I similarly I gratify.   swart dark   12 When
. . . even i.e., by saying that, when sparkling stars do not twinkle or
peep out, you make bright the evening

## 29

When, in disgrace with fortune and men's eyes,
I all alone beweep my outcast state,
And trouble deaf heaven with my bootless cries,
And look upon myself and curse my fate, 4
Wishing me like to one more rich in hope,
Featured like him, like him with friends possessed,
Desiring this man's art and that man's scope,
With what I most enjoy contented least; 8
Yet in these thoughts myself almost despising,
Haply I think on thee, and then my state,
Like to the lark at break of day arising
From sullen earth, sings hymns at heaven's gate; 12
   For thy sweet love remembered such wealth brings
   That then I scorn to change my state with kings.

**29 · 3 bootless** useless  **4 look upon myself** consider my predicament
**5 more rich in hope** with better prospects of success  **6 Featured**
formed, i.e., having good looks.  **like him, like him** like a second man,
like a third  **7 art** literary skill (?)  **scope** range of powers  **8 most
enjoy** possess the most  **10 state** state of mind  **14 change** exchange

## 30

When to the sessions of sweet silent thought
I summon up remembrance of things past,
I sigh the lack of many a thing I sought,
And with old woes new wail my dear time's waste.                4
Then can I drown an eye, unused to flow,
For precious friends hid in death's dateless night,
And weep afresh love's long since canceled woe,
And moan th' expense of many a vanished sight.                   8
Then can I grieve at grievances foregone,
And heavily from woe to woe tell o'er
The sad account of fore-bemoanèd moan,
Which I new pay as if not paid before.                           12
   But if the while I think on thee, dear friend,
   All losses are restored and sorrows end.

**30 · 1 sessions** (The metaphor is that of a court of law, continued in
*summon up*, l. 2.)   **3 sigh** sigh for   **4 new . . . waste** lament anew the
wasting of precious time or time's erosion of those things held precious   **5 unused to flow** not prone to weep   **6 dateless** endless
**7 canceled** paid in full (by grieving)   **8 expense** loss   **9 grievances**
**foregone** sorrows past   **10 heavily** sadly.   **tell** count   **11 The sad . . .**
**moan** the distressing total of previously-uttered laments

## 31

Thy bosom is endearèd with all hearts,
Which I by lacking have supposèd dead,
And there reigns love and all love's loving parts,
And all those friends which I thought burièd.                    4
How many a holy and obsequious tear
Hath dear religious love stol'n from mine eye
As interest of the dead, which now appear
But things removed that hidden in thee lie!                      8
Thou art the grave where buried love doth live,
Hung with the trophies of my lovers gone,
Who all their parts of me to thee did give;
That due of many now is thine alone.                            12
   Their images I loved I view in thee,
    And thou, all they, hast all the all of me.

31 · 1 **endearèd with all hearts** (1) beloved by all (2) made dear to me by
representing and including those I have loved  2 **lacking** not having
3 **parts** attributes  5 **obsequious** suitable to mourning  6 **religious**
dutiful  7 **interest** that which is rightfully due.  **which** who  8 **But . . .
lie** i.e., no more than absent persons (now dead) whose best qualities are
to be found concealed in you  10 **lovers** loved ones, friends  11 **parts**
shares  12 **That due of many** that which was the due of many
13 **I loved** which I loved  14 **all they** (you) who comprise all of them

# 32

If thou survive my well-contented day
When that churl Death my bones with dust shall cover,
And shalt by fortune once more re-survey
These poor rude lines of thy deceasèd lover,                4
Compare them with the bettering of the time,
And though they be outstripped by every pen,
Reserve them for my love, not for their rhyme,
Exceeded by the height of happier men.                      8
O, then vouchsafe me but this loving thought:
"Had my friend's Muse grown with this growing age,
A dearer birth than this his love had brought
To march in ranks of better equipage;                       12
   But since he died and poets better prove,
   Theirs for their style I'll read, his for his love."

32 · 1 my . . . day i.e., the day of my death, which will content me well
3 fortune chance  4 rude unpolished.  lover friend  5 bettering i.e.,
improved writing, greater cultural sophistication  7 Reserve preserve.
rhyme i.e., poetic skill  8 height superiority, highest achievement.
happier more gifted  9 vouchsafe me but deign to bestow on me just
11 dearer birth i.e., better poem, better artistic creation  12 of better
equipage i.e., more finely wrought verse  13 better prove turn out to be
superior

## 33

Full many a glorious morning have I seen
Flatter the mountaintops with sovereign eye,
Kissing with golden face the meadows green,
Gilding pale streams with heavenly alchemy;                    4
Anon permit the basest clouds to ride
With ugly rack on his celestial face,
And from the forlorn world his visage hide,
Stealing unseen to west with this disgrace.                    8
Even so my sun one early morn did shine
With all-triumphant splendor on my brow.
But out, alack! He was but one hour mine;
The region cloud hath masked him from me now.                  12
  Yet him for this my love no whit disdaineth;
  Suns of the world may stain when heaven's sun
     staineth.

**33 • 1 Full** very   **5 Anon** soon afterward.   **basest** darkest; also, far below
the royal glory of the sun in dignity and in altitude   **6 rack** mass of
cloud scudding before the wind   **12 region** of the upper air   **14 Suns**
i.e., great men (with a pun on *sons of the world*, mortal men).   **stain**
grow dim, be obscured, soiled.   **staineth** is clouded over

## 34

Why didst thou promise such a beauteous day
And make me travel forth without my cloak,
To let base clouds o'ertake me in my way,
Hiding thy bravery in their rotten smoke?                    4
'Tis not enough that through the cloud thou break,
To dry the rain on my storm-beaten face,
For no man well of such a salve can speak
That heals the wound and cures not the disgrace.            8
Nor can thy shame give physic to my grief;
Though thou repent, yet I have still the loss.
Th' offender's sorrow lends but weak relief
To him that bears the strong offense's cross.              12
　　Ah, but those tears are pearl which thy love sheeds,
　　And they are rich and ransom all ill deeds.

---

**34 · 3 To** only to   **4 bravery** finery.   **rotten smoke** foul vapors
**8 disgrace** i.e., the scar, the disfigurement caused by his friend's neglect
or harsh treatment; the *loss* mentioned in l. 10   **9 shame** repentance for
the wrong done.   **physic** remedy   **12 cross** affliction   **13 sheeds** sheds

## 35

No more be grieved at that which thou hast done.
Roses have thorns, and silver fountains mud,
Clouds and eclipses stain both moon and sun,
And loathsome canker lives in sweetest bud.                    4
All men make faults, and even I in this,
Authorizing thy trespass with compare,
Myself corrupting, salving thy amiss,
Excusing thy sins more than thy sins are.                       8
For to thy sensual fault I bring in sense—
Thy adverse party is thy advocate—
And 'gainst myself a lawful plea commence.
Such civil war is in my love and hate                          12
   That I an accessary needs must be
   To that sweet thief which sourly robs from me.

**35 · 3 stain** dim, obscure   **4 canker** cankerworm   **6 Authorizing** sanctioning, justifying.   **compare** comparisons (as in this sonnet)   **7 Myself . . . amiss** i.e., excusing your misdeed, thereby bringing blame on myself   **8 Excusing . . . are** i.e., going further to excuse your sins than they warrant   **9 sensual** pertaining to the flesh.   **sense** pertaining to the rational faculty (i.e., I reason away your fleshly offenses with sophistical justifications)   **10 Thy . . . advocate** I who profess to be your accuser find myself instead pleading your case   **13 That . . . be** that I am compelled (by my love) to be a guilty accomplice

## 36

Let me confess that we two must be twain,
Although our undivided loves are one;
So shall those blots that do with me remain,
Without thy help, by me be borne alone.                    4
In our two loves there is but one respect,
Though in our lives a separable spite,
Which though it alter not love's sole effect,
Yet doth it steal sweet hours from love's delight.         8
I may not evermore acknowledge thee,
Lest my bewailèd guilt should do thee shame,
Nor thou with public kindness honor me
Unless thou take that honor from thy name.                 12
    But do not so; I love thee in such sort
    As, thou being mine, mine is thy good report.

36 • 1 **twain** parted   3 **blots** defects, stains of dishonor   5 **but one
respect** i.e., a mutual regard, singleness of attitude   6 **separable spite**
spiteful separation   7 **sole** unique   9 **not evermore** nevermore.
**acknowledge** admit my acquaintance with   12 **Unless . . . from** without
consequent loss of honor to   13 **in such sort** in such a way   14 **As**
that.   **report** reputation

## 37

As a decrepit father takes delight
To see his active child do deeds of youth,
So I, made lame by Fortune's dearest spite,
Take all my comfort of thy worth and truth.                    4
For whether beauty, birth, or wealth, or wit,
Or any of these all, or all, or more,
Entitled in thy parts do crownèd sit,
I make my love engrafted to this store.                        8
So then I am not lame, poor, nor despised,
Whilst that this shadow doth such substance give
That I in thy abundance am sufficed
And by a part of all thy glory live.                          12
    Look what is best, that best I wish in thee.
    This wish I have; then ten times happy me!

**37 · 3 made lame** handicapped in life.   **dearest** most bitter   **4 of** in,
from   **5 wit** intelligence   **7 Entitled . . . sit** sit enthroned in first place
among your qualities   **8 I make . . . store** I add my love to this abundance (and thereby flourish by drawing on their strength)   **10 shadow**
idea (in the Platonic sense).   **substance** actuality   **13 Look what** whatever

# 38

How can my Muse want subject to invent
While thou dost breathe, that pour'st into my verse
Thine own sweet argument, too excellent
For every vulgar paper to rehearse?                    4
O, give thyself the thanks, if aught in me
Worthy perusal stand against thy sight,
For who's so dumb that cannot write to thee,
When thou thyself dost give invention light?          8
Be thou the tenth Muse, ten times more in worth
Than those old nine which rhymers invocate;
And he that calls on thee, let him bring forth
Eternal numbers to outlive long date.                 12
   If my slight Muse do please these curious days,
    The pain be mine, but thine shall be the praise.

**38 · 1 want . . . invent** lack something to write about  **2 that** you who
**3 Thine . . . argument** yourself as subject  **4 vulgar paper** common
piece of writing.  **rehearse** recite, repeat  **5 in me** of my writing
**6 stand against** meet  **7 dumb** silent, lacking in subject  **12 numbers**
verses.  **date** duration  **13 curious** critical  **14 pain** labor

## 39

O, how thy worth with manners may I sing,
When thou art all the better part of me?
What can mine own praise to mine own self bring?
And what is 't but mine own when I praise thee?          4
Even for this let us divided live,
And our dear love lose name of single one,
That by this separation I may give
That due to thee which thou deserv'st alone.             8
O absence, what a torment wouldst thou prove,
Were it not thy sour leisure gave sweet leave
To entertain the time with thoughts of love,
Which time and thoughts so sweetly dost deceive,        12
   And that thou teachest how to make one twain
   By praising him here who doth hence remain!

**39 · 1 with manners** decently, becomingly   **4 mine own** i.e., praise of
myself   **5 Even for** precisely because of   **6 name** reputation
**11 entertain** pass, occupy   **12 dost deceive** (you) do beguile away
**13 that** were it not that.   **make one twain** i.e., divide one beloved person
into two   **14 praising him here** i.e., invoking his presence here through
my praising of him

## 40

Take all my loves, my love, yea, take them all;
What hast thou then more than thou hadst before?
No love, my love, that thou mayst true love call;
All mine was thine before thou hadst this more.         4
Then if for my love thou my love receivest,
I cannot blame thee for my love thou usest;
But yet be blamed, if thou this self deceivest
By willful taste of what thyself refusest.              8
I do forgive thy robbery, gentle thief,
Although thou steal thee all my poverty;
And yet love knows it is a greater grief
To bear love's wrong than hate's known injury.          12
    Lascivious grace, in whom all ill well shows,
    Kill me with spites; yet we must not be foes.

**40 · 1 all my loves** (1) all those whom I love (2) all the love I have. (The
young man addressed has taken away the poet's mistress.)   **3 No . . .
call** i.e., any love more than you had already—my complete affection—
cannot be called true love   **5 my love . . . my love** love of me . . . her
whom I love   **6 for** because.   **thou usest** you enjoy (sexually)   **7 this
self** i.e., this other self of yours, the poet. (Often emended to *thyself*.)
**8 willful taste** i.e., sensual enjoyment.   **thyself** i.e., your true self (?)
**10 steal . . . poverty** take for your own the poor little that I have
**12 known** undisguised   **13 Lascivious grace** i.e., you who are gracious
even in your lasciviousness

## 41

Those pretty wrongs that liberty commits
When I am sometimes absent from thy heart,
Thy beauty and thy years full well befits,
For still temptation follows where thou art.                    4
Gentle thou art, and therefore to be won;
Beauteous thou art, therefore to be assailed;
And when a woman woos, what woman's son
Will sourly leave her till she have prevailed?                  8
Ay me, but yet thou mightst my seat forbear,
And chide thy beauty and thy straying youth,
Who lead thee in their riot even there
Where thou art forced to break a twofold truth:               12
  Hers, by thy beauty tempting her to thee,
  Thine, by thy beauty being false to me.

---

**41 · 1 pretty** minor; sportive.  **liberty** licentiousness  **3 befits** (The subject is *wrongs*, l. 1.)  **4 still** constantly  **9 seat** place, that which belongs to me (i.e., my mistress)  **11 Who** which.  **riot** debauchery **12 twofold truth** i.e., her plighted love and your plighted friendship

# 42

That thou hast her, it is not all my grief,
And yet it may be said I loved her dearly;
That she hath thee is of my wailing chief,
A loss in love that touches me more nearly.                    4
Loving offenders, thus I will excuse ye:
Thou dost love her because thou know'st I love her,
And for my sake even so doth she abuse me,
Suff'ring my friend for my sake to approve her.               8
If I lose thee, my loss is my love's gain,
And, losing her, my friend hath found that loss;
Both find each other, and I lose both twain,
And both for my sake lay on me this cross.                    12
 But here's the joy: my friend and I are one.
 Sweet flattery! Then she loves but me alone.

**42 · 3 is ... chief** is chief cause of my lamentation   **7 abuse** betray,
wrong   **8 Suff'ring** allowing.   **approve** try, test (in a sexual sense)
**9 my love's** hers whom I love, my mistress's   **10 losing her** i.e., I losing
her   **12 for my sake** out of love for me.   **cross** torment   **14 flattery**
gratifying deception

## 43

When most I wink, then do mine eyes best see,
For all the day they view things unrespected;
But when I sleep, in dreams they look on thee,
And, darkly bright, are bright in dark directed.                    4
Then thou, whose shadow shadows doth make bright,
How would thy shadow's form form happy show
To the clear day with thy much clearer light,
When to unseeing eyes thy shade shines so!                          8
How would, I say, mine eyes be blessèd made
By looking on thee in the living day,
When in dead night thy fair imperfect shade
Through heavy sleep on sightless eyes doth stay!                   12
  All days are nights to see till I see thee,
  And nights bright days when dreams do show
    thee me.

**43 · 1 wink** close my eyes in sleep   **2 unrespected** unnoticed, unregarded; not deserving notice   **4 And . . . directed** and, able to see in the
darkness, are directed toward your brightness in the dark   **5 whose . . .
bright** whose image makes darkness bright   **6 thy shadow's form** the
substance of the shadow, i.e., your presence.   **form happy show** make a
gladdening sight   **8 unseeing eyes** i.e., closed eyes of the dreamer
**11 imperfect** unsubstantial, indistinct as in a dream   **12 stay** linger,
dwell   **13 All . . . to see** all days are gloomy to behold   **14 me** to me

## 44

If the dull substance of my flesh were thought,
Injurious distance should not stop my way;
For then despite of space I would be brought,
From limits far remote, where thou dost stay.                    4
No matter then although my foot did stand
Upon the farthest earth removed from thee;
For nimble thought can jump both sea and land
As soon as think the place where he would be.                    8
But, ah, thought kills me that I am not thought,
To leap large lengths of miles when thou art gone,
But that, so much of earth and water wrought,
I must attend time's leisure with my moan,                      12
   Receiving naught by elements so slow
   But heavy tears, badges of either's woe.

44 • 1 dull heavy   4 limits regions, bounds.   where i.e., to the place
where   6 farthest earth removed that part of the earth farthest removed   8 he i.e., thought   9 ah, thought ah, the thought   11 so . . .
wrought i.e., I, compounded to such an extent of the heavier elements,
earth and water. (The lighter elements are fire and air.)   12 attend
time's leisure i.e., wait until time has leisure to reunite us   13 by
from   14 badges signs, tokens.   either's i.e., both earth's and water's,
because the earth is heavy and the sea is salt and wet, both like tears

## 45

The other two, slight air and purging fire,
Are both with thee, wherever I abide;
The first my thought, the other my desire,
These present-absent with swift motion slide.          4
For when these quicker elements are gone
In tender embassy of love to thee,
My life, being made of four, with two alone
Sinks down to death, oppressed with melancholy;        8
Until life's composition be recured
By those swift messengers returned from thee,
Who even but now come back again, assured
Of thy fair health, recounting it to me.               12
   This told, I joy; but then no longer glad,
   I send them back again and straight grow sad.

**45 · 1 other two** i.e., of the four elements discussed in Sonnet 44.   **slight**
insubstantial.   **purging** purifying   **4 present-absent** now here and
immediately gone   **7 life** living body.   **two alone** i.e., earth and water
**8 melancholy** a humor thought to be induced by an excess of earth and
water   **9 composition** proper balance among the four elements.
**recured** restored   **10 swift messengers** i.e., fire and air, thought and
desire   **14 straight** straightway

## 46

Mine eye and heart are at a mortal war
How to divide the conquest of thy sight;
Mine eye my heart thy picture's sight would bar,
My heart mine eye the freedom of that right.    4
My heart doth plead that thou in him dost lie—
A closet never pierced with crystal eyes—
But the defendant doth that plea deny
And says in him thy fair appearance lies.    8
To 'cide this title is impanelèd
A quest of thoughts, all tenants to the heart,
And by their verdict is determinèd
The clear eye's moiety and the dear heart's part,    12
 As thus: mine eye's due is thy outward part,
  And my heart's right thy inward love of heart.

**46 · 1 mortal** deadly  **2 conquest** spoils.  **thy sight** the sight of you
**3 Mine . . . bar** i.e., my eye would issue an order prohibiting my heart
from enjoying the sight of your picture  **4 My . . . right** i.e., my heart
would deny to my eye the privilege of looking on your picture  **6 closet**
small private room  **9 'cide** decide  **10 quest** inquest, jury  **12 moiety**
portion  **13 mine . . . part** i.e., the eye gets the mere appearance of the
young man only (since the jury is composed entirely of those who are
loyal to the heart, its *tenants*)

## 47

Betwixt mine eye and heart a league is took,
And each doth good turns now unto the other.
When that mine eye is famished for a look,
Or heart in love with sighs himself doth smother,          4
With my love's picture then my eye doth feast
And to the painted banquet bids my heart;
Another time mine eye is my heart's guest
And in his thoughts of love doth share a part.             8
So, either by thy picture or my love,
Thyself, away, are present still with me;
For thou not farther than my thoughts canst move,
And I am still with them and they with thee;               12
  Or, if they sleep, thy picture in my sight
    Awakes my heart to heart's and eye's delight.

47 · 1 a league is took an agreement is reached   3 When that when
4 Or heart or when my heart.   himself itself   5 With i.e., on   6 painted
banquet i.e., visual feast, perhaps an actual picture of the friend
12 still constantly

## 48

How careful was I, when I took my way,
Each trifle under truest bars to thrust,
That to my use it might unusèd stay
From hands of falsehood, in sure wards of trust!          4
But thou, to whom my jewels trifles are,
Most worthy comfort, now my greatest grief,
Thou best of dearest and mine only care,
Art left the prey of every vulgar thief.                  8
Thee have I not locked up in any chest,
Save where thou art not—though I feel thou art—
Within the gentle closure of my breast,
From whence at pleasure thou mayst come and part;         12
  And even thence thou wilt be stol'n, I fear,
  For truth proves thievish for a prize so dear.

**48 · 1 took my way** set out on my journey  **2 truest** most trusty  **3 to
my use** for my own use and profit  **3–4 stay From** remain out of
**4 hands of falsehood** the hands of thieves  **5 to** compared to  **6 worthy**
valuable.  **grief** anxiety, cause of sorrow (i.e., because of your absence
and likeliness of being stolen)  **8 vulgar** common  **12 part** depart
**14 truth** i.e., even honesty itself

## 49

Against that time, if ever that time come,
When I shall see thee frown on my defects,
Whenas thy love hath cast his utmost sum,
Called to that audit by advised respects;                        4
Against that time when thou shalt strangely pass
And scarcely greet me with that sun, thine eye,
When love, converted from the thing it was,
Shall reasons find of settled gravity—                           8
Against that time do I ensconce me here
Within the knowledge of mine own desart,
And this my hand against myself uprear
To guard the lawful reasons on thy part.                        12
    To leave poor me thou hast the strength of laws,
    Since why to love I can allege no cause.

**49 • 1 Against** in anticipation of   **3 Whenas** when.   **cast ... sum** added
up the sum total. (The metaphor is from closing accounts on a dissolution of partnership.)   **4 advised respects** careful consideration
**5 strangely** as a stranger   **8 of settled gravity** for a dignified reserve or
continued coldness (?) of sufficient weight (?)   **9 ensconce** fortify,
shelter   **10 desart** i.e., deserving, such as it is. (This quarto spelling of
desert, *desart,* indicates the rhyme with *part.*)   **11 this ... uprear** I raise
my own hand (as a witness) against my own interest   **12 To ... part** i.e.,
to testify in behalf of the lawful reasons on your side of the case
**14 Since ... cause** since I can urge no lawful cause why you should
love me

## 50

How heavy do I journey on the way,
When what I seek, my weary travel's end,
Doth teach that ease and that repose to say,
"Thus far the miles are measured from thy friend!"          4
The beast that bears me, tired with my woe,
Plods dully on, to bear that weight in me,
As if by some instinct the wretch did know
His rider loved not speed being made from thee.              8
The bloody spur cannot provoke him on
That sometimes anger thrusts into his hide,
Which heavily he answers with a groan,
More sharp to me than spurring to his side;                 12
　　For that same groan doth put this in my mind:
　　My grief lies onward and my joy behind.

---

**50•1 heavy** sadly   **2–4 When . . . friend** i.e., when the ease and repose I
seek at journey's end will merely remind me that I have gone so many
miles from my friend   **8 speed being made** (1) speed that is made
(2) speed when he is being carried

# 51

Thus can my love excuse the slow offense
Of my dull bearer when from thee I speed:
From where thou art why should I haste me thence?
Till I return, of posting is no need.                          4
O, what excuse will my poor beast then find
When swift extremity can seem but slow?
Then should I spur, though mounted on the wind;
In wingèd speed no motion shall I know.                        8
Then can no horse with my desire keep pace;
Therefore desire, of perfect'st love being made,
Shall neigh—no dull flesh—in his fiery race.
But love, for love, thus shall excuse my jade:                12
  Since from thee going he went willful slow,
  Towards thee I'll run, and give him leave to go.

**51 · 1 love** affection.  **slow offense** offense consisting in slowness   **2 my
dull bearer** i.e., the horse   **4 posting** riding swiftly   **6 swift extremity**
extreme swiftness   **8 In . . . know** even at the speed of flight I won't
perceive the motion at all, won't feel as though I'm moving   **11 Shall
. . . race** i.e., shall neigh proudly in its fire-swift race, since it, composed
like fire of a lighter element, is not held back by the heavy flesh. (See
Sonnet 45.)   **12 for love** for love's sake.   **jade** nag   **14 go** walk, as
contrasted with running

## 52

So am I as the rich whose blessèd key
Can bring him to his sweet up-lockèd treasure,
The which he will not every hour survey,
For blunting the fine point of seldom pleasure.       4
Therefore are feasts so solemn and so rare,
Since, seldom coming, in the long year set,
Like stones of worth they thinly placèd are,
Or captain jewels in the carcanet.                     8
So is the time that keeps you as my chest,
Or as the wardrobe which the robe doth hide,
To make some special instant special blest,
By new unfolding his imprisoned pride.                 12
  Blessèd are you whose worthiness gives scope,
  Being had, to triumph, being lacked, to hope.

---

**52·1 as the rich** like the rich man  **4 For blunting** lest he blunt.  **fine**
delicate; splendid.  **seldom pleasure** pleasure sparingly enjoyed
**5 feasts** feast days.  **solemn** ceremonious, festive.  **rare** excellent;
uncommon  **8 captain** principal.  **carcanet** necklace of jewels  **9 as**
like  **12 his** its.  **pride** splendor, proud treasure  **13–14 gives . . . hope**
gives me opportunity, when you are with me, to rejoice, and when you
are away from me, to hope for reunion

## 53

What is your substance, whereof are you made,
That millions of strange shadows on you tend?
Since everyone hath, every one, one shade,
And you, but one, can every shadow lend.                    4
Describe Adonis, and the counterfeit
Is poorly imitated after you;
On Helen's cheek all art of beauty set,
And you in Grecian tires are painted new.                   8
Speak of the spring and foison of the year;
The one doth shadow of your beauty show,
The other as your bounty doth appear,
And you in every blessèd shape we know.                     12
   In all external grace you have some part,
   But you like none, none you, for constant heart.

**53 · 2 strange** (1) exotic (2) not belonging to you.  **tend** attend, wait
upon  **3 shade** shadow (as cast by the sun)  **4 And . . . lend** and yet you,
being only one person, can cast all sorts of shadowy images or reflections (such as Adonis, Helen, etc.)  **5 Adonis** beautiful youth beloved of
Venus.  **counterfeit** likeness, portrait  **7–8 On . . . new** set forth the
entire art used to beautify the cheek of Helen of Troy, and the result
will be a portrait of you in Grecian attire or headdress  **9 foison** abundance, i.e., autumn  **14 But . . . heart** but in the matter of constancy
you resemble no one and no one can resemble you

## 54

O, how much more doth beauty beauteous seem
By that sweet ornament which truth doth give!
The rose looks fair, but fairer we it deem
For that sweet odor which doth in it live.      4
The canker blooms have full as deep a dye
As the perfumèd tincture of the roses,
Hang on such thorns, and play as wantonly
When summer's breath their maskèd buds discloses.    8
But, for their virtue only is their show,
They live unwooed and unrespected fade,
Die to themselves. Sweet roses do not so;
Of their sweet deaths are sweetest odors made.     12
   And so of you, beauteous and lovely youth,
    When that shall vade, by verse distills your truth.

**54·2 By** by means of.   **truth** (1) constancy (2) substance, reality
**5 canker blooms** dog roses (outwardly attractive, but not as sweetly
scented as the damask rose).   **dye** tincture   **7 wantonly** sportively
**8 discloses** causes to open   **9 for** because.   **their show** in their appearance   **10 unrespected** unregarded   **11 to themselves** i.e., without profit
to others   **12 Of . . . made** i.e., perfumes are made from the crushed
petals of these roses   **13 of you** (1) distilled from you (2) with regard to
you.   **lovely** (1) lovable (2) handsome   **14 When . . . truth** when your
physical beauty fades, your true substance will be distilled and preserved by (my) verse. (See Sonnet 5.)   **vade** (1) fade (2) go away

## 55

Not marble nor the gilded monuments
Of princes shall outlive this powerful rhyme,
But you shall shine more bright in these contents
Than unswept stone besmeared with sluttish time.       4
When wasteful war shall statues overturn,
And broils root out the work of masonry,
Nor Mars his sword nor war's quick fire shall burn
The living record of your memory.                       8
'Gainst death and all-oblivious enmity
Shall you pace forth; your praise shall still find room
Even in the eyes of all posterity
That wear this world out to the ending doom.           12
  So, till the judgment that yourself arise,
  You live in this, and dwell in lovers' eyes.

**55 · 3 these contents** i.e., the contents of my poems written in praise of
you  **4 Than unswept stone** than in a memorial stone that has been left
unswept, unattended.  **with sluttish time** by neglectful time  **5 wasteful**
laying waste  **6 broils** uprisings, battles  **7 Nor Mars his sword** neither
Mars' sword (shall destroy)  **9 all-oblivious enmity** i.e., oblivion, at
enmity with everything  **12 That ... doom** that will last from now till
doomsday. (*That* refers to *eyes*.)  **13 till ... arise** until the Judgment Day
when you will arise from the dead

## 56

Sweet love, renew thy force; be it not said
Thy edge should blunter be than appetite,
Which but today by feeding is allayed,
Tomorrow sharpened in his former might.                    4
So, love, be thou; although today thou fill
Thy hungry eyes even till they wink with fullness,
Tomorrow see again, and do not kill
The spirit of love with a perpetual dullness.             8
Let this sad interim like the ocean be
Which parts the shore where two contracted new
Come daily to the banks, that, when they see
Return of love, more blest may be the view;               12
　　As call it winter, which being full of care
　　Makes summer's welcome thrice more wished,
　　　　more rare.

**56 · 1 love** i.e., the spirit of love. (The friend is not directly mentioned in
this sonnet.)  **2 edge** keenness.  **should blunter be** is blunter.  **appetite**
lust, craving  **3 but** only for  **4 his** its  **6 wink** shut  **9 sad interim**
i.e., the period of love's abatement or absence  **10 parts the shore**
separates the shores.  **contracted new** newly betrothed  **11 banks**
shores  **12 love** the loved one  **13 As** just as appropriately

## 57

Being your slave, what should I do but tend
Upon the hours and times of your desire?
I have no precious time at all to spend,
Nor services to do, till you require.                          4
Nor dare I chide the world-without-end hour
Whilst I, my sovereign, watch the clock for you,
Nor think the bitterness of absence sour
When you have bid your servant once adieu.                      8
Nor dare I question with my jealous thought
Where you may be, or your affairs suppose,
But, like a sad slave, stay and think of naught
Save where you are how happy you make those.                   12
    So true a fool is love that in your will,
    Though you do anything, he thinks no ill.

**57 • 1 tend** attend · **5 world-without-end** interminable   **6 my . . . you**
watch the clock for you, my sovereign   **7 Nor think** nor dare I think
**9 question with** (1) debate with (2) seek to know by means of
**10 suppose** make conjectures about   **11 sad** sober   **13 true** (1) constant
(2) utter.   **will** desire. (This word, which is capitalized in the 1609
quarto, is regarded by some as a pun on Shakespeare's first name;
see Sonnet 135.)

## 58

That god forbid that made me first your slave
I should in thought control your times of pleasure,
Or at your hand th' account of hours to crave,
Being your vassal, bound to stay your leisure!                    4
O, let me suffer, being at your beck,
Th' imprisoned absence of your liberty,
And, patience-tame to sufferance, bide each check,
Without accusing you of injury.                                   8
Be where you list, your charter is so strong
That you yourself may privilege your time
To what you will; to you it doth belong
Yourself to pardon of self-doing crime.                           12
  I am to wait, though waiting so be hell,
  Not blame your pleasure, be it ill or well.

58 • 3 th' account . . . crave should crave an accounting of how you
spend your time   4 stay await   6 Th' imprisoned . . . liberty i.e., the
lack of freedom I suffer in being absent from you, arising from (of) your
freedom and free behavior   7 And . . . check and, trained to endure any
suffering, let me put up with each rebuke   9 list please.   charter
privilege   10 privilege authorize   12 self-doing committed by yourself   13 am to must

# 59

If there be nothing new, but that which is
Hath been before, how are our brains beguiled,
Which, laboring for invention, bear amiss
The second burden of a former child!                          4
O, that record could with a backward look,
Even of five hundred courses of the sun,
Show me your image in some antique book,
Since mind at first in character was done!                    8
That I might see what the old world could say
To this composèd wonder of your frame;
Whether we are mended, or whe'er better they,
Or whether revolution be the same.                            12
    O, sure I am the wits of former days
    To subjects worse have given admiring praise.

---

**59 • 1 that** everything  **3–4 laboring . . . child** i.e., striving to give birth
to a new creation, merely miscarry with the repetition of something
created before  **5 record** memory, especially memory preserved in
writing  **6 courses . . . sun** years  **8 Since . . . done** since thought was
first expressed in writing  **10 composèd wonder** wonderful composition  **11 mended** improved.  **whe'er** whether  **12 revolution . . . same**
i.e., the revolving of the ages brings only repetition  **13 wits** i.e., poets

## 60

Like as the waves make towards the pebbled shore,
So do our minutes hasten to their end;
Each changing place with that which goes before,
In sequent toil all forwards do contend.                    4
Nativity, once in the main of light,
Crawls to maturity, wherewith being crowned,
Crookèd eclipses 'gainst his glory fight,
And Time that gave doth now his gift confound.              8
Time doth transfix the flourish set on youth
And delves the parallels in beauty's brow,
Feeds on the rarities of nature's truth,
And nothing stands but for his scythe to mow.             12
    And yet to times in hope my verse shall stand,
    Praising thy worth, despite his cruel hand.

60 · 3 **changing place with** replacing    4 **In . . . contend** one after another
all struggle onward    5 **Nativity** i.e., the newborn infant.    **once** (1) no
sooner (2) formerly.    **main** main body, expanse. (The child is seen as
dwelling in the main or ocean of light.)    7 **Crookèd** perverse, malig-
nant    8 **confound** destroy    9 **transfix the flourish** pierce through and
destroy the decoration or embellishment, i.e., physical beauty
10 **delves the parallels** digs the wrinkles, furrows    11 **Feeds . . . truth**
consumes the most precious things created by the fidelity of nature
12 **but . . . mow** i.e., that can escape the mowing of Time's scythe
13 **times in hope** times to come

## 61

Is it thy will thy image should keep open
My heavy eyelids to the weary night?
Dost thou desire my slumbers should be broken
While shadows like to thee do mock my sight?            4
Is it thy spirit that thou send'st from thee
So far from home into my deeds to pry,
To find out shames and idle hours in me,
The scope and tenor of thy jealousy?                    8
O, no, thy love, though much, is not so great;
It is my love that keeps mine eye awake,
Mine own true love that doth my rest defeat,
To play the watchman ever for thy sake.                 12
   For thee watch I whilst thou dost wake elsewhere,
   From me far off, with others all too near.

61 • 4 **shadows** images (but also suggesting spirits)   **8 The scope . . .
jealousy** the aim and purport of your suspicion (probably modifying
*shames and idle hours*)   **13 watch** stay awake.   **wake** revel

# 62

Sin of self-love possesseth all mine eye,
And all my soul, and all my every part;
And for this sin there is no remedy,
It is so grounded inward in my heart.                          4
Methinks no face so gracious is as mine,
No shape so true, no truth of such account;
And for myself mine own worth do define,
As I all other in all worths surmount.                         8
But when my glass shows me myself indeed,
Beated and chapped with tanned antiquity,
Mine own self-love quite contrary I read;
Self so self-loving were iniquity.                            12
   'Tis thee, myself, that for myself I praise,
   Painting my age with beauty of thy days.

---

**62 • 5 Methinks** it seems to me   **7 for myself** (1) by my own reckoning
(2) for my own pleasure   **8 As** (1) inasmuch as (2) as if.   **other** others
**9 indeed** i.e., as I actually am   **10 Beated** battered, weather-beaten.
**tanned antiquity** i.e., leathery old age   **12 Self . . . iniquity** i.e., it would
be wicked for the self to love such an aged and unattractive self
**13 thee, myself** i.e., you, with whom I identify myself.   **for** as   **14 days**
i.e., youth

## 63

Against my love shall be, as I am now,
With Time's injurious hand crushed and o'erworn;
When hours have drained his blood and filled his brow
With lines and wrinkles; when his youthful morn          4
Hath traveled on to age's steepy night,
And all those beauties whereof now he's king
Are vanishing or vanished out of sight,
Stealing away the treasure of his spring;                8
For such a time do I now fortify
Against confounding age's cruel knife,
That he shall never cut from memory
My sweet love's beauty, though my lover's life.          12
   His beauty shall in these black lines be seen,
   And they shall live, and he in them still green.

---

**63 · 1 Against** anticipating the time when.  **love** beloved  **2 crushed and
o'erworn** creased and worn threadbare (like a long-used garment)
**5 steepy** precipitous, i.e., descending swiftly toward death  **9 For such a
time** (Parallel in construction with *Against* in l. 1.)  **fortify** raise works
of defense  **10 confounding** destroying  **11 That** so that  **12 though** i.e.,
though he cut  **13 black** (1) inscribed in ink (2) the opposite of fair or
beautiful  **14 green** i.e., as in springtime and youth

## 64

When I have seen by Time's fell hand defaced
The rich proud cost of outworn buried age;
When sometime lofty towers I see down-razed
And brass eternal slave to mortal rage;                    4
When I have seen the hungry ocean gain
Advantage on the kingdom of the shore,
And the firm soil win of the watery main,
Increasing store with loss and loss with store;            8
When I have seen such interchange of state,
Or state itself confounded to decay,
Ruin hath taught me thus to ruminate:
That Time will come and take my love away.                 12
   This thought is as a death, which cannot choose
   But weep to have that which it fears to lose.

**64 · 1 fell** cruel **2 The rich . . . age** i.e., those monuments that were the
product of proud wealth and magnificent outlay in times now past and
forgotten **3 sometime** formerly **4 brass . . . rage** i.e., seemingly inde-
structible brass subdued to the destructive power of mortality **7 of** at
the expense of **8 Increasing . . . store** i.e., one gaining as the other
loses, and losing as the other gains **9 state** condition **10 state** pomp,
greatness; condition in the abstract. **confounded to decay** destroyed to
the point of being in ruins **12 love** beloved **13 which cannot choose**
(Modifies *thought*.) **14 to have** i.e., because it now has

# 65

Since brass, nor stone, nor earth, nor boundless sea,
But sad mortality o'ersways their power,
How with this rage shall beauty hold a plea,
Whose action is no stronger than a flower?                        4
O, how shall summer's honey breath hold out
Against the wrackful siege of battering days,
When rocks impregnable are not so stout,
Nor gates of steel so strong, but Time decays?                    8
O fearful meditation! Where, alack,
Shall Time's best jewel from Time's chest lie hid?
Or what strong hand can hold his swift foot back?
Or who his spoil of beauty can forbid?                            12
  O, none, unless this miracle have might,
  That in black ink my love may still shine bright.

---

**65 · 1 Since** i.e., since there is neither  **2 But** but that.  **o'ersways**
overrules  **3 with this rage** against this destructive force (the *mortal
rage* of 64.4).  **hold** maintain (as in a legal action)  **4 action** case (in
law)  **6 wrackful** destructive  **7 stout** sturdy, impregnable  **8 decays**
brings about their decay  **10 from Time's chest** i.e., away from being
deposited by Time in his repository of forgetfulness  **12 spoil** despolia-
tion, ravaging

# 66

Tired with all these, for restful death I cry:
As, to behold desert a beggar born,
And needy nothing trimmed in jollity,
And purest faith unhappily forsworn,                                    4
And gilded honor shamefully misplaced,
And maiden virtue rudely strumpeted,
And right perfection wrongfully disgraced,
And strength by limping sway disablèd,                                    8
And art made tongue-tied by authority,
And folly doctorlike controlling skill,
And simple truth miscalled simplicity,
And captive good attending captain ill.                                    12
   Tired with all these, from these would I be gone,
   Save that, to die, I leave my love alone.

---

**66 · 1 all these** i.e., the following   **2 As** for instance, namely.   **desert** i.e.,
those who have merit, as contrasted with *needy nothing* in the next line,
those insignificant persons who deserve nothing, or those who in beg-
garly worthlessness squander what little they have on *jollity* or finery
**4 unhappily forsworn** evilly betrayed   **5 gilded** golden, splendid (not
here suggesting mere appearance of splendor)   **7 right** true.   **disgraced**
banished from favor   **8 limping sway** halting leadership   **9 art** literature, learning.   **made tongue-tied** i.e., censored, stifled   **10 doctorlike**
assuming a learned bearing.   **controlling** dominating, curbing
**11 simplicity** foolishness, naivete   **12 attending** waiting on, subordi-
nated to   **14 to die** in dying

# 67

Ah, wherefore with infection should he live,
And with his presence grace impiety,
That sin by him advantage should achieve
And lace itself with his society?                                    4
Why should false painting imitate his cheek
And steal dead seeing of his living hue?
Why should poor beauty indirectly seek
Roses of shadow, since his rose is true?                            8
Why should he live, now Nature bankrupt is,
Beggared of blood to blush through lively veins,
For she hath no exchequer now but his,
And, proud of many, lives upon his gains?                          12
   O, him she stores, to show what wealth she had
   In days long since, before these last so bad.

**67 • 1 wherefore** why.  **with infection** i.e., with the world's ills as enu-
merated in the preceding sonnet.  **he** i.e., the poet's friend  **3 That . . .
achieve** with the result that sin should flourish by his means  **4 lace . . .
society** (1) adorn itself with his company (2) weave its way into his
company  **6 dead seeing of** lifeless appearance from  **7 poor** inferior.
**indirectly** imitatively, or falsely  **8 Roses of shadow** i.e., painted roses,
cosmetically applied  **9–10 now . . . veins** i.e., seeing as Nature is
bankrupt through supplying him all her arts, and is therefore now
destitute of healthy blood to make red the veins  **11 For** since.  **exchequer** i.e., treasury of natural beauty  **12 proud** i.e., though proudly
boasting.  **gains** endowments  **13 stores** preserves, keeps in store
**14 last** i.e., recent days, the present

## 68

Thus is his cheek the map of days outworn,
When beauty lived and died as flowers do now,
Before these bastard signs of fair were born,
Or durst inhabit on a living brow;                              4
Before the golden tresses of the dead,
The right of sepulchers, were shorn away
To live a second life on second head;
Ere beauty's dead fleece made another gay.                      8
In him those holy antique hours are seen
Without all ornament, itself and true,
Making no summer of another's green,
Robbing no old to dress his beauty new;                        12
  And him as for a map doth Nature store,
  To show false Art what beauty was of yore.

---

**68 · 1 map** picture, image   **3 bastard . . . fair** i.e., cosmetics   **4 inhabit**
dwell   **6 The right of** rightly belonging in. (Wigs were made of dead
persons' hair.)   **8 gay** lovely, gaudy   **9 holy antique hours** blessed
ancient times   **10 all** any   **13 store** preserve

# 69

Those parts of thee that the world's eye doth view
Want nothing that the thought of hearts can mend;
All tongues, the voice of souls, give thee that due,
Utt'ring bare truth, even so as foes commend.          4
Thy outward thus with outward praise is crowned,
But those same tongues that give thee so thine own
In other accents do this praise confound
By seeing farther than the eye hath shown.             8
They look into the beauty of thy mind,
And that, in guess, they measure by thy deeds;
Then, churls, their thoughts, although their eyes were
    kind,
To thy fair flower add the rank smell of weeds.        12
    But why thy odor matcheth not thy show,
    The soil is this, that thou dost common grow.

69 • 2 **Want** lack.  **mend** improve upon  **3 the voice of souls** i.e., uttering
heartfelt conviction.  **give thee that due** allow that as your due
**4 Utt'ring . . . commend** i.e., thus saying what even your enemies would
concede to be the bare truth  **5 outward praise** the kind of praise suited
to mere outward qualities  **6 thine own** your due  **7 In other accents** in
other terms and with another emphasis.  **confound** confute, destroy
**10 in guess** at a guess  **12 To . . . weeds** i.e., to the flower of your outward beauty they contrastingly suggest something putrid within
**13 odor** i.e., reputation  **14 soil** (1) blemish, fault (2) origin, source,
ground.  **common** stale, vulgar (like a weed)

# 70

That thou are blamed shall not be thy defect,
For slander's mark was ever yet the fair;
The ornament of beauty is suspect,
A crow that flies in heaven's sweetest air.                    4
So thou be good, slander doth but approve
Thy worth the greater, being wooed of time,
For canker vice the sweetest buds doth love,
And thou present'st a pure unstainèd prime.                    8
Thou hast passed by the ambush of young days,
Either not assailed, or victor being charged;
Yet this thy praise cannot be so thy praise
To tie up envy evermore enlarged.                             12
　　If some suspect of ill masked not thy show,
　　Then thou alone kingdoms of hearts shouldst owe.

**70·1 defect** fault　**2 mark** target　**3 The . . . suspect** i.e., beauty is
always attended by suspicion (*suspect*), as though suspicion were a
necessary ornament to beauty　**5 So** provided that.　**approve** prove
**6 being . . . time** i.e., since you are courted by the world　**7 canker vice**
i.e., slander that is like the cankerworm　**8 unstainèd prime** unspotted
youth (like the pure unspoiled flower that attracts the cankerworm)
**9 ambush . . . days** i.e., temptations of youth　**10 being charged** when
you were assailed　**11 so** sufficiently　**12 To . . . enlarged** i.e., as to
silence malice, which is always at liberty　**13 If . . . show** if some
suspicion (*suspect*) of illdoing did not partly obscure your outward
attractiveness　**14 owe** own

# 71

No longer mourn for me when I am dead
Than you shall hear the surly sullen bell
Give warning to the world that I am fled
From this vile world, with vilest worms to dwell.          4
Nay, if you read this line, remember not
The hand that writ it, for I love you so
That I in your sweet thoughts would be forgot
If thinking on me then should make you woe.               8
O, if, I say, you look upon this verse
When I perhaps compounded am with clay,
Do not so much as my poor name rehearse,
But let your love even with my life decay,               12
   Lest the wise world should look into your moan
   And mock you with me after I am gone.

**71 · 2 bell** a passing bell for one who has died, rung once for each year
of that person's life   **8 on** of, about.   **make** cause   **10 compounded**
mingled   **11 rehearse** repeat   **12 even with** at the same time as
**14 with** because of, for loving

# 72

O, lest the world should task you to recite
What merit lived in me that you should love
After my death, dear love, forget me quite;
For you in me can nothing worthy prove,          4
Unless you would devise some virtuous lie
To do more for me than mine own desert,
And hang more praise upon deceasèd I
Than niggard truth would willingly impart.        8
O, lest your true love may seem false in this,
That you for love speak well of me untrue,
My name be buried where my body is,
And live no more to shame nor me nor you.      12
   For I am shamed by that which I bring forth,
    And so should you, to love things nothing worth.

---

**72 · 1 recite** tell   **7 hang** (as in hanging trophies on a funeral monument)   **10 untrue** untruly   **11 My name be** let my name be   **12 nor . . . nor** neither . . . nor   **13 that . . . forth** (Perhaps a deprecatory reference to the author's acting and writing of plays, but more probably his verse or his written work generally.)   **14 should you** i.e., you ought to be ashamed

# 73

That time of year thou mayst in me behold
When yellow leaves, or none, or few, do hang
Upon those boughs which shake against the cold,
Bare ruined choirs, where late the sweet birds sang.     4
In me thou seest the twilight of such day
As after sunset fadeth in the west,
Which by and by black night doth take away,
Death's second self, that seals up all in rest.     8
In me thou seest the glowing of such fire
That on the ashes of his youth doth lie,
As the deathbed whereon it must expire,
Consumed with that which it was nourished by.     12
   This thou perceiv'st, which makes thy love more
     strong,
   To love that well which thou must leave ere long.

**73 · 4 choirs** those areas of churches where the service is sung, here
viewed as in ruins and resembling the arched shape of bare trees. **late**
lately **8 seals** closes **10 That** as. **his** (1) its (2) his

## 74

But be contented when that fell arrest
Without all bail shall carry me away;
My life hath in this line some interest,
Which for memorial still with thee shall stay. 4
When thou reviewest this, thou dost review
The very part was consecrate to thee.
The earth can have but earth, which is his due;
My spirit is thine, the better part of me. 8
So then thou hast but lost the dregs of life,
The prey of worms, my body being dead,
The coward conquest of a wretch's knife,
Too base of thee to be rememberèd. 12
   The worth of that is that which it contains,
    And that is this, and this with thee remains.

---

**74 · 1 be contented** do not be distressed. **that fell arrest** i.e., death.
**fell** cruel  **3 line** verse.  **interest** legal concern, right, or title  **4 still**
always  **5 reviewest this** see this again (and view it with a critical eye)
**6 part was** part (of me) that was.  **consecrate** dedicated solemnly (as in
a religious service)  **7 his** its  **11 The coward . . . knife** i.e., the cowardly conquest that even such a poor wretch as Mortality, or Death, can
make with his scythe  **12 of . . . rememberèd** to be remembered by you
**13–14 The worth . . . remains** the only worth of my body is the spirit it
contains—i.e., this verse, which will remain with you

# 75

So are you to my thoughts as food to life,
Or as sweet-seasoned showers are to the ground.
And for the peace of you I hold such strife
As twixt a miser and his wealth is found:                    4
Now proud as an enjoyer, and anon
Doubting the filching age will steal his treasure;
Now counting best to be with you alone,
Then bettered that the world may see my pleasure;           8
Sometimes all full with feasting on your sight
And by and by clean starvèd for a look;
Possessing or pursuing no delight
Save what is had or must from you be took.                   12
   Thus do I pine and surfeit day by day,
   Or gluttoning on all, or all away.

75 • 1 **as food to life** what food is to life   2 **sweet-seasoned** of the sweet
season, i.e., spring   3 **of you** to be found in loving you   6 **Doubting**
suspecting, fearing that.   **filching** thieving   7 **counting** (1) thinking it
(2) reckoning, like a miser   8 **bettered** made happier, better pleased.
**see my pleasure** i.e., see me with you, enjoying your company   10 **clean**
completely, absolutely.   **a look** (1) a glimpse of you (2) an exchange of
glances   12 **from you** (Modifies both verbs, *had* and *must be took*.)
13 **pine and surfeit** starve and overeat   14 **Or . . . or** either . . . or.   **all
away** i.e., all food being taken away

# 76

Why is my verse so barren of new pride?
So far from variation or quick change?
Why with the time do I not glance aside
To newfound methods and to compounds strange?          4
Why write I still all one, ever the same,
And keep invention in a noted weed,
That every word doth almost tell my name,
Showing their birth and where they did proceed?          8
O, know, sweet love, I always write of you,
And you and love are still my argument;
So all my best is dressing old words new,
Spending again what is already spent.          12
  For as the sun is daily new and old,
  So is my love still telling what is told.

76 • 1 **pride** ornament   2 **quick change** fashionable innovation   3 **time**
way of the world, fashion   4 **compounds strange** literary inventions, or
perhaps compound words, neologisms   5 **still all one** continually one
way   6 **invention** literary creation.   **noted weed** familiar garment
8 **where** whence   10 **still** always.   **argument** subject, theme   14 **telling**
(1) retelling (2) counting over. (Continuing the financial wordplay of
*Spending* and *spent* in l. 12.)

# 77

Thy glass will show thee how thy beauties wear,
Thy dial how thy precious minutes waste;
The vacant leaves thy mind's imprint will bear,
And of this book this learning mayst thou taste.      4
The wrinkles which thy glass will truly show
Of mouthèd graves will give thee memory;
Thou by thy dial's shady stealth mayst know
Time's thievish progress to eternity.                 8
Look what thy memory cannot contain
Commit to these waste blanks, and thou shalt find
Those children nursed, delivered from thy brain,
To take a new acquaintance of thy mind.               12
   These offices, so oft as thou wilt look,
   Shall profit thee and much enrich thy book.

77 • 1 glass mirror. wear wear away   2 dial sundial   3 vacant leaves
blank pages. (Apparently these lines accompanied the gift of a book of
blank pages, a memorandum book.) thy mind's imprint i.e., your
reflections and ideas, to be set down in the memorandum book   4 this
learning i.e., mental profit derived from reflecting and keeping a jour-
nal, as explained in ll. 9 ff.   6 mouthèd all-devouring, gaping. memory
reminder   7 shady stealth slow progress of the shadow on the dial
9 Look what whatever   10 waste blanks blank pages   11 nursed i.e.,
preserved and matured. delivered from having been produced by
12 take . . . of i.e., provide fresh insight to, be freshly remembered by
13 offices duties (of meditation and reflection)   14 and . . . book i.e.,
and you will set down your reflections in the memorandum book, where
they will profit you

# 78

So oft have I invoked thee for my Muse
And found such fair assistance in my verse
As every alien pen hath got my use,
And under thee their poesy disperse.                    4
Thine eyes, that taught the dumb on high to sing
And heavy ignorance aloft to fly,
Have added feathers to the learnèd's wing
And given grace a double majesty.                       8
Yet be most proud of that which I compile,
Whose influence is thine and born of thee.
In others' works thou dost but mend the style,
And arts with thy sweet graces gracèd be;               12
    But thou art all my art, and dost advance
    As high as learning my rude ignorance.

**78·2 fair** favorable    **3 As** that.    **alien pen** i.e., other poet.    **got my use**
adopted my practice    **4 under thee** i.e., with you as their muse or
patron; under your influence.    **disperse** circulate    **5 on high** aloud
**6 aloft to fly** i.e., to get off the ground    **7 added . . . wing** i.e., enabled
learned poets to fly higher still. (A falconry metaphor; birds could be
given extra wing feathers.)    **8 And . . . majesty** and have added to the
majesty of poets already capable of it    **9 compile** compose, write
**10 influence** inspiration (with suggestion of astrological meaning)
**11 mend the style** correct or improve the style (but with a suggestion of
repairing the point of a writing quill or stylus, continuing the metaphor
of *pen*)    **12 arts** learning, literary culture    **13 advance** lift up

# 79

Whilst I alone did call upon thy aid,
My verse alone had all thy gentle grace,
But now my gracious numbers are decayed
And my sick Muse doth give another place.          4
I grant, sweet love, thy lovely argument
Deserves the travail of a worthier pen,
Yet what of thee thy poet doth invent
He robs thee of and pays it thee again.            8
He lends thee virtue, and he stole that word
From thy behavior; beauty doth he give,
And found it in thy cheek; he can afford
No praise to thee but what in thee doth live.      12
   Then thank him not for that which he doth say,
   Since what he owes thee thou thyself dost pay.

**79 · 3 numbers** verse   **4 give another place** yield place to another   **5 thy lovely argument** the theme of your lovable qualities   **6 travail** labor **7–8 Yet . . . again** i.e., yet whatever a poet under your patronage discovers as a literary subject concerning you he merely robs from you and gives you back your own again   **11 afford** offer to pay

# 80

O, how I faint when I of you do write,
Knowing a better spirit doth use your name,
And in the praise thereof spends all his might
To make me tongue-tied, speaking of your fame!                    4
But since your worth, wide as the ocean is,
The humble as the proudest sail doth bear,
My saucy bark, inferior far to his,
On your broad main doth willfully appear.                         8
Your shallowest help will hold me up afloat,
Whilst he upon your soundless deep doth ride;
Or, being wrecked, I am a worthless boat,
He of tall building and of goodly pride.                          12
    Then if he thrive and I be cast away,
     The worst was this: my love was my decay.

---

**80 • 1 faint** grow weak, falter   **2 better spirit** i.e., rival poet, whom the
speaker admires   **5 wide . . . is** as wide as is the ocean   **6 as** as well
as   **8 main** ocean.   **willfully** perversely, boldly, in spite of all
**10 soundless** unfathomable   **11 wrecked** shipwrecked   **12 tall building**
i.e., sturdy construction.   **pride** splendor   **13 cast away** (1) shipwrecked
(2) abandoned   **14 decay** ruin

## 81

Or I shall live your epitaph to make,
Or you survive when I in earth am rotten,
From hence your memory death cannot take,
Although in me each part will be forgotten.                    4
Your name from hence immortal life shall have,
Though I, once gone, to all the world must die;
The earth can yield me but a common grave,
When you entombèd in men's eyes shall lie.                    8
Your monument shall be my gentle verse,
Which eyes not yet created shall o'erread,
And tongues to be your being shall rehearse
When all the breathers of this world are dead.                    12
   You still shall live—such virtue hath my pen—
   Where breath most breathes, even in the mouths
     of men.

**81 · 1 Or** whether   **3 hence** (1) this poetry (2) the earth (also in l. 5)   **4 in . . . part** every quality of mine (as distinguished from the poetry)   **5 from hence** (1) from this poetry (2) henceforth   **11 to be** i.e., of persons yet unborn.   **rehearse** recite   **12 breathers** living people.   **this world** this present time   **13 virtue** power

# 82

I grant thou wert not married to my Muse,
And therefore mayst without attaint o'erlook
The dedicated words which writers use
Of their fair subject, blessing every book.                    4
Thou art as fair in knowledge as in hue,
Finding thy worth a limit past my praise,
And therefore art enforced to seek anew
Some fresher stamp of the time-bettering days.                 8
And do so, love; yet when they have devised
What strainèd touches rhetoric can lend,
Thou, truly fair, wert truly sympathized
In true plain words by thy true-telling friend;                12
   And their gross painting might be better used
    Where cheeks need blood; in thee it is abused.

---

**82 · 2 attaint** blame, discredit.  **o'erlook** look at, peruse   **3 dedicated**
devoted (with suggestion of *dedicatory*).  **writers** i.e., other writers
**4 blessing every book** i.e., you bestowing favor thus on the writings of
others   **5 hue** complexion, appearance   **6 a limit** an extent   **8 Some . . .
days** some more recent and current literary product of this culturally
advanced age   **11 wert truly sympathized** would be faithfully matched
and described   **13 gross** extravagantly flattering.  **painting** (The imagery sees flattering praise as a kind of cosmetic.)   **14 abused** misused,
misapplied

# 83

I never saw that you did painting need,
And therefore to your fair no painting set;
I found, or thought I found, you did exceed
The barren tender of a poet's debt;                                    4
And therefore have I slept in your report,
That you yourself, being extant, well might show
How far a modern quill doth come too short,
Speaking of worth, what worth in you doth grow.         8
This silence for my sin you did impute,
Which shall be most my glory, being dumb;
For I impair not beauty, being mute,
When others would give life and bring a tomb.            12
　　There lives more life in one of your fair eyes
　　Than both your poets can in praise devise.

83 · **2 fair** beauty.  **set** applied   **4 barren tender** paltry offering.  **debt**
payment   **5 slept . . . report** been neglectful in writing praisingly of
you   **6 That** because, so that.  **extant** still alive and much in the public
eye   **7 modern** commonplace   **7–8 doth . . . grow** comes too short, in
describing your worth, of the actual worth that flourishes in you
**9–10 This . . . dumb** you imputed my silence to sinfulness when in fact
it will prove most to my credit   **11 being mute** (Modifies *I*.)   **12 a tomb**
i.e., an inadequate monument that conceals lifelessly rather than enhancing   **14 both your poets** i.e., (probably,) I and the rival poet

## 84

Who is it that says most which can say more
Than this rich praise—that you alone are you,
In whose confine immurèd is the store
Which should example where your equal grew?          4
Lean penury within that pen doth dwell
That to his subject lends not some small glory;
But he that writes of you, if he can tell
That you are you, so dignifies his story.            8
Let him but copy what in you is writ,
Not making worse what nature made so clear,
And such a counterpart shall fame his wit,
Making his style admirèd everywhere.                 12
  You to your beauteous blessings add a curse,
    Being fond on praise, which makes your praises
      worse.

---

**84 • 1–2 Who . . . praise** what extravagant writer of praise can say more
than this in way of praise.  **which** who   **3–4 In . . . grew** i.e., in whose
person are contained all those rich qualities that would be needed as a
model to produce again your equal in beauty   **5–6 Lean . . . glory** i.e., it
is a poor piece of writing indeed that does not confer at least some
glory on its subject   **8 so** sufficiently, thus   **10 clear** glorious
**11 counterpart** copy, likeness.  **fame** endow with fame   **13 curse**
(1) defect in character (2) burden for those seeking to praise you
**14 Being fond** doting.  **which . . . worse** (1) which encourages false
flattery (2) which makes all praises seem inadequate in comparison to
you

# 85

My tongue-tied Muse in manners holds her still,
While comments of your praise, richly compiled,
Reserve thy character with golden quill
And precious phrase by all the Muses filed.                    4
I think good thoughts whilst other write good words,
And like unlettered clerk still cry "Amen"
To every hymn that able spirit affords
In polished form of well-refinèd pen.                          8
Hearing you praised, I say " 'Tis so, 'tis true,"
And to the most of praise add something more;
But that is in my thought, whose love to you,
Though words come hindmost, holds his rank before.            12
    Then others for the breath of words respect,
    Me for my dumb thoughts, speaking in effect.

85 • 1 in . . . still i.e., politely remains silent   2 comments . . . compiled
eulogies of you composed in fine language   3 Reserve thy character i.e.,
store up praise of you in their writings. (The quarto reading, Reserne
[i.e., Reserve] their Character, might mean "preserve their own writing.")   golden aureate, affected   4 precious affected.   filed polished
5 other others   6 unlettered clerk illiterate assistant to a priest.   still
cry "Amen" i.e., continually give my approval   7 hymn i.e., praising
verse.   that able spirit i.e., the rival poet (and others like him).   affords
provides   10 most utmost   11 that . . . thought i.e., that which I add is
added silently   12 holds . . . before considers its place to be before all
others   13 Then . . . respect then take notice of others for what they say
14 speaking in effect i.e., which convey what speech would say

# 86

Was it the proud full sail of his great verse,
Bound for the prize of all-too-precious you,
That did my ripe thoughts in my brain inhearse,
Making their tomb the womb wherein they grew?          4
Was it his spirit, by spirits taught to write
Above a mortal pitch, that struck me dead?
No, neither he, nor his compeers by night
Giving him aid, my verse astonishèd.                   8
He, nor that affable familiar ghost
Which nightly gulls him with intelligence,
As victors of my silence cannot boast;
I was not sick of any fear from thence.                12
    But when your countenance filled up his line,
    Then lacked I matter; that enfeebled mine.

---

86 • 1 his i.e., an unidentified rival poet's   2 prize capture, booty (as in a
seized cargo vessel)  3 inhearse coffin up   5 spirits i.e., literary ances-
tors or contemporaries (with a suggestion also of daemons)  6 pitch
height. (A term from falconry.)   dead i.e., dumb, silent   7 compeers by
night spirits (see l. 5) visiting and aiding the poet in his dreams or
nighttime reading   8 astonishèd struck dumb   9 ghost spirit (as in ll. 5
and 7)   10 gulls misleads, gorges.   intelligence information, ideas
12 of with   13 countenance filled up (1) approval repaired any defect in
(2) beauty served as subject for   14 lacked I matter I had nothing left to
write about

# 87

Farewell! Thou art too dear for my possessing,
And like enough thou know'st thy estimate.
The charter of thy worth gives thee releasing;
My bonds in thee are all determinate.                    4
For how do I hold thee but by thy granting,
And for that riches where is my deserving?
The cause of this fair gift in me is wanting,
And so my patent back again is swerving.                 8
Thyself thou gav'st, thy own worth then not knowing,
Or me, to whom thou gav'st it, else mistaking;
So thy great gift, upon misprision growing,
Comes home again, on better judgment making.            12
    Thus have I had thee as a dream doth flatter,
    In sleep a king, but waking no such matter.

---

**87 · 1 dear** precious   **2 like** likely, probably.   **estimate** value   **3 charter
of** privilege derived from.   **releasing** i.e., release from obligations of
love   **4 determinate** ended, expired. (A legal term, as throughout this
sonnet.)   **8 patent** charter granting rights of monopoly; hence, privilege.   **swerving** returning (to you)   **10 mistaking** i.e., overvaluing
**11 upon misprision growing** arising out of error   **12 on . . . making** on
your forming a more accurate judgment

# 88

When thou shalt be disposed to set me light
And place my merit in the eye of scorn,
Upon thy side against myself I'll fight
And prove thee virtuous, though thou art forsworn.      4
With mine own weakness being best acquainted,
Upon thy part I can set down a story
Of faults concealed, wherein I am attainted,
That thou in losing me shall win much glory.           8
And I by this will be a gainer too;
For, bending all my loving thoughts on thee,
The injuries that to myself I do,
Doing thee vantage, double-vantage me.                 12
   Such is my love, to thee I so belong,
   That for thy right myself will bear all wrong.

---

**88 · 1 set me light** make light of me, value me slightingly   **3 Upon thy side** supporting your case (also *Upon thy part* in l. 6)   **7 concealed** not publicly known.   **attainted** dishonored   **8 That** so that.   **losing** i.e., separating from (with a suggestion of *loosing*, setting free, the quarto spelling)   **12 vantage** advantage

# 89

Say that thou didst forsake me for some fault,
And I will comment upon that offense;
Speak of my lameness, and I straight will halt,
Against thy reasons making no defense.     4
Thou canst not, love, disgrace me half so ill,
To set a form upon desirèd change,
As I'll myself disgrace, knowing thy will.
I will acquaintance strangle and look strange,     8
Be absent from thy walks, and in my tongue
Thy sweet belovèd name no more shall dwell,
Lest I, too much profane, should do it wrong
And haply of our old acquaintance tell.     12
   For thee against myself I'll vow debate,
   For I must ne'er love him whom thou dost hate.

**89 • 1 Say** assert, claim   **2 comment** enlarge   **3 Speak . . . halt** i.e., if
you ascribe to me any kind of handicap, I immediately will limp to
show that you are right. (*Halt* also has the suggestion of ceasing to
object, remaining silent.)   **4 reasons** charges, arguments   **5 disgrace**
discredit   **6 To . . . change** to provide a pretext for (in the interest of
justifying) your change of affection, and to set it in proper order   **7 As
. . . disgrace** as I will disfigure and depreciate myself   **8 acquaintance
strangle** put an end to familiarity (with you).   **strange** like a stranger
**9 walks** haunts   **12 haply** perchance   **13 vow debate** declare hostility,
quarrel

# 90

Then hate me when thou wilt; if ever, now;
Now, while the world is bent my deeds to cross,
Join with the spite of fortune, make me bow,
And do not drop in for an after-loss.                           4
Ah, do not, when my heart hath scaped this sorrow,
Come in the rearward of a conquered woe;
Give not a windy night a rainy morrow,
To linger out a purposed overthrow.                             8
If thou wilt leave me, do not leave me last,
When other petty griefs have done their spite,
But in the onset come; so shall I taste
At first the very worst of fortune's might,                    12
    And other strains of woe, which now seem woe,
    Compared with loss of thee will not seem so.

90 • 2 bent determined.   cross thwart   4 drop . . . after-loss crushingly
add to my sorrow at some future time   5–6 when . . . woe i.e., follow
with an attack after I have overcome my present misfortune.   in the
rearward of behind. (A military metaphor.)   7 windy, rainy (Suggestive
of sighs and tears.)   8 linger out protract.   purposed intended, inevitable   11 in the onset at the outset   13 strains kinds

# 91

Some glory in their birth, some in their skill,
Some in their wealth, some in their body's force,
Some in their garments, though newfangled ill,
Some in their hawks and hounds, some in their horse;    4
And every humor hath his adjunct pleasure,
Wherein it finds a joy above the rest.
But these particulars are not my measure;
All these I better in one general best.                 8
Thy love is better than high birth to me,
Richer than wealth, prouder than garments' cost,
Of more delight than hawks or horses be;
And having thee, of all men's pride I boast—            12
    Wretched in this alone, that thou mayst take
    All this away and me most wretched make.

**91 · 3 newfangled ill** fashionably unattractive  **4 horse** horses  **5 humor**
disposition, temperament.  **his** its.  **adjunct** corresponding  **7 measure**
standard (of happiness)  **8 better** surpass, improve upon  **10 prouder**
more an object of pride  **12 of . . . boast** I boast of having the equiva-
lent of all that is a source of pride in other men

## 92

But do thy worst to steal thyself away,
For term of life thou art assurèd mine,
And life no longer than thy love will stay,
For it depends upon that love of thine.                    4
Then need I not to fear the worst of wrongs,
When in the least of them my life hath end;
I see a better state to me belongs
Than that which on thy humor doth depend.                  8
Thou canst not vex me with inconstant mind,
Since that my life on thy revolt doth lie.
O, what a happy title do I find,
Happy to have thy love, happy to die!                      12
   But what's so blessèd-fair that fears no blot?
   Thou mayst be false, and yet I know it not.

**92 · 1 But do** i.e., but even if you do  **2 term of life** i.e., my lifetime
**5–6 Then . . . end** i.e., I need not fear what most men would call the
worst of misfortunes, since the seemingly lesser misfortune—loss of
your friendship—would prove fatal to me  **7–8 I see . . . depend** i.e., I
see that I am happier than most men whose happiness ends when they
are cast from favor, since my very existence will cease when I am cast
from favor, and thus end my misery.  **humor** whim, fancy  **10 Since . . .
lie** since if you desert me it will cost me my life  **11 happy title** right to
be thought happy; fortunate legal right of ownership  **13 that fears** as
to fear  **14 Thou . . . not** i.e., my worst fate would be to lose your
affection without knowing it, and thereby live on in an unloved state,
unreleased by the death that certainty of your desertion would bring

## 93

So shall I live, supposing thou art true,
Like a deceivèd husband; so love's face
May still seem love to me, though altered new,
Thy looks with me, thy heart in other place.                    4
For there can live no hatred in thine eye,
Therefore in that I cannot know thy change.
In many's looks the false heart's history
Is writ in moods and frowns and wrinkles strange,              8
But heaven in thy creation did decree
That in thy face sweet love should ever dwell;
Whate'er thy thoughts or thy heart's workings be,
Thy looks should nothing thence but sweetness tell.            12
   How like Eve's apple doth thy beauty grow,
   If thy sweet virtue answer not thy show!

---

**93 · 1 So** (Continues the thought of Sonnet 92.)    **supposing** I supposing
(incorrectly)   **2 face** appearance   **3 new** to something new   **5 For**
since   **6 in . . . change** I won't be able to detect your changed affection
from your looks   **8 moods** moody looks.   **strange** unfriendly
**14 answer . . . show** does not conform with your outward appearance

# 94

They that have power to hurt and will do none,
That do not do the thing they most do show,
Who, moving others, are themselves as stone,
Unmovèd, cold, and to temptation slow,                         4
They rightly do inherit heaven's graces
And husband nature's riches from expense;
They are the lords and owners of their faces,
Others but stewards of their excellence.                       8
The summer's flower is to the summer sweet,
Though to itself it only live and die,
But if that flower with base infection meet,
The basest weed outbraves his dignity.                         12
  For sweetest things turn sourest by their deeds;
  Lilies that fester smell far worse than weeds.

---

**94·1 and . . . none** i.e., and do not willfully try to do hurt   **2 show** i.e.,
show themselves capable of; or, seem to do   **4 cold** dispassionate
**5 inherit** (1) receive through inheritance (2) enjoy, make use of
**6 husband** carefully manage, preserve.   **expense** waste, expenditure
**7 They . . . faces** i.e., they are completely masters of themselves and of
the qualities that appear in them   **8 but stewards** merely custodians or
dispensers   **10 it only** alone it   **12 outbraves his dignity** surpasses in
show its worth   **14 Lilies . . . weeds** (This line appears in the anonymous play *Edward III*, usually dated before 1595 and attributed in part
by some editors to Shakespeare.)

## 95

How sweet and lovely dost thou make the shame
Which, like a canker in the fragrant rose,
Doth spot the beauty of thy budding name!
O, in what sweets dost thou thy sins enclose!                    4
That tongue that tells the story of thy days,
Making lascivious comments on thy sport,
Cannot dispraise but in a kind of praise;
Naming thy name blesses an ill report.                          8
O, what a mansion have those vices got
Which for their habitation chose out thee,
Where beauty's veil doth cover every blot,
And all things turns to fair that eyes can see!                 12
    Take heed, dear heart, of this large privilege;
    The hardest knife ill used doth lose his edge.

95 · **2 canker** cankerworm that destroys buds and leaves  **3 name**
reputation  **6 sport** amours  **8 blesses** graces  **12 all . . . fair** either
(1) makes all things beautiful (the object of *veil*), or (2) all things become
beautiful  **14 his** its

## 96

Some say thy fault is youth, some wantonness;
Some say thy grace is youth and gentle sport;
Both grace and faults are loved of more and less;
Thou mak'st faults graces that to thee resort.                    4
As on the finger of a thronèd queen
The basest jewel will be well esteemed,
So are those errors that in thee are seen
To truths translated and for true things deemed.                  8
How many lambs might the stern wolf betray,
If like a lamb he could his looks translate!
How many gazers mightst thou lead away,
If thou wouldst use the strength of all thy state!                12
    But do not so; I love thee in such sort
    As, thou being mine, mine is thy good report.

**96 · 1 wantonness** amorousness   **2 gentle sport** gentlemanlike amorousness   **3 of more and less** by high and low   **4 Thou . . . resort** you
convert into graces the faults that attend you   **8 translated** transformed   **9 stern** cruel   **11 away** astray   **12 the strength . . . state** the
full power at your command—i.e., your wealth, charm, and social
rank   **13–14 But . . . report** (The same couplet ends Sonnet 36.)

# 97

How like a winter hath my absence been
From thee, the pleasure of the fleeting year!
What freezings have I felt, what dark days seen!
What old December's bareness everywhere! 4
And yet this time removed was summer's time,
The teeming autumn, big with rich increase,
Bearing the wanton burden of the prime,
Like widowed wombs after their lords' decease. 8
Yet this abundant issue seemed to me
But hope of orphans and unfathered fruit,,
For summer and his pleasures wait on thee,
And, thou away, the very birds are mute; 12
  Or, if they sing, 'tis with so dull a cheer
  That leaves look pale, dreading the winter's near.

97 • 5 **time removed** time of separation   **6 big** pregnant   **7 the wanton
. . . prime** the fruit or offspring of wanton spring, i.e., the crops planted
in springtime   **9 issue** offspring   **10 hope of orphans** orphaned hope
**11 his** its.   **wait on thee** attend on you, are at your disposal   **13 with
. . . cheer** in so melancholy a fashion

## 98

From you have I been absent in the spring,
When proud-pied, April dressed in all his trim,
Hath put a spirit of youth in everything,
That heavy Saturn laughed and leapt with him.                    4
Yet nor the lays of birds nor the sweet smell
Of different flowers in odor and in hue
Could make me any summer's story tell,
Or from their proud lap pluck them where they grew.       8
Nor did I wonder at the lily's white,
Nor praise the deep vermilion in the rose;
They were but sweet, but figures of delight
Drawn after you, you pattern of all those.                        12
   Yet seemed it winter still, and, you away,
   As with your shadow I with these did play.

98 · 2 proud-pied gorgeously multi-colored.   trim finery   4 That so
that.   Saturn (A planet associated with melancholy, *heavy*.)   5 nor the
lays neither the songs   6 different flowers flowers differing   7 any
summer's story i.e., any pleasant story   8 proud lap i.e., the earth
11 but sweet . . . delight mere sweetness, mere delightful forms or
emblems   12 after resembling   14 shadow image, portrait.   these i.e.,
the flowers

# 99

The forward violet thus did I chide:
"Sweet thief, whence didst thou steal thy sweet that
    smells,
If not from my love's breath? The purple pride
Which on thy soft cheek for complexion dwells       4
In my love's veins thou hast too grossly dyed."
The lily I condemnèd for thy hand,
And buds of marjoram had stol'n thy hair;
The roses fearfully on thorns did stand,       8
One blushing shame, another white despair;
A third, nor red nor white, had stol'n of both
And to his robbery had annexed thy breath,
But, for his theft, in pride of all his growth       12
A vengeful canker eat him up to death.
    More flowers I noted, yet I none could see
    But sweet or color it had stol'n from thee.

**99 · 1 forward** early, and presumptuous. (This sonnet has fifteen lines,
the first being introductory.) **2 thy sweet** your scent **3 pride** splendor **5 grossly** obviously and heavily **6 for thy hand** i.e., because it has
stolen its whiteness from your hand **7 And . . . hair** i.e., and I condemned the buds of marjoram for having stolen your hair. **buds of
marjoram** (These are dark purple red or auburn, and it may be that the
reference is to color, although marjoram is noted for its sweet scent.)
**8 on thorns did stand** grew on thorny stems (with a suggestion of being
apprehensive) **9 shame** i.e., red for shame **10 nor red** neither (purely)
red **11 to . . . annexed** to this robbery had added the robbery of
**12 But, for** although, in punishment for. **in pride . . . growth** in his
prime **13 canker eat** cankerworm ate **15 But** except. **sweet** scent (as
in l. 2)

# 100

Where art thou, Muse, that thou forgett'st so long
To speak of that which gives thee all thy might?
Spend'st thou thy fury on some worthless song,
Dark'ning thy pow'r to lend base subjects light?          4
Return, forgetful Muse, and straight redeem
In gentle numbers time so idly spent;
Sing to the ear that doth thy lays esteem
And gives thy pen both skill and argument.          8
Rise, resty Muse, my love's sweet face survey,
If Time have any wrinkle graven there;
If any, be a satire to decay,
And make Time's spoils despisèd everywhere.          12
　　Give my love fame faster than Time wastes life;
　　So thou prevent'st his scythe and crooked knife.

---

**100 · 3 fury** poetic inspiration  **4 Dark'ning** debasing  **5 straight**
straightway  **6 gentle numbers** noble verses.  **idly** foolishly  **7 lays**
songs  **8 argument** subject  **9 resty** inactive, inert  **10 If** to see if
**11 If any** if there are any.  **satire to** satirist of, here one composing a
satire on Time as a despoiler  **12 spoils** acts of destruction, ravages
**13 faster** (1) more quickly (2) more firmly  **14 thou prevent'st** you
forestall, thwart.  **crooked knife** curved blade

# 101

O truant Muse, what shall be thy amends
For thy neglect of truth in beauty dyed?
Both truth and beauty on my love depends;
So dost thou too, and therein dignified.                          4
Make answer, Muse. Wilt thou not haply say,
"Truth needs no color with his color fixed,
Beauty no pencil, beauty's truth to lay;
But best is best, if never intermixed"?                           8
Because he needs no praise, wilt thou be dumb?
Excuse not silence so, for 't lies in thee
To make him much outlive a gilded tomb
And to be praised of ages yet to be.                              12
    Then do thy office, Muse; I teach thee how
    To make him seem, long hence, as he shows now.

101 • 1 **what . . . amends** what reparation will you make   **3–4 Both . . .
dignified** i.e., both faith and beauty depend on my love for their proper
appreciation and recognition, and you, my Muse, depend for your very
office and dignity on that same function   **5 haply** perhaps   **6 no . . .
fixed** no artificial color (with suggestion of *pretense*) added to its natural and permanent color or hue   **7 pencil** paint brush.   **lay** apply color
to, as with a brush   **8 intermixed** adulterated   **9 dumb** silent   **12 of**
by   **13 office** function   **14 long hence** long in the future.   **shows**
appears

## 102

My love is strengthened, though more weak in seeming;
I love not less, though less the show appear.
That love is merchandized whose rich esteeming
The owner's tongue doth publish everywhere.                4
Our love was new and then but in the spring
When I was wont to greet it with my lays,
As Philomel in summer's front doth sing
And stops her pipe in growth of riper days.                8
Not that the summer is less pleasant now
Than when her mournful hymns did hush the night,
But that wild music burdens every bough
And sweets grown common lose their dear delight.          12
  Therefore like her I sometimes hold my tongue,
  Because I would not dull you with my song.

102 · 1 **seeming** outward appearance   3 **merchandized** degraded by
being treated as a thing of sale.   **esteeming** valuation   4 **publish** an-
nounce, advertise   6 **wont . . . lays** accustomed to salute it (our love)
with my song   7 **Philomel** the nightingale.   **front** forehead, beginning
8 **stops her pipe** stops singing.   **riper** i.e., those of late summer and
autumn   11 **But . . . music** i.e., but because a profusion of wild birds'
singing. (Refers to other poets.)   **burdens** weighs down (but with a
musical sense as well; a *burden* is a chorus)   14 **dull** surfeit

# 103

Alack, what poverty my Muse brings forth,
That, having such a scope to show her pride,
The argument all bare is of more worth
Than when it hath my added praise beside.          4
O, blame me not if I no more can write!
Look in your glass, and there appears a face
That overgoes my blunt invention quite,
Dulling my lines and doing me disgrace.            8
Were it not sinful then, striving to mend,
To mar the subject that before was well?
For to no other pass my verses tend
Than of your graces and your gifts to tell;        12
    And more, much more, than in my verse can sit
    Your own glass shows you when you look in it.

103 · 1 **poverty** poor stuff   2 **pride** splendor   3 **argument all bare**
subject alone, unadorned   5 **no more can write** i.e., cannot go beyond
what you yourself are, cannot excel my own poverty of invention
6 **glass** mirror   7 **overgoes** surpasses.   **blunt invention** unpolished
style, writing   8 **Dulling** i.e., making dull by comparison   11 **pass**
purpose, issue   13 **sit** reside

## 104

To me, fair friend, you never can be old,
For, as you were when first your eye I eyed,
Such seems your beauty still. Three winters cold
Have from the forests shook three summers' pride,               4
Three beauteous springs to yellow autumn turned
In process of the seasons have I seen,
Three April perfumes in three hot Junes burned,
Since first I saw you fresh, which yet are green.               8
Ah, yet doth beauty, like a dial hand,
Steal from his figure and no pace perceived.
So your sweet hue, which methinks still doth stand,
Hath motion, and mine eye may be deceived,                    12
    For fear of which, hear this, thou age unbred:
    Ere you were born was beauty's summer dead.

104 • 4 **pride** splendor   **6 process** the progression   **9 dial hand** watch
hand   **10 his figure** (1) the dial's numeral (2) the friend's shape.   **and
. . . perceived** i.e., imperceptibly   **11 hue** appearance, complexion.   **still
doth stand** remains motionless, unaltered   **13 of which** i.e., that my eye
may be deceived. (The poet, though wishing to believe that his friend
never can be old, concedes that this is a deception.)   **unbred** not yet
born

# 105

Let not my love be called idolatry,
Nor my belovèd as an idol show,
Since all alike my songs and praises be
To one, of one, still such, and ever so.                        4
Kind is my love today, tomorrow kind,
Still constant in a wondrous excellence;
Therefore my verse, to constancy confined,
One thing expressing, leaves out difference.                    8
"Fair, kind, and true" is all my argument,
"Fair, kind, and true" varying to other words;
And in this change is my invention spent,
Three themes in one, which wondrous scope affords.             12
  Fair, kind, and true have often lived alone,
   Which three till now never kept seat in one.

**105 · 2 show** appear   **3 Since** (1) simply because, or (2) since it can be said in my defense that   **4 still** always   **8 difference** variety of other literary subjects; any kind of diversity that detracts from the young man's constancy (including any suggestion of quarreling or fluctuation of mood)   **11 this change** variations on this theme.   **invention** inventiveness.   **spent** expended   **13 alone** separately (in different people)   **14 kept seat** resided; sat enthroned

# 106

When in the chronicle of wasted time
I see descriptions of the fairest wights,
And beauty making beautiful old rhyme
In praise of ladies dead and lovely knights,                    4
Then, in the blazon of sweet beauty's best,
Of hand, of foot, of lip, of eye, of brow,
I see their antique pen would have expressed
Even such a beauty as you master now.                           8
So all their praises are but prophecies
Of this our time, all you prefiguring;
And, for they looked but with divining eyes,
They had not skill enough your worth to sing.                   12
  For we, which now behold these present days,
  Have eyes to wonder, but lack tongues to praise.

106 • 1 **wasted** past, used up   **2 wights** persons   **3 beauty** (1) beauty of
style and language (2) beauty of the persons described   **5 blazon** i.e.,
glorification, cataloguing of qualities. (A heraldic metaphor.)   **7 see**
perceive (that).   **their** i.e., of antique poets.   **would have expressed**
wished to express   **8 master** possess, control   **11 for** because.   **divining** guessing or predicting as to the future   **13 For we** for even we
**14 praise** i.e., praise you worthily, sufficiently

# 107

Not mine own fears nor the prophetic soul
Of the wide world dreaming on things to come
Can yet the lease of my true love control,
Supposed as forfeit to a confined doom.                               4
The mortal moon hath her eclipse endured
And the sad augurs mock their own presage;
Incertainties now crown themselves assured
And peace proclaims olives of endless age.                            8
Now with the drops of this most balmy time
My love looks fresh, and Death to me subscribes,
Since, spite of him, I'll live in this poor rhyme,
While he insults o'er dull and speechless tribes;                     12
 And thou in this shalt find thy monument,
  When tyrants' crests and tombs of brass are spent.

**107 • 1–2 soul . . . world** collective consciousness of humanity **3 yet**
now. **lease** term, allotted time. **control** set a limit to **4 Supposed . . .
doom** i.e., though imagined to be destined to expire after a limited
term **5 mortal moon** (Probably a reference to Queen Elizabeth, ill or
deceased, most probably to her death in 1603; she was known as Diana,
Cynthia, etc.) **6 And . . . presage** and the solemn prophets of disaster
now mock their earlier predictions **7 Incertainties . . . assured** uncer-
tainties have triumphantly given way to certainties **8 olives** (Conventionally associated with peace, and probably pointing here to King
James VI's resolutions of war with Spain and strife in Ireland.) **of
endless age** i.e., without foreseen end **9 with the drops** i.e., healed as
though by a balmy dew. (Balm was employed in the coronation ceremony for James in 1603, as in all such coronations.) **10 subscribes**
yields **12 insults** triumphs **14 crests** trophies adorning a tomb.
**spent** expended, wasted away

# 108

What's in the brain that ink may character
Which hath not figured to thee my true spirit?
What's new to speak, what now to register,
That may express my love or thy dear merit?                    4
Nothing, sweet boy; but yet, like prayers divine,
I must each day say o'er the very same,
Counting no old thing old—thou mine, I thine—
Even as when first I hallowed thy fair name.                    8
So that eternal love in love's fresh case
Weighs not the dust and injury of age,
Nor gives to necessary wrinkles place,
But makes antiquity for aye his page,                          12
    Finding the first conceit of love there bred
    Where time and outward form would show it dead.

**108·1 character** write    **2 figured** revealed, represented.    **true** constant    **3 register** record    **7 Counting . . . thine** i.e., dismissing no old truth as out of date or shopworn, such as the truth that you are mine and I yours    **8 hallowed** (As in "hallowed be thy name" from the Lord's Prayer.)    **9 fresh case** new exterior and circumstance    **10 Weighs not** is unconcerned about    **11 place** consideration, primacy    **12 aye** ever. **page** servant, subordinate    **13 the first . . . love** i.e., the first conception of love, experienced as though for the first time.    **there** (1) in you (2) in my verse.    **bred** generated    **14 would** try to, wish to

## 109

O, never say that I was false of heart,
Though absence seemed my flame to qualify.
As easy might I from myself depart
As from my soul, which in thy breast doth lie.   4
That is my home of love; if I have ranged,
Like him that travels I return again,
Just to the time, not with the time exchanged,
So that myself bring water for my stain.   8
Never believe, though in my nature reigned
All frailties that besiege all kinds of blood,
That it could so preposterously be stained
To leave for nothing all thy sum of good;   12
   For "nothing" this wide universe I call
   Save thou, my rose; in it thou art my all.

---

**109 · 2 flame** passion.  **qualify** temper, moderate  **5 ranged** traveled,
wandered  **7 Just** punctual.  **the time . . . the time** the exact hour . . .
the period of separation.  **exchanged** changed  **8 So . . . stain** i.e., so
that I myself provide the means (my tears) of excusing my absence, of
washing away the stain  **10 blood** temperament, sensual nature  **12 for**
in exchange for

# 110

Alas, 'tis true, I have gone here and there
And made myself a motley to the view,
Gored mine own thoughts, sold cheap what is most
     dear,
Made old offenses of affections new;                    4
Most true it is that I have looked on truth
Askance and strangely. But, by all above,
These blenches gave my heart another youth,
And worse essays proved thee my best of love.           8
Now all is done, have what shall have no end.
Mine appetite I nevermore will grind
On newer proof, to try an older friend,
A god in love, to whom I am confined.                   12
　　Then give me welcome, next my heaven the best,
　　Even to thy pure and most most loving breast.

110•2 **motley** jester, fool.　**to the view** in the eyes of the world
3 **Gored** wounded　4 **Made . . . new** i.e., repeated old offenses or made
offense against old friendships in forming new attachments　5 **truth**
constancy　6 **Askance and strangely** disdainfully, obliquely and at a
distance.　**by all above** by heaven　7 **blenches** swervings　8 **essays**
experiments (in friendship)　9 **Now all** now that all that.　**have what**
**. . . end** take what is eternal (my friendship)　10 **grind** whet, sharpen
11 **newer proof** further experiment, experience.　**try** test　12 **A god**
godlike　13 **next my heaven** i.e., you, who are to me second only to
heaven itself

# 111

O, for my sake do you with Fortune chide,
The guilty goddess of my harmful deeds,
That did not better for my life provide
Than public means which public manners breeds.          4
Thence comes it that my name receives a brand,
And almost thence my nature is subdued
To what it works in, like the dyer's hand.
Pity me then, and wish I were renewed,                  8
Whilst, like a willing patient, I will drink
Potions of eisel 'gainst my strong infection;
No bitterness that I will bitter think,
Nor double penance, to correct correction.              12
    Pity me then, dear friend, and I assure ye
    Even that your pity is enough to cure me.

111·2 **guilty goddess** goddess responsible for   3 **life** livelihood   4 **Than
. . . breeds** i.e., than providing me a means of livelihood that depends on
catering to the public. (A probable reference to Shakespeare's career as
an actor.)   5 **receives a brand** is disgraced (through prejudice against
my occupation)   7 **like the dyer's hand** (The dyer's hand is stained by
the dye it handles, just as the poet's nature is almost overpowered by
the medium in which he works—the language of poetry and, more
particularly, the theater.)   8 **renewed** restored to what I was by nature,
cleansed   10 **eisel** vinegar, used as an antiseptic against the plague and
also as an agent for removing stains   11 **No bitterness** i.e., there is no
bitterness   12 **Nor . . . correction** i.e., nor will I think it bitter to undertake a twofold penance in order to correct what must be corrected
14 **Even that your pity** that very pity of yours

## 112

Your love and pity doth th' impression fill
Which vulgar scandal stamped upon my brow;
For what care I who calls me well or ill,
So you o'ergreen my bad, my good allow?                        4
You are my all the world, and I must strive
To know my shames and praises from your tongue;
None else to me, nor I to none alive,
That my steeled sense or changes right or wrong.              8
In so profound abysm I throw all care
Of others' voices, that my adder's sense
To critic and to flatterer stoppèd are.
Mark how with my neglect I do dispense:                      12
    You are so strongly in my purpose bred
    That all the world besides methinks are dead.

---

**112·1 th' impression fill** efface the scar   **2 vulgar scandal** i.e., notoriety (for being an actor?)   **4 So you o'ergreen** provided that you cover as with green growth.   **allow** approve   **5 my all the world** everything to me   **7–8 None . . . wrong** i.e., no one else but you affects my fixed and hardened sensibilities, whether for better or for worse   **9 In so profound** into such a deep   **10 Of** about.   **voices** i.e., criticism.   **adder's sense** i.e., deaf ears   **11 critic** fault-finder   **12 Mark . . . dispense** i.e., see how I excuse my disregard of the opinion of others   **13 You . . . bred** i.e., you are so nurtured in my thoughts and are such a powerful influence over my intentions

# 113

Since I left you, mine eye is in my mind,
And that which governs me to go about
Doth part his function and is partly blind,
Seems seeing, but effectually is out; 4
For it no form delivers to the heart
Of bird, of flower, or shape, which it doth latch;
Of his quick objects hath the mind no part,
Nor his own vision holds what it doth catch; 8
For if it see the rud'st or gentlest sight,
The most sweet-favor or deformedst creature,
The mountain or the sea, the day or night,
The crow or dove, it shapes them to your feature. 12
   Incapable of more, replete with you,
   My most true mind thus maketh mine eye untrue.

113 • 1 mine . . . mind i.e., I'm guided by my mind's eye   2 that . . .
about i.e., my physical sight   3 part divide.   his its, i.e., the physical
eye's (also in ll. 7 and 8)   4 Seems seeing seems to be seeing.   effectually in reality.   out out of commission, ineffectual   5 heart (Here
portrayed as capable of receiving sense impressions and of consciousness, as in Sonnet 47.)   6 latch catch or receive the sight of   7 Of . . .
part i.e., the mind, attuned to its inner eye, takes no part in the fleeting
and lively (quick) things seen by the physical sight   8 Nor . . . holds i.e.,
nor does the eye itself retain.   catch i.e., see glimpsingly   9 For . . .
sight for whether it see the most uncouth or most gracious sight
10 sweet-favor sweet-featured   12 shapes . . . feature makes them
resemble you

# 114

Or whether doth my mind, being crowned with you,
Drink up the monarch's plague, this flattery?
Or whether shall I say mine eye saith true,
And that your love taught it this alchemy,　　　　4
To make of monsters and things indigest
Such cherubins as your sweet self resemble,
Creating every bad a perfect best
As fast as objects to his beams assemble?　　　　8
O, 'tis the first, 'tis flattery in my seeing,
And my great mind most kingly drinks it up;
Mine eye well knows what with his gust is greeing,
And to his palate doth prepare the cup.　　　　12
　　If it be poisoned, 'tis the lesser sin
　　That mine eye loves it and doth first begin.

---

**114 · 1, 3 Or whether** (Indicates alternative possibilities.)　**1 crowned
with you** elevated by possession of you　**2 the monarch's . . . flattery**
this pleasing delusion to which all monarchs are prone　**4 your love** my
love of you.　**alchemy** science of transmuting base metals　**5 indigest**
chaotic, formless　**6 cherubins** angelic forms (suggesting the youth and
beauty of the friend)　**7 Creating** creating out of　**8 his beams** its (the
eye's) gaze　**9 'tis . . . seeing** my eye is flattering my mind (see ll. 1–2)
**11 what . . . greeing** what agrees with the mind's taste　**12 to** to suit
**13–14 'tis . . . it** i.e., it extenuates the eye's sinful deed (of misleading the
mind) that it first drinks in the poison itself　**14 doth first begin** i.e.,
tastes of the poison first, like an official taster sampling food before it
is given to the king

# 115

Those lines that I before have writ do lie,
Even those that said I could not love you dearer;
Yet then my judgment knew no reason why
My most full flame should afterwards burn clearer.        4
But reckoning Time, whose millioned accidents
Creep in twixt vows and change decrees of kings,
Tan sacred beauty, blunt the sharp'st intents,
Divert strong minds to th' course of altering things—     8
Alas, why, fearing of Time's tyranny,
Might I not then say, "Now I love you best,"
When I was certain o'er incertainty,
Crowning the present, doubting of the rest?               12
    Love is a babe; then might I not say so,
    To give full growth to that which still doth grow.

---

**115 · 5 reckoning Time** (1) Time, which we reckon up (2) Time, that
makes a reckoning.   **millioned** numbered in the millions   **6 twixt vows**
i.e., between the making of vows and their fulfillment   **7 Tan** darken,
i.e., coarsen.   **sacred** deserving worship   **8 to . . . things** i.e., into the
current that flows toward decay of all things   **9 fearing of** fearing
**10 Might . . . say** i.e., wasn't it understandable for me to say then, when
I wrote *Those lines* (l. 1)   **11 certain o'er incertainty** i.e., certain of my
love's perfection then, as contrasted with the uncertainty of the
future   **12 Crowning** glorifying.   **doubting of** fearing   **13 then might
. . . so** i.e., therefore it was wrong of me to say, "Now I love you best"
(l. 10)   **14 To give** thereby attributing

# 116

Let me not to the marriage of true minds
Admit impediments. Love is not love
Which alters when it alteration finds,
Or bends with the remover to remove.      4
O, no, it is an ever-fixèd mark
That looks on tempests and is never shaken;
It is the star to every wandering bark,
Whose worth's unknown, although his height be taken.    8
Love's not Time's fool, though rosy lips and cheeks
Within his bending sickle's compass come;
Love alters not with his brief hours and weeks,
But bears it out even to the edge of doom.     12
    If this be error and upon me proved,
    I never writ, nor no man ever loved.

116 • **2 Admit** concede that there might be, allow consideration of. (An echo of the marriage service.)   **3 alteration** i.e., in age, beauty, affection, health, circumstance   **4 Or . . . remove** or inclines to inconstancy simply because the person loved is inconstant   **5 mark** seamark, conspicuous object distinguishable at sea as an aid to navigation   **8 Whose . . . taken** whose value is beyond estimation, although its altitude above the horizon can be determined (for purposes of navigation)   **9 fool** plaything, laughingstock   **10 his** i.e., Time's (also in l. 11).   **bending** curved.   **compass** range   **12 bears . . . doom** endures or holds out to the very Day of Judgment

# 117

Accuse me thus: that I have scanted all
Wherein I should your great deserts repay,
Forgot upon your dearest love to call,
Whereto all bonds do tie me day by day;                      4
That I have frequent been with unknown minds,
And given to time your own dear-purchased right;
That I have hoisted sail to all the winds
Which should transport me farthest from your sight.          8
Book both my willfulness and errors down,
And on just proof surmise accumulate;
Bring me within the level of your frown,
But shoot not at me in your wakened hate;                    12
   Since my appeal says I did strive to prove
   The constancy and virtue of your love.

**117 · 1 scanted** come short in  **3 upon . . . call** i.e., to pay my respects to
your love, or to invoke your aid  **5 frequent** familiar.  **unknown minds**
strangers of no consequence  **6 given . . . right** squandered your rights
in me on temporary matters and alliances  **8 should** would  **9 Book . . .
down** record both my willful faults and errors  **10 on . . . accumulate** to
sure proof add surmise, suspicion  **11 level** point-blank range, aim
**13 appeal** legal appealing of the case.  **I . . . prove** my intention was to
test

# 118

Like as to make our appetites more keen
With eager compounds we our palate urge,
As to prevent our maladies unseen
We sicken to shun sickness when we purge:                    4
Even so, being full of your ne'er-cloying sweetness,
To bitter sauces did I frame my feeding
And, sick of welfare, found a kind of meetness
To be diseased ere that there was true needing.             8
Thus policy in love, t' anticipate
The ills that were not, grew to faults assured,
And brought to medicine a healthful state
Which, rank of goodness, would by ill be cured.            12
    But thence I learn, and find the lesson true,
    Drugs poison him that so fell sick of you.

118 · 1 **Like as** just as   **2 eager compounds** pungent, bitter concoc-
tions.   **urge** stimulate, prompt   **3 As** just as.   **prevent** anticipate,
forestall.   **unseen** not yet physically manifested   **4 sicken . . . sickness**
induce a kind of sickness, purging (i.e., evacuation of stomach or bowel),
in order to ward off greater sickness   **5 Even so** in just the same way
**6 bitter sauces** i.e., other loves, undesirable in comparison with you.
**frame** adapt, direct   **7 sick of welfare** surfeited and made ill by health
and happiness (in love).   **meetness** suitability   **8 ere . . . needing** before
there was any real necessity for it   **9 policy** shortsighted calculation.
**anticipate** forestall   **10 assured** actual   **11 to medicine** to a state of
needing medical care   **12 rank of goodness** gorged and sickened by
good health   **14 Drugs . . . you** i.e., the cure is worse than the disease.
**so** thus

# 119

What potions have I drunk of siren tears,
Distilled from limbecks foul as hell within,
Applying fears to hopes and hopes to fears,
Still losing when I saw myself to win!                              4
What wretched errors hath my heart committed,
Whilst it hath thought itself so blessèd never!
How have mine eyes out of their spheres been fitted
In the distraction of this madding fever!                          8
O, benefit of ill! Now I find true
That better is by evil still made better;
And ruined love, when it is built anew,
Grows fairer than at first, more strong, far greater.             12
   So I return rebuked to my content,
   And gain by ills thrice more than I have spent.

119 • 1 **siren tears** i.e., deceitful tears of a seductive woman. (The poet seems to speak of an affair like that with the Dark Lady in Sonnets 127–152.)   **2 limbecks** vessels used in distillation.   **foul as hell within** i.e., possessing an inner ugliness and evil contrasted with a beautiful and seductive appearance   **3 Applying . . . fears** i.e., trying vainly to control my wild hopes with a sense of fear and to assuage my fears with hope   **4 Still** always.   **saw myself** vainly expected   **6 so blessèd never** never before so fortunate   **7 How . . . fitted** how my eyes have popped out in convulsive fit   **8 distraction** frenzy.   **madding** maddening

# 120

That you were once unkind befriends me now,
And for that sorrow which I then did feel
Needs must I under my transgression bow,
Unless my nerves were brass or hammered steel.                    4
For if you were by my unkindness shaken
As I by yours, you've passed a hell of time,
And I, a tyrant, have no leisure taken
To weigh how once I suffered in your crime.                    8
O, that our night of woe might have remembered
My deepest sense how hard true sorrow hits,
And soon to you, as you to me then, tendered
The humble salve which wounded bosoms fits!                    12
   But that your trespass now becomes a fee;
   Mine ransoms yours, and yours must ransom me.

120 • 1 **befriends** gives me friendly advice   **2–3 for . . . bow** i.e., realizing
the sorrow I felt from your unkindness, I must now give up my unkindness to you   **4 nerves** sinews   **6 hell of** hellish   **7 have . . . taken** have
not taken the opportunity   **8 weigh** consider.   **in your crime** i.e., from
your unkindness. (If I suffered so, I should realize you've suffered too
from my unkindness.)   **9 that** would that.   **our night of woe** the dark
and woeful time of our earlier estrangement.   **remembered** reminded
**10 sense** consciousness, apprehension   **11 And . . . tendered** i.e., and
would that I had quickly offered to you, as you did to me   **12 humble
salve** i.e., apology and remorse.   **which . . . fits** which is just what
wounded hearts need   **13 that your trespass** that unkindness of
yours.   **fee** payment, compensation   **14 ransoms** redeems, excuses

# 121

'Tis better to be vile than vile esteemed
When not to be receives reproach of being,
And the just pleasure lost which is so deemed
Not by our feeling but by others' seeing.     4
For why should others' false adulterate eyes
Give salutation to my sportive blood?
Or on my frailties why are frailer spies,
Which in their wills count bad what I think good?     8
No, I am that I am, and they that level
At my abuses reckon up their own.
I may be straight though they themselves be bevel.
By their rank thoughts my deeds must not be shown,     12
   Unless this general evil they maintain:
   All men are bad, and in their badness reign.

121 • 1 **vile esteemed** (to be) considered vile  **2 When . . . being** when not
to be vile receives the reproach of vileness. (It's just as bad, or even
worse, to be unjustly accused of wickedness as to be truly wicked.)
**3–4 And . . . seeing** and to lose justifiable pleasure because its justifica-
tion has to depend not on our feelings but on the censorious attitudes of
others  **5 false adulterate eyes** i.e., the eyes of those whose own wickedness prompts them to misconstrue my innocent love  **6 Give . . . blood**
i.e., greet me, in my lusty merriment, with familiarity and with a knowing wink of the eye  **7 Or . . . spies** or why should there be more faulty
persons spying on my fleshly indulgences  **8 in their wills** i.e., by the
measure of their prurient, licentious minds  **9 am that** am what.  **level**
(1) aim (2) guess  **10 abuses** misdoings.  **reckon up their own** i.e.,
merely enumerate their own misdeeds  **11 bevel** out of square,
crooked  **12 rank** ugly, foul.  **shown** viewed, interpreted  **14 reign** i.e.,
prosper

# 122

Thy gift, thy tables, are within my brain
Full charactered with lasting memory,
Which shall above that idle rank remain
Beyond all date, even to eternity—                           4
Or at the least, so long as brain and heart
Have faculty by nature to subsist;
Till each to razed oblivion yield his part
Of thee, thy record never can be missed.                     8
That poor retention could not so much hold,
Nor need I tallies thy dear love to score;
Therefore to give them from me was I bold,
To trust those tables that receive thee more.               12
  To keep an adjunct to remember thee
  Were to import forgetfulness in me.

122 · 1 **tables** writing tablet, memorandum book  2 **charactered** written.  **with** by  3 **that idle rank** i.e., the relative unimportance of that
memorandum book (as compared with the memory itself)  6 **faculty . . .
subsist** natural power to survive  7 **each** i.e., brain and heart.  **razed
oblivion** obliterating forgetfulness. (*Razed*, effaced, destroyed, and *rased*,
erased, scraped away, often mean much the same thing.)  **his** its
8 **missed** lost. (The poet is apologizing for having given away or lost a
memorandum book written by the friend.)  9 **retention** i.e., the book, an
instrument for retaining memoranda.  **so much** i.e., as much as is in
my memory  10 **tallies** sticks notched to serve for reckoning. (The
notebook is such a mere *tally*.)  **score** reckon  11 **to . . . me** i.e., to give
away the writing tablet.  **bold** i.e., bold in taking the liberty  12 **those
tables** i.e., those of memory.  **receive thee more** retain more of you
13 **adjunct** aid  14 **Were** would be.  **import** imply, impute

## 123

No, Time, thou shalt not boast that I do change.
Thy pyramids built up with newer might
To me are nothing novel, nothing strange;
They are but dressings of a former sight.                              4
Our dates are brief, and therefore we admire
What thou dost foist upon us that is old,
And rather make them born to our desire
Than think that we before have heard them told.                        8
Thy registers and thee I both defy,
Not wondering at the present nor the past,
For thy records and what we see doth lie,
Made more or less by thy continual haste.                             12
  This I do vow and this shall ever be:
  I will be true, despite thy scythe and thee.

---

**123·2 pyramids** (May refer to obelisks or other structures erected in
Rome in 1586 or in London in 1603.)   **3 nothing** not at all   **4 dressings
. . . sight** reconstructions in new form of things from the past   **5 dates**
life spans   **7 make . . . desire** consider them newly created to our liking
and reinvented by us   **8 told** reckoned, told about   **9 registers** visual
records, monuments   **10 wondering** marveling   **11 doth lie** deceives
us   **12 Made more or less** i.e., raised one minute and ruined the next
(by Time), and alternately overvalued and undervalued by us

# 124

If my dear love were but the child of state,
It might for Fortune's bastard be unfathered,
As subject to Time's love or to Time's hate,
Weeds among weeds, or flowers with flowers gathered.   4
No, it was builded far from accident;
It suffers not in smiling pomp, nor falls
Under the blow of thrallèd discontent,
Whereto th' inviting time our fashion calls.   8
It fears not Policy, that heretic,
Which works on leases of short-numbered hours,
But all alone stands hugely politic,
That it nor grows with heat nor drowns with showers.   12
   To this I witness call the fools of Time,
   Which die for goodness, who have lived for crime.

**124 • 1 love** i.e., love for you. **but** merely. **child of state** result of (your) rank or power; or, of changing circumstance **2 for . . . unfathered** i.e., be declared to have no father or source other than (your) good fortune **3 As** i.e., and accordingly regarded as **4 Weeds . . . gathered** i.e., either despised as worthless like a weed or cherished like a flower, as Fortune dictates **5 accident** chance, fortune **6 It . . . pomp** i.e., it does not lessen or weaken in circumstances of pomp and finery **6–7 nor . . . discontent** nor does it weaken under the blows of adversity, turning melancholy. **thrallèd** enslaved, oppressed **8 Whereto . . . calls** i.e., to which the temptations of our present age expose all of us; or, which the age invites us to regard as fashionable **9 Policy, that heretic** cunning expediency, false to the spirit of love **10 Which . . . hours** i.e., which thinks only shortsightedly of short-term gain and makes only short-term commitments **11 hugely politic** i.e., prudent in a long-term sense **12 nor . . . heat** i.e., neither flourishes only in good times. **showers** i.e., adversity **13 witness call** call to witness. **fools** playthings, laughing-stocks. (See Sonnet 116.) **14 Which . . . crime** i.e., those who have lived evilly and then attempt to repent at their deaths or to die in a good cause

## 125

Were 't aught to me I bore the canopy,
With my extern the outward honoring,
Or laid great bases for eternity,
Which proves more short than waste or ruining?        4
Have I not seen dwellers on form and favor
Lose all, and more, by paying too much rent,
For compound sweet forgoing simple savor,
Pitiful thrivers, in their gazing spent?              8
No, let me be obsequious in thy heart,
And take thou my oblation, poor but free,
Which is not mixed with seconds, knows no art
But mutual render, only me for thee.                 12
    Hence, thou suborned informer! A true soul
    When most impeached stands least in thy control.

**125 • 1 Were 't . . . canopy** i.e., would it be anything to me if I did public
homage as one honors great persons by carrying over their heads a
cloth of state as they go in procession    **2 With . . . honoring** honoring
the external by means of external action    **3 laid . . . eternity** laid foun-
dations for supposedly lasting monuments    **5 dwellers on** those who
insist fulsomely upon (with pun on the idea of "tenants").    **form and
favor** (1) courtly etiquette and the achieving of status through influence
(2) figure and face    **6 Lose all, and more** i.e., lose all their wealth, and
then go into debt.    **by . . . rent** i.e., by overdoing their obligations to
mere ceremony    **7 For . . . savor** i.e., foregoing wholesome sincerity for
the sake of obsequious flattery    **8 Pitiful thrivers** i.e., those thriving
only in pitiful or worthless gains.    **in . . . spent** i.e., starved merely
by ceremonial observance    **9 obsequious** (1) courtly (2) devoted
**10 oblation** offering.    **free** freely offered    **11 seconds** inferior matter,
adulterants.    **art** artifice    **12 render** exchange    **13 suborned informer**
perjured witness, the envious one who has charged the poet with self-
interested flattery    **14 impeached** accused

## 126

O thou, my lovely boy, who in thy power
Dost hold Time's fickle glass, his sickle hour;
Who hast by waning grown, and therein show'st
Thy lovers withering as thy sweet self grow'st;                    4
If Nature, sovereign mistress over wrack,
As thou goest onwards, still will pluck thee back,
She keeps thee to this purpose, that her skill
May Time disgrace and wretched minutes kill.                       8
Yet fear her, O thou minion of her pleasure!
She may detain, but not still keep, her treasure.
Her audit, though delayed, answered must be,
And her quietus is to render thee.                                 12

**126 · 1** (This sonnet is made up of six couplets.)   **2 Time's . . . hour** i.e.,
Time's hourglass by which we are constantly betrayed and the hour of
final reckoning when all is cut down by Time's sickle (? The line may be
corrupt.)   **3 by waning grown** grown more youthful as age increases.
**show'st** i.e., show by way of contrast with yourself   **5 wrack** ruin.
(Nature is mistress over decay because of her power of restoration.)
**6 onwards** i.e., in life's journey   **7 to** for   **8 and . . . kill** i.e., and render
powerless the passing of the minutes   **9 minion** darling; slave   **10 She
. . . treasure** i.e., Nature may keep and restore you for a time, but Time
will ultimately triumph.   **still** always   **11 Her audit** i.e., the proverbial
paying of one's debt to Nature through death; also, Nature's account to
Time.   **answered** settled   **12 quietus** discharge, quittance.   **render**
surrender

# 127

In the old age black was not counted fair,
Or if it were, it bore not beauty's name;
But now is black beauty's successive heir,
And beauty slandered with a bastard shame.                    4
For since each hand hath put on nature's power,
Fairing the foul with art's false borrowed face,
Sweet beauty hath no name, no holy bower,
But is profaned, if not lives in disgrace.                    8
Therefore my mistress' eyes are raven black,
Her brows so suited, and they mourners seem
At such who, not born fair, no beauty lack,
Sland'ring creation with a false esteem.                     12
   Yet so they mourn, becoming of their woe,
   That every tongue says beauty should look so.

**127 · 1 old age** olden times.  **black** darkness of hair and eyes.  **fair**
(1) beautiful (2) light-complexioned  **2 it. . . name** i.e., it was not called
so  **3 now . . . heir** i.e., nowadays black has been named lawful succes-
sor to the title of beauty  **4 beauty** i.e., blonde beauty.  **slandered . . .
shame** i.e., declared illegitimate, created artificially by cosmetics  **5 put
on** assumed  **6 Fairing the foul** making the ugly beautiful.  **borrowed
face** i.e., cosmetics  **7 no name . . . bower** no reputation or pride of
family, and no sacred abode  **8 profaned** i.e., scorned, and violated by
those who use cosmetics.  **if not** or even  **10 so suited** decked out in
the same color and for the same reason  **11 At** for.  **no beauty lack** i.e.,
nonetheless make themselves attractive  **12 Sland'ring . . . esteem** i.e.,
dishonoring nature by a false reputation for beauty  **13 they** i.e., my
mistress's eyes.  **becoming of** gracing, or being graced by

# 128

How oft, when thou, my music, music play'st
Upon that blessèd wood whose motion sounds
With thy sweet fingers when thou gently sway'st
The wiry concord that mine ear confounds,                        4
Do I envy those jacks that nimble leap
To kiss the tender inward of thy hand,
Whilst my poor lips, which should that harvest reap,
At the wood's boldness by thee blushing stand!                   8
To be so tickled, they would change their state
And situation with those dancing chips
O'er whom thy fingers walk with gentle gait,
Making dead wood more blest than living lips.                    12
    Since saucy jacks so happy are in this,
    Give them thy fingers, me thy lips to kiss.

128 · 2 wood keys of the spinet or virginal.   motion mechanism   3 thou
gently sway'st you gently control   4 wiry concord harmony produced
by strings.   confounds i.e., pleasurably overwhelms   5 jacks (Literally,
upright pieces of wood fixed to the key-lever and fitted with a quill that
plucks the strings of the virginal; here used of the keys, and with a pun
on *jacks* in the sense of "common fellows," as in l. 13.)   8 by beside; or
with. (The poet stands beside the lady as she plays, blushing to his very
lips; and he blushes in vexation at the *jacks'* boldness with her hand.)
9 they i.e., my lips   13 jacks (with a pun on "knaves, fellows" as in l. 5)

# 129

Th' expense of spirit in a waste of shame
Is lust in action; and, till action, lust
Is perjured, murderous, bloody, full of blame,
Savage, extreme, rude, cruel, not to trust,                                    4
Enjoyed no sooner but despisèd straight,
Past reason hunted, and no sooner had
Past reason hated, as a swallowed bait
On purpose laid to make the taker mad;                                         8
Mad in pursuit, and in possession so;
Had, having, and in quest to have, extreme;
A bliss in proof, and proved, a very woe;
Before, a joy proposed; behind, a dream.                                      12
   All this the world well knows; yet none knows well
   To shun the heaven that leads men to this hell.

**129 · 1–2 Th' expense . . . action** lust being consummated is the expenditure or dissipation of vital energy in an orgy of shameful extravagance and guilt. (*Spirit* also suggests "sperm.") **2 till action** until it achieve consummation **3 blame** (1) guilt (2) recrimination **4 rude** brutal. **to trust** to be trusted **5 straight** immediately **6 Past reason** madly, intemperately **11 in proof** while experienced. **proved** i.e., afterward **12 Before** in prospect

## 130

My mistress' eyes are nothing like the sun;
Coral is far more red than her lips' red;
If snow be white, why then her breasts are dun;
If hairs be wires, black wires grow on her head.          4
I have seen roses damasked, red and white,
But no such roses see I in her cheeks;
And in some perfumes is there more delight
Than in the breath that from my mistress reeks.          8
I love to hear her speak, yet well I know
That music hath a far more pleasing sound.
I grant I never saw a goddess go;
My mistress, when she walks, treads on the ground.        12
   And yet, by heaven, I think my love as rare
   As any she belied with false compare.

**130 · 1 nothing** not at all   **3 dun** dull grayish brown, mouse-colored
**5 damasked** mingled red and white   **8 reeks** issues as smell   **11 go**
walk   **13 rare** extraordinary and unique   **14 she** woman.   **belied**
misrepresented.   **compare** comparison

# 131

Thou art as tyrannous, so as thou art,
As those whose beauties proudly make them cruel;
For well thou know'st to my dear doting heart
Thou art the fairest and most precious jewel.                    4
Yet, in good faith, some say that thee behold
Thy face hath not the power to make love groan;
To say they err I dare not be so bold,
Although I swear it to myself alone.                             8
And, to be sure that is not false I swear,
A thousand groans, but thinking on thy face,
One on another's neck, do witness bear
Thy black is fairest in my judgment's place.                    12
  In nothing art thou black save in thy deeds,
  And thence this slander, as I think, proceeds.

**131 · 1 tyrannous** pitiless and domineering.  **so as thou art** even as you
are (dark, not considered handsome)  **3 dear** fond  **9 to be sure** as
proof.  **false I** false that I  **10 but thinking on** when I do no more than
think of  **11 One . . . neck** one rapidly after another  **12 black** dark
complexion.  **my judgment's place** i.e., my opinion  **14 this slander**
(See ll. 5–6.)  **proceeds** originates

## 132

Thine eyes I love, and they, as pitying me,
Knowing thy heart torment me with disdain,
Have put on black, and loving mourners be,
Looking with pretty ruth upon my pain.                         4
And truly not the morning sun of heaven
Better becomes the gray cheeks of the east,
Nor that full star that ushers in the even
Doth half that glory to the sober west                         8
As those two mourning eyes become thy face.
O, let it then as well beseem thy heart
To mourn for me, since mourning doth thee grace,
And suit thy pity like in every part.                          12
    Then will I swear beauty herself is black,
    And all they foul that thy complexion lack.

**132 · 1 as** as if   **2 Knowing . . . torment** knowing that your heart torments   **4 ruth** pity   **6 becomes** adorns.   **cheeks** i.e., clouds   **7 that full
star** the evening star, Hesperus, i.e., Venus.   **even** evening   **8 Doth** i.e.,
lends.   **sober** somber, subdued in color   **9 mourning** (Spelled *morning*
in the quarto, suggesting a pun on l. 5.)   **10 beseem** suit   **12 suit thy
pity like** dress your pity alike, make it alike and consistent.   **in every
part** i.e., in the heart as well as the eyes   **14 And . . . that** and that all
those are ugly who

## 133

Beshrew that heart that makes my heart to groan
For that deep wound it gives my friend and me!
Is 't not enough to torture me alone,
But slave to slavery my sweet'st friend must be?    4
Me from myself thy cruel eye hath taken,
And my next self thou harder hast engrossed.
Of him, myself, and thee I am forsaken—
A torment thrice threefold thus to be crossed.    8
Prison my heart in thy steel bosom's ward,
But then my friend's heart let my poor heart bail;
Whoe'er keeps me, let my heart be his guard;
Thou canst not then use rigor in my jail.    12
  And yet thou wilt; for I, being pent in thee,
    Perforce am thine, and all that is in me.

**133 · 1 Beshrew** i.e., a plague upon   **2 it** i.e., *that heart* (l. 1), the cruel
heart of the Dark Lady   **4 slave to slavery** enslaved to slavery itself, to a
slavish infatuation   **6 And . . . engrossed** i.e., and you have put my
dearest friend, my other self, under even greater restraint.   **engrossed**
(1) driven into obsession (2) bought up wholesale   **8 crossed** thwarted,
afflicted   **9 Prison** imprison.   **steel bosom's ward** the prison cell of
your hard heart   **10 bail** set free by taking its place   **11 keeps** has
custody of.   **his guard** my friend's guardhouse   **12 rigor** harshness.
**my jail** i.e., my heart, where my friend is kept (and where I can protect
him from your harsh authority)   **13 pent** shut up   **14 and all** along
with everything

## 134

So, now I have confessed that he is thine,
And I myself am mortgaged to thy will,
Myself I'll forfeit, so that other mine
Thou wilt restore to be my comfort still.                    4
But thou wilt not, nor he will not be free,
For thou art covetous and he is kind;
He learned but surety-like to write for me
Under that bond that him as fast doth bind.                  8
The statute of thy beauty thou wilt take,
Thou usurer, that putt'st forth all to use,
And sue a friend came debtor for my sake;
So him I lose through my unkind abuse.                       12
　　Him have I lost, thou hast both him and me;
　　He pays the whole, and yet am I not free.

**134 · 2 will** (1) wishes (2) fleshly desire    **3 so . . . mine** provided that my
other self, my friend    **5 will not** does not wish to    **7 surety-like** as
security, as guarantor.    **write** sign the bond, endorse (suggesting that
the friend has taken the poet's place with the mistress)    **8 that bond . . .
bind** that mortgage or bond (of sexual enslavement) that now binds him
as securely as it does me    **9 statute** a usurer's security or amount of
money secured under his bond.    **take** call in, invoke. (The lady will
exact the full forfeiture specified in the mortgage as the amount to
which her beauty entitles her.)    **10 use** (1) usury (2) sexual pleasure
**11 sue** (with suggestion also of "woo").    **came** i.e., who became    **12 my
unkind abuse** your ill-usage and unkind deceiving (of me)    **14 pays**
(with sexual suggestion)

## 135

Whoever hath her wish, thou hast thy Will,
And Will to boot, and Will in overplus;
More than enough am I that vex thee still,
To thy sweet will making addition thus.                    4
Wilt thou, whose will is large and spacious,
Not once vouchsafe to hide my will in thine?
Shall will in others seem right gracious,
And in my will no fair acceptance shine?                   8
The sea, all water, yet receives rain still
And in abundance addeth to his store;
So thou, being rich in Will, add to thy Will
One will of mine, to make thy large Will more.            12
   Let no unkind no fair beseechers kill;
    Think all but one, and me in that one Will.

**135 · 1 Will** (This and the following sonnet and Sonnet 143 ring changes
on the word *will*—sexual desire, temper, passion, and the poet's name;
possibly also the friend's name. The word can also suggest the sexual
organs, male and female.)   **3 vex** (by unwelcome wooing).   **still** continually   **6 hide . . . thine** (with sexual suggestion)   **7 will in others** others'
will   **10 his** its   **13 Let . . . kill** let no unkind word kill any who seek
your favors; or, *Let "no" unkind*, etc., do not kill your wooers with the
word "no"   **14 Think . . . Will** i.e., think all your wooers and their wills
to be but one, all comprised in me

# 136

If thy soul check thee that I come so near,
Swear to thy blind soul that I was thy Will,
And will, thy soul knows, is admitted there;
Thus far for love my love suit, sweet, fulfill.          4
Will will fulfill the treasure of thy love,
Ay, fill it full with wills, and my will one.
In things of great receipt with ease we prove
Among a number one is reckoned none.                     8
Then in the number let me pass untold,
Though in thy store's account I one must be;
For nothing hold me, so it please thee hold
That nothing me, a something, sweet, to thee.            12
   Make but my name thy love, and love that still,
   And then thou lovest me for my name is Will.

---

**136 · 1 check** rebuke.  **come so near** i.e., come so near the truth about
you (in my previous sonnet); with suggestion of physical nearness also
**2 blind** unperceptive  **4 fulfill** grant  **5 fulfill the treasure** fill full the
treasury (with sexual suggestion)  **6 my will** (suggesting "my penis").
**one** one of them  **7 receipt** capacity (suggesting profligacy)  **8 one . . .
none** (A variant of the common saying "one is no number.")  **9 untold**
uncounted  **10 in . . . account** in your (huge) inventory (of lovers)
**11–12 For . . . thee** i.e., consider me too insignificant to think of, provided that you deign to hold insignificant me to you, my sweet, thereby
making me something of worth. (*Something* is sexually suggestive.)
**13 my name** i.e., "will," that is, desire.  **still** continually  **14 for**
because

# 137

Thou blind fool, Love, what dost thou to mine eyes
That they behold and see not what they see?
They know what beauty is, see where it lies,
Yet what the best is take the worst to be.                    4
If eyes corrupt by overpartial looks
Be anchored in the bay where all men ride,
Why of eyes' falsehood hast thou forgèd hooks,
Whereto the judgment of my heart is tied?                     8
Why should my heart think that a several plot
Which my heart knows the wide world's common
    place?
Or mine eyes seeing this, say this is not,
To put fair truth upon so foul a face?                        12
  In things right true my heart and eyes have erred,
  And to this false plague are they now transferred.

137 • 1 **Love** Cupid, portrayed as blind   2 **see not** do not comprehend
3 **lies** resides   4 **Yet . . . be** yet take the worst for the best   5 **corrupt by
overpartial looks** corrupted by doting and frankly prejudiced gazing
6 **Be . . . ride** have brought me to anchor in a bay used by everyone (with
sexual suggestion of a wanton woman)   7 **Why . . . hooks** why have you,
Love, fashioned snares out of my eyes' delusion   9 **think . . . plot** think
that to be a private field, i.e., that woman to be the exclusive property of
one man   10 **knows** knows to be.   **common place** (1) a commons, a
common pasture (2) a woman's body that is open, promiscuous   11 **Or**
i.e., or why should.   **not** not so   14 **false plague** (1) plague of judging
falsely (2) false woman

## 138

When my love swears that she is made of truth
I do believe her, though I know she lies,
That she might think me some untutored youth,
Unlearnèd in the world's false subtleties.                    4
Thus vainly thinking that she thinks me young,
Although she knows my days are past the best,
Simply I credit her false-speaking tongue;
On both sides thus is simple truth suppressed.                8
But wherefore says she not she is unjust?
And wherefore say not I that I am old?
O, love's best habit is in seeming trust,
And age in love loves not to have years told.                12
　　Therefore I lie with her, and she with me,
　　And in our faults by lies we flattered be.

**138·1** (A version of this sonnet appears in *The Passionate Pilgrim*.)
**truth** fidelity, constancy   **2 believe** i.e., pretend to believe   **5 vainly
thinking** acting as though I thought   **7 Simply** pretending to be foolish.   **credit** give credence to   **9 unjust** unfaithful   **11 habit** demeanor
(with, however, a suggestion of *garb*, i.e., something put on).   **seeming
trust** apparent fidelity   **12 age in love** an aging person in love, or, in
matters of love.   **told** (1) counted (2) told   **13 lie with** deceive (with
sexual pun)   **14 And . . . be** and so by lies we flatteringly deceive our-
selves about our moral lapses

# 139

O, call not me to justify the wrong
That thy unkindness lays upon my heart;
Wound me not with thine eye but with thy tongue;
Use power with power and slay me not by art.                4
Tell me thou lov'st elsewhere, but in my sight,
Dear heart, forbear to glance thine eye aside;
What need'st thou wound with cunning when thy might
Is more than my o'erpressed defense can bide?               8
Let me excuse thee: "Ah, my love well knows
Her pretty looks have been mine enemies,
And therefore from my face she turns my foes,
That they elsewhere might dart their injuries."            12
    Yet do not so; but since I am near slain,
     Kill me outright with looks and rid my pain.

139 · 1 call ask.  justify i.e., condone something actually taking place
under my eyes  2 unkindness i.e., flagrant infidelity  3 with thine eye
i.e., with a roving eye. (See ll. 5–6.)  4 with power i.e., candidly, directly.  art artifice, cunning  7 What why  8 bide abide, withstand
11 foes i.e., the *pretty looks* or wanton glances of l. 10  13 near nearly
14 rid end. (*Rid my pain* also suggests "satiate my craving.")

## 140

Be wise as thou art cruel; do not press
My tongue-tied patience with too much disdain,
Lest sorrow lend me words, and words express
The manner of my pity-wanting pain.                          4
If I might teach thee wit, better it were,
Though not to love, yet, love, to tell me so,
As testy sick men, when their deaths be near,
No news but health from their physicians know.               8
For if I should despair, I should grow mad,
And in my madness might speak ill of thee.
Now this ill-wresting world is grown so bad,
Mad slanderers by mad ears believèd be.                      12
    That I may not be so, nor thou belied,
    Bear thine eyes straight, though thy proud heart
        go wide.

---

**140 · 4 The manner . . . pain** the nature of my pain, on which you bestow
no pity   **5 wit** wisdom, prudence   **6 Though . . . so** even though you
don't love me, yet, love, to tell me that you do   **8 know** i.e., hear   **11 ill-
wresting** misinterpreting in an evil sense.   **bad** bad (that)   **13 so** i.e., a
*mad slanderer*.   **belied** slandered   **14 wide** astray. (The image is from
archery.)

## 141

In faith, I do not love thee with mine eyes,
For they in thee a thousand errors note;
But 'tis my heart that loves what they despise,
Who in despite of view is pleased to dote.          4
Nor are mine ears with thy tongue's tune delighted,
Nor tender feeling to base touches prone,
Nor taste, nor smell, desire to be invited
To any sensual feast with thee alone.               8
But my five wits nor my five senses can
Dissuade one foolish heart from serving thee,
Who leaves unswayed the likeness of a man,
Thy proud heart's slave and vassal wretch to be.    12
　　Only my plague thus far I count my gain,
　　That she that makes me sin awards me pain.

**141 · 2 errors** flaws in beauty　**4 Who ... view** which (i.e., the heart), in spite of what the eyes see　**6 Nor ... prone** nor (is) my delicate sense of touch inclined toward carnal contact (with you)　**9 my five wits** (neither) my five intellectual senses, i.e., the common sense, imagination, fancy, estimation (judgment), and memory　**11 Who ... man** i.e., which heart abandons the proper government of my person, leaving me the mere likeness of a man　**13 thus far** to the following extent　**14 That ... pain** i.e., that the sin brings with it its own punishment and contrition, thus presumably shortening my torment after death (with a suggestion in *pain* of "sexual pleasure"; see Sonnet 139)

# 142

Love is my sin, and thy dear virtue hate,
Hate of my sin, grounded on sinful loving.
O, but with mine compare thou thine own state,
And thou shalt find it merits not reproving;          4
Or, if it do, not from those lips of thine,
That have profaned their scarlet ornaments
And sealed false bonds of love as oft as mine,
Robbed others' beds' revenues of their rents.          8
Be it lawful I love thee as thou lov'st those
Whom thine eyes woo as mine importune thee.
Root pity in thy heart, that when it grows
Thy pity may deserve to pitied be.          12
   If thou dost seek to have what thou dost hide,
   By self-example mayst thou be denied.

142 • 1–2 Love . . . loving i.e., my sin is to love you, and your best virtue
is to hate—hate that sin in me, the sin of loving you. (The bitter paradox
here is that hatred of sin must be virtue, and yet the lady is herself
deeply implicated in this sin; her hatred is more a disdainful rejection
of the poet's love than a noble virtue.) 4 it i.e., my state 6–7 That . . .
mine i.e., that have forsworn themselves in love as often as my lips. (The
*scarlet ornaments* are lips and also red wax used to seal documents;
they *seal* with a kiss.) 8 Robbed . . . rents i.e., and committed adultery
with other women's husbands. (The metaphor is of income-yielding
estates, *revenues*, whose *rents* or payments made by tenants are not
properly paid; the husband does not pay what is owed to the wife in
terms of marital affection and producing children.) 9–10 Be . . . thee
i.e., I am as justified in loving you and imploring you with my eyes as
you are in pursuing other men. (*Be it lawful* is a legal phrase meaning
"let it be considered lawful that.") 12 deserve make you deserving
13 what . . . hide what you withhold, i.e., pity

## 143

Lo, as a careful huswife runs to catch
One of her feathered creatures broke away,
Sets down her babe and makes all swift dispatch
In pursuit of the thing she would have stay, 4
Whilst her neglected child holds her in chase,
Cries to catch her whose busy care is bent
To follow that which flies before her face,
Not prizing her poor infant's discontent; 8
So runn'st thou after that which flies from thee,
Whilst I, thy babe, chase thee afar behind;
But if thou catch thy hope, turn back to me,
And play the mother's part: kiss me, be kind. 12
   So will I pray that thou mayst have thy Will,
   If thou turn back and my loud crying still.

---

**143 · 1 careful** distressed, full of cares, busy.   **huswife** housewife
**5 holds her in chase** chases after her   **7 flies** flees   **8 Not prizing**
disregarding   **13 Will** (See Sonnets 135, 136.)   **14 still** hush, make quiet

# 144

Two loves I have, of comfort and despair,
Which like two spirits do suggest me still:
The better angel is a man right fair,
The worser spirit a woman colored ill.                          4
To win me soon to hell, my female evil
Tempteth my better angel from my side,
And would corrupt my saint to be a devil,
Wooing his purity with her foul pride.                          8
And whether that my angel be turned fiend
Suspect I may, yet not directly tell;
But being both from me, both to each friend,
I guess one angel in another's hell.                           12
    Yet this shall I ne'er know, but live in doubt
    Till my bad angel fire my good one out.

**144 · 1** (This sonnet appears, somewhat altered, in *The Passionate Pilgrim.*) **2 suggest** urge, offer counsel, tempt. **still** continually **4 ill** i.e.,
dark of complexion **11 from me** away from me. (The poet suspects
they are together.) **both . . . friend** friends to each other **12 I . . . hell** I
suspect that she (the evil angel) has him in her power (i.e., her sexual
embracement; *hell* is slang for the pudenda) **14 fire . . . out** drive out
my good angel, stop seeing him (with the suggestion of driving him out
of the lady's sexual body as one would use fire and smoke to drive an
animal out of its burrow, and with the further suggestion that the *fire* is
venereal disease. *Bad angel* also hints at bad coinage driving out good
money.)

# 145

Those lips that Love's own hand did make
Breathed forth the sound that said "I hate"
To me that languished for her sake;
But when she saw my woeful state,                    4
Straight in her heart did mercy come,
Chiding that tongue that ever sweet
Was used in giving gentle doom,
And taught it thus anew to greet:                    8
"I hate" she altered with an end,
That followed it as gentle day
Doth follow night, who like a fiend
From heaven to hell is flown away.                   12
　"I hate" from hate away she threw,
　　And saved my life, saying "not you."

145•1 (This sonnet is in eight-syllable meter.)  5 **Straight** at once
7 **used** . . . **doom** accustomed to passing a mild sentence   13 **"I hate"**
. . . **threw** i.e., she separated the phrase "I hate" from the hatred I
feared it expressed, from hateful meaning

## 146

Poor soul, the center of my sinful earth,
Thrall to these rebel powers that thee array,
Why dost thou pine within and suffer dearth,
Painting thy outward walls so costly gay?                    4
Why so large cost, having so short a lease,
Dost thou upon thy fading mansion spend?
Shall worms, inheritors of this excess,
Eat up thy charge? Is this thy body's end?                   8
Then, soul, live thou upon thy servant's loss,
And let that pine to aggravate thy store;
Buy terms divine in selling hours of dross;
Within be fed, without be rich no more.                     12
   So shalt thou feed on Death, that feeds on men,
   And Death once dead, there's no more dying then.

**146 · 1 sinful earth** body   **2 Thrall to** (One of several conjectures; the
quarto repeats *My sinfull earth* from l. 1.)   **rebel powers** i.e., rebellious
flesh.   **array** dress, clothe   **4 outward walls** i.e., the body, decked out in
finery, cosmetics, etc.   **5 so short a lease** (because we are lent the
*mansion* of our body for so short a time)   **6 mansion** dwelling, i.e., the
body   **8 thy charge** that on which you have expended so much, and that
was put in your *charge* or custody   **9 thy servant's** i.e., the body's
**10 that . . . store** the body starve to increase your stock of riches
**11 Buy . . . dross** i.e., purchase eternal life in return for giving up
(selling) mere hours of wasteful pleasure; arrange *terms* that only God
can provide

# 147

My love is as a fever, longing still
For that which longer nurseth the disease,
Feeding on that which doth preserve the ill,
Th' uncertain sickly appetite to please.     4
My reason, the physician to my love,
Angry that his prescriptions are not kept,
Hath left me, and I desperate now approve
Desire is death, which physic did except.     8
Past cure I am, now reason is past care,
And frantic-mad with evermore unrest;
My thoughts and my discourse as madmen's are,
At random from the truth vainly expressed;     12
   For I have sworn thee fair and thought thee bright,
   Who art as black as hell, as dark as night.

**147 · 1 still** always   **3 preserve the ill** sustain the illness   **4 uncertain**
finicky   **7 desperate** in despair.   **approve** demonstrate, show by experience that   **8 Desire . . . except** (that) desire, which the advice of medicine (i.e., reason) proscribed, proves fatal   **9 care** medical care. (The line
is an inversion of the proverb, "things past cure are past care," i.e.,
don't worry about what can't be helped. Reason, the physician, has
ceased to care for his patient.)   **10 evermore** constant and increasing
**12 vainly** to no sensible purpose

## 148

O me, what eyes hath love put in my head,
Which have no correspondence with true sight!
Or, if they have, where is my judgment fled,
That censures falsely what they see aright?            4
If that be fair whereon my false eyes dote,
What means the world to say it is not so?
If it be not, then love doth well denote
Love's eye is not so true as all men's "no."           8
How can it? O, how can love's eye be true,
That is so vexed with watching and with tears?
No marvel then though I mistake my view;
The sun itself sees not till heaven clears.            12
    O cunning love, with tears thou keep'st me blind,
    Lest eyes well-seeing thy foul faults should find.

---

**148 · 4 censures** judges  **7 love** i.e., the self-deceiving nature of my
love.  **denote** indicate, demonstrate (that)  **8 eye** (with a pun on *ay*,
yes)  **10 vexed** troubled.  **watching** remaining awake  **11 mistake my
view** err in what I see

# 149

Canst thou, O cruel, say I love thee not,
When I against myself with thee partake?
Do I not think on thee when I forgot
Am of myself, all tyrant for thy sake?                        4
Who hateth thee that I do call my friend?
On whom frown'st thou that I do fawn upon?
Nay, if thou lour'st on me, do I not spend
Revenge upon myself with present moan?                        8
What merit do I in myself respect
That is so proud thy service to despise,
When all my best doth worship thy defect,
Commanded by the motion of thine eyes?                        12
    But, love, hate on, for now I know thy mind:
    Those that can see thou lov'st, and I am blind.

**149 · 2 partake** take part (against myself)   **3 think on thee** put consideration of you foremost   **3–4 when … sake** when I am tyrannously neglectful of, or oblivious of, myself and my best interests on your behalf.   **forgot** forgotten   **7 spend** vent   **8 present moan** immediate suffering   **9 respect** value   **10 thy … despise** as to think it demeaning to serve you   **11 all my best** all that is best in me.   **defect** insufficiency   **14 Those … blind** i.e., you scorn one who loves you in a blind passion, in defiance of reason, and are drawn instead to those who worship your looks only

## 150

O, from what power hast thou this powerful might
With insufficiency my heart to sway?
To make me give the lie to my true sight
And swear that brightness doth not grace the day?          4
Whence hast thou this becoming of things ill,
That in the very refuse of thy deeds
There is such strength and warrantise of skill
That, in my mind, thy worst all best exceeds?          8
Who taught thee how to make me love thee more,
The more I hear and see just cause of hate?
O, though I love what others do abhor,
With others thou shouldst not abhor my state.          12
    If thy unworthiness raised love in me,
    More worthy I to be beloved of thee.

**150·2 With insufficiency** by means of all your shortcomings.  **sway**
rule  **3 give the lie to** accuse flatly of lying  **4 And . . . day** i.e., and
swear that what is so is not so, that what is fair and beautiful is not fair
and beautiful since you are dark  **5 becoming . . . ill** i.e., ability to show
ill things in a becoming light  **6 in . . . deeds** in the most debased of
your actions  **7 warrantise of skill** warrant or assurance of expertise
**12 state** i.e., condition of being helplessly in love

# 151

Love is too young to know what conscience is;
Yet who knows not conscience is born of love?
Then, gentle cheater, urge not my amiss,
Lest guilty of my faults thy sweet self prove.          4
For, thou betraying me, I do betray
My nobler part to my gross body's treason;
My soul doth tell my body that he may
Triumph in love; flesh stays no farther reason,          8
But, rising at thy name, doth point out thee
As his triumphant prize. Proud of this pride,
He is contented thy poor drudge to be,
To stand in thy affairs, fall by thy side.          12
   No want of conscience hold it that I call
    Her "love" for whose dear love I rise and fall.

**151 • 1 too young** (Love is personified as the young Cupid.) **2 conscience**
guilty knowing, carnal knowledge (playing on *conscience*, "moral
sense," in l. 1) **3 urge** stress, invoke. **amiss** sin **5 betraying**
(1) exposing (2) leading into temptation **6 nobler part** i.e., soul **8 stays**
awaits. **reason** reasoning talk **9 rising** (with bawdy suggestion of
erection, continued in *point, Proud, stand, fall*) **10 triumphant prize**
spoils to be enjoyed in victory. **Proud of** swelling with. **pride** splendor; erection **12 stand** (1) serve, undertake business (2) be erect. **fall**
(as in battle; with sexual suggestion of detumescence) **13 want** lack

## 152

In loving thee thou know'st I am forsworn,
But thou art twice forsworn, to me love swearing;
In act thy bed-vow broke, and new faith torn
In vowing new hate after new love bearing.                    4
But why of two oaths' breach do I accuse thee,
When I break twenty? I am perjured most,
For all my vows are oaths but to misuse thee,
And all my honest faith in thee is lost;                      8
For I have sworn deep oaths of thy deep kindness,
Oaths of thy love, thy truth, thy constancy,
And, to enlighten thee, gave eyes to blindness,
Or made them swear against the thing they see;               12
    For I have sworn thee fair. More perjured eye,
    To swear against the truth so foul a lie!

**152 · 1 forsworn** i.e., faithless to my vows of love (perhaps marriage
vows) **3 act** sexual act. **bed-vow** marriage vows to your husband
**3–4 new . . . bearing** i.e., a new contract of fidelity is torn up by your
swearing hatred toward me to whom you have only recently professed
love. (Or the *new faith* that is torn up may be that which the lady has
sworn to the friend.) **7 but to misuse** merely to misrepresent; or,
deceive **8 And . . . lost** i.e., and by loving you I forfeit all claim to
integrity **11 And . . . blindness** i.e., and, to invest you with brightness,
I made my eyes testify to things they did not see **13 eye** (with a pun
on *I*)

# 153

Cupid laid by his brand and fell asleep.
A maid of Dian's this advantage found,
And his love-kindling fire did quickly steep
In a cold valley-fountain of that ground;                        4
Which borrowed from this holy fire of Love
A dateless lively heat, still to endure,
And grew a seething bath, which yet men prove
Against strange maladies a sovereign cure.                       8
But at my mistress' eye Love's brand new-fired,
The boy for trial needs would touch my breast;
I, sick withal, the help of bath desired,
And thither hied, a sad distempered guest,                       12
   But found no cure. The bath for my help lies
   Where Cupid got new fire—my mistress' eyes.

**153·1** (This sonnet and the following seemingly have no direct connection with those preceding. They are adaptations of epigrams in the *Palatine Anthology*, Greek poems of the fifth century translated into Latin in the sixteenth century.) **brand** torch **2 maid** attendant virgin, votaress. **Dian** Diana, goddess of chastity **4 of that ground** i.e., nearby **6 dateless** endless, eternal. **still** always **7 grew** became. **seething bath** spring of hot medicinal waters. **yet** even today. **prove** discover to be **8 sovereign** efficacious **9 new-fired** having been re-ignited **10 for trial** by way of test **11 withal** from it **12 hied** hastened. **distempered** sick. (The bath is suggestive of the sweating cure for venereal disease.)

# 154

The little love god lying once asleep
Laid by his side his heart-inflaming brand,
Whilst many nymphs that vowed chaste life to keep
Came tripping by; but in her maiden hand       4
The fairest votary took up that fire
Which many legions of true hearts had warmed,
And so the general of hot desire
Was, sleeping, by a virgin hand disarmed.       8
This brand she quenchèd in a cool well by,
Which from Love's fire took heat perpetual,
Growing a bath and healthful remedy
For men diseased; but I, my mistress' thrall,       12
     Came there for cure, and this by that I prove:
     Love's fire heats water, water cools not love.

---

**154·7 general** inspirer and commander, i.e., Cupid    **9 by** nearby
**11 Growing** becoming    **12 thrall** slave, bondman    **13 cure** (with suggestion of treatment for venereal disease, as in 153.7–14).   **this** i.e., the following proposition.   **that** i.e., my coming, which failed to cure me

# Date and Text

On May 20, 1609, "Thomas Thorpe Entred for his copie vnder thandes of master Wilson and master Lownes Warden a Booke called Shakespeares sonnettes." In the same year appeared the following volume:

> SHAKE-SPEARES SONNETS. Neuer before Imprinted. AT LONDON By *G. Eld* for *T. T.* and are to be solde by *Iohn Wright,* dwelling at Christ Church gate. 1609.

Some copies of this same edition are marked to be sold by William Aspley rather than John Wright; evidently Thorpe had set up two sellers to distribute the volume. The sonnets were not reprinted until John Benson's rearranged edition of 1640, possibly because the first edition had been suppressed or because sonnets were no longer in vogue. The 1609 edition may rest on a transcript of Shakespeare's sonnets by someone other than the author, and the edition itself is marred by misprints, though Thorpe was a reputable printer. Clearly the sonnet sequence was not supervised through the press as were *Venus and Adonis* and *The Rape of Lucrece.* All the evidence suggests that it was obtained without Shakespeare's permission from a manuscript that had been in private circulation (as we know from Francis Meres's 1598 allusion, in his *Palladis Tamia: Wit's Treasury,* to Shakespeare's "sugared sonnets among his private friends"). Two sonnets, 138 and 144, had appeared in 1599 in *The Passionate Pilgrim.* On questions of dating and order of the sonnets, see the Introduction to *Sonnets* in this volume.

# Textual Notes

These textual notes are not a historical collation; they are simply a record of departures in this edition from the copy text. The reading adopted in this edition appears in boldface, followed by the rejected reading from the copy text, i.e., the quarto of 1609. Only major alterations in punctuation are noted. Corrections of minor and obvious typographical errors are not indicated.

Copy text: the quarto of 1609 [Q].

**2.14 cold** could   **6.4 beauty's** beautits   **8.10 Strikes** Strike   **12.4 all** or   **13.7 Yourself** You selfe   **15.8 wear** were   **17.12 meter** miter   **18.10 [and elsewhere] lose** loose   **19.3 jaws** yawes   **20.2 Hast** Haste   **22.3 furrows** forrwes   **23.6 rite** right   **23.14 with** wit   wit wiht   **24.1 stelled** steeld   **25.9 fight** worth   **26.12 thy** their [also at 27.10, 35.8 (twice), 37.7, 43.11, 45.12, 46.3, 46.8, 46.13, 46.14, 69.5, 70.6, 85.3, 128.11, 128.14]   **27.2 travel** trauaill   **28.12 gild'st** guil'st   **28.14 strength** length   **31.8 thee** there   **34.2 travel** trauaile   **34.12 cross** losse   **38.2 pour'st** poor'st   **38.3 too** to   **41.7 woos** woes   **41.8 she** he   **42.10 losing** loosing   **44.13 naught** naughts   **45.9 life's** liues   **46.9 'cide** side   **46.12 the** he   **47.2 other.** other,   **47.4 smother,** smother;   **47.11 not** nor   **50.6 dully** duly   **51.10 perfect'st** perfects   **55.1 monuments** monument   **56.3 [and elsewhere] today** too daie   **58.7 patience-tame to sufferance,** patience tame, to sufferance   **59.6 hundred** hundreth   **59.11 whe'er** where   **61.14 off** of   **too** to   **62.10 chapped** chopt   **65.12 of** or   **69.3 due** end   **72.1 lest** least [also at l. 9 and elsewhere]   **73.4 ruined** rn'wd   **choirs** quiers   **76.7 tell** fel   **77.1 wear** were   **77.10 blanks** blacks   **83.7 too** to   **85.3 Reserve** Reserne   **88.8 losing** loosing   **90.11 shall** stall   **91.9 better** bitter   **93.5 there** their   **98.11 were** weare   **99.4 dwells** dwells?   **99.9 One** Our   **102.8 her** his   **106.12 skill** still   **111.1 with** wish   **112.14 are** y'are   **113.6 latch** lack   **113.14 mine eye** mine   **118.5 ne'er-cloying** nere cloying   **118.10 were not, grew** were, not grew   **119.4 losing** loosing   **126.8 minutes** mynuit   **127.2 were** weare   **127.10 brows** eyes   **129.9 Mad** Made   **129.11 proved, a** proud and   **132.9 mourning** morning   **138.12 to have** t' haue   **140.5 were** weare   **144.6 side** [adopted from *The Passionate Pilgrim*] sight   **144.9 fiend** [adopted from *The Passionate Pilgrim*] finde   **146.2 Thrall to** My sinfull earth   **147.7 approve** approoue.   **153.14 eyes** eye

# Index of Sonnet First Lines

# Further Reading

## Venus and Adonis

Dubrow, Heather. " 'Upon Misprision Growing': *Venus and Adonis.*" *Captive Victors: Shakespeare's Narrative Poems and Sonnets*. Ithaca and London: Cornell Univ. Press, 1987. Dubrow explores the poem's formal strategies of characterization. Focusing mainly on Venus, Dubrow argues that Shakespeare transforms the Ovidian mythological poem into a mode "conducive to the creation of complex characters and to the evocation of complex responses to them."

Hulse, Clarke. *Metamorphic Verse: The Elizabethan Minor Epic*, pp. 143–175. Princeton, N.J.: Princeton Univ. Press, 1981. Hulse examines the "iconographic" technique in *Venus and Adonis* that enables Shakespeare to hold "conflicting attitudes towards love in an aesthetic balance." The poem is structured like a formal debate in which one set of images alternates with another without any resolution of the contradiction and with unity provided only "by the repetition of the image itself."

Kahn, Coppélia. "Self and Eros in *Venus and Adonis.*" *Centennial Review* 4 (1976): 351–371; Rev. and rpt. in *Man's Estate: Masculine Identity in Shakespeare*. Berkeley, Los Angeles, and London: Univ. of California Press, 1981. Kahn views Adonis' rejection of Venus as "a *rite de passage* in reverse": instead of forging an adult sexual identity, Adonis flees from the possibility of intimacy, regressing into narcissistic isolation. His narcissism masks a deep desire for dependence, a wish ultimately fulfilled in his transformation into a flower that Venus nurtures as her child.

Keach, William. "*Venus and Adonis.*" *Elizabethan Erotic Narrative*. New Brunswick, N.J.: Rutgers Univ. Press, 1977. Examining Shakespeare's alterations of Ovid's version of the story, Keach finds "an antithetical, bipartite structure" in *Venus and Adonis* that organizes the poem's "tragic parody of the Platonic doctrine that love is the desire for beauty."

Muir, Kenneth. "*Venus and Adonis:* Comedy or Tragedy?" *Shakespeare the Professional, and Related Studies.* Totowa, N.J.: Rowman and Littlefield, 1973. Finding that the poem's fundamental ambivalence extends even to its "mingling of wit and seriousness," Muir sees *Venus and Adonis* neither as praise of chastity nor a paean to sensuality, but as a self-consciously Ovidian poem, imaginatively engaged with both Venus and Adonis and equally dismissive of Neoplatonic and Puritan arguments for "the denial of the flesh."

Rabkin, Norman. *Shakespeare and the Common Understanding,* pp. 150–162. New York: Free Press, 1967. Rabkin argues that the poem explores contradictions and unresolved tensions between spiritual and sensual love: Adonis' idealized conception of love's purity is juxtaposed with Venus' emphasis on love as sensual desire. The poem's provocative ambivalence mirrors the paradoxical treatment of love found in Shakespeare's plays.

# The Rape of Lucrece

Allen, D. C. "Some Observations on *The Rape of Lucrece.*" *Shakespeare Survey* 15 (1962): 89–98. Allen argues for the predominance of Christian over classical perspectives in the poem, a view implicitly critical of Lucrece, whose actions, he finds, are largely motivated by her "love of pagan honour." Allen suggests that the poem invites an allegorical reading that confirms this harsh view of Lucrece's fate, despite the sympathy aroused for her plight.

Donaldson, Ian. " 'A Theme for Disputation': Shakespeare's Lucrece." *The Rapes of Lucretia: A Myth and Its Transformations.* Oxford: Clarendon Press, 1982. Donaldson's book considers the interpretations and transformations of the Lucrece story from Ovid to Giraudoux, and his account of Shakespeare's treatment focuses on the poem's movement between the conflicting ethical demands of Roman and Christian perspectives on the action.

Dubrow, Heather. " 'Full of Forged Lies': *The Rape of Lucrece.*" *Captive Victors: Shakespeare's Narrative Poems and Sonnets.* Ithaca and London: Cornell Univ. Press, 1987. Dubrow probes the poem's elaborate rhetorical surface to discover Shakespeare's "preoccupation with the moral and psychological issues expressed through—or even raised by—such adornment."

Hulse, Clarke. *Metamorphic Verse: The Elizabethan Minor Epic*, pp. 175–194. Princeton, N.J.: Princeton Univ. Press, 1981. Hulse argues for the importance of pictorial elements in the poem in establishing the poem's characteristic "movement between incident and analysis." In the tapestry of the fall of Troy, Lucrece sees the analogy between the Trojan fate and her rape, enabling her to recognize her innocence and to demand her revenge through her own vivid portrayal of her suffering.

Kahn, Coppélia. "The Rape in Shakespeare's *Lucrece.*" *Shakespeare Studies* 9 (1976): 45–72. The focus of Kahn's essay is on the complex moral, social, and psychological ramifications of Lucrece's rape. The rigid structure of Rome's patriarchal society, where chastity is the "only value which gives meaning to her as a Roman wife," determines her tragic fate. Only by her death can she recreate her "ideal self" and restore Collatine's honor.

Miola, Robert S. "*The Rape of Lucrece*: Rome and Romans." *Shakespeare's Rome.* Cambridge and New York: Cambridge Univ. Press, 1983. Focusing on the poem's imagery of Lucrece herself as a city under attack by a barbarian, Miola sees the poem as part of Shakespeare's ongoing exploration of Rome and Romans, and he finds in Lucrece's fate—a suicide chosen as an act of Roman honor and piety—the origins of Shakespeare's disillusioned scrutiny of Roman values.

Vickers, Nancy J. " 'The Blazon of Sweet Beauty's Best': Shakespeare's *Lucrece.*" In *Shakespeare and the Question of Theory*, ed. Patricia Parker and Geoffrey Hartman. London and New York: Methuen, 1985. Vickers examines the language of praise in the poem to discover the limits and dangers of a descriptive rhetoric that "displays" women as part of an aggressive rivalry between men. Her analysis reveals the complex relationship of the poem to its own insight, as it exposes the disturbing implications of rhetorical competition and yet "remains embedded in the descriptive rhetoric it undercuts."

# The Phoenix and Turtle

Alvarez, A. "William Shakespeare: 'The Phoenix and the Turtle.'" In *Interpretations: Essays on Twelve English Poems*, ed. John Wain. London: Routledge and Kegan Paul, 1955. Alvarez offers a close and detailed reading of the logical, philosophical, and linguistic complexities of "The Phoenix and Turtle" that reveals the "stringent logic" of the poem's paradoxical presentation of mysterious love.

Ellrodt, Robert. "An Anatomy of 'The Phoenix and the Turtle.'" *Shakespeare Survey* 15 (1962): 99–110. Ellrodt's thorough account of the poem's symbolism and philosophical assumptions leads him to recognize the "originality of Shakespeare's handling of the Phoenix theme" and his sobering awareness that "truth may seem but cannot be," for "Love and Constancy are dead."

Empson, William. "'The Phoenix and the Turtle.'" *Essays in Criticism* 16 (1966): 147–153. Empson suggests that Shakespeare's poem must be understood in terms of its appearance in an anthology by Robert Chester designed to celebrate the knighting of Sir John Salusbury. He examines the genesis of the anthology as well as the relationship of Shakespeare's poem to the other poems included in the celebratory collection.

Garber, Marjorie. "Two Birds with One Stone: Lapidary Re-Inscription in 'The Phoenix and Turtle.'" *The Upstart Crow* 5 (1984): 5–19. Garber sees the poem as triumphing over its conventional subject matter and the restrictions of its occasion through the "highly self-conscious formal structure" and the fusion of elegy and epithalamion that permit its witty subversion of its own formal and logical authority.

Matchett, William H. *"The Phoenix and the Turtle": Shakespeare's Poem and Chester's "Loues Martyr."* The Hague and Paris: Mouton; New York: Humanities Press, 1965. Matchett provides a patient analysis of the poem's language and structure before turning to the poem's literary and historical contexts. He sees the poem as a political allegory about Elizabeth (the Phoenix) and Essex (the Turtle) and finds its terms of praise qualified by the elegiac quality of the threnos and the "insistence" of the final line.

# A Lover's Complaint

Jackson, MacD. P. *Shakespeare's "A Lover's Complaint": Its Date and Authenticity.* Auckland, N.Z.: Univ. of Auckland Press, 1965. By examining the poem's vocabulary, phrasing, imagery, stylistic mannerisms, and subject matter, Jackson's thirty-nine-page pamphlet affirms Shakespeare's authorship.

Muir, Kenneth. " 'A Lover's Complaint': A Reconsideration." In *Shakespeare 1564–1964: A Collection of Modern Essays By Various Hands,* ed. Edward A. Bloom. Providence, R.I.: Brown Univ. Press, 1964. Muir considers the question of authorship and concludes, on the basis of stylistic as well as bibliographic indications, that the poem was written by Shakespeare, probably sometime near 1600. He also provides an account of the poem's paired thematic concerns: "the difficulty of distinguishing between appearance and reality" and "the battle of the sexes."

Warren, Roger. " 'A Lover's Complaint,' *All's Well,* and the Sonnets." *Notes and Queries* n.s. 17 (1970): 130–132. Warren finds verbal echoes of the sonnets and *All's Well That Ends Well* in "A Lover's Complaint," which leads him to posit a connection "in Shakespeare's mind (and perhaps in date of composition) between the Helena/Bertram relationship and the lovely but deceitful boy of both sonnets and poem."

# Sonnets

Booth, Stephen. *An Essay on Shakespeare's Sonnets*. New Haven, Conn.: Yale Univ. Press, 1969. Booth sees the sonnets as being "multiply ordered" by a variety of formal patterns, and he traces their function and interaction as they structure the reader's experience of the poems.

_____, ed. *Shakespeare's Sonnets, Edited with Analytic Commentary*. New Haven, Conn.: Yale Univ. Press, 1977. Booth's edition includes almost 400 pages of commentary on the diction, syntax, idiom, and background of individual sonnets, focusing on the "fusions by which incompatible and contradictory truths are voiced simultaneously."

Fineman, Joel. *Shakespeare's Perjured Eye: The Invention of Poetic Subjectivity in the Sonnets*. Berkeley, Los Angeles, and London: Univ. of California Press, 1986. In this dense and provocative study of the sonnets, Fineman finds in Shakespeare's complex response to the Renaissance poetry of praise a profound disruption of its idealizing strategies, dependent upon the recognition of a divided self-consciousness and permitting the development of "a genuinely new poetic subjectivity."

Herrnstein, Barbara, ed. *Discussions of Shakespeare's Sonnets*. Boston: D. C. Heath, 1964. The collection includes nineteen essays, ranging from John Benson's preface to the 1640 edition of Shakespeare's poems to an essay by C. L. Barber written in 1960, encompassing a wide variety of critical responses "to the themes, attitudes, and experiences which the poems reflect, to their value as literary achievements and to their characteristics as poetic art."

Hubler, Edward, ed. *The Riddle of Shakespeare's Sonnets*. New York: Basic Books, 1962. Hubler provides a text of the sonnets, plus essays by Northrop Frye, Leslie A. Fiedler, Stephen Spender, and R. P. Blackmur. Hubler also includes his own "Shakespeare's Sonnets and the Commentators" and Oscar Wilde's "The Portrait of Mr. W. H." (1895).

Krieger, Murray. *A Window to Criticism: Shakespeare's Sonnets and Modern Poetics*. Princeton, N.J.: Princeton Univ. Press, 1964. Rejecting both mimetic and formalistic critical approaches, Krieger argues for a "contextual-ism" that reveals, through his supple reading of individual sonnets, the ways in which Shakespeare's poetry is both a "window" and "mirror," at once opening out to an historical existence and reflecting the "insistent" reality of the aesthetic object itself: "word and thing—indeed word and world—are made one."

Landry, Hilton, ed. *New Essays on Shakespeare's Sonnets.* New York: AMS, 1976. Landry's collection of nine specially commissioned essays includes studies by Winifred Nowottny on the sonnets' "form and style," W. G. Ingram on the poems' "internal poetic organization," Anton M. Pirkhofer on their "dramatic character," and Landry's own "defense" of the sonnets against the criticism of John Crowe Ransom and Yvor Winters.

Leishman, J. B. *Themes and Variations in Shakespeare's Sonnets.* New York: Hillary House, 1961. Leishman examines the central themes and strategies of organization in the sonnets and their sources in the classical and Renaissance literary traditions available to Shakespeare.

Melchiori, Giorgio. *Shakespeare's Dramatic Meditations: An Experiment in Criticism.* Oxford: Clarendon Press, 1976. Melchiori's subtle analysis of sonnets 20, 94, 121, 129, and 146, focusing on the poems' linguistic, literary, and socio-historical resources, reveals them as "meditations *in action*," dramatic engagements with the contradictions and unresolved tensions of their originating idea or emotion.

Muir, Kenneth. *Shakespeare's Sonnets.* London and Boston: George Allen and Unwin, 1979. Muir's sensible introduction to the sonnets includes a discussion of their date, the text, and the sonnet order, as well as a consideration of their relation to the sonnet tradition and an essay examining the themes and attitudes of the sequence.

Pequigney, Joseph. *Such Is My Love: A Study of Shakespeare's Sonnets.* Chicago: Univ. of Chicago Press, 1985. Pequigney's interpretation focuses on the drama of human desire articulated by Shakespeare's sonnet sequence, usefully differentiating Renaissance conventions of friendship from the erotic (including homoerotic) relations he finds delineated in the poems.

# Contributors

DAVID BEVINGTON, Phyllis Fay Horton Professor of Humanities at the University of Chicago, is editor of *The Complete Works of Shakespeare* (Scott, Foresman, 1980) and of *Medieval Drama* (Houghton Mifflin, 1975). His latest critical study is *Action Is Eloquence: Shakespeare's Language of Gesture* (Harvard University Press, 1984).

DAVID SCOTT KASTAN, Professor of English and Comparative Literature at Columbia University, is the author of *Shakespeare and the Shapes of Time* (University Press of New England, 1982).

JAMES HAMMERSMITH, Associate Professor of English at Auburn University, has published essays on various facets of Renaissance drama, including literary criticism, textual criticism, and printing history.

ROBERT KEAN TURNER, Professor of English at the University of Wisconsin–Milwaukee, is a general editor of the New Variorum Shakespeare (Modern Language Association of America) and a contributing editor to *The Dramatic Works in the Beaumont and Fletcher Canon* (Cambridge University Press, 1966–).

JAMES SHAPIRO, who coedited the bibliographies with David Scott Kastan, is Assistant Professor of English at Columbia University.

# THE BANTAM SHAKESPEARE COLLECTION

## The Complete Works in 29 Volumes

*Edited with Introductions by David Bevington • Forewords by Joseph Papp*

------------------------------------------------------------